BY STARK YOUNG

FELICIANA

SO RED THE ROSE

THE STREET OF THE ISLANDS

RIVER HOUSE

THE TORCHES FLARE

HEAVEN TREES

THEATRE PRACTICE

GLAMOUR: Essays on the Art of the Theatre

THE THREE FOUNTAINS

THE FLOWER IN DRAMA

So Red the Rose

So Red the Rose

By

Stark Young

New York
Charles Scribner's Sons

TO
LOUISE STEWART

"I sometimes think that never blows so red
The rose as where some buried Cæsar bled;
    That every hyacinth the garden wears
Dropt in her lap from some once lovely head.

And this reviving herb whose tender green
Fledges the river-lip on which we lean—
    Ah, lean upon it lightly! for who knows
From what once lovely lip it springs unseen!"

CHARACTERS OF THE BOOK

The principal scenes in this novel are two neighboring plantations, Portobello and Montrose. This list of the principal characters is therefore grouped under the names of these two estates:

PORTOBELLO
(HOME OF THE BEDFORDS)

MALCOLM BEDFORD ("Darlin'," "Mac")
MRS. SARAH TATE BEDFORD, his wife ("Sallie," "My Dumplin' ")
DUNCAN, their son, 21, absent at the University of Virginia
JULIA VALETTE SOMERVILLE, their adopted daughter, child of a friend in New Orleans
MARY HARTWELL } their two little daughters
FRANCES SCOTT
ROSA TATE, Mrs. Bedford's sister ("Auntie," "Rosie," "Aunt Piggie")
HENRY FAIRFAX TATE, senile brother of Mrs. Bedford
MISS GILBERT, the governess
MIDDLETON, 5, Malcolm Bedford's nephew, child of his dead sister
DUNCAN'S MAMMY (Aunt Tildy)
UNCLE THORNTON, her husband; the four Celies; Abner; Billy McChidrick; Dock, the Indian; and other family servants

VISITORS AT PORTOBELLO

CAPTAIN RUFFIN a United States senator, and MRS. RUFFIN

MONTROSE
(HOME OF THE MCGEHEES)

HUGH MCGEHEE, brother of Malcolm Bedford's first wife, Mary Hartwell McGehee
AGNES BEDFORD MCGEHEE, his wife, sister of Malcolm Bedford
EDWARD, their son, 18, absent at the Louisiana Military Academy
LUCINDA, their daughter ("Lucy")
MISS WHIPPLE, seamstress, from Iowa
WILLIAM VEAL, the family butler

VISITORS AT MONTROSE

SHELTON TALIAFERRO, a cousin, and his son, Charles
MRS. CYNTHIA EPPES, a cousin from New Orleans, and her son, Francis
EDWARD MCGEHEE, a brother, and his wife, Mary, from Woodville
MILES MCGEHEE, a brother
MR. MUNGER and MR. TRIPPLER, invalids from the North, guests at Montrose for the climate

VISITORS AT PORTOBELLO AND MONTROSE

MARY CHERRY, a spinster of 60, who has no kin of her own in the State, but moves from house to house for long or short stays, as the case may be
ELIZA TURNER QUITMAN, of Monmouth, widow of a famous Mexican War general

So Red the Rose

I

"WHEREAS, the Creator," Malcolm Bedford wrote, "has seen fit to remove from the earthly scene our beloved friend, Hugh McGehee, and, whereas, Zachary Taylor, President of the United States of America, stated that Edward McGehee of Woodville, brother of the deceased, was the best man he ever knew, making him, furthermore, executor of his estate, it is the opinion here that the virtues of said Hugh McGehee were no less great."

The light autumn wind stirring in his direction carried the sheet of paper from the arm of Malcolm Bedford's chair, along with a moment's drift of oak leaves, to the porch floor. When he had drunk a little too much, he used to write obituaries of people. He looked now at the paper where it lay, hesitated, let it stay there, and began another.

"On Thursday last, the 2nd of November, the noble womanhood of our parish was bereft of one of its noblest ornaments, nay, its very flowers, Eliza Turner Quitman—nay, its fairest blossoms——"

But he was not pleased with the effort and brushed it aside; it too fell fluttering to the floor and under his chair.

"Whereas, God in his mercy"—he began another—"has removed from our midst our sister Mary Cherry—" He chuckled at something that came into his mind and went back—"in his mercy and infinite wisdom," he wrote, inserting the phrase, with a caret beneath the line, "be it said. Hallelujah——"

He stopped writing and sat brushing his lips with the tip of his silver penstaff, smiling and thinking. Then he took a sip from the toddy on a chair beside his.

"Darlin', Eliza Quitman's not dead," said his wife's voice behind him. He had not heard her light step in the doorway. "I declare, Darlin'." She came around and stood by one of the pillars.

"Yes, my dear."

"Darlin', I declare."

She leaned over and straightened his stock, and took up one of the sheets of paper—" 'Mary Cherry, et cetera, et cetera—be it said she was lofty in her mien, eloquent in her discourse, a lioness in her spirit.' Well, Miss Mary brings it on herself, I reckon. Look, Yellow Ab's bringing you out some coffee. We must have something to clear your head."

"And what's the objection to my head?"

"Nothing much, provided it's clear. I told him to make it black as ink." She turned to the boy who had come with the coffee. "Give Major Bedford the coffee, Abner, and hand me those sheets of paper off the floor. Never mind," she went on, seeing the negro was afraid to touch the papers; he knew they concerned death. She stooped quickly and picked up the obituaries herself, with one eye on her husband, who sat drinking the coffee, in his broadcloth coat with the velvet lapels. She skimmed what he had written, holding the paper in the small, busy hands that were still delicate and white like porcelain. She smiled to see the name of Hugh McGehee, the very man whose birthday party they were going to. But she said nothing. She was a woman who naturally, in whatever ways a man seemed to her to be like a man, let him alone. These obituaries were nothing new.

"Why won't you wear your rings?" Malcolm said, taking one of her hands, which he was very proud of.

"Very well, I will if you drink your coffee and get ready." She sent the servant to tell Celie to bring the diamond rings and the brooch with the column and leaves, from the box on her dressing-table. There were four maids named Celie in the house, it saved trouble. You merely called Celie and said tell Celie. So she said, "Call Celie, and if she can't find them tell her to tell Celie, she'll know where they are."

Mrs. Bedford wore a prune silk, as plain as she dared. The little face might have been called grim but for the eyes, which were gray, downright, and shone with some humor both friendly and tart. This was what led her to such things as saying that she enjoyed having children, it gave her a chance to lie in bed and read as much as she liked. She had been in Natchez all this time, twenty-three years since Malcolm had brought her from Alabama, and people were not yet used to this side of her.

"Where are Middleton and Frances and Hartie?" Malcolm asked, speaking of his little nephew and two daughters.

"They're gone on in the carriage with Rosa and Valette. Miss Gilbert's not going, for the simple reason," said his wife —referring to the children's governess, as she buttoned her gloves, which like all the Natchez ladies of that day, she wore too tight—"that there's so much feeling now it's embarrassing for the poor thing. It's a blessing she's going back North to her own people."

Celie came with the rings, and Mrs. Bedford put them into her reticule, hoping if possible to escape wearing them.

The barouche was waiting before a little white building with columns, like a small temple, which stood near the house at that side and served for the plantation office. Twilight was coming on, and the shadow of the oak trees and the thick leaves of the camellia bushes fell on the barouche and the horses, one of which was champing the ground now and then. There was a soft shade everywhere in that spot of the garden.

In a corner of the barouche, sitting upright against the cushions, was a lady in a black silk, and black bonnet with sprays of wired beads on the front of it. She sat high, as it were, on the seat but yet gaunt, like some great Amazonian in buckram. She was Mary Cherry, and had taken her place some time before.

Miss Cherry had these last two years deserted the north part of the State, Panola County, where she had lived so long visiting the diverse houses, mostly the McGehees; and had come to their cousins and connections here in the Natchez neighborhood and Woodville farther south. She would arrive for a week, a month, or several months, as things turned out. She had been, this time, at Portobello since the end of June.

"Well," Miss Mary said to her hosts, giving her skirt a slap out of their way, "I was about to take root."

Mrs. Bedford took her place on the front seat of the barouche. "Never mind, Miss Mary," she said, "we'll be there soon."

"Aye." Miss Mary turned away her head abruptly. Her left eye was blind, so that by turning her head like that she could put them out of her range of vision.

"Darlin', you sit there," said Mrs. Bedford.

"She calls me darlin' when she scolds me, and darlin' when she pets me," Malcolm said, as he obeyed his wife and took the seat beside Miss Cherry. "So I never know whether she loves me or not."

"Go on, go on, and sit down, Brother Malcolm. All I say is no all-fired man ever lived that I'd sit backward for. I'd as soon ride the waves. Phew, my goodness!" she went on, waving her handkerchief before her nose at the smell of the whiskey.

At the end of the avenue the driver got down to open the big gate and took the carriage through. Something about the chain to be adjusted kept him busy for a moment and they were left sitting there, the horses headed for the town. The three in the carriage sat looking back at the house they had just come from. Along the avenue the light struck here and there on the statues with their marble pedestals, and on the walks with their green borders; and at the far end you saw the house, on which the last glow of the twilight rested, standing out among the garden trees. It was not like the usual house of the day, a classic front with a pediment and tall columns. Two galleries with fluted columns, one row above the other, ran across the main portion of the house, beyond whose gabled ends were one-story wings with little columned porches set deep into the garden. The whole air of the house was that of a retreat, a lovely and secret place, strangely formal and domestic at the same time, extravagant but never beyond taste, the product of romantic feeling and thought.

Of the three people there, Malcolm Bedford should have been the one to know best what this place meant. He had built it for his first wife, who had died soon afterward. She was Mary Hartwell McGehee, the young sister of the man whose birthday they were on their way to celebrate. Malcolm had taken her to Europe while the house was building, and they had travelled there, buying the furniture with rose-red damask, the brocade curtains in the same color, the carpets, silver, the lustres, and candlesticks, with which the house was full. They had bought the classic statues along the avenue, the statues in the Louis XV style of the four continents that stood in a semi-circle facing the house, and the fluted alabaster vases, sending back with them from France an artist to design a garden. And in Philadelphia on their journey home they had stayed to be painted by Sully; the pictures hung in the dining-room.

Two lovers forever young: Malcolm saw them always as if they were people in a dream. They had named the place Portobello after a Virginia house in her family, though this Mississippi house was nothing like the one in Virginia, which was designed to suggest a ship. On Mary Hartwell's mother's side, a young Collier had gone off with Lawrence Washington to the British war in the Caribbean; and when they returned they had built two houses, and in their enthusiasm named them out of the war. Lawrence Washington named his house for the admiral: Mt. Vernon; and Collier named his for the battle: Portobello.

It was all here still: the house Malcolm Bedford had built for his bride, and what was in it; the garden with the box walks, the tiny pavilions in blue lattice, the camellias, roses, azaleas, jasmines, gardenias. He had brought home its second mistress, but little at Portobello had changed. It was all here still, and Sallie had seen her husband looking back at the house in the evening light and had turned her head away. Malcolm had not forgotten the days this house was built, but he loved her too, what more could she ask? And if the house had been for another woman, she had kept it well and when her first little girl was born she had named her for Mary Hartwell, who had died childless—what more was there to do?

As they drove along Mrs. Bedford heard Mary Cherry asking if Malcolm's nephew Edward would be coming up for his father's birthday, and Malcolm reply that the military academy had given Edward leave.

"He may be at home by now," Malcolm said.

"On what?"

"The *Princess.*"

"Not from what I hear of that steamboat. She backed into the bank her last trip, at Bayou Sara, so they tell. The captain's not got his mind on his business more'n likely. My, your sister Agnes is proud of Edward!"

"And well she might be."

"Yes, Edward's mighty fine. Though I prefer your Duncan. I must say give me Duncan any day. There's a young man for you. I don't care if he is way off in Virginia. Duncan I can tell you is A Number One."

"I won't deny that, Miss Mary. But Edward McGehee's a fine boy."

"Aye," she said, "the McGehees are fine men, but they need a woman to pull 'em."

"Well, I'd say push 'em."

"First they push 'em, and then they pull 'em."

They were on the old Natchez Trace, the Indian road that had run nobody knew how many centuries northward to what was now Nashville. Like many of the old roads it was sunk below the banks at either side, in places higher than the carriage top. The trees rose in a high wall of green, now almost black; the sky, swept with rose light and the dusk, shone in a bright lane far overhead; the horses' hoofs sounded clear and hard.

It had not taken long for the settlers pouring over the Southern States to find their levels and divide. There were the adventurers, the drifters, the scum, and wreckage of life in the older colonies and abroad; they lingered, dropped lower, or passed on. There were those who wished to make homes, to own land, to found a society in which their families might live. At the same time, scattered here and there in the South, were certain communities that from the very start had been made up of a special class who in their turn drew others like them.

This old town, toward which the Bedfords' carriage was rolling along the hard, dry dirt of the road, lay high up on the bluffs above the Mississippi, which spread out below in a vast curve, with its yellow current and its timeless air of volume and full movement to the gulf. It was this elevation, in contrast to the woods, the swamps, the low-lying river lands—the richest land in the world—for miles about Natchez and also across the river to the west, that had given the town its fortunes. The village of the Natchez tribe, coming up from Mexico nobody knew when, was found here by De Soto's

Spaniards, in the year 1543, and he himself was thought to be buried in Lake St. John. The French came, then the British, then the Spanish again for nineteen years, until 1798 when Natchez became a United States territory. Tobacco and indigo gave place to cotton; for which the climate and soil were so richly adapted that it was not uncommon to see a piece of land pay itself out of the purchase price in two or three seasons. Most of the fine houses of Natchez belonged to the planter class.

There were still a world of the piney-woods whites, the squatters, the people back among the bayous, the people on their way to the West. Natchez-under-the-Hill was still a proverb for vice over all America and even in Europe: the place most of all where met fantastic river romance, scum, and all that the frontier had spelled. But neither of these, the rough frontier nor the human dregs of the river, concerned the town of Natchez itself nor the society of the great plantation houses.

All the people the Bedfords or the McGehees knew, except for a preacher now and then, or a mechanic or clerk, belonged to this planter class. All their virtues, all their faults were characteristic of it.

The evening cool had restored Malcolm and he sat watching the scenery along the road, with now and then a glance at his wife and Mary Cherry.

"Speaking of houses," said Miss Mary—nobody had mentioned a house, "for the life of me I can't see what Hugh McGehee wants with that old Spanish house rambling around. You say Spaniard to me, and I say black wretch, he'll cut your heart out." Along the quiet road her voice was like a trumpet.

Malcolm crossed his legs smiling:

"As a matter of fact that house was built a hundred years ago, by a Scotchman. He called it Dundee, but nobody could pronounce it to suit him so he changed to something or other,

and then Hugh changed it to Montrose. Of course, it is like
the Spanish governor's house, however, Concord."

"Riding along like this, when it's all so green and rich,
so lush and abundant," Sallie Bedford said, "I think of all
the things have happened in this country. I think of what
calamity will be hanging over us now."

Neither Malcolm nor Mary Cherry made any reply, and
a silence fell.

They entered the town itself, driving past Green Leaves and
then Arlington, whose columns they saw faintly in the grove
about it. The road had passed into the open, with a sweep
of sky above. The east was already starry, and the evening
star, with its small star near, had risen. How sweetly the day
had drawn to its due close! Mrs. Bedford sat looking up
around her quietly. She had a knowledge like a shepherd's
of the heavens and the signs in the night sky.

II

"There's your sister watching out for you now," Mary
Cherry said to Malcolm Bedford when they had been ushered
to the drawing-room by William Veal, a grave, fine-looking
mulatto who was the Montrose butler. "There's Sister Agnes,"
she went on, pointing boldly toward the centre of the room,
where, with one hand leaning on the table and a lace fan
in the other, stood a quiet figure in a flowered amber silk.
Agnes McGehee had a ribbon stitched with pearl clusters
around her neck and a spray of pearl flowers in her dark
hair.

The room was filling with guests for the party, and the air
was fragrant with the mounds of roses and the vases of gardenias and cinnamon pinks.

"I see Captain Ruffin too," Miss Mary went on, with her elbow pushing Mrs. Bedford a little off from her. "Ah, Senator——"

"So you did get here?" Mrs. Bedford said, as she kissed her husband's sister and turned to greet Captain Ruffin, who bowed low over her hand. "We were expecting him, Agnes, at our house."

"I have just been telling Mrs. McGehee," he bowed in his hostess' direction, "the *Resolute* was tardy, and so we proceeded here to meet you. Colonel Harrod, who was at the landing, courteously offered us seats in his carriage. We knew we should meet you here."

Miss Mary took away the hostess' lace fan and began to fan herself as if it were a sturdy palm leaf. "And so you did, for here we be, eh?" she said. "What more?"

"Captain, you may not get everybody straight," Agnes McGehee said, looking at her hand, now empty of the fan, and then around the room with her gentle, brown eyes, and smiling to some of the guests whose glance she met, "but it's no matter, you can take it all as just one company. I always say to strangers in Natchez they would make a mistake trying to remember each separate person. Yes, I say, they must take it all as one——"

"Bouquet?" Captain Ruffin said, as if the words inside his head were oiled and perfumed as the raven locks outside it. He had made the outside at least into a Roman senator, according to the busts in the Capitol at Washington.

Mary Cherry smacked the lace fan shut and returned it to its owner. "Come, Senator, there's something I want to discuss with you, sir." He bowed again and gave her his arm.

"Supper will be later in the dining-room," Agnes said. "But the punch is here." She pointed to the long console table between the windows. "Rosa made it for us, so you can be sure——"

Miss Mary stopped and turned back a step, jerking Captain Ruffin up to a sudden halt, "I can be sure it's that Pope punch Rosa makes."

Agnes smiled. "Tea—green tea—and guava jelly, Miss Mary, and burnt brandy, rum, sherry, Château Margaux, lemon peel."

" 'Tought to be good, Sis Sallie, with all creation in it. I say she makes it at Portobello sometimes out of plain popery. But I'm a Methodist. You can't tell me there's a man alive can't sin, pope or no pope."

Agnes' eyes twinkled as she turned to the captain. "The recipe was given by the valet of Pius VII to Napoleon's valet, Constant, who gave it to my grandfather's old Philo, in Paris. So you see, Miss Mary."

"You'd think the Catholic Church would have something better to think about than brewing punches. However——" She moved away toward a quieter spot in the library, taking with her Captain Ruffin, who was stroking his chin as if to say that life in Washington had taught him discretion. "But tell me, now, Senator Ruffin——"

The entertainment at Montrose, the McGehees' house, was not so gay as at Arlington, Magnolia Vale, and other Natchez places, nor so romantic and fanciful as at Clifton, where the gardens, famous up and down the whole Mississippi, were turned sometimes into a paradise of lanterns and music, or river boats stopped for their passengers to see. But Montrose was cordial and warm, full of kindness; and the china and silver were the rapture of guests. To this store a great deal of glass had lately been added. Hugh McGehee's nephew, George, from Woodville, making the grand tour abroad, had developed an enthusiasm for Bohemian glass. All during the past spring, boxes of this glass had arrived through Mr. Lanux, the Montrose cotton-factor in New Orleans. It was white, cut with clear medallions, in which were clusters of enamelled flowers. Not only Bowling Green, George's own home, but Montrose also overflowed with this glass, and Agnes McGehee had begun to send it quietly away for presents.

"You couldn't say George's father cared very much," Mrs. Bedford said, turning to Judge McGehee, who was up from Woodville for the birthday and had at that moment joined them at the table, "so long as his son came back safe and sound; we were talking of all that glass you let your son buy."

Judge McGehee stood looking down from his great height into her droll eyes and smiled, but said nothing—"let" was a strange word for his son George, who could play any instrument he ever touched, would buy ten at a time, take them off with him and nobody ever hear of them again. He saw Mrs. Bedford's face growing serious as she added, "I tell Darlin', soon it'll be no time for boys galavantin'. As Lord Byron says, 'and we'll go no more a roaming by the light of the moon.' That's the way it seems to me." She was thinking of her son Duncan in Virginia at the university. "Though there's nothing yet. I reckon Washington is only too full of Southern oratory and Yankee tricks."

Malcolm Bedford's face, naturally proud, reddened angrily. "It's the hot heads will ruin us yet"—he said bitterly.

The subject of the Union and the South was uppermost in every one's mind, but was to be avoided for the moment because the evening belonged to pleasure and happiness. And yet there were the debates going on in Washington; and the great questions of state's rights and the extension of slavery into the new territories were in the air. People even at a Natchez party, a thousand miles from Washington, could not very well look into each other's eyes without coming to it. The subject was fortunately switched by a movement at the far end of the room. Guests were standing around the piano there, the young men were showing ladies to seats and taking their places beside them, leaning over and putting up their hands to see if their stocks were in place, as they stood to listen. At the long concert piano, which Hugh McGehee had himself selected in New York and sent down to Montrose, clearly seen by all now, as if she were a prima donna on the stage, sat a young girl in a dress of white tulle without ornaments. She was not very tall, with dark hair, pale olive skin, and a red mouth. Word had somehow passed to the servants that Miss Valette was going to sing, and two or three of them had stolen into the room along the wall. Miss Whipple, the little seamstress from Iowa, had also stolen in and taken a good armchair near the door. Their mistress made a sign to one of the maids to snuff the candles on the mantelpiece; and, with the lights thus brighter, the face, the young neck and arms, the hands on the piano keys seemed to grow more shining and fragile. No one spoke. You could hear only Mary Cherry clear her throat at the library door, where she had come with Captain Ruffin; and then the captain clearing his throat somewhat more positively. The girl made a little run over the keys of the piano, whose tone they were so proud of at Montrose. Then she turned the lovely eyes to Rosa Tate, who sat not far away, with Hugh McGehee, his hand on the back of her armchair, standing beside her.

"Auntie, what shall I sing?"

Rosa Tate looked up at Hugh McGehee, and he leaned down and whispered in her ear.

"I dreamt I dwelt"—she said.

"I dreamt I dwelt—I'd like to sing that," the girl said, with a pretty gravity, already absorbed in the thought of the song, and beginning the accompaniment before the hum of approval in the company could cease.

"I dreamt I dwelt in marble halls"

It was one of those voices, very pure and fresh, which the moment they begin are a singing sound and no other. And though she had for some time had lessons with the Chevalier

La Tour, who came up twice a month from New Orleans to his pupils in Natchez, what she did was more or less natural to her; and, since she sang for the sense, for the words rather than the mere melody, the persuasion and feeling were felt by every listener in the room.

The voice stopped, there was a second's hush. Many of the ladies had put on romantic expressions. To every one there she was a figure of youth, and, as the case might be, the dream of some desire, or the ghost of memory.

"Bravo!" Captain Ruffin shouted above all the applause and the sighs, clapping his hands so that the seals of his watch chain jingled. "Now, 'The Last Rose of Summer,' 'The Last Rose of Summer,' ah, could you not, Miss Valette?"

When she had sung it, Valette rose, touching the fingers of one hand lightly to her bosom, and smiling to the applause and the compliments. She was on the way to Miss Rosa when she stopped suddenly before an old lady with long dark eyes and a face as white as alabaster, who sat on the sofa. This lady was known to all Natchez as Miss Percy. The Duc d'Orleans, accompanied by his brother, the Duc de Montpensier, and the Comte de Beaujolais, travelling in exile, had visited Natchez as the guest of her father; and later on, when he came to the throne as Louis Philippe, Miss Percy had been lady-in-waiting at the French court. A slight, stooped little figure, she wore a gown of white silk with cascades of lace, and across her breast a spray of diamond flowers given to her by the Queen of France. Valette caught the look of those eyes, and all at once, as if unexpectedly even for herself, dropped on her knee, lifted the shaky hand with its heavy rings, and kissed it.

"*Mais cette petite—elle faisait mon travail léger*—I forget everything, but Victor Hugo himself recited the poem for me—*faisait mon ciel bleu—doux ange aux candides pensées,*" said the little old lady, with her strong Parisian accent, and with an air of listening to what she herself had just said. She spoke French as a delicate compliment, for she remembered Valette's New Orleans origin.

"*Merci, chère Mademoiselle,*" Valette replied, in the softer speech of Louisiana. "*Chère Mademoiselle, comme vous êtes belle*"—she hesitated and tears came into her eyes, "*et vous êtes triste.*"

The old lady bowed with a formal grace, putting her satin slipper, on which were paste buckles with some of the sets missing, out a little from her skirt; she had heard in Paris that the great Goethe once said that the only beauty time cannot take from a woman is her foot.

"What'd the child say, Sis Sallie?" Mary Cherry asked, watching Valette cross the room.

"She said Miss Percy was beautiful, then she said 'and sad.' "

"No use being sad, but she shows proper respect. I never could abide that *polly vous français* fracas."

"She wasn't ten years old when I took her, but the poor little thing has that ear for French. Yes, an ear's an ear."

"The epidemic of 1853 was about the worst yellow fever ever did, I presume," said Miss Mary.

"Yes, *faisait mon ciel bleu,* that was what Monsieur Hugo wrote," said Miss Percy quickly, as if she expected Miss Mary to say more, which she did:

"It's a blessing for the little thing you were caught there at the time and quarantined in town, Sis Sallie. You went one morning to see your friend, and there at the gate was the garbage cart and the man yelling bring out your dead, bring out your dead, and that cart already piled up with packages, corpses wrapped in sheets, so they just carted them off to the cemetery and trampled them down in trenches."

"*Mon dieu, mon dieu, mademoiselle!*" Miss Percy gasped, dabbing her brow with a lace handkerchief.

Agnes changed the subject, hoping to escape the memory of

the plague; "William Veal tells me we have forty-three varieties of our roses tonight, Miss Mary."

"All I'm saying and I repeat it, it's a good thing you were there to adopt that child."

"Fortunate for me, I'd lost my own little girl not long before."

"Be that as it may, Sis Sallie."

Valette called her foster mother "My Dumplin'," not Mamma, like the other children. They had not changed her name, Julia Valette Somerville. Her father was a Virginian. The Julie Valette, which it should have been, not Julia, was for an old French countess, a family friend, perhaps a distant cousin of her mother's when they lived in Chartres Street— la Comtesse Julie Valette de—everybody had forgotten the rest of it; but Valette had some of her lace.

"It's a good thing all the New Orleans boats are not as slow as the *Princess,* Sis Sallie," Mary Cherry said. "I reckon every livin' soul's asking Sister Agnes when her Edward will get here. It's going on nine o'clock now. How old's Edward, Sis Sallie."

"Edward's eighteen."

"Well, it's going on nine o'clock."

Valette, who had been beckoned to the window by the little boy Middleton, returned to them. She threw her arms around her foster mother's neck and kissed her and Mrs. Bedford gave that low chuckle of hers, "Who said you were a nightingale, you little wretch?"

"I'd rather have you say it, My Dumplin', than anybody."

"Go way from here."

Valette had already left them when Mrs. Carroll from Crescent Hood Plantation came up with her son Francis, a very stiff young man that people who did not dislike him said was on his way to being president of the bank where he was cashier. He stuck to his mother because he was more at ease when he was admired.

"My son tells me," Mrs. Carroll said, "that King Cotton is already in danger. What will happen to our Southland if that's true? I mean—but you say it, Francis."

"If cotton falls below wheat and if the Northern manufacturers control the government," said Francis.

"Exactly," said Miss Percy, in her charming voice, and looked at him as if to say, "I suppose now we shall hear about a surplus of cotton and that power is passing from us to the industrialists."

Francis went on to explain just that. He was one of those people with whom everything they say we know to be true and yet each time wonder why they said it. Mrs. Carroll, not understanding anything said, gave a motherly smile.

Presently they saw Valette with young Walworth on the gallery outside, where other young people were sitting, and where four negroes with their guitars, who had planned this birthday surprise for their master, were playing in the garden In the dusk of the porch they could see Valette's cloudy dress, and hear her laughter.

III

AT the end of the room, where the portrait of their cousin Winfield Scott that the general had sent to Montrose twenty years ago hung over a long rosewood sofa, the political discussion had grown animated. They talked as if Secession had already come, and after years of possibility was now a fact. A judge from the county court had just told them that for all intents and purposes there had been a war on for ten years. "Between," he said, "the industrial North and the landed South."

"But, Judge Winchester," said a tall man who now and then smoothed the hair over a bald spot on his crown, "why

should anybody deny that our life in this plantation country
has long ere this begun to rest on sand? Our staples have
declined, the Northern grist mills have the same value as our
cotton has."

Judge Winchester spoke of the restless industrial communities of the North as contrasted with the stability of life
in the South.

"But we must admit," said Mr. Harrod, again smoothing
his bald spot, "that the possibilities of industry are unlimited.
And it's well known Lincoln favors industrialism. And now
they finally have got the agreement between Indiana and
Ohio and the Eastern States about a tariff. That tariff agreement strikes me as ominous, Judge, so far as concerns our
interests." Mr. Harrod's father had been of that despised profession, the slave traders; but the son had become a rich, Whig
planter.

"Tariff aside, and slavery aside—for Mr. Lincoln, though
he does not approve of slavery, has stated that there is no
Constitutional right to abolish it," said Judge Winchester,
"the issue to his mind is the Union. Do this or do that, the
Union must be preserved. So he has said."

"Said so repeatedly in his campaign speeches, that's about
all anybody ever heard of Lincoln so far."

"Can any man imagine being dictated to in this case?"
Francis Carroll exclaimed, glancing at the young ladies who
had gathered as the conversation had grown lively enough
almost for drums and flags. "Independence is almost a defini-
tion of a man," he added, taking up a gold and enamel patch-
box from a what-not near by, looking at its design of Napoleon's bees, and replacing it with the finality of a national
decision. "Else I have failed to understand what a man is and
what a State is!"

"Quite so. I cannot see it as a matter of debate, this attempt-
ing to dictate the course of a State. It's almost personal, as if

we were all one man," Judge Winchester said. And aware at the same moment that this was not the place for such vehemence, he went on in a casual voice, scratching with his nail the lapel of his waistcoat, "What is this spot?"

"When our family took the part it did in the War for Independence, are we to be told now whether to go free or not, and by a lot of Yankees we could whip five to one?" said Mrs. Carroll, the black fringes waving on her full gown of white alpaca. "No. Hardly!"

"If," said the judge, "Mr. Lincoln is elected, it's the end of us. And why?"

"For the simple reason—" Mrs. Carroll began, but turned to her son, "you say it, Francis."

"But Lincoln won't be elected," Captain Ruffin interrupted.

"Assuredly, sir," Francis said, "with the Democratic party split between Bell and Douglas— And Mr. Lincoln—for the first time in our history we have a party that is entirely sectional—his party is entirely Northern."

"Split or no split, our party won't lose this election," Captain Ruffin broke in, "ah, no!" as if he found the proof of this in the tone of his own voice.

"But," Francis exclaimed, "the wishy-washy policy pursued by President Buchanan——"

"You'll knock that box off, pretty soon," said Mary Cherry, coming up to join the conversation, with a glass of punch in her hand, and fixing her good eye on the young man. "What are you going on like forty about with Senator Ruffin? What do you say to this, Bro' Hugh? You seem to be keeping out of the argument."

Before Hugh McGehee could make any reply, she had turned and was looking through a large album of colored plates on the table. "I know Audubon roamed, as they say, one of the McGehee plantations, but that's no reason for eternally drawing birds, even pelicans, being the national flag bird of Louisiana, as 'tis." She glanced at the pelican, then at the Senator and back at the pelican. "However," she added, grinning a little and in the kindest tone, as if to say nobody could help what they looked like, "they say pelicans—it's only the first sight of 'em, I reckon."

It was true, as Mary Cherry said, that Hugh McGehee had taken no part in the discussion. He had not done so, first, because he thought idle or hot words North and South, most of all among newspapers and orators, had blown the national situation too close to the point of explosion; second, because he was a Union man, not from the secession proposals' being anything new in the history of the United States, and not from any fancy patriotic talk, but from a conviction that the Union of the States was best practically and wise politically, or so, at least, up till now; and, third, because he believed that, even if Mr. Lincoln was elected, the new administration should be given a chance.

IV

WHILE all this talk of politics and North and South was going on, Agnes McGehee sat on a sofa by the library window with her sister-in-law, Edward McGehee's wife, who had come up from Woodville with him for the birthday.

Tonight these two women, who had so much affection for each other and so often exchanged notes between the two plantations, sat there together, both silent. Both had the same foreboding, and for both this talk of the war had the same dangerous burden. Through the long window they could see Mrs. Ruffin, the Captain's wife, on the gallery with the children. She had spent the evening there, doing as she pleased like a child herself. The sound of the talking, the negroes' guitars strumming in the garden, and Mrs. Ruffin's tiny voice telling a story, was suddenly broken off when the children sprang up, shouting "Cousin Edward! Cousin Edward!" ran to meet him. Mrs. Ruffin flew in to find Agnes.

"You could see him from the gallery," she said, as they rushed down the steps. "He must have left the boat and driven up—there he is—will you look, a uniform!—from Bayou Sara!"

A few minutes later the guest that so many of the family had been asking about entered by the door at the far end of the drawing-room. His father and mother followed. The two Bedford children had got themselves somehow past everybody and rushed to their cousin again. Mary Cherry, as if charging their attack, advanced to be the first who should greet this young man. He did not lean down and kiss them then, but put his left arm around both their necks, holding out his right to Miss Cherry and saying he was glad to see her.

"My goodness, you look healthy, Edward!" she said, looking at the red lips and the white teeth.

People crowded around him. He had to kiss a score of the family, and many of the girls now had to be called more formally by the *Miss,* not merely by their names, so fast were they growing into young ladies. What had been Louise was now Miss Louise Prynelle, Felicia Fleming was Miss Felicia, and so on; these were delicate matters not to be forgotten. "But not Miss Valette," he said, laughing as she leaned toward him for a light kiss.

Mary Cherry's exclamations on Edward's healthy looks may have been partly because he was blushing a little at so much commotion. It ended at last, however, and he was left free among the others there.

Sallie Bedford thought Edward lacked a certain fire which

she required in men and which no one could say her own son Duncan, at the University of Virginia, was without. Edward's was one of those faces that are in no sense childish, but that remind you of a child. The light brown hair, fine as a child's, was parted at one side and brushed across the wide forehead, the nose was straight, the gray eyes were too clear not to be a little sad. People looked at him, expecting him to smile, a smile that they would take, perhaps, more as a sign of sweetness and character than of happiness.

Captain Ruffin had started the political discussion again. "Did not President Buchanan himself declare in his message that the general government has no power to coerce a State? Were not those his exact words? I myself was present and heard them."

The Captain paused then, smiling affably. He was one of those lucky men who, in their way, have grown more attractive as they have grown vainer.

Miss Percy, from her seat on the yellow sofa, had beckoned Edward's mother, and drawing her down to her said something in her ear, with a gesture of the transparent little hand, so heavily jewelled, in his direction. The hand, or its finger-tips, alighted finally at her bosom, on a spray of diamond flowers, as if to say there were thoughts more precious than mere nature.

It was not one of those elaborate Natchez parties with half the town there and Monsieur Le Roi's orchestra up from New Orleans to play for the dancing, but merely people coming in for the birthday. William Veal had carried notes around the day before. Taking each note from his pocket he would present it with a bow at the door of Clifton, Monteigne, Arlington, Monmouth, Melrose, Rosalie, or Kenilworth, and, however snobbishly he might frown along the roadside, with the same formality at whatever other houses were not so fine.

Double doors, all save those of the dining-room, where

supper would be announced at any moment, had been thrown open and the whole first floor of the house could be seen. Sixty feet away the mirrors at the end of the second drawing-room reflected the lights of the chandeliers, the crystals of the candelabra on the two mantelpieces, the single candles in the hurricane shades on the console tables, and the company in their midst.

Agnes McGehee leaned down again to Miss Percy's lips, as she saw Colonel Harrod, a Natchez millionaire and a windbag, coming to offer his arm.

"Is that not Colonel Harrod coming for me?" Miss Percy whispered.

"No less."

"I shall be blown quite away. My dear, what a pleasure to see your Edward! *La beauté d'homme!*" The lovely old voice went on: "He will not go to war because it defends his interests. Nor because he hates the North. He'll go because it's right for himself to go. For no reason. And for a young man that's the best of all reasons! That's the noblest."

"It's the reason most like Edward," said Agnes.

"It's what I should expect from the son of his charming mother."

The eyes of Agnes shone with pleasure. She was subject to flattery, not out of vanity but from a kind of loneliness, perhaps.

V

FATHER and son were standing in the library, where, without planning it, they presently found themselves for a few moments before supper.

"'Tain't worth while, I suppose, asking if you young

gentlemen at Alexandria are feeling the excitement?"
Hugh McGehee said, watching his son's face. "The excitement
of these times, I mean."

"As I wrote you, Father, our 130 cadets are divided into
two companies. Arms have been issued, and drills have
begun."

The Louisiana Seminary of Learning and Military Academy had opened its doors for the first time the past January,
with sixty cadets and Colonel William Tecumseh Sherman
as superintendent. The examinations at the end of July
wound up with a ball, Edward had come home to Montrose
for the summer, and in November had returned.

"It seems," his father said, "that the seminary is all in order,
and running, but Colonel Sherman hasn't fetched his family
yet?"

"Everybody knows, Father; all the cadets know. We've
been there only three weeks."

His father sat down in an armchair, and Edward went
over and stood by him. "My friend Governor Moore of
Louisiana writes me," he said, "that Colonel Sherman loves
Southern living and has won himself many friends in this
part of the country."

"He says he's too red-headed for patience. But if you like
him at all, you——"

"Like him very much. It's what Governor Moore says,
red-headed but has character and heart. And yet the fact
remains that in this country down here, and down there in
Rapides Parish, everybody knows of his brother, John
Sherman, as an Abolitionist who's running for Congress, for
Speaker of the House, in fact. Do the cadets talk about all
this?"

"And their letters from home talk about it," Edward said.
He slid his forefinger along the table to the familiar inkstand.
It was a replica of one at Concord with which the Spanish

governer signed the English treaty. At places on the sides
of the drum the cords had lost their gilt. "I remember one
day René Beauregard had a long letter from his father."

The McGehee men had voices that carried a long way, and
Hugh McGehee began speaking louder than he knew. "We
have over a thousand people" (he never said slaves), "you
know that, and Brother Edward still more; and I don't
believe in the system. Brother Edward doesn't believe in it,
and Brother John in Panola didn't believe in it. One of the
last things he advised his sons was to get rid of their slaves.
But I don't see the way out; not as it is now. Down in the
Feliciana parishes six blacks to one white, six to one. And
I don't believe in secession, nor does your uncle. Nor in slavery.
You know how Brother Edward as an officer of the Coloniza-
tion Society worked to send negroes back to Africa. More than
500 were sent before the scheme collapsed. No telling how far
it was worth the trouble. We are both Union men, and meantime we all know—well, what is the solution?"

The tone of Hugh's voice had softened; and though he
did not go on with his thought, it was clear that he looked
only into discouraging visions of the future. He got up out
of the chair and went and stood at the window, taking hold
of the curtains with his small, firm hand, as if to still their
soft movement in the air.

It was when he was silent, far off, not moving, like this
that Edward most felt what it was in his father that touched
his heart. It was not so much the thought, the conviction
his father held, but rather a rightness and depth in the blood,
which he himself seemed to share and to live in. It was this
inner thing of feeling and goodness, so beloved, that bound him
to his father. Though he might not have put it into words or
even thought it out so, he felt half unconsciously that his father's
father also had had this feeling and this goodness, and his
father before him, and so on.

Edward was of medium height, his father just over six feet, so that when he heard him speaking again, the young man looked up as if the voice were strangely above him.

"If it keeps up as 'tis now yonder in the North and down here in this country, there'll be war; and I reckon you'll be enlisting. That's about the size of it. You'll be going?"

Edward hesitated, then he said simply, "Yes, sir."

"You'll enlist."

"I think I will."

"You'll be just eighteen at that. Listen, something I'm not likely to say again." Edward could scarcely hear what his father was saying. "You're my son: there's nothing about you I'd want to see changed. Nothing at all. God bless and keep you what you are."

The young man started to make some reply but did not; instead he rested his hands on the back of the armchair to stop their trembling.

Hugh McGehee turned and walked toward the drawing-room, beyond which they now could see the lights of the supper table. "We've got to hurry up," he said. "Your mother'll be waiting on us." But at the door he stopped short.

"There's one thing promise me, Edward. You'll come home first and go from here, if there's war. You give me your word?"

"I give you my word."

"Not rush off from anywhere with some crew because some fool is beatin' a drum."

"No, Father."

"That's not our style."

VI

THE Ruffins, as the plan was, had returned in the carriages to Portobello, their travelling trunks up with the drivers. The Captain sat beside Mrs. Bedford, facing Mary Cherry and the host; Mrs. Ruffin, at her own insistence, was put in the other carriage with Rosa and Valette and the children, for whom there was a little seat that pulled out from the side.

Except for Green Leaves, where the sound of a piano came through the garden and lights shone, or a few smaller houses along the way, the town was asleep; for it was later than any one at Montrose had thought. The new moon, whose bright crescent had glimmered through the trees here and there on their journey over, was long since down. But the November night was warm and starry around and above the travellers on that road, and lanes of perfume seemed to lie across their road, from the autumn flowers and leaves.

Malcolm had drunk a good deal of the Montrose punch made from the papal recipe that did not call for water, and sat looking at the trees and the sky, indifferent to conversation and gazing out on the mysterious, shadowy world through which they passed. Mary Cherry was asleep. Now and then she awoke, with a jerk of her head upward, and cleared her throat.

The Captain and Mrs. Bedford were talking of the trip to Minnesota from which Hugh McGehee and his family had returned a few weeks since. She was one of those people who are the soul of truth and not afraid to say anything they believe; but often, if it was something from which conclusions were to be drawn, her account would be stretched to suit her feelings. Sometimes, considering the downrightness of her nature, it was strangely different from the precise facts. She now told Captain Ruffin of Agnes McGehee's pleasure in

getting back home to Montrose from Carpenter's, near
St. Paul. The disturbance with the servants of two Louisiana
families had startled the whole covey and away they flew.
Colonel Christmas' woman had left her master, under the
persuasion of her Northern friends; and when Mrs. Prince
saw what had happened, she had put all servants in charge of
a man and sent them back South to Natchez. The McGehees
could hear the drum beating in the evening and the marching,
one night a company of the "Little Giants," another the "Wide
Awakes," and so on. They attended a Presbyterian, not their
own Episcopal, church, lest it should result as unhappily as
the day they had heard the rector discourse at Saratoga from
the text, "Free, indeed," and were so outraged and disgusted.
As Mrs. Bedford told it the account was true to what had
been said at Montrose, but the sum of it was more violent
and in that lay all the difference. What she said aroused the
Captain; he spoke vehemently of certain Northern editors and
their tirades against slavery.

Meantime, as Mrs. Bedford was feeding brimstone to the
Captain, in the other carriage the conversation was as happy
and innocent as the twitter of birds in a nest. Mrs. Ruffin
did all the talking and the three children, Mary Hartwell and
Frances and Middleton, listened with the delight of fairy tales.
Now and then their aunt gave a little laugh, pure and bright
like a child's, when the ecstasy of Mrs. Ruffin's stories would
pass endurance. and Frances or Mary Hartwell would cry,
"Listen, Aunt Rosa," "Oh, Auntie," "Listen, Aunt Piggie,"
which were different names they had for her. She sat holding
lightly on her lap a great bouquet of roses from Montrose.

Mrs. Ruffin and the Captain had often been in Natchez,
stopping off on their way from Panola County to New
Orleans, and everybody knew her story. At a Memphis res-
taurant, where she was a waitress, he had noticed first her
white hands. She was fifteen, and a girl from the Cumberland

Hills, and terrified of him. He married her, took a governess to give her lessons for a year or so, and it had been a happy marriage. They had four children of their own, now all married. People said that the children, in the rambling old house at Panola, had brought themselves up. For example, it was said that the children's laundry was all thrown into one chest, each child getting out at need whatever he could find. When the four children were married and gone to homes of their own, Mrs. Ruffin had no one to talk to at all. She was not very tall and was short-waisted, and her hair was the wrong shade of sandiness. There were only the lovely smile and the low voice. She liked to wear red, and the pendant of old diamonds from her husband's family had one tiny ribbon string of pink and one of blue. She wore gloves constantly out of doors, so that her hands were as fair as ever. Her husband still saw her in a mirage of white-handed maidenhood, which left her in a sort of romantic void; and still treated her with the old gallantry, which still slightly terrified her. Her lasting terror, however, was thunderstorms. Whenever there was thunder and lightning, she sent a servant for her husband and went to bed and pulled the cover up over her head; and he closed his office and came to lie by her side. If he was not there, she shut up the cook in a clothes closet and sat in her lap.

"There's the Petersons'," she said suddenly to Rosa Tate, as they passed a faded house by the roadside; once when a storm had overtaken her, Mrs. Ruffin had rushed into it and gone upstairs to a room and got into bed. "When the lady came upstairs she told me her name was Peterson—what thunderclaps there were! I must say she was very kind."

But leaning back in the carriage now, as if they were all on their way to Cinderella's ball, Mrs. Ruffin was telling the children about Bailey Springs in Tennessee where you went in the summer—Captain Ruffin was famous for a whist game

he had played there once. Bailey Springs sounded like
Mammy Tildy's picture of heaven. There was a grand ball to
open the season, and a big barbecue. There was a tenpin alley,
four parlors; and you went from spring to spring of water,
which were marked to show you what each spring would
cure you of if you were sick. City girls came out from
Memphis, Mobile, and Montgomery. Elocution was the
fashion just then and one of these girls would recite. She
was dressed in black, with a black lace scarf over her head,
and would recite, "I am not mad but soon will be." The
girl's mamma had a white tea gown with lavender bows
down the front of it.

"Why was the girl mad, Aunt Piggie?" Frances wanted to
know. She was not so quick as her sister, but was always
serious about the truth.

Mary Hartwell squeezed her hand. "Didn't you hear Mrs.
Ruffin say she isn't mad? She soon will be."

"Oh," said Frances; that seemed to be different.

Next morning before eight o'clock they were all in the
dining-room at Portobello. Breakfast was in the style familiar
to the plantation country, chicken, ham, eggs, hominy or
rice, spoon bread, biscuits, preserves and jellies, waffles and
Louisiana molasses, and coffee. The Bedfords were said to
be divided into two kinds, the eating Bedfords and the
Bedfords who did not eat. Those at Portobello were the
eating Bedfords. Malcolm sat at the head of the table; but
his wife, instead of sitting at the other end, sat on his right.
This had to be; it was his habit to eat nothing unless it came
by her direction. She had either to pass a dish to him and
say "Darlin'?" or else to say to the servant, "Pass your master
so and so."

"Well," said Captain Ruffin, as Valette, after coming in
somewhat late and stopping to kiss Malcolm and Mrs.

Bedford on the cheek, took her seat beside him, "we have a fine morning after the festivities."

Valette, as she knew how to do when she thought of nothing to say, laughed.

"But like summer, 'tis," he went on. "Yes, if the heat increases as the sun progresses, it will be very warm today."

"Oblige me by passing the syrup," Mary Cherry said. Since she did not look up, every one, along with Ben, the footman, and Celie, the waitress, felt constrained to locate the little silver molasses pitcher, and the conversation stopped.

Miss Mary had the habit in the houses she visited of declining a dish offered to her with, "No. It's been cooked to death," or, shaking her head, "it should have been stewed." Up in Panola County at Mr. John McGehee's or Doctor Tait's, where she visited so much, she went further sometimes and sent dishes away from the table; "Here, gal, take this away, there's too much pepper in it." She could have done so at Portobello as far as Malcolm went, but Sallie Bedford was not the kind to put up with it. Nobody would have nursed Mary Cherry through a fever more patiently, but there was also justice. "Right under your nose, Miss Mary," Sallie said, fixing her eyes sharply on the molasses pitcher.

At Doctor Tait's house in Panola Miss Mary had professed to be tired of going around a corner of the hall leading from her room, and they had cut a door for her near the head of the stairs. "It will be a sweet day when we go to cuttin' up this house to suit Miss Mary," Mrs. Bedford said, when she heard of it. She did, however, allow Mary Cherry to do at Portobello what she did at every house she visited, which was to go down some afternoon that suited her, put all the servants out of the kitchen and bake cakes. The recipe for these cakes was kept secret from every one. When they were done Miss Mary put them in a black box and locked them in her wardrobe.

"And who did we like at the party?" Mrs. Bedford said to Valette, her eyes twinkling. "Drink your milk, honey. Now what of the young Lochinvar from Woodville?"

"Who, My Dumplin'?"

"You know perfectly well, George McGehee. Why does he say *ond* for *and,* pray?"

"Because Henry Walsworth and that Fentriss chap and the Dunbar and the heir of Clifton pronounce it the other way," Malcolm said. "You sang to all their hearts, I suppose."

"No, Uncle, I sang for Miss Percy," Valette said, half laughing, her eyes clouding at the same time. She had left her chair and was standing by him. "I sang for her."

"Don't weep about it."

"I should say not," Mary Cherry said. "Are the hot waffles comin', Sister Sallie?" Ben was at the door with them and Celie was taking the platter out of his hands. "As for Mistress Percy, I've no objection to the diamonds if Napoleon wanted to give 'em to her——"

"But, Miss Mary," said Valette, laughing outright at this, " 'twasn't Napoleon's court, 'twasn't Napoleon."

"And why not?"

"Because Napoleon was dead then."

"So's she from the looks of her. What's the point of looking like you'd stuck your head in a flour barrel?"

"Oh, no," Mrs. Ruffin put in, very boldly for her. "She's a vision, I think. The French for it"—she looked about her shyly and finished her remark,—"is *charmante."*

"Go way from here," Sallie Bedford said, giving Valette a little push. "Pretending to love us or anything else that will let you out of your breakfast. And your auntie's no better," she went on, turning to her sister, as Valette sat down again at the table.

"Aunt Piggie's worse than I am," Valette said. "Uncle Mac says it's a sin not to eat and that a Christian needn't fast."

"Not on peppers," he said, eyeing the saucer of cherry peppers that was always put at Rosa's plate. It delighted him to think of that angelic voice asking for this food that would knock you backwards.

Rosa laughed and pushed the saucer across to him. She had a way of talking very little but of being never out of the conversation.

"I thought Christians used to fast like everything, My Dumplin'," Valette said to Mrs. Bedford.

"What your Uncle Mac means, honey, is he thinks nothing necessary to a Christian that would be unsuitable for the Bedfords."

The conversation turned on the party split that might give the victory to the other side. The public knew very little about Lincoln, the Republican candidate. Captain Ruffin was discussing what might happen if Lincoln was elected.

Valette did not listen. She sat with her own thoughts looking out toward the avenue of live-oaks. From her seat at the table she could see, past the fluted marble vases near the house, the trees and the moss hanging down, flecked with sunlight. Of all the houses in the world it seemed to be the beloved of its own trees and gardens.

At the south end, running straight back, was a wing with chambers for guests. There was a gallery with columns, slender and square, along this wing, and steps that led down into a garden set apart for roses. On the inner side of this wing ran another gallery; it looked across a brick-paved court toward the pantries and an arcade, open, with brick pillars and a flat roof, that led to the kitchens.

From this gallery during the last of breakfast came a commotion, children's cries and laughter mingled with the sound of a parrot squawking and screaming. There could be only the two Bedford children and their little cousin Middleton Dandridge, the child of Malcolm's dead sister, and with them their little darkeys, for each one of the children had his play-mate. But the air rang.

"My gracious, Darlin', you'd think there was a regiment!" Mrs. Bedford said, as the noise on the gallery burst out afresh. "Really!"

"Let the floods clap their hands," he laughed, while the parrot and children seemed to chime their screeching together, "Eh? let the hills be joyful together before the Lord."

"Amen," said Mary Cherry, not looking up from her plate, but recognizing the Bible rhythm. "Amen!"

VII

"Ir's Billy McChidrick's parrot," Mrs. Bedford explained to Captain Ruffin.

Billy McChidrick had belonged to Malcolm's father, who had bought him from South Carolina. Nobody knew just how old he was, but when the elder Bedford died, Billy had fallen to Agnes with her part of the estate. She took him to Montrose. He was a rice-field negro, half savage. Long ago he had built a sort of stockade of bamboo cane and split post-oak around his cabin, with his own fruit trees enclosed and three ferocious bloodhounds running loose. Both Hugh McGehee and Agnes knew of Billy McChidrick's stealing off at night into Natchez, where he could get hold of rum. They knew that he plucked birds alive, and that if he discovered some piece of spoiled meat, he would sit down at once with his jackknife, knocking the maggots off and eating it. Plenty of times they had threatened him with punishment. But a month ago the negroes at the quarters had reported that Billy had punched his plough horse's eyes out to stop them looking back and putting a ha'nt on him. Not only because of this brutality, but as an example to the other negroes something had to be done. The two punishments most dreaded by the plantation slaves were either to be turned over to poor whites or to be sold down the river to the cane fields. Agnes would not let Billy McChidrick be sold to the poor whites, she could not bear to see him broken like that; and so he was sent off to New Orleans; she cried when they took him away.

"Good-bye, Ole Miss," he said, half drunk, chuckling to himself, with tears in his eyes.

"Good-bye, Uncle Billy. Don't lose the quinine I gave you."

"Yes'm. Hit's sholy good, anybody's got um chills, Ole Miss."

"Good-bye, Uncle Billy."

"Yas, m'am!"

A week later her brother Malcolm, after a visit to Montrose, came home and dispatched one of his overseers to find Billy McChidrick and bring him to Portobello. This was easy enough, for M. Prudhomme, of Parlange, who had bought Billy, had already returned him to the dealer, with a scorching letter.

Malcolm was telling the Ruffins of how, out of pride, perhaps, Billy McChidrick had so shaved his head and body and greased himself up that in a lot of eleven auctioned off, he passed for much younger than he was. There was nothing new to it. Billy had only remembered an ancient trick of the slave-traders landing African cargoes. And now he was living at Portobello, where he had his cabin apart from the other negroes but not the stockade. Mrs. Bedford had put her foot down about that. She thought it enough to have him shambling about the grounds, wheezing and jabbering at the children, though Malcolm said the children loved him much more than they did their parents. That at least was true of Sallie Bedford's brother Henry, old Henry Tate, whose tall figure you saw sometimes wandering about the lot. Five years before, he had turned up at Portobello, nobody knew from where. He lived in one of the cabins, and no matter what his sisters did, would have nothing to do with the family or the house. He and Billy used to sit talking for hours. One way or another, Billy McChidrick had brought back a parrot with him from his travels.

A little boy, with a round face and wide gray eyes, came to the door from the back gallery and paused a moment.

"Well, Master Middleton?" Mrs. Bedford asked.

"Aunt Sallie, who's Mrs. Shaw?"

"Mrs. Shaw? Why, Aunt Sallie don't know. Come here, honey, you poor little orphan, he's Aunt Sallie's pet is what he is. Listen," she went on, putting her lips to his ear. "Say good-morning, and tell Miss Mary she's looking well, can't you?"

"Oh, wife, don't plague the child," said Mr. Bedford, winking at him.

"No, Middleton may as well learn right now to make himself pleasant; he can't just act the way he feels."

Middleton turned to his uncle. "Uncle Mac, do you know where Mrs. Shaw lives?"

"Ask me no questions and I'll tell you no lies." He made a pass to catch the little boy, who eluded him, bending his small body unconsciously like a flower stem, on his way to Mary Cherry.

"Are you Mrs. Shaw?"

"Why, Middleton," Valette cried, trying not to laugh at the sight of that look on Miss Mary's face, like a noiseless snort. "That's Miss Mary. You know her. You like Miss Mary, don't you?"

"I love Miss Mary," the sweet child voice repeated. No one in the family had laughed at him. They sat listening politely for what he might tell them.

But the little boy stood looking at various people, as if to say it was strange they would not know such a simple thing as who Mrs. Shaw was. Then, as another burst of laughter came from the other children outside, he went to take Valette by the hand and drew her out with him.

It was like this every morning at breakfast except when Malcolm had had more to drink than was good for him the day before. Then his wife kept the children quiet, sat watching to see that the coffee in his cup was hot, and talked to him as on any other morning. But this did not often happen.

VIII

AFTER breakfast they went to sit till the mail came from town, in the library.

"The only Shaws I know were poor wretches we sent the coffee and meat to," said Mrs. Bedford, "some of those piney woods people." Along the Jackson road some miles to the east the shanties of these people could be seen, poor whites who owned no slaves, were too shiftless to work more than mere patches of land, and, so far as the planter society went, might as well not have existed. The Bedford children had never seen any people of this sort, except on the roads and two or three times, perhaps, some Saturday in Natchez. "The old man came here to the steps one day, you remember, Darlin'."

"If Billy McChidrick thought that parrot of his was calling those people, he'd wring her neck. If you want a snob give me a darkey. And ours at Portobello are worse than at Montrose."

"Yes, Senator," Mrs. Bedford said, turning to Captain Ruffin, "what snobs the darkeys are! And how did you explain it to

some of those Abolitionists—? Field hands are another matter, but there's been many a black skin a servant in this house.
Whatever they may think of freedom I never saw one yet
who believed in equality."

As they sat there expecting at any moment the mail from
town to arrive, they began to speak of the negroes at the two
plantations. As always Mrs. Bedford quoted the Biblical utter-
ance that the Ethiopian was given us to the uttermost, to be
broken with rods—meaning not, of course, she said, hit him
over the head, but to rule him.

Captain Ruffin was, as Malcolm used to say, a fine man,
naturally keen and obtuse. He spoke usually in the style of
Plutarch, and spoke often; but at the moment the good breakfast he had eaten rather disposed him to listen to others. He
concurred in Mrs. Bedford's opinion.

"And this I believe," she went on, "with things in the state
they are in the South—no matter what happens, even if the
Abolitionists win and the blacks are freed, take my word for
it, in a thousand years they'll all be slaves again."

"Look at Hugh McGehee and his brother Edward, two of
the largest slaveowners in the world, and it's on their con-
sciences," said Malcolm. "They are worried to desperation and
don't know any way out of it. Well, on my plantations the
overseers run things, and it goes well enough."

"Plenty well," said Miss Mary, shaking her heavy old finger, "and listen to me! Hugh McGehee's always worrying over
'em, and he's got the worst niggers in the country."

Mrs. Bedford nodded her head and turned to Senator Ruffin.
"You know, Captain, how plenty of people let the darkies raise
their own patches of Nankeen cotton for pocket money. It's
brown and so they can't steal the master's cotton and mix
with it. But at Montrose, thank you, they can raise white or
anything they please. You can imagine——"

"I can indeed. Our old Gussie avows the rest of them on

our place in Pontotoc will steal the money off a dead man's eyes. You were about to say——?"

"I was going to say I declare poor Agnes McGehee! You'd think every darkey was stolen separately from his home in Africa by the traders. When, as a matter of fact, we all know it's the African chiefs and traders of their own blood do the selling. I tell Agnes that, but she goes right on wondering if Aunt Eve or Uncle David had a good night's rest and their rheumatism's better this morning."

"But nobody has a kinder heart than you, my dear friend."

"Sis Sallie's just as kind to a lame mule," said Miss Mary. "Here, Thornton," she saw the old negro outside on the lawn beneath the window, "go up to my room and bring me my other specs; don't fall down with 'em either."

"Yes, mam," came the friendly old voice.

"Is that Uncle Thornton, Miss Mary? I'd like to tell him to——" Mrs. Bedford began.

"'Twas Thornton. But he's gone for my specs, so that I can see better than with these I've got on. I told him not to fall down and break 'em either."

"He won't fall."

"He looks like he might."

"What makes you think that, Miss Mary?"

"Well, carrying those shears in his hip pocket is one thing. Just let him try fallin' on a pair of shears. So I said don't fall with my specs."

"It will be all right, Miss Mary."

"To be sure it'll be all right. If he don't fall. That's exactly why I said don't fall on my specs, Thornton."

Sometime during this conversation the children had stolen into the room. They came in quietly, taking their places on the chairs near the wall. Mary Hartwell, the tallest of the three, carried the parrot on her wrist. When she sat down it hopped away and perched on the back of her chair.

Presently Valette followed the children in from the gallery and joined Mrs. Ruffin on the sofa.

"This spring when I was at Montrose—" In her strong, hard voice Miss Mary began to tell what pains Hugh McGehee took, whenever he acquired new slaves, to buy their children or husbands or wives, if possible. He would send sometimes all the way back to Virginia, so that families would not be separated. "But he had to laugh himself about Nettie. They bought her from Virginia for a seamstress, and when they found she had left a husband on a neighbor's place, there in Green County, Brother Hugh wrote and offered to buy him. But the offer was declined by the darkey himself, and, bless my soul, come to find out Nettie had been writin' back about the terrible ocean she'd had to cross on the way down to Mississippi! What's the matter with that ocean was that Nettie had found a man she liked better, you know Brother Hugh's Big Dave, one of those buck niggers as strong as a horse."

The parrot meantime had sat still, only turning her head this way and that, as if what one eye had seen the other had reason to doubt.

"I vow the way the Montrose darkies are indulged—" Miss Mary was describing how often you were interrupted in an evening at Montrose when all at once the sound of some one sniffling was heard.

"You are sitting on the porch conversing, when——"

Miss Mary stopped short, looking about the room to see who it was that had such a cold. Plainly nobody, and with a general glare at the four children, she went on. "It's 'Marse Hugh, I'm got a fever.' 'Who's there?' 'Hit's Jim, Marse Hugh. Ed's stuck a nail in he foot.' And that's the way it goes."

Sounds of clearing the throat began, *"harwk,"* one after another, embarrassingly literal. The children had sat looking at each other, their lips pressed close, as if about to laugh. They held on to themselves, exchanging glances as if there were better yet to come. Miss Mary stood up and faced them, her hand planted on the chair back.

"Well, what a fool bird!" she almost shouted.

At that the parrot gave a great belch.

Malcolm Bedford, trying to address some remark or other to Miss Mary and seeing her look past him, was convulsed with laughter, the children joining in, delighted and shrieking all together. In the excitement the parrot began bobbing up and down on her feet, batting her eyes and this time producing delightedly a loud series of belches.

Mrs. Bedford glanced up with an air of stern inquiry at Valette, who only rose and, coming to stand behind the chair, laid her arm around the fragile shoulders, taking pains not to look at anybody for fear she should lose her composure. Miss Mary had resumed her seat and sat pulling down her cuffs. The children now kept still.

What delighted Malcolm was the idea as to why, with all the sounds there are in this world to choose from, the creature should pick out those so very special to the natural man. On that basis, he reflected, nevertheless, the belch would be a good place to stop. A very good place to stop.

"Better ring for Celie to take Polly out," he said to Mary Hartwell.

But the little girl begged to carry the parrot herself, who as soon as she was taken up began to call for Mrs. Shaw. The three smaller children shot down from their chairs and crowded up close, as they went through the door and outside, the parrot screaming as loud as possible: "Mrs. Shaw! Mrs. Shaw! Mrs. Shaw!"

Sallie Bedford's eyes were twinkling. "You'll have to excuse the rascals. Maybe when Dock brings the mail, there'll be a letter from Mrs. Shaw, who knows?" She spread out her white, small hands on her lap, and sighed, as if to say Heaven knows there was plenty to do at Portobello.

"You talk about pets," Miss Mary said, "but it's always a surprise to me, Sis Sallie, that anybody wants to feed a beast like that when there are so many people need it. Not that I'm speakin' of myself."

"Miss Mary, honey, what that bird eats you could put on your thumb nail."

"That's just it. Who wants to carry parrot food around on his thumb nail?"

The parrot, however, had spoiled a plan that, in spite of his wife's remonstrances, Malcolm had thought of trying. There was a little mulatto boy on the place named Lester, who had taken an infatuation for Captain Ruffin, and by hanging about the windows listening to the Captain's talk, had mastered the same accent and delivery. Malcolm, sitting on the gallery some of these afternoons, had conceived the idea of teaching Lester to say by heart a peroration to one of the Senator's Washington speeches, and Lester was now perfect at it. To have him in, to watch the Senator's astonishment when the little yellow boy with his curly head should give them word for word, eloquence for eloquence—he could hear that,

"A thousand nays, rather shall we perish from the earth——"

But not after the parrot, and not with Captain Ruffin on his way now to Jackson where they were planning a convention to consider secession. As against the North the majority was united. But they were divided between those who thought secession should await the joint co-operation of a number of slave states and those who were for immediate secession. Captain Ruffin was among the second, following Senator L. Q. C. Lamar, the leader. Nevertheless, to give up Lester's speech seemed to Malcolm a pity. If war came, he himself would be among the first to go—but a man can laugh——.

IX

THEY had an Indian at Portobello employed to hunt. He had a salary of six dollars a month plus his living and was to keep them in game. He had been there since he was a very young man, and was now thirty-four or thirty-five. His name, or at least a portion of it, was Ophio, but he was called Dock. He was not the stale Indian of the tales, but a Choctaw who had stayed behind with the Bedford family when his tribe was robbed and sent West by the United States Government. By that time the Choctaws were no longer nomadic but had settled down with land and possessions. Dock rarely spoke at all, but once when out hunting he had told Malcolm Bedford —Malcolm had never forgotten it—of seeing his people, when they departed, touching the twigs, the leaves, the tree trunks about their homes, saying good-bye to them forever.

On most mornings it was Dock who rode into town for the post; and that day at Portobello when he stood at the door of the library, his eyes on the floor, Mrs. Bedford, from where she sat by the centre table, asked him to bring the newspapers and letters to her. There were, also, a packet of garden seeds, a book, and a small box with red seals on it.

"Here, child," she gave to Valette all but a letter and the box, on which she was already untying the strings. "Those are for you, Darlin', barring the seeds," she said, as Valette put the newspapers into Malcolm's hands and came back to stand beside her chair.

Malcolm read *The National Intelligencer*. He used to maintain his subscription by sending thirty dollars at a time. And now, when Valette handed him this issue, he ripped off the journal's wrapper with his index finger, and handed over another paper to Captain Ruffin, who opened it with a silver-and-ivory paper-knife that lay on the table.

"But it's *The New York World*," Captain Ruffin said, "sent to me marked by somebody. Now what under the sun? See here 'tis," he said, as he went on down the column.

His wife looked at him apprehensively for a moment, until he began to read aloud. If they were not to be his own words but some one else's they were at least from his lips. Captain Ruffin read to them and every one had to listen.

"Letter to the editor. From the South, yes. 'If our'—et cetera, et cetera—'I am a native of Virginia, a graduate of New England, a resident of Mississippi, a taxpayer of Louisiana. I loved to be national and I was. I have loved the Union with a worshipping love, with a grand look at the future. If Southern precipitancy has made the North a unit, Northern threats have made and are making the South a unit. Whatever was the difference as to the "mode and measure of redress," we are now one in the position in which we find ourselves. You are for war, for turning loose upon us the horrors of a war to which a servile war will be added. Slave uprisings will be added to civil war."

"Why not allow, advise and aid a peaceable Secession? You cannot arrest the course of things here; nothing less than extermination can do it. Why not aid in the establishment and consolidation of two nations closely bound by every bond of interest and blood? J. W. Burruss, Woodville, Mississippi."

The hands that held the paper were shaking. "And by God Almighty, he's right! Why not?" said the Captain.

"I agree," Malcolm said, "though we could spare a little of that *l'état c'est moi* tone, eh, wife?"

"No mind about that, Darlin'. You know how 'tis with Mr. Burruss, he's always got to be the one shot the bear."

It was well known that a great difference between the industrial North and the planter South lay in the fact that where in general the captains of industry sent lawyers to Washington to look after their interests, the planters sent members of their own class. When Mr. Daniel Webster wrote Mr. Biddle, the banker, suggesting that his check had not arrived, it could have been assumed that his fiery orations in the Senate halls for certain interests were, though none the less sincere, less closely connected with himself than the speeches of Mr. Calhoun were to himself, who argued for his own possessions and prejudices, which were also those of the people he represented. If the ground was not higher it was at least his. The planter voted for himself, as it were, voiced in Washington his cause, his home, and the society in which both materially and passionately he belonged. It happened thus that such a man as Captain Ruffin, who might otherwise have been a mere windbag or politician in the Senate, and at this moment in the drawing-room that morning at Portobello might have been a mere florid ranter, was suddenly caught up into something larger than his own self. His voice, naturally flexible and rich, now darkened and stung, its rhythm was that of feeling. There was no one in the room who did not feel the persuasion of what, apart from right or wrong, wise or foolish, is deep within a man's nature.

His wife looked at Captain Ruffin with adoration. And thus, too, it happened that in this woman, also, short waisted, homely, with small eyes and thick red hair, something beautiful appeared in her stead. "The South, my country," she thought, smiling with her lovely smile. "My dear lover, how wonderful he is, my husband!" She had put her hand up to her mouth, as if to say, "Don't speak. As for me I shall not even breathe. And you, don't speak!"

Captain Ruffin folded up the newspaper, as if a treaty had been concluded. "Is there any man who would desire to bring war to this fair land?" he said. "Only the militarist monsters of hell and Messrs. Wendell Phillips and Company desire it."

He had fallen into an orator style that had little to do with what he felt, which had the exactness of passionate emotion.

But every one understood this. Sallie Bedford almost at the first, out of politeness, had left off trying to read the letter that had come for her, though she could let her eyes rest on the daguerreotype. Presently she forgot the picture. What she saw in place of it was her son—Duncan—Captain Ruffin was speaking of war—her eyes no longer saw the face in the daguerreotype—they were merely looking.

"All this hue and cry about the sinfulness of Secession spells nonsense," Malcolm said. "William Lloyd Garrison called for Secession of the Northern States if Texas entered the Union as a slave State, back yonder in 1836."

"But, Darlin', are you sure of the date?"

His wife used to say that Malcolm knew nothing correctly but Byron's *Mazeppa*. He shook his finger at her and repeated,

"1836."

"Bless my soul, bless my soul!" he went on, winking at Valette. "She's all eyes, she's all blushes, this little rose of ours!" Valette, who had stood with her eyes on the picture all this time, moved away from Mrs. Bedford's shoulder and then, without looking up or speaking, went out of the room. Mrs. Ruffin watched her.

"Miss Sallie," she said, "that child seems sad to me."

"Who?" Mrs. Bedford said, drily.

"Valette, Miss Sallie."

"Did she?"

"I expect she misses having kin of her own. I mean her not gettin' mail like the rest of you all this morning."

"We are her family."

"I know, I know, there's no difference between her and your own. But isn't there one blood kin for her? Not a single one?"

"So far as we know."

"It's like a scourge on us that yellow fever." She sighed and Sallie Bedford turned to Malcolm.

"Darlin', I don't much care about the date; what I was going to say was we've heard from Duncan, and here's his picture."

"Let's see it," said Mary Cherry, reaching up for the little black case before Malcolm had had time to open it. She leaned back in her armchair to look at the picture, turning it so that her good eye caught the light.

"Yes, that's right. That's Duncan. Yes, sirree." She did not return it but sat looking at the face in the picture, as she went on. "And, furthermore, what I'd say is, Julia Valette's lost her heart to him, and that's why."

"Why what, Miss Mary?" said Malcolm, frowning. "Excuse me, pray." He took the case out of her hand.

"Why she went out just now so white in the gills."

"Did she?" Mrs. Bedford said.

"And Duncan's equally enamored with Valette?"

"Aren't all the young men. You saw 'em last night, Miss Mary."

"I saw that Walworth boy and that young George McGehee from Woodville."

"My me, but George eats out of her hand!"

"You talk about Virginia"—nobody had spoken of Virginia. "I thought Duncan was at St. Luke's Academy in Maryland." She turned her head and looked straight at Malcolm Bedford, but his wife answered.

"Duncan was, but he changed," she said, in an indifferent tone. "Darlin', show our guests Duncan's picture."

"With pleasure. You'd know what a horseman he is by the way he sits by that table, eh? After all why shouldn't he go to Charlotteville, his grandmother Randolph was first cousin to Mr. Jefferson who built the university. We could hardly ask more, now could we?" Captain Ruffin made a deep bow, as of agreement, of full acknowledgment.

The young man who looked out at them from the case of dark morocco tooled with gold and fitted with the line of rose velvet, gold frame and gold mat, appeared at first sight to be in a fury of some sort; the fury then, when you glanced at him again, spread into impulsive pride, and from that suddenly it became the most astonishing air of generous youth and elegance combined. He was twenty-one, perhaps, and sat with his left hand on his crossed legs, his right on the table beside him. He wore a silk waistcoat, double-breasted; the points of his necktie, with the large knot in its bow, extended at each side beyond the velvet collar of his coat. The linen collar opened at the front stiffly, above the bow. His hair was parted far to the right and was left full at the back of his head and neck.

"He looks like for the drop of a handkerchief he'd knock the stuffin' out of you," Mary Cherry said, "ha!" in a tone that implied that this was the way a young man should look.

"And he'd take his heart out and give it to you," Mrs. Bedford said. She was standing by Mrs. Ruffin, looking at the daguerreotype with her. Mrs. Ruffin put her short plump arm around her waist and Sallie pressed her own elbow gently against it.

"You haven't seen our son! Then I'll tell you," she said, pointing with her little finger to each feature, as if their names were not enough. "The eyes are gray, his hair's brown, the complexion naturally fair, but the hot sun, of course— What is Duncan, Darlin', six feet?"

"No. Your son's seven feet six, Mrs. Bedford, or is it eight feet?"

"Ha, yes," Miss Mary said suddenly. "I do recollect! 'Twas some goin' on of Duncan up at that Maryland place. At any rate they sent him away for it."

"What was it?" Mrs. Bedford said politely, as if willing to hear some piece of news that was not very interesting.

"Seems to me he sassed the president about the mess halls or something—anyhow it was discipline, Sis Sallie. I can't remember these things."

"I don't imagine they set them down to feasts of Lucullus at that, do you?"

"No, I reckon not," said Mary Cherry, pushing down her basque front and fixing her gaze out of the window, as if she were as cool and detached as the great white camellia then covered with blossoms, full blown. "You can't believe anything you hear."

Malcolm Bedford smacked a fist into the palm of his left hand. "And yet, Miss Mary, you must admit, you——"

"Nor half, you see," Mary Cherry said, strongly. She spaced these words apart to down any reply, since she mistook his remark for an argument. He burst out laughing.

"No, I mean you must admit—when the rascal set fire to the cornstacks on the campus just to see the theologues from the seminary run— Running around in their nightshirts— I mean—" He was laughing so that he could scarcely talk.

"Oh, Darlin'," his wife said. "Little rascal! Well, I always said a child with any sense was full of the old imp. All my chillun were like that. You take Agnes McGehee when she used to bring Lucinda here, all you had to do was set Lucy on the floor and give her her mamma's ring to play with, and she'd sit there all day. So with Duncan—" She stopped, smiling fondly, then sighed.

Mary Cherry leaned back and gave a tremendous laugh. She laughed but seldom, but when she did it was like that. "Those theologues running around, bare-legged. Reminds me of old Sut Lovingood when he fell through the loft." This was the Georgia story of Sut Lovingood who left the party dancing the reel and went up to the loft overhead to go to bed. When he put on his nightshirt he slipped through the poles of the loft floor and fell till he caught on his armpits, and hung there dangling his legs over everybody.

"Oh, my goodness!" Mrs. Bedford said. The story was well known but generally considered rather broad; and Mary Cherry was a captain, which was, as Mrs. Bedford half knew, something of her own reputation in the county.

"So the president called Duncan up, Miss Mary, and expelled him," Malcolm said.

"Did 'em good. Did 'em good, Brother Bedford. I'm positive I enjoy a good sermon as well as anybody. But I never could understand a young man worth a rap studyin' to be a preacher."

"I'm afraid Duncan would agree with you."

Mary Cherry now appeared to be very much pleased with everything. "And what do you reckon he said about the table-board got the president so almighty roused up," she said, grinning so broadly that the gap showed between her large front teeth.

"Now, if it comes to that I can tell you," Sallie said. "He said the vegetables were full of sticks—and doubtless they were. Duncan never told a lie in his life—and when the president called him up to apologize, and said young man it has been reported to me you said the vegetables on my table had sticks in them, Duncan said, Well, I didn't say they were fence rails."

"He wasn't there long," Malcolm said. "He came home and taught his mother to ride fast horses and to shoot."

During this conversation Captain Ruffin sat over by the window with his head thrown back reading again the article in *The World*. His wife was divided between trying to keep an eye on him and trying to hear the conversation at the same time.

"Yes, to teach his mother to ride fast horses and to shoot,

and in the meantime to fall himself in love with Valette,"
said Mrs. Bedford. "And he courted her. She flirted him,
smiling at another young man, or so he thought anyhow, and
said so, and she flung him his ring back. He came in my room
and told me his troubles. We went down to Mammy Tildy's
cabin to saw the diamond ring off his finger where he'd put it
in his rage. The diamond flew out of the setting and rolled
off into the cracks of the floor somewhere. Much Duncan cared,
he was mad."

"What'd I tell you?" Miss Mary said. "I saw the little wretch
lookin' at that daguerreotype."

"But you must say, Darlin'," Mrs. Bedford said, as if his
father had somehow reflected on the young man, "Duncan
was eternally busy with his Mario horses, and, Miss Mary, you
know's well as I do, we and our Arabians are all one family."

"I've got my opinion of a man that don't like horses," Mary
Cherry said. "Yes, indeed, Sis Sallie."

"You'd see his little colts following him in droves."

X

YOUNG George McGehee had stayed on at Montrose, and
two days after the birthday party he rode over in the evening
to Portobello. He was riding Fancy, whose grandmother had
been the Arabian intended as a gift to General Winfield
Scott when he visited his Woodville cousins on his way north
from the Mexican War. George's grandmother had been
Nancy Scott from the Virginia Portobello, near Williamsburg.

George's father, Edward McGehee, was a man of great
character and reflection, his mother was a college president's
daughter, and the library at Bowling Green ran past nine thousand volumes. But George himself was a very happy young

man in his own fashion, who liked music and staying in New Orleans, where he played duets with various young ladies, whom he regarded as angels, and learned to admire the French Emperor Louis Napoleon. The mustache and imperial that he wore to imitate the emperor made him look older than his twenty years.

Valette and he had last seen each other in the starlight of the gallery at Montrose—she had thought of it since and had not been pleased with herself for the way she had allowed him to gaze into her eyes and had laughed as if some special happiness existed between them two alone out of the whole wide world. About this she had said nothing last night to Miss Mary Cherry; and now on his visit to Portobello the plain prose of a mere room made it easier to be natural and sensible.

"Do you remember the time, George," Valette said, "we were at your papa's lodge at the camp meeting and they burnt pine knot fires in front of the door?"

"They got us up at five o'clock," he said.

For reasons of their own they laughed at everything remembered, and more than an hour passed with childhood recollections interesting to themselves, or at least more interesting than silence to George, and for Valette more comfortable than his making sheep's eyes at her. She wished now with all her heart that she had frowned a little when he looked at her in the starlight at Montrose.

Presently, after a silence, when the recollections seemed to have run out, George said that last week a letter had come from Micajah McGehee in California. This was George's half brother, who had been away twelve years. Immediately Valette got up from her chair and, bringing her hands together as if to applaud, stood looking down eagerly to hear. "Cousin Micajah!" He was not her cousin, but there was no reason why, as it were, he should not have been, what with

Montrose and Bowling Green and all. "I can remember when I was a little girl—I must have been ten—sitting on the arm of Cousin Micajah's chair. I just touched like this"—she held out her little finger—"his hair and then his cheek. I thought 'what beautiful curly brown hair, what white skin! I love him, I love him!' I remember it exactly. 'Oh, how I love him!' I said to myself."

She did not know that this was worse than looking into his eyes for George, who stood up suddenly and then sat down, with a bump, on the sofa.

"Is it really so that he was in love with the girl his brother loved and that's why Cousin Micajah didn't come home at all after the university but just went away?"

"And joined Frémont's expedition, and Brother Francis won the young lady."

"Will he ever come back?" Valette sighed.

"Cage?" he asked.

"Don't call him that."

"Father calls him Cage."

"I call him Micajah," her tone was so devout that one of their elders, hearing it, would have laughed. "I say 'Cousin Micajah.'"

"Last year when Father heard he was sick he sent Brother Francis out to California to bring him back, but he came home without Micajah."

"Haven't you ever felt," Valette said, sitting down again and looking past George, "that there are certain people you'd like to ask things? I always think I could say to somebody like Cousin Micajah, 'Cousin Micajah, you just gave up what you desired in your heart and kept away, have you found there's a sort of peace, as if you dreamed it? Or are we wasted, just thrown away?'" She blushed, as she added quickly, "I don't know. But that's the way it seems to me."

George felt himself less gay and happy than he had been.

Girls should be lighter than that, like flowers, like birds, exactly; their emotions should be like a song in a bird's throat. He could only change the subject.

"There's one personage missing here, I can tell you, I'd like mighty well to see."

"How empty his handsome eyes are!" Valette thought, collecting herself and reaching up her hand to feel if the little comb of silver and cameos was in place. "Who?"

"Old Duncan."

A second time she blushed. "Oh, Duncan." She was angry at his saying Old Duncan like that.

When she spoke of the daguerreotype Duncan had sent from Virginia, George wanted to see it. But she said that would have to be another time, the daguerreotype was on My Dumplin's table upstairs, in her room. How was Duncan? He was very well.

"I mean, do you mind if I ask you, Valette," said George, "if there was any sort of promise before Duncan left for college?"

"No, of course not, what is there to promise? There's the guitar, but don't carry it off," she said gaily.

She began singing in a low voice the Swedish air the Chevalier la Tour was teaching her; and George, who could play anything he touched, followed. He knew the song, after Jenny Lind's concert half of New Orleans hummed it; but at first they were not together. Then it went better, and that flutter of sweet sound like wings that was a part of her voice came into her singing. George could not be blamed for taking to himself some of this feeling. It was only the voice itself, which seemed compelled to listen to its own heart to find its way. They were apart again, he had struck the wrong chords, and stopped playing; and Valette suddenly, taking a high note as if flying into a tree, burst out laughing.

But George McGehee, instead of laughing, put down the

guitar and buried his face in his hands. So it had got to that. She wished George had not come and that he would let her alone. Then she leaned down and kissed his sleeve just below the shoulder. She was glad for a knock at the door and to have Celie come in with a silver tray on which was Malcolm's watch, the lid open. His father before him had used this way of reminding young men that it was half past ten o'clock and time to say adieu. For George as well as Valette Malcolm's watch was a relief.

"I'll do it if it wakes up the dead," Valette said to herself twenty minutes later, as she stood in her nightgown before her dressing-table. She left the door open into the hall and went back to blow out her candle.

XI

MRS. BEDFORD had blown out the candle half an hour before, but she and Malcolm lay awake talking of the state of things. The problem of the moment was Miss Gilbert, the children's governess. She had been with them a year. Her cousin, Mrs. Burruss, mistress of Elleray, at Woodville, had been the cause of Miss Gilbert's coming South; their two families lived side by side in Winsted. Miss Landon, the cousin, had gone from governess to wife; her sensible and sincere feelings and deep piety had made her beloved. With Miss Gilbert, though she was her cousin's age, not yet thirty, it was different. She had an aggravated sense of responsibility that dulled her, as if some final judiciality had been assigned her for life and had lodged in her insides. She might well have married a planter husband. Many a governess came down to this country from the North and did so; but the look around her nose had

frozen the rising compliment on the lips of various gentlemen.

"If it weren't so grim, she'd have a pretty face," Mrs. Bedford said.

"Well, no," said Malcolm, "what I maintain about her face
is how could anything be so strong and amount to so little?"

"No, Darlin'. She's prettier than that, though she does look
as if she'd swallowed a ramrod. And the truth is all of us
trust her entirely. And love her, except the darkies. They
don't.'

A year ago Malcolm had written in the most approved
elegance to Miss Gilbert, offering her the position of governess
and, in a second letter, extending to her the most cordial
welcome to Portobello; and Mrs. Bedford herself had driven
down to fetch her from the boat. She saw this newcomer
looking at the maroon velvet of the carriage seats, the harness
of the horses, and, as they passed one house after another, at
Monmouth and D'Evereux back among their trees; and saw
the pleasure in her eyes when Silas jumped down to open
the gate and there came into full view the live-oak avenue,
with the statues alongside, the house shining white at the end.
But it was only later that Malcolm and Sallie Bedford learned
that this pleasure was a good deal pure surprise.

They showed Miss Gilbert through the garden, but since
she had never seen so formal a garden before she had merely
asked what variety this flower was or that. They took her over
the ground floor of the house, and she exclaimed at the library,
between nine and ten thousand books, many of which,
Malcolm explained, with his off-hand air, had belonged to
his father, and some to his great-grandfather on his mother's
side, who had been a Randolph, Thomas Jefferson's grandfather also. Miss Gilbert had said nothing to that, for she had
thought little about Thomas Jefferson; Jonathan Edwards was
her hero in the past, and in the present Mr. Emerson and Mr.

Whittier. It was only later that they realized at Portobello and at Montrose that Miss Gilbert's father, a Unitarian preacher, had a collection of pioneer Americana, and that she had expected to find in this river country some wild and uncouth society of people, squatters and pirates for the general mass, and for her own employers, slave-holding rich renegades, as it were. Then why did she ever agree to come? Malcolm wondered: to earn a salary and to save souls? Gradually, as the months passed, it appeared from conversations and silences, that after her frontier reading in her father's collection, Miss Gilbert had two ideas of love among the pioneers.

First, that there was only brutal sex, women as instruments, or bearing children, wife after wife worn out and buried—how abhorrent to refined instincts, how antagonistic to the idea of woman's equality with man, the equal suffrage that Miss Harriet Martineau and others were preaching!

Second, that the hard lean life of the pioneer had a mistrust of the love between men and women; regarding it as a sin; and this Miss Gilbert's Puritan-conscience muddle caused her to feel that she understood.

These two attitudes in combination made no sense; but there was no machinery in Portobello society to discuss them with, and so on this subject it merely ended in silence with Malcolm Bedford saying privately to his wife, "Miss Gilbert resents being treated as a lady, don't she?"

"She'd be insulted if she were not," said Mrs. Bedford.

"Exactly. What she wants is a sort of court gazette where every day she'd state what she wanted a lady to be, the discussion of delicate matters to follow accordingly."

"Darlin', I declare sometimes I think if you hadn't read so much Rousseau's *Confessions* at the university you'd been a nicer man."

"What you mean is Miss Gilbert would think Rousseau would have been a nicer man if he hadn't confessed so much."

"Just as you say, of course, Darlin'."

"I say there's such a thing as too much stale virginity. Where does it get her?"

"I say what you've so often said, where is there to get?"

"And as Hamlet says the rest is silence."

"Yes, Darlin', you and Hamlet."

When the McGehees at Montrose had learned of Miss Gilbert's pioneering expectations they joined the Bedfords in a sly teasing, for soon they all liked her; Agnes most of all admired her clear, shy expression. "As honest as the day," Agnes said, "and down here among us looks like a child at his first earthquake; I remember how I felt when the water pitcher rattled one summer night. But I didn't think it mattered. I was sleeping on the trundle-bed in father's room, I didn't mind an earthquake, I thought father'll take care of me."

"So you thought we had come in our wagons, rude sons of toil, and hewn our simple cots from the sturdy oak," said Hugh.

Miss Gilbert laughed and looked at the Meissen teacup in her hand, with the gold flowers. She had a natural eye for good things.

"Now this old house," he said, "was first Spanish, nearly a hundred years ago, and some of the timbers in the basement are out of a ship, clearly. So we are only rough customers. With twenty-nine rooms, notwithstanding, and not an alligator in them; but, of course, my wife's an excellent house-keeper."

"Mr. McGehee, you're teasing me," said Miss Gilbert.

"But," he went on, "there's Stanton Hall, for example. What an advantage Natchez being a port, a boat was chartered to bring the fluted columns, the mantels, the arches, the mirrors, the chandeliers, et cetera, from France and Italy."

"Perhaps," Malcolm said, "the ship was drawn by oxen

across the prairies of the ocean main—*bipedum currus equum*
—bullocks of the deep."

Miss Gilbert, who would have been inhuman not to have
liked these people who all liked her, burst into one of her fits
of laughter that she could not control.

"And at D'Evereux," Agnes McGehee said, laughing too,
"the china was all done by M. Honoré of Paris in a green to
match the color on the walls. And just shipped here direct to
the redskins."

Malcolm Bedford said that they should take Miss Gilbert to
see what was going on at Longwood. Doctor Nutt, who was
building it, had named the place—an odd fancy—for Napoleon's last home on St. Helena. Doctor Nutt had experi-
mented with crossing Egyptian with the local staple, and had
given away to his friends right and left the new type known
as Little Mexican, worth millions to this country, had im-
proved Whitney's cotton-gin, and at Longwood there was a
rose garden of ten acres. "And thus," Malcolm said, "there was
nothing to do if Doctor Nutt kept on travelling abroad but to
order marbles and other matters right and left in Europe. So
much for the river pirates and land pirates in these parts."

"Just the same," Miss Gilbert said, "I saw some odd characters on that boat coming down. I feel certain some of them
were gamblers."

"And I'm sure they were all cousins of ours. But you must
go with us to Arlington tomorrow. Mrs. Boyd calls it tea,
but there'll be a bearfight you'll like in the parlor and in a
dark room Mr. and Mrs. Boyd will fight it out with daggers."

The truth was, as they all saw, Miss Gilbert liked it and
would have missed being teased about her expectations before
coming to this country.

When it came to Miss Whipple, the little seamstress from
Iowa, the case was different. Her ideas and expectations had
been like Miss Gilbert's. But Hugh McGehee had given what

amounted to orders at Montrose that Miss Whipple was not to
be plagued with arguments. It was a different case from Miss
Gilbert's because Miss Whipple did not have any sense.

Nevertheless, now that it had come, in the year 1860, what
with jarring sections and parties, to an issue between points
of view, Miss Gilbert had reverted to type: blood, after all,
is thicker than water.

For some weeks now her letters from home, the newspapers
they sent, full of anti-slavery editorials, and the discussions
everywhere to be heard, had perplexed her till she grew pale
and more serious than ever. As soon as this happened Mrs.
Bedford, in her sort of hard, straight humanity of feeling,
thought less of the issue and more of this unhappy young
woman; but Malcolm grew tired of the notion of a whole
house on the watch lest a young woman's feelings be hurt.

One morning after breakfast, reading a letter from her
father, Miss Gilbert had turned to the others and quoted
from it the lines:

"Dearer the blast round our mountains which raves
 Than the sweet summer zephyr that breathes over Slaves."

This was what the conversation was about. Both Malcolm
and his wife had decided that Miss Gilbert had best take the
cars back home, though as yet neither had said so, as they lay
talking in the bed that was part of a set long ago intended
as a present to Henry Clay, but for some reason when he was
not elected president never presented.

"We must admit—" Mrs. Bedford said, on her pillows with
only a light coverlid, and her arms outside. She paused, thinking Malcolm might be asleep. He lay on his side, one arm
under his head and his bare, right foot sticking out from the
covers at the foot of the bed, as it did summer and winter.

"Admit what, my treasure?"

"In some ways Miss Gilbert is not a fool."

"That's beyond peradventure," he said. He passed to the other, his real grievance against the children's governess: "But the thing I can't tolerate is that fetid idealism."

It is well known that, thanks to Thomas Jefferson, its founder, the University of Virginia was established in its scientific and social studies long before such Northern colleges as Harvard or Yale, where the theological tradition held on. The influence of French skepticism, humanism, and science had worked in the Virginia university from the start. This was what Malcolm Bedford meant as he went on:

"If I haven't kept up as I ought to, it's no sign I didn't get a little light from my studies. I'm familiar with the idea of progress. I read Condorcet, and I read Adam Smith's *Wealth of Nations,* much as I mayn't recollect it now."

"Of course. And Lucretius; on the tariff."

"Progress. It was that new conception that shook up the parsons, who, up till then, had thought we'd have to go to heaven if we wanted to find improvement anywhere."

"You get to talking about that and you'll never go to sleep. You know how 'tis. So hush."

"But that's a horse of another color from Miss Gilbert's notion."

"I agree with you."

"Well, then agree with me that I could stand my children being taught transcendentalism, witch burning, even abolition, but I'm damned if I'll have 'em taught that all things work together to make life sugar-coated."

"It's a pity we ever got on the subject, this time o' night."

"Sugar-coateder and sugar-coateder every day. Making fools out of helpless children. New England Puritan old-maid idealism!"

"When all that's needed," she said, "is to get a little sleep."

Presently she heard him turn abruptly over and lie on his back.

"Sallie, why does she want to say *stun* when she means *stone?*"

His wife chuckled, but made no answer. In the stillness she heard the flutter of the ruffled curtains in the light gulf breeze, and the birds here and there in the trees outside. "Never quite silent, never still out there," she thought, listening. She loved all the natural life of the world; little pigs snouting each other at the bran trough or the sound she was listening to now—it was the constant source of her tolerance with men and children.

Valette in her nightgown and slippers came along the hall as softly as she could. The new moon had set, but there was enough light from the clear stars of the autumn sky to show dimly the room. The thin white of its curtains poured into the soft darkness, where the vague square of the bed was, with its black tester and posts, the shadow of the bed steps crouching beside it. She could smell My Dumplin's orris, which was the only perfume she used and which would be in every drawer, faint like early violets. Valette paused to take a long, noiseless breath and to step out of her slippers.

"You won't find it there," Mrs. Bedford's voice said, from the dim white of the bed.

"My Dumplin'!" Valette burst into a smothered giggle.

"I took him off that table, and put him over here. I wanted to look at him too. Why aren't you in bed, I'd like to know?"

Valette had run on tiptoe across the room, and buried her face in the other's shoulder. "Sh! You'll wake your Uncle up, you little wretch!"

"He's awake. Uncle's exactly like me, I can feel him chuckling."

"Well, he'd like to be asleep and so would I. You're smothering me, Julia Valette."

"You're as skinny as a little bird, My Dumplin'!"

"Get up, I tell you! And go to Guinea!"

Valette raised her head and seated herself on the steps beside Mrs. Bedford.

"What is it you want, Valette?"

"I'd get sick to death of climbing these steps to bed."

"This bed belonged to——"

"I know. Thomas Jefferson's Aunt Kate. If she'd just fallen out of it once——"

Malcolm on his side of the bed kept still and said nothing. These conferences with his wife in the dark room were not new. Some of Duncan's chief crises had been settled thus, with Duncan stamping up and down the middle of the carpet; even Middleton had stolen out and come here about some of his secrets one night when Aunt Sophie, his nurse, was dozing in her bed.

"Look here," said Mrs. Bedford, pretending to whisper. "Why don't we like Mr. George McGehee, pray? Because you don't admire those side curls?"

"My Dumplin'," Valette said, reproachfully. "You know they're not side curls."

"They're brushed over the finger, then, like Napoleon the Third's."

"But you make him sound like that old lady in Jackson when Uncle spoke, who came up and said, 'Sir, I give you this apple because I like you.'"

"Yes, and that was your Uncle's one and only speech."

"I don't believe any apple would stop Captain Ruffin, do you, My Dumplin'?"

"So you thought you'd steal Duncan's picture? Why don't you steal George McGehee's picture from somebody?"

She heard Valette drop her head in her hands and begin to sob.

"Honey, it's no matter, we're just foolin'." The sobs went on. "Then what's the matter, you've been coquetting with George?"

There was no answer.

"Great God A'mighty," Malcolm said, as if, now that he had spoken at last, he might shout in a moment. "Now look, wife, what you've done. Gone and made her cry."

"No, it's all my fault," Valette sobbed, "it's not you, My Dumplin'."

"Then I reckon you must have let him kiss you?"

"No. He felt so sad. I kissed him on the sleeve."

Malcolm burst out laughing, "And it's not even full moon," he said, "and no serenade. So you see. So now hush."

Valette stopped sobbing and lifted to her lips the slight little hand that clasped hers.

But blood is thicker than water after all: Duncan was her son; and there was resentment in Mrs. Bedford's voice when she took her hand away and asked why any girl had to go on like milliners and matchmakers with the men.

"I just don't know," Valette said. "But you must know. You know more about me than I do, My Dumplin'!"

Nobody but Valette could have made that speech.

The scolding voice said kindly:

"It's youth, child, when we're young—and you felt sorry for George; I feel sorry for George. But that's no reason why you should think you can just flash yourself around all the time, honey, like a cluster of diamonds. We've got to do something about this child's eyes, Darlin', and that smile."

"And something about that sweet voice," he thought. It reminded him sometimes of another voice that had once been at Portobello, but he rarely spoke of his first wife.

"Here," his wife was saying to Valette, "kiss My Dumplin' good-night. I'll bet you've got your slippers off. Yes, and then we'll hear some singin' indeed, like a hoarse crow! You'd better leave the picture tonight, that's wiser. You can get it in the morning. There, honey, don't you know Duncan well enough to know if he won't write a word he loves you? I didn't say *don't*, I said *won't*. Now run to bed."

"Yes, sirree," Malcolm said, "and if my son exploded like a steamboat, ten to one t'would be when he loved you most."

The next morning word came out from town that Mr. Lincoln had been elected.

XII

"But do you see, it was just along the river bluff stood De Soto's men—" Rosa Tate would say to the children. "Perhaps it was sundown when they saw it first, and they thought my, that's a wide river, we will tell the king in Spain!" Or the soldiers of five nations had drilled on the esplanade looking down on the river.

It had nothing to do with their governess, but this was the way she taught the Portobello children, and Valette, too, a sort of dream of history. This was the way, too, she taught them astronomy; so that all of them went about not only on the ground but under the sky's vaulted dome, with its morning, its evening, its golden fires. And the fine names there among the stars and constellations, Aldebaran, Orion, The Big Dipper, the Pleiades, Mars, red in the east, with Cassiopeia's Chair near the horizon, were not too different from the garden leaves or the camellias. Even Duncan later on, when he was almost a man, coming from some tavern with too much whisky in him, would feel at his heart the tenderness of the new moon when there was one, or watched for the full moon in the trees. And this was the way Rosa taught the children the language of the Bible. She had her Catholic Bible but she read also—and would have done so if Father Maury had reproved her, which he was too wise to try—the King James's version that her father had given her, how long ago!—its cover was blue velvet with a flower-painted medallion.

"There is one glory of the sun, and another glory of the moon, and another glory of the stars; for one star differeth from another star in glory," she would say to a child, sitting on the porch steps, as if nothing could be more natural than to say it so in such magnificence.

Judge Tate, celebrated as the lifelong friend of President Jackson, and as hot tempered as the general himself—they once came near fighting a duel but ended by presenting each other with gold-headed canes—had sent his two little girls, Sarah and Rosa, to a convent in Mobile, according to him, in order to keep them unspotted from the world, and, according to his wife, in order to spite the Episcopal bishop in Huntsville. But at the end of one session he took them out again, having learned from Sallie how her younger sister took to the Catholics. The child, it turned out, all winter long had stolen from her bed to light one of the sisters' fire in the morning, had tended Our Lady's altar, and had announced that some day she would take the veil. She had not taken the veil and her father had taken them out of the convent, but when she left Alabama and came with her sister to Natchez, Rosa was already a Catholic. On Sundays she drove in to early mass at St. Mary's, and with her went old Matilda, sitting up in a starched white dress, a black *tignon* on her head, beside the driver. Tildy had belonged to the Bedfords since she was fifteen, but she had been born not far from Natchitoches, on the plantation of the Cloutiers. Her full name was Matilda Marie Josephine de Renne, and she had never forgotten her religion. None of the McGehees were Catholics, and with their stubborn Scotch forefathers, they might easily have been hostile. In fact, there were, during Rosa's first months in Natchez, a few of the old jibes about doing what you like and being forgiven by the priest, and so on, mostly banter, until Hugh McGehee, however little it may have been anybody's business at Montrose, had put his foot down, and in his own way settled the business once and for all. The fact was, both he and his brother Edward at Woodville admired Rosa more than they did her sister. Sallie Bedford had a certain harshness or finality hard for the McGehee men to understand. At Portobello it was her sister who set the note for Rosa's treatment. Sometimes when Sallie Bedford looked at that face, delicately aquiline, the skin so white, the eyes blue, and its strange look of original youth, her own eyes filled with tears. "I don't know whether I've only another child," she would say, "or whether an angel troubles the waters. May God bless my little sister." "You tell him, Darlin', for me," she said once to Malcolm, when a circuit-riding preacher who had stopped for dinner had seen fit to exhort her sister as a Papist, "he needn't trouble to come back, the poor simlin-headed jackass! Tell him while Rosie plays her golden harp he'll be roasting in hell. For that matter she plays the guitar now."

Except when she was with the children, Miss Rosa did not talk a great deal, though she never seemed out of the company and nobody ever felt embarrassed by her silence. But she could play the guitar any evening, on the gallery, or in the garden or by the fire in the parlor, as if she were a girl of sixteen. She had learned the guitar from a Spanish teacher, half in love with her. "Only you mustn't ask me to sing now," she said. "It's a sin to squawk like a crow when the song's sweet."

Rosa had grasped some centre of her religion by which she appeared to move in a vision, and to be simple and clear and impalpable like light. She said she had a quick temper, but about that her sister said, "There's nothing to it, Rosa, but a weak heart occasionally makes you irritable, though it may be eating peaches does it. However, if Rosa warn't so quiet, I reckon she'd sin a little with the unruly member sometimes. I'll never forget the time she said of a certain clan, 'How unfortunate 'twould be to be a McGehee if you didn't like one!'"

Toward sundown on the day Duncan's picture had arrived, Valette stood at her Aunt Rosa's door upstairs, about to knock. Then she ran on light feet down the hall to the window on the avenue, her steps soundless on the thick carpet. It would be better to walk in the garden. She had taken a rose from a vase in her room and put it in her hair. She drew it out now and balanced it on the knob, so that when the door was opened from the inside, it would fall at Miss Rosa's feet. One does this because one is sixteen and in love.

At the south end of the porch the children were sitting with Mammy Tildy. Mary Hartwell sprang off the bench, ran to Valette and threw her arms around her neck for a kiss. "Oh, you've got on your blue dress. Stay with us just a minute, Lette. Listen!"

The three children were sitting with Mammy, who was listening as solemnly as they to the sound of Miss Mary's voice coming from the wing upstairs. Wherever she visited, it was Mary Cherry's custom to sit in her room and sing hymns. She would put her rocking-chair in the middle of the room and sing at the top of her voice. Sometimes you could hear it all over the house.

Middleton caught hold of Valette's hand and hugged it. "Stay with us, Lette."

"No, this time Lette's got to walk in the garden."

"Why don' Miss Mary——?"

"Which *don't!* You ain't no nigger chile. *Doesn't,*" Mammy said, looking severely at the little boy.

"Doesn't. Lette, why doesn't Miss Mary be like you or Auntie? She sings like one of Duncan's horses."

"No, no," Valette said, laughing and hugging him. "Miss Mary has a nice sweet voice."

"Is it like the lark?" Frances asked.

"It's not like the lark but it's a nice sweet voice all the same. What do you think, this morning Duncan sent his picture! He looks very handsome, he has a big tie."

"Duncan's got a big tie," Middleton said to the other children, who doubled up with laughter about nothing at all.

They could hear faint thuds from Mary Cherry's heels on

the floor as she rocked, her voice rose louder than ever. Mammy Tildy looked up toward the room in the wing. "Listen at Miss Mary. She sho' ain' bust her goozle yit."

"Will Miss Mary bust her goozle?" Frances asked, her eyes troubled.

"No, Sweetness," Valette said. "She's been singing with it a long time. Here, give Lette a kiss. That's *Bear Me Away on the Wings of a Dove,* she's singing. That's the hymn Cousin Abner up at Panola wrote us about. One day in church the choir and congregation had begun singing *The Bread of Life* when Miss Mary jumped up and began *Bear Me Away on the Wings of a Dove* as loud as she could, till she drowned them out, and the organist found the place and the choir changed their hymn. She didn't like the selection."

The children did not laugh at this, but listened solemnly, as if considering how one would do that.

"Mammy," Middleton said suddenly, leaning his head against the full bosom of her white apron, "tell us about the sweet potato."

Valette had a way of ordering the servants about like a young tyrant, and the negroes at Portobello adored her. When she walked down to the quarters sometimes and sat with Aunt Lucy, Silas' mother, or in her own maid Liddy's cabin, you might have thought a young goddess had stepped out of the sky. Mammy Tildy was one exception; she was always respectful but grave with Valette, who had flirted with Marse Duncan, who was right to file that engagement ring off his hand. Everybody knew the story about the potato. When Duncan was a little fellow his Mammy was always catching him and hugging him. One day he went to the kitchen when they were baking and asked for a hot potato. He stood on the porch waiting with his hands behind him, and this time when Mammy threw her arms around him he slashed out with the hot potato and mashed it on the back of her neck. But she was not going to tell that story now with Miss Valette there. "Go on," she said, "y'all talkin' about things I disremember."

"I can tell y'all one thing," Frances said, "jes let any boy mash potato on my neck, I'd scratch his eyes out."

"Oh, you ain' scratchin' nothin' out. Keep still." Frances had climbed into the old woman's lap. "If Marse Duncan done sumpn' like 'at, he ain' meant nothin'. Anyhow, I forgit, back yonder. Hit's time for y'all to go on to Aunt Sophie anyhow. Hey, stop standin' on your knees in my lap, rumplin' me to death. All right, if you keep still." The little girl, resting against Mammy's shoulder, leaned off to admire the red *tignon* on the round old head. With one finger she touched lightly the *tignon,* wishing she could wear one.

"Sing 'On Jordan's stormy banks I stand,' " said Middleton.

" 'An' cast a wishful eye.' "

" 'To Canaan's fair and happy land, Where my possessions lie.' Sing it to us, Mammy," the little boy went on.

This was the verse Mammy Tildy sang to boil eggs by, three times for soft boiled, five for hard. But she now said only, "I can't sing nothin' today, de Lawd ain' wid me."

"Where is he?" asked Frances.

"Whar who?"

"De Lawd," said Frances.

"Well, then, talk some the way you did when you were little," Middleton said, and Frances patted the fat shoulder: "Say that about the two birds."

"What's the matter wid y'all? *Los dos ozos.*"

The children tried to repeat the Cajun French to each other, again doubling up with laughter.

It was a good moment for Valette to slip away.

Between the bay hedge and the line of live oaks and statues parallel to it on each side of the avenue, ran a walk carpeted with moss. The blue lattice pavilion seemed solitary and the boxwalks *triste,* and she felt happy, as if she herself were the good angel that walked with her. She went slowly on young feet over the green path. The high corridor of boughs above the driveway was denser and closer in the yellow dusk of the fading light, and from these trees the hanging moss was now blurred into a mist. She heard the sound of fowls going to roost. The yard behind the stables quieted; in the hedges the small noises fluttered for a moment. As she paused half way to the gate and would have turned back, she saw suddenly one of the statues where the sky through some gap in the trees touched it. Lifted on the pedestal the nymph stood, holding up with her white arm, her wrist curving lightly, a wreath. Valette raised her arm as the arm was in the nymph's figure, and stood there looking up at her hand, so lightly held, and felt as if the flowers of the wreath rained down from her own finger tips.

"Why not?" she said to herself.

XIII

"Look, come to my room," Mary Cherry said, taking Valette by the arm that night. On the way up from the company downstairs the sharp old eyes had found her standing alone by the hall window.

"Now what's the matter?" She closed the door behind them and, taking a ring of keys from her skirt pocket was unlocking the wardrobe. "Today you were all smiles, but I watched you at supper. You ate about as much as a sparrow. Here, eat some of these." She held the black box from the wardrobe open for Valette. "Go on, I made 'em myself. Do you want to starve to death? Well, I won't let you. You're very soft and kittenish and they all swallow it, but you don't fool me. You've got sense. I like you. Sit down."

"Never were such cakes, Miss Mary," Valette said, when she had swallowed a piece. "But I couldn't eat another one, and so pray excuse me."

"You needn't brighten your eyes at me. My name's Mary Cherry. I saw you."

Valette laughed outright, and took hold of the finger Miss Mary was shaking at her, heavy like an old man's finger. Nobody else at Portobello would have been so free. The old woman drew the girl's head against her shoulder for a brief moment; it was like leaning against some granite monument.

"Because Duncan didn't write us, eh?" She pushed Valette away from her as if to indicate that the court would now come to order. "Eh?" she repeated.

"He hasn't written since he left—it's two months." Tears came into the soft eyes.

"Which only shows he loves you. That's a man all over."

Valette did not argue the point about men, but went and stood by the window looking out.

"Whyn't he write you, tell me? What struck him?"

"He thinks I'm fickle."

"Why do you carry on and stir him up?"

"In my heart I never think of anybody but Duncan, it's Duncan."

"That's just it. You ought to give him something to worry about."

Valette's lips were trembling, but she made no reply to Mary Cherry, who sat down and began to rock: "He's quite a dandy in that daguerreotype, with all that finery. As splendid an eye as ever I see in a mortal head. I'd just forget him. When I was a young gal there warn't a man couldn't say I'd not forgotten him, and those I remembered

I wished I'd forgot. Draw up a chair and sit by me, or on the trunk if you're mind to."

Mary Cherry always had her two trunks put in the middle of her room and left there, they were leather carriage trunks and not very large. In one of these, the larger, were her clothes. In the other she always carried a little hearth broom, a shovel and tongs, her favorite cake pan, her hymn book, and a certain familiar article sometimes fancifully known as a vessel of dishonor, because, she said, it fit better.

Valette sat down on the smaller trunk, and Mary Cherry quit rocking and leaned over kindly to take the fluttering little hands in her own. She was going on to sixty years old: she had whiskers on her chin which she sometimes made the children of the family pluck for her, sometimes giving them a cake and sometimes not; she had never fallen in love; and yet leaning over and looking into the girl's eyes, so rashly bright and wild and tender, she felt humble and curiously happy in her soul. When she heard Valette saying that you couldn't blame Duncan and that it was her own fault, and heard at the same moment through the open windows the leaves on the trees outside stir like a whispering, she felt as if the sweet voice close to her ear was out there too, the beating of some gentle heart that said, "The strong belong to the weak, through love."

"It's a question if you ain't wrong, child," she said, patting Valette's hand awkwardly with the hard bones of her fingers. "I'm positive you are. Duncan got some of that wild Tate blood, his ma's brothers were tearing all over North Alabama. But he's a fine boy, and he will be yours, as they say. You watch and see." She wanted to say something more of comfort but felt she was not very good at it. "Look here," she said so suddenly that Valette looked up, startled for an instant at the rough tone, "nobody, I mean out of church ever saw Mary Cherry pray. I'm a-goin' to pray. Yes, sirree."

She threw herself on her knees, the great old frame looking high-shouldered and full of huge angles, and resting her elbows on the lid of the trunk in which travelled her absurd collection of articles, the hearth broom, shovel and tongs, the cake pan, hymn book, and chamber pot, and closing her eyes, she prayed: "May the words of my mouth and the meditations of my heart be acceptable to Thee, O, Lord, my strength and my redeemer. Hallelujah, Amen."

She rose clumsily and without looking at her young friend, walked over to the table for the box.

"Here, sit where you are. Eatin' will do you good."

Valette choked down several of the cakes, the tears streaming down her cheeks unnoticed.

"Don't you know tears are salty?" Miss Mary said. "With my cakes, what sort of a mess is that?" She began a low chuckling to herself like a grandmother, and Valette was obliged to laugh, brushing away the tears and the crumbs from her cheeks as she rose to go.

"You precious Miss Mary!" she said, raising the bony hand and kissing it on the palm.

"And if you feel like eatin' some more tomorrow, come back. There's plenty."

XIV

"I MYSELF truly believe," Mrs. Quitman said, "that children ought to be exposed to everything, none of this dodging life for them by their parents. If I had a child with measles I'd put the others in bed with it."

For this last week of December many people in Natchez filled the bowl with egg-nog, or syllabub, on the two festivals of Christmas and New Year's; Malcolm Bedford had egg-nog every night. It was Christmas Day, in the evening, after Christmas dinner was long over, and Mrs. Quitman had driven over to Portobello in a single-seated trap with her mulatto driver. The season had all the air of summer returning, the soft breeze, roses in bloom, and the moon clear and shining. The road ahead as she drove floated away in vague silver tides of shadow and light.

"And I go farther," she went on, turning to Hugh Mc-Gehee, after some of the company had expressed a difference of opinion, and begun a livelier conversation of their own on other subjects. "I quite agree with your notion, Mr. McGehee, that children and young people should not be spared the sorrows and deaths and crises that come to families. After all, these are high lights, children grow by them, and I feel sure of it."

"So I think," he said, "exactly."

She reached out her hand lightly to touch Edward's. "I haven't forgotten what your father said to me when my husband died. That a sacred memory is the most valuable thing one may have, to live by through the years."

"I know Father says that," Edward replied, confused at the trembling of her voice and then at her silence.

"We must admit," his mother said, having heard only the word and not what Mrs. Quitman had been saying so seriously, "that a Natchez child is born into a perfect academy of memories, I won't say all sacred."

"You agree with me, Ed?" Mrs. Quitman went on.

"Yes, Mrs. Quitman; if I didn't, Father and I would have wasted a lot of time talking on the porch." He turned to Valette on the piano stool, "and Valette thinks so too, fifty times more."

Mrs. Bedford said to Valette, "You needn't be leaning over here and your eyes growing bigger and bigger like the wolf in Little Red Riding Hood; this is all meat and drink to you. Don't I remember when you came home from Montrose and cried your eyes out over Fanny Lintot and Philip Nolan they'd been telling you about. That 'Man Without a Country' story is all taffy, but we all know the Mexican general had Philip Nolan shot, yes, madam."

"Yes, and madam yourself, My Dumplin'. I know lots more sad stories about Natchez places now than I did then."

"You don't have to tell me that."

"I don't cry over them now, because my heart's grown callous. You mean I did when I was thirteen years old, My Dumplin'."

"I'll tell you what I mean the next time a kitten dies."

"Did you hear that, Uncle Mac?" Valette turned to Malcolm, who had been refilling the cups, and emptying more than one, as he motioned Edward to do the honors of the house.

"It's beyond me the modus operandi of this controversy. Sing nightingale," said Malcolm. "And after this morning's joys, how weary, stale, flat, and unprofitable seem to us all the uses of this world."

"Shakespeare, before he began that, remarked 'Oh, God, oh, God,' Darlin'," said his wife.

"All right, oh, God, oh, God!" He burst out laughing. "Can you imagine four Celies at one time knocking at our door before breakfast and hollerin' 'Christmas Gift, Christmas Gift'?"

"Remember last year," said Mrs. Bedford, "our Connecticut governess was astonished. She thought one should say 'Merry Christmas.'"

"So she did, and I thought, all right, go ahead and be as merry as you want, I love to see you merry, and see what you get. Her idea of Christmas morning was family prayers and a pair of mitts you'd knitted for father. My father gave me a horse and a Spanish saddle and an English rifle, and by sunrise had proposed so much syllabub he didn't know which was which. Nevertheless, today was Christmas morning. And Christmas Gift!"

He meant that his wife and he had spent a long time that day giving the slaves presents. She had given the women dresses; he gave the men felt hats and shoes and coffee and flour. There was a four days' holiday. The slaves went into town to buy gifts for their children, and in the evening would dance and have suppers.

Valette sang the Echo Song which, difficult as it was, Madame Jenny Lind, in her New Orleans concerts, had made a favorite among the young lady singers in those parts.

"Well," said Mrs. Quitman speaking out in her downright fashion when the music ended, "you did get through it, my dear. I heard Jenny Lind sing it, General Quitman and I, nine years ago in New Orleans, when Mr. D'Arcy the hatter paid $245 for his seat, which we certainly did not, I can tell you. You haven't the musical education, but your voice is just as true as Jenny Lind's, who wasn't anybody's pretty child either, and your shoulders are better. The general said that evidently Swedish nightingales enjoy great health. She wore a dark blue dress draped with lace."

The old lady sighed at the thought of times past, and Valette sighed, smiling and so pleased at the compliment that she repeated the song, pushing the puffed sleeves farther down her white shoulders and singing the flowery parts more carefully. Afterwards she ran over and whispered in Mrs. Quitman's ear, who nodded her head and gave her young friend a little push toward the door. Then the old lady, taking the last cup of syllabub from Edward, motioned him to follow Valette.

"Sing something Southern," Malcolm said. "That la-di-da's all very delectable, but—" Then, not seeing her, he asked, "Where's Valette? Where's Ed?"

"Gone to Charleston," said Mrs. Quitman.

"No, honestly, Mrs. Quitman," he said, pushing back his thick hair, "tell me where they are."

She rose and held open one of the curtains, where the bright moonlight fell on the columns of the gallery outside and on the alabaster vases beyond.

"They've taken the hint from our conversation, my dear sir. They've borrowed my trap and gone on a tour of the places where the stories are. And a very good idea."

"A sort of *tournée de sentiment,* I gather," he said, very much pleased. "Sentimental journey, shall we say?"

"Eh bien?" said Mrs. Quitman, "but of course we all know that at that age you don't go to look for some romantic spot, you go to look for yourself."

"It's *eh bien* and all my little rascal's doings," Mrs. Bedford said, "she's the one got it up, you may be sure; she's the fertile one for inventing things. I tell her she wasn't ever born; she was hatched out of an egg and is a little bird. 'Do you think you're one of the apostles, madam,' I said to her, 'and can be in two places at once?' Ah, well, bird or apostle, it's only once in this world." She gave a sigh, her gaze resting on the moonlit scene beyond the window.

In the bright moonlight Edward and Valette drove the fast horses, seeing the leaves and shadows, the magical fields of silver, the moon ahead of them, high in the sky, though the night was not yet far advanced. He drove as naturally as the horses themselves took their gait.

"We'll pretend the places are shrines," Valette said, laughing.

"Are you thinking of romance, romance, nothing but romance?"

"No," she said, thinking of the lovely Fannie Lintot, of the Spanish woman's solitary grave on the edge of the Devil's Punch Bowl—a hundred years ago was that?—of the chapel at Windy Hill Manor, and of Duncan if he went off to the war. "No, I was wishing I could have heard Jenny Lind sing the Echo Song."

"Hear Jenny Lind?"

"So as to phrase better, Edward McGehee." She knew he was ready to laugh, and so she began to sing in a low clear voice the song's last movement, ending with the trill and its echo. "A place in the song like that," she said.

"I can't see how it could ever be better," Edward said, quietly and in the same tone of sincerity that his father often used. It made Valette feel that her singing had meant more to him than to herself, the singer.

"Now I hear his heart," she thought. "There's nobody like Edward. You'd think the girls in Natchez——"

She smiled at him that happy reckless smile that My Dumplin' had so often warned her about, lifting her young face so that her eyes were in their own shadow, and he could see the moon flash on her white teeth.

"Duncan hasn't heard you sing that yet, has he?" Edward said. He knew for whom she was so filled with sadness and delight.

"No, but—" She let it go at that. The last letter was folded down in her bosom. "Before we know it," she said, "Duncan'll be going off and enlisting."

"I expect so, if war comes now."

"It will."

"How do you know, Valette?"

"I know it," she said, throwing out both her small hands to the soft, near, shining night with its shades and its smell of the warm, moist fields. "I know it by all this. By all this now. I just know it."

They drove in silence past Concord where Mrs. Minor, wife of Don Estevan, Spain's governor, had lived. Natchez had known her as the Yellow Duchess because in her house the gold mirrors, the brass fireplace, the brocade of the curtains and furniture had been in that color, and her coach was lined with yellow silk and painted in gold and buff and drawn by clay-bank horses. Edward knew all there was to know at Concord from the stories told at Montrose, and Valette had heard often the Concord story. On the Concord walls hung the portrait of Don Estevan himself, in blue and crimson velvet and satin and gold braid.

"Is the back of this seat too straight for you?" Edward asked presently.

Valette did not answer. In her mind was the picture of Frances Lintot, waiting for Philip Nolan, and then walking up and down in the garden of her sister's house, after the news that he had been shot.

"Mrs. Quitman will want the trap or we could go to Laurel Hill," Edward said. "You know the Mercer Chapel." The chapel had been built for a wife and three children who had died suddenly in the yellow fever, and later the builder, who loved them, had asked in his will to be buried under the chancel. Valette's thoughts travelled there. On the statues of angels and the floor of marble mosaic the moonlight now must be falling through the rose window. Falling like the light on snow. The laurels around it would be black.

" 'Twould be easy enough, barrin' Mrs. Quitman," he went on, "she will want her trap."

But their way home led easily past Clermont and the Devil's Punch Bowl. From the cliffs surrounding it they could see down on the treetops below. Legend said it had been sunk by a falling meteor, that river pirates had buried their treasure there, and outlaw gangs made it their retreat. Everybody knew that, farther down nearer the stream, men dying on their river courses were buried; and had heard the superstition that the river, rising in flood at times, came to claim them again, washing them out of their graves. But here, high on the edge of that wooded hollow of the Devil's Punch Bowl, was the tomb of the Spanish lady buried there alone, whoever she may have been. Valette and Edward left the trap to go and stand there, in the moonlight that shone over the ruined spot.

"Edward, tell me. What do you feel when you are at a place like this? I want to know about you men."

"What do women think?"

Neither had answered the other's question. Edward tightened the reins as the horses struck out down the road that would bring them back to Portobello. She said to herself, "I could ask Edward questions I'd never dare ask Duncan, even though I do live in the same house with Duncan. And why?" The answer was that she was in love with Duncan. So that was what love was like! And that was why the moon tonight made you want to cry. She was trying to remember some poetry about the tears of things, and leaned her shoulder against Edward's.

"Once we started a fox along here," Edward said.

"I know, Mr. McGehee, you're the best shot of all the

planters' sons in the country," she replied, in a tone that made him defend himself.

"Hold your horses, now, there's a poem to the moon, chaste and fair, that says queen and huntress."

"It's just men poets."

"I'm sorry. And here's the gate, it seems only two seconds."

"Do you know—" Valette broke into happy laughter, "Look!" The trap had stopped inside while he closed the gate; and she pointed to where the moonlight fell through the live-oaks and the faint moss, down on the statues, gleaming and broken with shadow, and on the broad ground of the avenue. At the very end hung the cloudy white of the house.

"Isn't it really—? It's more beautiful here than any of them!" Valette said. "Anywhere we've been."

She saw him standing there, and thought, "And how beautiful Edward is!"

When he sprang into the seat beside her, she gave him the reins with a lovely gesture, as if she were giving a flower. Her mind was filled with the sweetness of life. She looked at the statues, her eyes half closed.

"Do you know, Edward, if I too were a marble goddess, I could go on forever."

"Yes—then. Forever," he said, in his young, rich voice, and so low that she scarcely heard the words.

The horses broke into a trot, quickening the flashes of the moon on the harness.

XV

It was two weeks since Edward had returned to the academy. His sister Lucinda McGehee had been away in Kentucky at the Worthington Female Seminary, where her two sisters had been graduated before her. But, with the uncertain times and

Lucinda's own annoyance at the indecision of Kentucky people in choosing between North and South, her father by the second week in January had thought it well enough to have her back at Montrose. "Has Buddie come yet?" she said to her father, her face shining as she kissed him. She had been the first off the boat.

His father hoped to keep Edward at the academy as long as possible, judging it, in such a state of things, a steadier place for a young man of eighteen to be in. In his letters home Edward wrote of the weekly exercises in reading and oratory devised by Colonel William Tecumseh Sherman, their superintendent, and that the students selected pieces by Yancey, Calhoun, and other Southern orators, all praising the defense of their slaves and home institutions as the patriot's highest duty. A year before, Captain Rickett's company at the Baton Rouge arsenal had been ordered to Texas, and the Governor of Louisiana had remonstrated with the Secretary of War at Washington for leaving unguarded so many arms in a country where the slave population was five or six to one white. Major Hoskin's company of forty men had been sent to take over the arsenal. On January 8, 1861, a convention was to meet at Baton Rouge to consider the state of the Union. Before Louisiana secession had been passed by the convention, telegrams came from her senators at Washington and Governor Moore ordered all the United States forts seized, along with the arsenal at Baton Rouge. The night of January 9 Colonel Wheat, with the New Orleans militia, came up and took the arsenal, allowing Major Hoskins to embark for St. Louis. The big store of arms was sent to various places, a large quantity put in Colonel Sherman's charge at the academy. Edward's father read his letter aloud with the family, several of the servants standing by the door to listen. Colonel Sherman was a Union man, he considered secession treason, war. He had been ordered to receive goods stolen from the United States. He had sent his resignation to Governor Moore. How, in a state of affairs like that, Edward wrote, could any cadet keep his mind on studies? "Won't you write, Father, and give me leave to come home?"

"Here's a copy of Sherman's letter," Hugh McGehee said, drawing out a paper that his friend Governor Moore had sent him. He sighed and began a passage from the letter:

"In the event of a severance of the relations hitherto existing between the Confederate States of this Union, I would be forced to choose the old Union. It is barely possible all the States may secede, South and North, that new combinations may result, but this process will be one of time and uncertainty, and I cannot with my opinions await the subsequent development.

"I have never been a politician, and therefore undervalue the excited feelings and opinions of present rulers. But I do think, if this people cannot execute a form of agreement like the present, that a worse one will result.

"I will keep the cadets as quiet as possible. They are nervous, but I think the interest of the State requires them here, guarding this property, and acquiring a knowledge which will be useful to your State in aftertimes."

"But, Papa," Lucinda said, the moment her father stopped reading. "You certainly intend to let Buddie come home, with a superintendent going on like that." She had a downright but engaging voice, as if she meant to be blunt only to pass the time for everybody.

"Lucy's right," Agnes said.

"The whole subject is a muddle."

"I think Lucinda's right," his wife repeated, as she rose and went over to stand beside his chair and laid her hand on the frowning brow.

"We had the academy report yesterday," Hugh said. "As you saw, it was merely our boy's rank in his studies."

"Not the top rung of the ladder, but good enough, my stars! I don't see how he can study at all."

"Maybe not. Will you write today, Agnes, and give him my leave to quit?"

She went over to the mantelpiece and leaning her face in her hands, stood there silent for a long time. With no one speaking they seemed to hear suddenly the sounds from outside, birds there, and then Aleck in the garden singing along, snatches to himself. Upstairs struck faintly the bell of the little silver clock with its beryl columns at the side that her brother Malcolm had given Agnes at her wedding. Presently, without looking at her husband, she asked what the day was.

It was the twentieth. "He'll be here before the end of the month. He'll be here with us, and then— I'm almost sorry I spoke. So that's it."

"That's it," said Hugh. "You hear what your mother says, Lucy? You've missed your brother, I know."

Lucy, without a word, faced around and went out of the room.

"Lucinda!" he called after her. "She doesn't answer me."

Agnes turned to him, "We'll just have to understand Lucy," she said. But the plain, level voice in which she spoke was only assumed. She was gazing at the expression on his face, on which she saw now that sad, lonely quietness, asking all, asking nothing, that most made her love him. The look in his eyes at the moment expressed everything on which we can rely in this world.

A week later Edward rode one afternoon into the court, dismounted from his horse, which William Veal had taken down to the docks to meet him, and ran up to his mother's room. She had just risen from her siesta and had on a Watteau teagown of dark blue challis that he had not seen before. When his mother saw him standing at the door from her sitting-room into the hall, she said nothing, only a little cry as she ran and buried her face in his shoulder. He put his cheek down on her head, his arm around her. William Veal, who had followed Edward upstairs, with the small portmanteau, turned away and walked slowly down the hall, shaking his head and talking to himself.

XVI

"BUDDIE," Lucy asked, in a cold tone, already prepared to resent it in case there were those who lacked the spirit, "would all you cadets enlist? I mean if it came to that."

"They say all will." He began to tell her of the various cadets from Louisiana and Mississippi families and what one or another of them had said or done.

"*Noblesse oblige,*" said Lucy, as if to say that to enlist was nothing, but not to enlist sheer white trash.

Edward had been home more than an hour, and the talking had not stopped for a moment. Everybody talked, as only a Southern family can, talking to each other for the love of all; whatever subjects of conversation there might be were knocked down like a feather.

"I certainly wouldn't take any foolishness from Washington. Those new towels of Mamma's, you might as well wipe your face with a sheet of wax!" Lucy had followed Edward to his room and sat on the bed while he washed his face and hands. "But Mamma likes this French damask and that fringe. Buddie, I thought my hair was fine enough, goodness knows, but yours is like a cloud of silk. Is that the way gentlemen of fashion in Alexandria must brush it now? It's like General Beauregard in his pictures."

Edward was always very susceptible to Lucy's moods, and her happiness on seeing him again shone back to her from him. General Beauregard had visited his two sons at the military academy, he said laughing, and for weeks there were nothing but little Beauregards marching about.

"Well, isn't he handsome!" said Lucy. "I always wanted to know what men think a handsome man is. Is that where you get that stock? Honestly, Buddie, I'd think it would choke you to death, but you look mighty sweet."

This reminded him, Edward said, that he must go and speak to Mr. Munger and Mr. Trippler, their two convalescent guests, and the sewing mistress, Miss Whipple. Mr. Munger was in the vapors, said Lucy, at the thought of Mississippi seceding. His own State of Wisconsin a year ago had threatened to secede till the United States Government put a foot down; but this was different, the Southerners were rebels, by the living God, Mr. Munger had said, the other day when Mrs. Wilson came over from Rosalie with the present of one of the hams she took such pride in, and had declared that secession was nothing new. "Yes," said Mr. Munger, "all men are brothers."

"No doubt of it," Mrs. Wilson said, "brothers and sisters."

She made this reply solely because she saw, as everybody at Montrose had seen, that Mr. Munger had been a preacher and would go on repeating things long after it is obvious they will never be clear to any one.

Lucy searched a fresh linen handkerchief out of the portmanteau and handed it to Edward:

"Go on and see them, Buddie, and sober up, and then all will be left is the sweet memory of a welcome from Miss Whipple. She has another bundle of tracts from Massachusetts, so she's calling us Mack Gee Hee again, and stuck a pin in me yesterday when we were fitting my blue silk Papa brought up from New Orleans and two brooches to go with it for my birthday, after Mamma and he'd already given me this necklace." She tipped her chin up for him to see the necklace of amethysts, like little bunches of grapes capped with gold leaves. "Mamma says not, but I saw Mamma laughing, and don't tell me about that pin, 'twas when I said no, Miss Whipple, McGehee rhymes with McFee. She said, which McFee? hold still."

When Edward came downstairs the ladies were absent at their toilettes, and he and his father went out to look at the new camellias, which were blossoming this year for the first time, and at the three Arabians brought from the plantation in West Feliciana. Then they walked for half an hour up and down a path, where hedges of clipped althea divided the quince orchard from the garden.

"You and Uncle Edward at Woodville are antislavery men, aren't you, Papa?" Edward said, "and so was Uncle John up in Panola." He knew what anxiety his father had always felt about the mistreatment of the negroes belonging to him.

"There were plenty of antislavery men in this country till the northeast part of Mississippi was opened up, and later on the industrial North began to grow solid against us."

When Hugh began to explain to his son the convictions that moved him, Edward himself replied with such point that his father was delighted. He was surprised also, as the older generation always is at the younger when it shows thought, and even accuracy, in a sober field and an argument close to preference and life. Evidently these young men at the military academy had not been devoted only to that artificial oratorical defense of states' rights that Colonel Sherman had mentioned; they had made a check on history. Hugh McGehee could see the cadets, as Edward talked, informing and correcting one another in the historical facts. He listened, as parents do, with astonishment but with pride to his son saying things that people were accustomed to think of as better known to his elders.

Who did not know, Edward said, that in the Revolution it

was the South that had led in the fight for freedom, and freedom, therefore, was beyond all price? It might be that one Union would be more profitable, economically, but what of that? If the State's being sovereign would make it hard for any secession government of these States to organize into one central power, well, what of that? In a country that might take over territory of another, and plan at any moment to annex Cuba or Haiti or Mexico, imagine talking of the Union! But if union is so holy why plot to break up union in Mexico? Any one of these is annexed to the Union, and, presto, some holy unity has come upon it! And then to talk of a State seceding as if some crime were about to happen that had never been heard of before!

The sound of laughter and quarrelling, then an accordion, all together, came through the orchard trees from the quarters. Hugh, glancing up, saw his son smiling at him, and silence fell between them. His father understood. The young hear what the old say; it seems to be reason and to be exact cause, but it is not the point. To Edward, his son, though he had not got it expressed for himself, the movement toward war represented something larger.

The sounds at the quarters stopped, it was supper time there and all would be indoors, except for a boy's voice, high and clear, which went on singing for a little, then left off; and Hugh MeGehee, who had paused to hear it, for he loved all that children did, moved on. It was strange to be walking with his son and listening to him in the double light of an old affection and the new state of affairs that would be taking him away.

As Edward spoke of the plantation and some of the old negroes he had always known, and then of the journeys when he was a little boy with his father to the plantation in Parish Ascension, and the festival of the sugar cane, when they tied a ribbon on the stalk to be the last cut before the shouting and rum began, he felt a sense of going back to his own, and said to himself that this soil, on the soft, brief herbage of which his feet now moved, would last forever. These feelings, though he did not see his way to develop them into ideas, he knew were stirring in him and that they could carry him, through some sort of *action,* farther than he had ever been into himself. He was one of those blest natures, based on health, rightness and sense, who want always not to be different but finer in the qualities of the average man.

Paralee's little grandson, Swamp, came out on to the gallery with the supper bell and rang it twice as long for Mr. Edward's having come home; and at the supper table, loaded down with the white Roman hyacinths, spoonbread, and brandied peaches, the afternoon conversation went on as if it had never been interrupted. Miss Whipple, who, however thin, was a hearty eater, kept her eyes first on her plate, then on Edward, then on Lucy, as if wondering at this conversation like a cage of birds.

"Lucy, my child," her mother said, "drink your milk, at least. You'll be worse than Cousin Lizzie Boone."

"If I may ask, Mrs. Mack Gee Hee," said Miss Whipple, "who is Mistress Lizzie Boone?"

"Oh, she's our cousin Lizzie Boone, in De Soto County."

"I said to myself I wouldn't go far wrong guessin' it's a cousin, norram I."

"And, Miss Whipple, ever since the day I was born," said Lucy, "I've had Cud'n Lizzie Boone thrown up to me, now haven't I, Mamma?"

"The thinner Cousin Lizzie gets the less she eats."

"Cud'n Betty Bullock when we were there always said Cud'n Lizzie wasn't like that at all, she was a pantry nibbler."

"Which is all moonshine," said her father, laughing, "lock, stock, and barrel."

"There, you see how 'tis, nobody in this family will ever let you say Cud'n Lizzie ever took a bite to eat in her life. Miss Whipple, you see?"

"I say a person has to eat, Miss Lucy, to keep the flesh on their bones."

"You're taller, Buddie," said Lucy, looking at her brother with rapturous eyes.

XVII

"Our nephew, I notice, is not remarking on the subject," Mrs. Miles McGehee said. "Are you a Davis man, little Edward?"

She was a plump woman with bright eyes, who had a way of resting her fingertips on her hoop as if she would soon be floating. They said that in the romantic first years of marriage her husband had gone off to his Georgia plantations if he meant to get drunk; but now Miles would say that he had ruined his health laughing at his wife's jokes. It was a successful transition and they got on well enough. He always planned the breakfast for Sunday morning, and before sitting down went out to the kitchen to inspect it. They were as generous as they were rich.

"If little Ed's for Mr. Jefferson Davis he must not have seen his Uncle Edward lately," Miles said. "Eh, son?"

"It amounts to the same thing, Uncle Miles, I've seen Father," Edward said, smiling at the creaks of his uncle's chair, a huge hickory rocker—his wife said it was built from a ship's timbers—in the midst of the French horsehair and brocade of the room.

"McGehee Brothers, Limited," his aunt said, "are all McGehees, all Whigs, all Anti-Secessionists, all against oratory, as 'tis well known."

"Nothing's well known in these God-forsaken days, my dear Puss," said Miles.

"And I reckon the McGehees being friends of Zack Taylor's didn't help. He hated Davis."

There was a pine fire on the hearth, but the long windows were open, and already by the end of this first week in February the air was like spring. The strong fragrance of the sweet-olive filled the room, confused at times with the peach trees blossoming. The lights from the room sifted out into cloudy shapes where the peach and cherry blossoms of the orchard came almost up to the walls of the house. From the outside you must have said that the large, friendly house rambled on into the orchard, and the orchard to the river, and so the name River Orchards seemed right and proper for the Miles McGehees' plantation. They had four other plantations but lived here.

"I know that we have always," Edward said, without any thought, and speaking as if from a clan, "been on the side of a Constitutional Union Party: destroy abolitionism in the North, destroy disunionism in the South."

"Less than a year ago Mr. Davis was opposing Secession, said he thought slavery and property were better under national government. Well, now, by God, he don't think so," Miles said "oh, no, not by a jug full, don't think so at all!"

"Both parties have gone to extremes, haven't they, Uncle Miles."

"Aye, aye. And much water's flowed under the bridge since Buchanan, saying his prayers every forty seconds, was President. And now this same Mr. Davis who last year was likely to be run for President of the United States is just as likely to be elected President of the Confederate States of America by the Congress of Delegates at Montgomery. And should he be, in my humble opinion it's no go."

"You know it's remarkable how much strength a delicate man can have if you stir him up," said one of the guests. He was the doctor from St. Joseph's, a neighbor of the Davis brothers.

"Anybody with a modicum of sense," said Mrs. McGehee, "knows Jeff Davis is ambitious. Ambitious and a politician. And a military man. That V formation of his in the Mexican War, whatever they did with a V formation it was the most celebrated V in the world's alphabet. Jeff Davis and General Zachary Taylor returned from the war, and had the ovation in Natchez, crowned by Miss Julia Montgomery, the fair, chosen by the citizens as their voice."

Edward watched his aunt's hands as they made a motion that implied a determined and comical planting of crowns on heroes' heads, and smiled when Uncle Miles winked at him.

"And everybody knows," she went on, "the Davises are plain people. Jeff Davis is handsomely educated, of course, he's cultivated himself. And Mrs. Davis, honey, goes up like a dome."

She was speaking with the ease, irritation, and prose of a neighbor. Joseph Davis lived on the next plantation to the north of them; and Brierfield, the thousand acres he had given to his brother, was nearby. Joseph Davis, by profession a lawyer, had become, also, a rich planter, with theories of agriculture and slave management.

She turned to her nephew, whom she admired and loved.

"But they just don't inherit what you've got, my dear, that's it. I don't know if you know the Davises; yes, I do, of course, I remember three or four years ago your uncle took you to The Hurricane, and both of you went from there with Mr. Joe Davis to Brierfield. That was the time he gave you the horse."

"Black Solo, Auntie," Edward said. "I rode him up here. They are like we are at Montrose; never sell horses but often give one to some friend." She asked him graciously to ring for the toddy tray, it was bedtime.

Her husband was absorbed with what he was saying about Mr. Davis as the orator of the South, and the crowd in Washington to hear his farewell speech. "The voice, the voice," he said, wrinkling up his eyes and laughing, for some reason.

"Your Uncle Miles," his aunt said to Edward, "got himself

sent to the State Legislature once—at Jackson. Didn't you, Mr. MeGehee?"

"To fight the bond measure. Then I resigned."

"He made a speech calling Senator Duval so many dreadful names that he jumped up and took a shot at your Uncle Miles, who was just saved by his bowie knife. Miles drew it out. 'Look at it,' said he coolly. 'Why, Duval, you've dented the handle of my knife.' So the whole Jackson, Mississippi, legislature applauded."

Miles McGehee looked annoyed and the chair squeaked loudly. "What sort of fool wants to be in politics?"

Nevertheless, for all this familiar criticism of Mr. Davis, Edward, when he got to his room, found his mind full of him. For a long time he lay awake in the wide Empire bed. At first the image of his uncle with his 400 pounds or more alternated with the tall, slender, military figure he remembered at Brierfield three years before, the large blue-gray eyes, the fine brow, the voice that people and newspapers were always comparing one way or another to music. Then there remained only the one image, of Jefferson Davis. At Brierfield, after the death of his young wife, President Taylor's daughter, Mr. Davis had been a recluse for eight years, talking with his brother, reading, sometimes for a year not leaving the plantation. Then he had married Miss Howell, one of the Howells at the Briars, neighbors of Montrose, and returned to be a leader in Washington. And now with the secession of his State he was no longer a leader in the Senate, and had come home again. And so Edward lay thinking, and before he fell asleep had decided to ride over next morning to Brierfield and call.

Mr. Davis, stopping to leave a pruning knife on the post, came through the gate to meet Edward.

"So you've come again to see us, how long is it?" he said, bowing formally and taking Edward's hand in his own, which was fine and slender but strong. His face was full of pleasure at seeing this young man whom he remembered as a boy of fifteen. Edward after the first greetings had pointed to Black Solo, and thanked Mr. Davis again for such a gift.

"This is a pacing country, Mr. Davis," he said in his slow, friendly voice, "but I tell people I've got the best pacer of all." Horses were in the Davis blood.

They stood there talking. Edward could not quite remember moment by moment what Mr. Davis had just said, standing there with his hand resting on the saddle, but the old magnetism which he remembered three years ago came back. This whole visit was to move in the glamor of that memory of a boy walking about Brierfield with one of the greatest orators of the day. He could remember his father saying, "I know, Mr. Jeff Davis can talk about Homer, loggerhead turtles, Roman law, Italian poets, astronomy, the American Revolution, but——"

To Edward the beautiful face, that of a dreamer, scholar, and soldier strangely mingled, looked tired and older. Mr. Davis put an arm through his, and talking of first one thing and then another, led him along the garden. His tone seemed to say that there must be nothing near to him that his young friend should not know. At the same time he gave the impression of taking for granted that others agreed with him. The *Gloire de France,* the finest of all tea roses, had provided cuttings for the circular rosebed. The other roses needed pruning. He was proud of the system at Brierfield, which, though there were only thirty-six negroes instead of the usual hundreds, had a special code, and a jury system among the negroes themselves, the pardoning power residing with the master.

Then suddenly he began to speak of a State like South Carolina withdrawing from the Union. Which was one thing. "But," he said, "if there should be an attempt to coerce her

back into the Union, that act of usurpation, folly, and wickedness would enlist every Southern man for her defense." The
fine clear eyes turned now and again to his young visitor,
the long slender hands made now and then a gesture. Mr.
Davis was talking to him now as he had talked before to a
boy, with that same openness and persuasion. He was a man
who was generous in feeling but not in mind; and thus he
had a ready approach to the young, because with them he had
the sense of not being misjudged.

Edward's father had read to him from some journal a sen-
tence that said Mr. Jefferson Davis had the power to stir
rather than to win men's hearts. His eyes rested on the finely
cut lips, which now and then were compressed into the old
and austere line that he had heard Mr. Davis' critics speak
of. But most of the time the expression of these lips seemed
to him only delicate and mobile, the music of the voice had
not changed.

Overhead now and then the white herons from the swamps
and lagoons along the river to the north came flying against
the cloudless sky. The soft morning warmth filled the air
with violets, sweet-olive, and scents from the orchard.

Upon the secession of Mississippi, Jefferson Davis, Mexican
hero, former Secretary of War, United States Senator, had been
appointed by Governor Pettus Major-General of the State
Militia; and in the event of war, which was generally thought
certain, it was known that Davis would like to head the Southern armies. As he was asking Edward about the sentiment
among the cadets at the seminary and the seizure of the arsenal
at Baton Rouge, they reached the gallery, where Mrs. Davis
came from indoors to join them.

"Pray allow me to present," her husband began, but she
also remembered Edward and began to inquire of his family
at Montrose. She was younger than her husband. To Edward,
who at this period of life must judge women by his mother,

the poise that she had taught herself seemed rather something pompous. But when he saw the passionate attraction and pride that came into the dark eyes as she looked at her husband, he forgot this impression of cold self-confidence. In the library, crowded on all its walls to the ceiling with books, a servant brought a decanter of Madeira; and Mr. Davis repeated his questions about the cadets and the superintendent, Colonel Sherman. Edward answered these inquiries quietly and exactly. He never considered what he was going to say, and so you always believed it sincere, which it was.

On their way to the gate, where Black Solo was standing with his ears up, waiting, Mr. Davis spoke of Edward's uncle at Woodville.

"Judge McGehee," he said, in his fine, quick rhythm of speech which made Edward feel as if he were stepping to music, "I trust he is well. When I think of him I am always reminded of Madame de Maintenon's remark anent sincerity, you will remember: sincerity, she said, does not consist in saying a great deal but in saying all. Only a few words are necessary to open the heart, if you are sincere." The tone, as Mr. Davis said this, was half like an orator's, perhaps; but Edward heard only the enchantment of the idea and the words as they were spoken.

Two days later they heard at River Orchards that yesterday Mr. Jefferson Davis had been elected President of the Confederate States by the Congress of Delegates meeting at Montgomery. It was the 9th of February. Alexander S. Stephens had been elected Vice-President and a constitution had been formulated. The delegates of the seven States thus far seceded had pushed forward in order to establish definitely the Confederacy before the day of Mr. Lincoln's inauguration on the 4th of March. It was a morning like spring and he and Mrs. Davis had been making rose cuttings from the *Gloire de France* that grew near the gate when a messenger rode up on horseback with a telegram. Mr. Davis had opened it, read and re-read the message, then told Mrs. Davis. The messenger later had described to people how the President looked at the message a long time, with a grave, sad face.

While they were discussing the news at his Uncle Miles' house, Edward, for some reason he himself could not have explained, decided that he would leave next morning for home.

XVIII

"CIVIL war has only horror for me," Mr. Davis had said. He had dreaded war and hoped up to the very last that it would be averted. But should any attempt be made to coerce the seceding States to return to the Union, that act of usurpation, folly, and wickedness would enlist every true Southern man for her defense.

Edward as he rode along heard in his thoughts Mr. Davis' words.

He had lingered at his uncle's house for a while listening to the discussion of the new President of the Confederate States. Three or four neighbors had come to dine, and what would have been at other times gossip and hunting talk now buzzed around the political situation. On devotion to the State there had been no disagreement. Every one there shared Mr. Davis' conception of Mississippi as a commonwealth, a whole in itself, free under the Constitution to withdraw from the Union of States when she saw fit. But about Jefferson Davis as the man best suited for the Presidency of the seceded States no two persons in the company thought the same thing.

In the first place, who were the Montgomery delegates to take things thus into their own hands?

"Mr. Davis is a military politician," some one said, "he is not an administrator."

"That Jeff Davis is a scholar we all know, and you know it, Miles," Mrs. McGehee said, and spoke of Mr. Davis' Latin and Greek, his reading in Spanish literature and in the Italian poets, and French. "Five languages, besides his own, ought to be enough for anybody, not to mention those Indian dialects he's conversant with, which seems a waste of time the way they grunt what they mean anyhow. And I myself have heard him quote poetry by the yard. Melodies and lyrics, in that angel voice. And science he knows, all that about fishes and geologies."

"You see that, gentlemen?" said Miles. "My wife's the kind of lady if she drowned would float upstream!"

"I heard Jeff Davis speaking once. He brought in Justinian, and he made law persuade, from him law seemed melodious like music. But thinker, no," the lawyer said, "not sufficiently dispassionate. But when he gets his tooth into an idea he won't let go. I suppose that gives a sort of philosophy."

"I think it does," said Miles, "it's a philosophy of character at least."

"Take his education, however," continued the lawyer, "nevertheless, notwithstanding, it's not Southern. I've known Mr. Joe Davis these many years, as his lawyer and as his friend. I recall when he sent his beloved brother Jefferson off to Kentucky. Born in Kentucky, then moved to this country, then sent off again to school. Six years a scholar in one college or another, his teachers not Southerners but English, then Scotch, New England, French and Irish. Catholic, Presbyterian, Unitarian, Deist, Socian influences. I will say one thing: his contact with the Catholic Church for a time must have helped his literary style. He's had a training about as little Southern as possible and West Point removed him still further from Southern influences. Mr. Davis may represent but he was not born to the Southern system that your family represents, Mr. McGehee. A great orator he is, yes, that's another matter."

"Is he! He can charm a bird off a bough," said Mrs. McGehee. "And he's a kind enough man and it's delightful to be in his company. Eddie was there yesterday. He's positively in love with Mr. Davis."

Some of the guests turned to look at the young man standing by the armoire. Edward made no answer; he kept his eyes on the carpet, and could feel his face and his lip twisting with anger.

Miles McGehee pushed himself up out of his chair and turned toward his nephew, chuckling. "No matter, son, keep your hero, don't let us——"

"It's a fine lot anybody here knows of Mr. Jefferson Davis," Edward said. His loud and arrogant tone surprised even himself.

"Miles! Miles!" he heard his aunt say; his Uncle Miles was cursing angrily in the huge family voice.

"I apologize," Edward said, bringing his heels together in the style learned at the military academy, and with a stiff bow. "I beg your pardon, sir. Au revoir, sir."

"Now, Miles! What'd I tell you?" he could hear his aunt saying as he went out. "I never get a McGehee red in the face. Tell me not, sweet, I am unkind—to wars and arms I fly—" her voice followed him on his way to the gallery, as if she were reciting, and when the words were lost he could still hear her bright laughter.

While the servant, a short, lively boy named Lige, was tying Edward's saddle bags on the horse, his Uncle Miles came out, the fat, proud, kind face troubled.

"Get that girth tight enough, Lige," he said.

"Yas, suh, yas, suh. Seems lak today Mr. Ed cusses ev'ything he teches."

Miles McGehee looked tenderly at his nephew, and said he was sorry, in such times as these nothing bitter must come into families. "Why don't you wait till in the morning? It'll be after sundown before you get there. But I know you'll cut right out once you've started. So come and see us. So goodbye."

Edward kissed his uncle and sprang into the saddle. From the gate he saw Miles McGehee going toward the house, walking slowly and every now and then stopping to gaze out across his fields.

The road followed the river, the expanse of which sometimes was visible. Sometimes there was only the glint through the trees and the hanging moss. He rode along half seeing the river, or the road ahead, or the green of the fields, and with nothing at all of the scene at his uncle's house left in his thoughts. His mind was filled with the glamour and magnetism and conversation of the man whose voice and words came back to him. If his mind was filled with this man, his heart was resting on his father, who was in Edward's feeling the background of all true things. On all sides everybody was talking the questions of the day: and all these things his father said or knew: his father heard all the arguments, and remained alone; and felt something about life and about the future, comprehended it, as it were, under God. And Edward saw how this was different from most men's chatter.

Mr. Davis may have been chosen over better men for President of the Confederate States: it may have been the politics of the delegates; the States might have seceded in too much haste; Mr. Lincoln might, as he promised in his inaugural address, not interfere with slavery. So people talked, and so men argued.

Mr. Davis remained. This Southern country that Edward loved remained. "And I go with it," he thought; for he was one of those people who follow something inner, some com-

pulsion like a cloud; something in him was like the balancings
of the clouds.

In the young soul there is a certain universal element by
which causes and events are simplified and weighed so that
they take a form that is like what, eventually, time will give
them. The report of events that later history gives is often
only what they were to the youth who were in the midst of
them. And so at this moment Edward could not but have
believed that his feeling was right about these things. If he
had consciously thought in those terms he would have seen
himself as the prophecy of what would some day be the story
of this Southern cause.

The striking of his horse's hoofs on the ground seemed all
at once to him louder, and Edward saw that dusk was coming
on. The first stars were out in the east, the fields and pastures
were fading. As he passed through town and saw people
going along the streets to their homes after the day, he was
filled with egotism, and he thought how low and sordid the
world was, compared to what he was feeling. At the edge
of the town he could feel Black Solo step out into a pace, and
leaned down and patted his shoulder. At the same moment
he decided that he would not join a cavalry regiment; not
cavalry, some humility beyond the dash and show and caval-
cade seemed to fill his young spirit.

As he turned into the Montrose road, he seemed to be
turning into the gate at Briarfield three years ago, on that first
visit to Mr. Jefferson Davis. A boy of fifteen, and the tall
man with the fine brow and eyes, courteous and deferential,
as if you were not a mere boy, talking in that voice like music
and in such words as nobody else ever used, about the horses,
the soil, what planets belonged to the month; walking along
with him in the garden paths, past the hedges, where they
saw the orchard there, and there the melon patch, quoting
the Latin poetry—Edward had found it afterward and learned

it by heart—about the whitening melons on their sea-green leaves——

At Montrose, William Veal came to open the stable gate. Edward learned that his father when he heard that Jefferson Davis had been elected had walked the floor all night.

XIX

"Tell me, Buddie," Lucinda said, as they sat in the hammock at the end of the south gallery one morning in the languid ten o'clock hour, "do you think talking brings you closer to people or just keeps them farther off?"

"I only wish now at the seminary we'd been able to talk—from the way it looks nobody there will be meeting again."

"But why do you say you won't see the cadets again?"

"You know as well as I do. War."

"Do you remember the time at the Easter party General Quitman scented himself all out? He roared about the Mexican War and annexing Cuba, which he said everybody in the country was crying for."

"I remember he had taken you up in his arms and you had long curls, and climbed down to the carpet," Edward said, giving the hammock a swing with his foot against the floor.

"That was because I knew that what he was talking about was his big self."

"Then Mamma whispered to you to go take the general's hand, he was the most popular hero in the United States; but you wouldn't. So you came and sat by me on the corner sofa. You said he smelled like cake."

"He kept vanilla beans in his armoire to scent his linen, but we didn't know that. I sat by you and felt very sad because I thought a hero could eat up all the cake if he wanted to."

"If we'd always done the way Mamma wanted us to we'd have been angels by now."

"Buddie, do you think Father's dull, well, say simple?" Lucy asked suddenly.

He stopped the hammock with his root.

"Plague take it, what do you mean, simple?"

"Plague take it yourself, Mr. Edward McGehee, I am always wondering why he won't just pack off these old psalm singers out of the house."

What she referred to was the way they had at Montrose of giving shelter every winter to two or three invalids from the North, recommended to Hugh McGehee by some minister or other in the church. Two rooms in the south wing were reserved for this charitable practice. The two now were Mr. Munger from Wisconsin and Mr. Tripler from Providence. Lucy went on: "Father'd let Mr. Munger bring his medicine bottles to the table if Mamma hadn't put her foot down and yet look at the sense Papa's got, what he says about people like Mr. Munger's ancestors!"

"What does he say?"

"Says it's not so much that these people are not well-born, they don't want to be well-born."

"Born better but don't like it," Edward said, laughing.

"It's not that you're trying to descend from Alfred the Great, Papa says, what you want is to be connected with something larger than yourself. But it's no use telling Mr. Munger. If you're Mr. Munger, you want to be self-made."

"Certainly. Then you're the first to get there."

" 'Twould be rude with a bang," said Lucy, "to tell Mr. Munger just where he's got. You know, Buddie, Papa's certainly got sense sometimes."

"I thought you said he was dull."

"I said sometimes. I think he'd be smart, though, if he'd wring Miss Whipple's neck. That's what your sister'd do."

"You sound like Aunt Sallie," he said, smiling.

"Well, let me sound like Aunt Sallie. I remember one day over there she said to me, 'Honey, what does your father mean letting those Yankee divines sit around Montrose with their sharp noses?'"

"Yes, and what does Aunt Sallie do? She'd sit up all night with a crippled goslin."

"That's different. You should have heard them yestiddy, I mean our two theologues and Miss Whipple." Lucinda told of the conversation of the three Northerners about slavery and secession. God would punish every man, woman, and child in the South, they said. Except that Miss Whipple did not think darkies should be slaves; she thought they ought to be all taken out and shot. You ask for a glass of water, Miss Whipple said, you may get it in a quarter of an hour and you may never get it at all.

"What I wish is," Lucy continued, "I could bray the way I used to. You remember the time Miss Whipple told Papa on me because I asked her why she didn't say Mc Gee Hee Haw? Haw hee haw hee haw hee! I said. All the same, though I like our old donkey Pike better, I like her more than I do the theologues." Lucy's voice suddenly changed, as he put her hand through his arm. "Edward, are you really going to enlist?"

He turned and looked into her eyes quietly, then kissed her brow.

"I know you are right. I know you are right, because you are good," she said, as if to her own thoughts.

Presently, as they talked, Lucy began to complain of how everybody talked of secession and the war to suit themselves, but her mother interrupted by coming to say there were guests who wanted her to sing. Judge and Mrs. Winchester and Colonel Harrod were in the parlor.

"Mamma, I'd rather not," Lucy said, frowning. "You know I ought to stop trying to sing until Monsieur la Tour has taught me a little at least."

"Colonel Harrod's just been praising your voice to the skies."

"*Pour les sots acteurs—*" Lucy said, turning to Edward. "Monsieur la Tour says for stupid actors God made stupid spectators."

"I know it's considered a most elegant tendency to run into the French, but my child had better give up French if it's going to make her so tart," her mother said, stroking the brown head.

"Mamma, you know it's not French, it's that old Colonel Harrod. If he'd just hush up!"

"Sh! Your voice carries. I'm sorry, but I didn't propose it, honey."

"I know, I'm sorry," Lucinda said, rising, but not touching her mother as they moved toward the long window that would take them through the library to the parlor. "I'll try gladly. I don't know what's come over me lately, Mamma. Sometimes I think I'm the sort will live on and on till they have to put out poison for me."

"Precious, don't always jump to the bottom of the well. Judge Winchester has an ear for music."

When Edward heard Lucy singing a few moments later he understood that he could see deeper into her nature than his mother could. As he heard now the low, rich voice moving through the song, he leaned his head on his hands and sat motionless, listening, solitary and eager. Both his father and mother loved Lucy and admired her; but they would sometimes look at her as if nothing they could do or say would make their love reach her.

Lucy was too handsome a young lady not to draw Colonel Harrod's loud applause, and Edward heard it with his young lips curled in contempt. Colonel Harrod was a tall man of fifty with two plantations and a house then building, called Stamboul, and designed with the idea of rivalling Longwood, Doctor Haller Nutt's house at the other end of town, thirty-two octagonal rooms with an octagonal rotunda for the five stories. For some months the colonel had talked their heads off about tyranny and tasting the steel of Southern manhood. At the same time he had been able to explain that he must accept the proposed terms of exemption from military service for planters with more than twenty slaves. He could, he declared, best serve the South by the raising of supplies. He was the kind that if such a law of exemption for planters were abolished, would likely turn preacher.

Colonel Harrod, Edward could forget. But there were men like his father, like Judge Winchester, and thousands of others who had talked from so many sides about the war. There was so much to be considered, so many rights, leaders, policies and laws, sections, interests. As if these things were the point— As if there were not within you——

The singing went on. His heart was restless, tragic and rebellious; he wanted the cause he fought for to be simple and single; he knew that it was not. He wanted his country to be perfect just as one thinks of a beloved girl as perfect. He knew that he was going to the war; he had not any girl that he was in love with, and the Southern cause passed through his mind like a face that was still vague but would be beautiful yet, and a voice whose sweetness he felt but had not heard.

XX

"WHAT would you do, Aunt Piggie?" Valette asked Rosa one day, "if the war gets down here?"

"As it certainly will," Malcolm said. He had just read aloud a letter written by Mr. Burruss in *The Gazette*.

"I think I would help with the nursing, in a place the size of Natchez they'd need nurses you'd think," Rosa said.

Her sister looked sternly at her. "Sis Pig, child, I'd like to know where you'd get the strength to be a nurse?"

Rosa put her arm around Valette's shoulder. "Tell my sister I always was a fraud and she knows it. I'm plenty strong."

"It all looks to me [said the writer whose letter in *The Gazette* Malcolm had read to them], now that war is thundering north of us, very puerile. You may hardly believe it, but until late years I have been friend, defender, admirer of Northern ways and men. My first political controversy was in defense of J. Q. Adams, twenty years ago; this is a sample of my politics. In social life I showed the same feeling. My house was sought by Northern men. I gave cordial fellowship to them *because* they were Northern men; some of my most cultivated correspondents were Northern men. In the developments of Northern politics came out purposes that startled me. I felt a rebuff and with indignation. Next came this dissolution of the Union caused by the election of Lincoln. In my sorrow for the dissolution and righteous rage against its authors, I have not yet learned to love the Southern Confederacy as I shall, I trust. The breaking of the Union has at times almost broken my heart. Now I am Southern solely and am ready to do anything that can secure Southern independence.

                                        J. W. BURRUSS."

"His opinion is all well enough," the major said, "but, wife, I'll swear I could do without some of the I, I, I business— *l'état, c'est moi.*"

"Darlin', you know Mr. Burruss. He's always shot the bear, he's got to be the one."

Rosa Tate did not carry out her plans for nursing. On a March day, late in the afternoon, a sudden pain in her heart was so intense that she fainted. The season that year was already like summer, the windows open, the garden full of hyacinths, roses, verbenas, and heliotrope, and the air fragrant with them. The vegetable garden had come in. Next morning it was languid and overcast; and Rosa did not offer to get up, but lay motionless in her bed, scarcely speaking. The symptoms were what Doctor Martin had long since said they would be; he came at once, there was nothing he could do. Notes were sent to Mrs. Wilson at Rosalie and other friends and cousins. Lucy and Edward had gone with their mother on a visit to Baton Rouge; the note to Montrose asked that Hugh McGehee bring Father Carey out from town.

Rosa's eyes, still blue as when she was a girl, looked up at him.

"Hugh McGehee, it's always given me so much pleasure to think of you and Agnes. These things are good for me."

"Ain't there anything you want?"

Rosa shook her head and paused. Then she began to speak in an odd whimsical tone. "I know I'm dying. I've never done anything but I'm not jealous, I'm not prejudiced, and I'm well balanced. If I'd stop talking, I'd be restful."

Her sister chuckled, and smoothed the sheet at the foot. "I declare, Rosa, you're a captain," she said, without raising her eyes.

"Brother Malcolm," Rosa said, "don't cry—my own brother couldn't have been better to me—or loved me more, I reckon."

"At least I meant"—Malcolm began, but turned quickly away and went out into the hall.

"Sis Sallie," Rosa said, "tell him he oughtn't to feel like that. In my Father's house are many mansions, if it were not so— I was never worthy of Christ, never worthy." The voice went on. "You remember back at home, Sis Sallie, they had to put the schoolhouse for the children off in the grove so we couldn't hear the noise the grown-ups made at the big house; they had such a good time. So that we could keep our minds on our studies, you see, that's how 'twas."

"Yes, honey."

"Father used to think we were perfect ignoramuses."

"You'll tire yourself all out, child," Mrs. Bedford said. "Don't tire yourself out entertaining us."

"What harm does it do? But I can tell you our mother didn't think so. Mamma thought her daughters were such classical young ladies. Do you know I got six Abbot's histories as a prize for diligence. Can you imagine anything more ridiculous?" She closed her eyes, and seemed to be asleep, still smiling at the comical notion.

They went to bring the priest for the extreme unction. Valette came with the children, who knelt with her along one side of the room, looking on with curious, wide eyes as the priest went through his ministrations. Frances, her little face quivering and tense, held on to Valette's hand, as she kept peering into her mother's face. At that time Sallie Bedford was not religious, or only conventionally so. The deism of her father, who had somewhat pompously professed to follow the belief of certain founders of the Republic, had left its traces on her. So that now she would not meet the child's eyes, asking of her things nobody could know; and instead fixed her attention on the priest's face. The priest looked like a dull man, but he was only an instrument; the power of the great Catholic service and the depth of the moment made every one present understand the plan and meaning of it.

Some of the servants had come in and stood against the wall. With so many people there the room was crowded. Mary Hartwell stood with her arm around Middleton's shoulder, leaning over to stroke his hair with her other hand, as if she were the little boy's mother. When the service was over, Frances began to sob aloud and Hugh McGehee took her up in his arms and carried her into the hall. The two other children were taken over to kiss their aunt, whose eyes were still closed. Every one but Sallie Bedford then left the room.

In the silence that filled the room Rosa suddenly opened her eyes and saw her sister looking at her with an expression of love and pain. Then all at once in place of her sister and this love and pain, she saw what seemed to be figures in a ritual, a march, a sort of childlike glory. And at that moment it seemed to Rosa that for the first time she understood the movement in herself of her religion:

In every Christian church men laid their sorrows before God. But life was not merely sorrow. The Catholic Church had a visible form to contain the abounding life, the beloved pride, the show and energy of us; and through this form we gave ourselves to the church; so that, also, God should possess our joy.

She repeated that thought to herself: so that, also, God should possess our joy.

Sallie Bedford touched her sister's shoulder, which to the hand felt thinner even than appeared, in that thin body which she had carried like a light.

"Are you in such pain, Rosa, honey?" She had to lean down to hear.

"All my life I've known so much love. I should be able now to endure a little discomfort."

"Oh, Darlin', you talk like a book. Nobody ever loved you enough."

"Yes, they did."

"Go to sleep, Rosa."

"You must take care of Brother Henry," Rosa said, her eyes seeking the portrait, not very large, that hung on the opposite wall. It was a little boy in a white suit, standing by a table with a vase of flowers. Mrs. Bedford also glanced at the picture before she replied.

"Henry? I will. I will. The very best I can. Go to sleep." She had sent twice and had gone herself out to his room the day before, but her brother would not put his foot in the house.

"I didn't get to tell Hennie good-bye."

"No, you know how he is. I think he must have gone off for a long walk."

"Sis Sallie, listen," Rosa went on, after a silence. "I want you to do something. I want you to kiss me, kiss me good-bye and then go, honey. You stay there in the hall, don't you go away. I want to die by myself."

Mrs. Bedford did not answer. The figure on the bed seemed to sink downward and to be quieter, the eyes smaller till they closed. The hands, after making some strange weaving motion, were laid at the sides.

"So kiss me," Rosa said.

She kissed her, and as she went out, until the door was closed, she saw the white face with its delicate aquiline features, and the blue eyes following her.

XXI

By that time it was late morning. As Mrs. Bedford brought a chair and put it before the door of her sister's room and took her place there, she saw how the trees outside no longer cast shadows into the hall, or varied the colors of the wreaths in the carpet. A warm light fell over everything.

The plantation would be going on as it had gone every day for more than twenty years, but the house negroes tiptoed about downstairs and talked with low voices in the kitchen. On the bench by the kitchen cistern, little darkeys had sat all morning huddled in a line close together, frightened and still. Miss Rosa had talked to them every day, when she was feeding cottage-cheese to the young turkeys, or had paid them cakes to pick up the feathers if the geese had molted on the lawn, the most cakes for the most feathers. The servants were thinking that tomorrow they would go into the parlor and see Miss Rosie in her coffin. If they were not allowed to, their feelings would be hurt.

Mrs. Bedford sat there squarely before the door. Rosa had asked to be alone, and had asked her not to go away; and that was the way it was going to be. It did not seem to her strange that her sister wished to die with no one in the room. "Love that was in her whole heart," Sallie thought—"will she go, depart, with this sense of love? Can she take it with her? Or is it only something warm within?" Rosa had been open like a book in all things, even about her religion; that was true, and yet it was not true. Something about her life with God,—was it some dream of God in a life that is only a sleep?—Rosie could not share. Was that a weakness? Nobody could answer such a question; but if it was a weakness, Rosa had a right to it; let everybody live his own life.

She heard Valette's voice and then her brother Henry's

downstairs, but not what they were saying. Then she heard old Henry's voice say, "What's it to you if I go?" and his heavy tread like a drunkard's coming up the stair. He reached the head of the stair and stepped a foot or two forward and then stopped. His haggard frame in the baggy suit appeared to be even taller as she looked at him from where she sat in the chair. His long hair was wilder than usual.

"Listen to me, Bud Henry," she said, folding her small arms across her breast. "You listen to me. Yesterday I went out there myself and begged you to come see Piggie before she died, and you wouldn't do it. Swore you wouldn't. And now you can just stop in your tracks right where you are."

She could see the shine of perverse meanness in his dim, shrewd eyes under their wiry eyebrows. He had put his hands into the side pockets of his coat, from one of which a worn leather book stuck out, and as he spoke he assumed a sort of lazy swagger.

"Eh?" he said. "Then I judge I'm *de trop*."

"This is no time, Henry. Rosie's dying. Go on down-stairs," she said, looking not at him but at the floor.

"Who's in there with her?"

"Nobody, she's by herself. She asked me to leave her by herself."

"Don't let me intrude, I am always the last to intrude. As you know."

A blush spread over his sister's face, but she made no reply. She unfolded her arms and clasped her hands around her knees; and he waited until he saw her look up at him.

"And you carry out her wish. You tell yourself what Rosa wants Rosa shall have, just as you let your brother stay out in a nigger cabin, because he wants to."

"Whyn't you tell the truth, Henry? You know a hundred times we've begged you to come in and have your room up here," she said, squinting as she spoke, in order to examine him. He was clean at least, his linen white; Aunt Sophie had orders to see to that. "A hundred times I've begged you to come on in the house."

"As if I wouldn't o' perished," he said, with a smirk. "All the blather in this house!"

"Shh! Don't talk so loud." She looked at the door behind her.

"All right. Then listen. I'm not fooled. This letting people have their own way, this taking care of us. Don't you think I think it's love. It's just vanity—and it's no more'n you'd do for a sick dog. I know. What you feel, my darling sister, is animal pity. Animal pity."

"Oh, Henry, oh, please hush! You'll break Sis Piggie's heart."

He repeated the harsh phrase that had been in his mind. "Animal pity! That's all 'tis, not human love. Animal pity!"

"Curse me out, but talk low," she said. Then as she saw him glaring at her, his head craned forward, and the wretched look in the old eyes, she remembered in anguish how handsome he had been when he was a young man; she thought of the child's picture on the wall; and with a gasp like a sob she buried her face in her hands.

Then she heard the door to her bedroom open down the hall and raised her head to see her husband standing there. He stood just outside the door. She saw by that air of control and concentration that he was drunk. Drink whiskey to escape! Malcolm had a book open in his hand.

"What is it?" he said, quietly, closing the book and glancing at her brother, who had turned his head away.

She said nothing, inside she felt hard; and at the same time she was surprised to see that she recognized the book, it was her own copy of *La Rochefoucauld*. She saw in her mind that first page, his portrait of himself; *Je suis d'une taille médiocre, libre, et bien proportionée*—I am medium height, easy, and well proportioned—oh, Malcolm, trying to drown this grief in whiskey! At the same time she heard her brother Henry's phrase, "animal pity—animal pity."

"I asked what is it?" her husband repeated, but not moving from where he stood. "This commotion up here?"

"Vanity of vanities, saith the preacher," old Henry burst out mocking, as he saw his sister motioning his brother-in-law back into his room. "Saith the preacher!"

Malcolm listened to these words and began to grin. Then he stopped grinning and stood gazing at his wife, with eyes full of confusion and distress, as he stood wavering slightly on his feet.

"*Vanitas vanitatum,*" old Henry said, his voice rising "Hypocrites!"

Mrs. Bedford rose, but put her hand backward on the frame of the door, her arm across it.

"Hush, Henry! Your being an atheist don't matter. Malcolm, go back to your room!" she said, hissing under her breath. "Go back!"

"Why died I not from the womb?" Henry mocked. "Why did I not give up the ghost when I came out of the belly?"

She made a violent gesture to Malcolm with her hand, and he turned gravely back to his room and shut the door. When the door was shut, she turned to her brother, stepping out nearer to him and away from Rosa's room,

"Hush your mouth, you crazy dog! I'll cut your throat."

"All right, all right, I can hiss, too. Did she ever tell you she used to bring me cakes? Your cook makes 'em from Mamma's recipe, back in the old days that was. But I gave them to the niggers. And she saw me do it. I don't need her damned religion. After that she wouldn't come, not so often."

Mrs. Bedford forgot her anger thinking of Rosa, her taking the cakes to him like that——

"Hennie," she said, gently, calling him the childhood name

for the first time in years. "Hennie, you're in the presence of death."

She saw the look of fear that came into his eyes—"Then the idea of death haunts the poor wretch," she thought.

Her brother looked timidly at Rosa's door. "That's so," he said, and turning on his heel walked clumsily down the stair.

Sallie hesitated a moment; and then going to the stair rail, she leaned down and in a low voice kept calling till Valette answered.

"Come help me," she said, as Valette fell on her knees beside the chair and put her arms around her. "Seems like I can't stand it; it's just the way it is, but I seem—I can't stand it."

"I wanted to come. I tried to keep Uncle Henry away," the girl said, drawing the light body close in her arms.

"You've cried your eyes red, but don't. Not for Aunt Rosie."

"No," Valette said, in her sweet voice, leaning back to look at Mrs. Bedford and stroking her brow.

"When I was a young slip, just a fool, I was jealous of Rosie's red lips; and she was jealous because I could catch up a snake by his tail and pop his head off, like a whip-cracker. Of course Rosie was not really jealous, 'twarn't like her."

"Nor you, My Dumplin'," Valette said, but Sallie Bedford went on:

"Precious child, I tell you—we've begun now to have death in this house. And, I reckon you've thought of it, too—we've begun death in our country."

Valette only closed her eyes and rose to her feet, her lips quivering. Mrs. Bedford had also stood up.

"Listen, now maybe you might open the door a little and just see. No, wait, give her a little more time."

Valette, without heeding the hand that made a weak gesture

of restraining her, opened Rosa's door a few inches. She quickly drew back, closing the door again softly, and bowing her head as if to say yes.

Mrs. Bedford took hold of Valette's wrists. "Keep your hands down. Don't cry. Here, you've heard your Aunt Piggie say this, we'll say it now. 'I am the resurrection and the life' —if you cry for her it's wrong and you just stop it. 'I am the resurrection'—now you say it, too." She paused and was silent, listening to Valette's voice:

"I am the resurrection and the life——"

XXII

The McGehees had a distant cousin over in Amite County, Shelton Taliaferro. He had married a Miss Mary Dabney and brought her home to his plantation, Belle Grove, which at his father's death had been one of the finest in all that part of Mississippi. In his early years Shelton Taliaferro had ridden far and wide, paying visits, courting, dancing, and playing the races. His wife was a beautiful woman who wore her beauty with an indifference that puzzled people, especially Southern people. She had two interests. Religion was one; St. John Dabney, her grandfather, had been converted to Methodism by John Wesley. The other interest was her husband, whom she loved with passionate worship and surrounded with a devotion that drew alternately the contempt and the reverence of the neighbors. Several years passed without children, then a son was born, and at his birth Mary Taliaferro died.

Her husband, though he had neglected her, or at least not by any means devoted himself to her, when she was dead seemed all at once to be transformed. The power of love seemed to envelop him. Her memory was like the memory of a saint to him; he became gentle, absorbed, almost abstract, and began to divide his life between going to the church meetings and reading, solitary brooding, or meditation. You heard in Amite County that grief for his wife had been too much for him, and that he had gone daft. He knew what some of the hunting planters thought; and he spoke serenely to them when, for the first months before they left him to his ways, they called like gentlemen and friends at Belle Grove. "It's strange," he told them, "how, when you've heard them blindly all your life, all of a sudden you understand what the old phrases mean—'the communion of saints,' 'the fellowship of the Holy Ghost'." When he said that, they took it to mean, since they were not very strong on saints, that a man must love his family, and that Shelton Taliaferro should marry again. After a while they stopped coming to Belle Grove.

The child born was named Charles Edward de Jarnette, Charles Edward de Jarnette Taliaferro. He was brought up by his black mammy, Dorsey Bond, who gave him whatever training he got. Because the child had no mother and because his face resembled the dead Mary Taliaferro's, Shelton never punished him. The passionate and wilful boy did as he pleased, now defying his father, now throwing his arms wildly around his neck in a burst of tears, now sulking. It was understood that anybody at the plantation, even his mammy, who laid so much as a finger on him would have to settle with the master; and so the boy's natural arrogance was increased. Tom, Dorsey's son, of about the same age, was given to Jarnette, to be his playmate, to be ordered about, and later to be his valet. Shelton called his son Jarnette, a family name from Virginia—often at Belle Grove they said Jarrie—until at fifteen the boy himself decided that he would not have the name any longer, but would be called by his first name, Charles.

Meanwhile, the plantation fell into even worse neglect than it had suffered since the death of Charles' grandfather, its first owner. It was mortgaged and re-mortgaged; parts of it were sold off. Two or three times Shelton Taliaferro had written Hugh McGehee and borrowed money to pay the Belle Grove taxes. He knew he was welcome to the money, but always felt that he must give the most elaborate reasons for requesting it.

In the autumn of 1859 Charles, taking along his man Tom, his guns and hounds, rode up to Oxford to the University, from which he came home in April. The following November he enrolled with Edward, his cousin, at the Seminary of Learning in Alexandria; but at the close of the first examinations Colonel William Tecumseh Sherman, the superintendent, who had no patience with young Southern gentlemen of Charles' type, called him into his office and read to him the comment he intended to write on the report about to be sent his father; and Charles, who thought even worse of Colonel Sherman than Sherman did of him, without a word walked out and took the first boat to New Orleans.

Since his wife's death, Shelton Taliaferro would never leave the plantation unless he was obliged. Just before Charles went off to Oxford, however, they came for a visit to Montrose, driving over in an old rockaway that had itself seen better days, but at least was drawn by two fine horses belonging to Charles. The visit was less than a week. Shelton did not like to be away from home, where some revivalist preacher or circuit rider was often staying, and where he used to read in his library sometimes till dawn, or walk about the neglected place, under the old trees and by the outhouses, with a strange, rapt movement as if speaking with God. Some of the negroes, if they awoke at such times, were afraid to look out at him.

One day at Montrose, during Shelton's visit, when they were sitting on the gallery, they saw the tall, thin figure in its black suit, walking thus. He was far down at the end of the garden, where the last of the box walks led to a small orchard of quinces.

"Well, wife," Hugh McGehee said, gazing at the figure, walking, walking, "I reckon these days Shelton's just not all there."

"Who knows? Sometimes, I declare, I think poor Cud'n Shelt's real self is in heaven."

"We can't argue that," he said, with a dry smile, "can we, Lucy?"

Lucy said abruptly, "What I think is the thing to do is to mend him up, he's all ravelled out, did you see his clothes? So clean and pitiful, but nobody cares how he looks, not a soul cares a rap. And do it now, while he's not in his room." She called to a servant crossing the court below to send Aunt Aurora to her upstairs. "I know it's just as you say, Mamma, Cousin Shelt's got land enough to dress like a prince if he'd manage it; but just the same Aunt Aurora and I might as well take care of the poor old thing."

"I'm not so sure he's such a poor old thing, precious. His face is so sweet."

"I know how you think, Mamma, and that's all right for angels, they've got their wings to cover them. But I look at his waistcoat. It looks as if he buttoned it with a fork."

On Wednesday, Mrs. Quitman, with Doctor and Mrs. Martin, came to supper at Montrose, bringing along beside the driver's box a basketful of some new water lily, shell pink with a yellow centre. Pretty soon Sallie and Malcolm Bedford with Valette arrived. During supper Malcolm Bedford was telling stories of Natchez-under-the-Hill, before the days when the town on the bluffs above was much of anything. He loved the story of James Willing, who owned a shop there, went away to join the Revolutionary armies, was promoted to captain of a company, and his patriotism thus reinforced, said Malcolm, he came back home with his soldiers and looted his old friends.

"They'd taken the oath of allegiance to the Colonies, but Captain Willing skipped that," Malcolm laughing and winking at Lucinda, whom he liked for that look of honest pride and wit. "He made them prisoners, to row his boats on the river. *Sic semper tyrannis,* which was in 1778. The sins of the whole Mississippi Basin were washed down to that Natchez of those days."

Malcolm knew stories about the pirate Lafitte's sending

barges of stolen cattle up to be sold and was cheered on to tell them. Even Shelton Taliaferro listened with a child's delight; he was one of those rare people who lead intensely religious lives without taking much stock in weighing the sins of others. As Malcolm spread himself, everybody therefore laughed except Mr. Munger, the older consumptive.

"Nevertheless, notwithstanding, sir, our great Constitution stands like a rock," he said to Malcolm.

"You've got it mixed up with the burial service," Malcolm said: "brethren, we are gathered together."

"Tell about Murrell perhaps," said Agnes quickly. "Murrell, Mr. Munger, had a sort of club on the bandit order."

"Murrell's gang," said Malcolm, bursting out laughing at so innocently elegant a description. He began an account of the famous highwayman.

Afterwards Charles rode in as far as town with them, and next day, looking the worse for wear, fell asleep in the parlor after dinner. Everybody else knew what it was; he had done the town and ended with Natchez-under-the-Hill; but they saw his father gaze at Charles, rosy around the eyes and nodding in company like that, as if it were only a child resting. When their cousin Shelton spoke of starting for Belle Grove, Lucy and Edward begged that Charles might stay. She was fifteen and the two boys were not much past seventeen; and it seemed to the three of them that the visit had just begun.

"Uncle William could drive him home," they said, and William Veal, with an admiring glance at this young man who seemed to him very stylish and quality, said, nodding his round, gray head,

"Gladly, sir, gladly."

But their dashing young cousin surprised them by linking his arms through theirs and walking with them toward the window: "No," he said, quietly, in his engaging voice, and putting a gentle stress on the last word, "I'll go back with *him.*"

It was a Sunday, and they were to depart for Belle Grove early Monday morning. A chicken had been fried for their lunch basket and the rest ordered: green tomato pickle, stuffed eggs, ham, beaten biscuit, peach chips, cup cakes, and a bottle of punch. Paralee, the cook, was to keep an eye on the preparations and see that they were ready in good time. Every morning at the Montrose quarters this old woman waked the servants. She passed along by the cabins and in her great voice would call,

"Get up, you lazy niggers, the stars are down!"

That last afternoon of the visit, Charlie had been telling his cousin Edward some of his New Orleans stories, which now and then he would compare with Natchez-under-the-Hill; and that night when everybody had said good-night and gone to their rooms and shut the doors, Edward lay for a long time awake in his bed by the window. The things his cousin talked about, the stories he told, were disturbing. The soft air poured over him, and the leaves outside moved softly with a sound like waves. Shortly after midnight he heard, or half heard, some one at the stable-lot; and, looking out of the window, saw Charles riding at a walk down the drive.

XXIII

It was a year and six months later, that day in May, 1861, when Charles Taliaferro rode over to Montrose and told them that he was going away with Edward to the army. Eighteen months, plus Charles' manner of living them, had done everything. He was now a young man, going on to twenty, tall, slender, with languid movements and muscles as strong as wire. His complexion was all white and red and black, the color strongest in his cheeks, and pink around the brown eyes, the brow white, the dark hair compact and rich. He was a perfect example of a certain Southern type, planters' and lawyers' sons, who knew horses, rode well, hunted—were fine shots, had manners, a certain code of their own, and would not have been afraid of the devil himself. He had never taken an education, had never worked and never intended to. Life with its powers and magnetisms came to him easily, as the sun and growing came to the vegetation in that country. He read slowly and talked easily, in a low voice, persuasive and alive.

By one of the ironies of human life it was this young man who was devoted to Edward McGehee. Reckless, headstrong, dashing, sure to be, until his marriage at least, forever after women, oblivious and wilful, Charles gave to Edward a great, impetuous affection and complete admiration. They had been together the few months at the seminary until Colonel Sherman proved too much for Charles' patience. And now Charles also was going to enlist under General Beauregard. He had ridden over to go with Edward to Virginia. It could have been said that his father and Edward were the only two people he loved in the world.

From the parlor Charles and Edward could be heard talking of the January state convention to consider the relations between the government of the United States and the government of the people of Mississippi, after which the commissioners were sent to visit the other slave states. At all the Southern capitals they were received in diplomatic style, as ambassadors from foreign republics.

"For these three days now those boys have talked nothing but General Beauregard," Hugh McGehee said, having just heard the young men comparing their hero with Napoleon. His wife and Lucinda were near him in the library, where they were writing down a list of things to be bought in town for Edward to take along. "Can't be much to Charles, one war's as good as another to him; he'd fight a buzz saw, I reckon. It's all Edward, Charlie just follows him."

"It won't do him any harm, Edward's example," Agnes said, smiling. "Let's put him in his fine-tooth comb," she said to Lucy, who gave a shudder at the thought of what this was for

"Well," Hugh said, "Charles Edward de Jarnette Taliaferro—at least he's got all the family names, whatever credit he may do them."

"And plenty of castile soap," her mother said to Lucy.

"Yes, plenty," Hugh said. "Cousin Cindy Eppes is a case," he went on, picking up one of the morning's letters from the table. It was from a fifth cousin of theirs in New Orleans, who had buried her husband, mortgaged the plantation and for a while lived in Paris bringing up a son, whom she planned to make a diplomat. "What do you reckon she wanted us to think, Agnes, when she wrote this about Charlie?"

"Cud'n Cynthia will let us know in her own sweet time what she wants us to think."

"What's it she says, Papa?" Lucy asked.

"A little disposed to be Creolized and I gave him such a lecture about balls, plays, and so forth, that I think I restrained him a great deal."

Agnes shook her head with a grin. "There's no use talking about it, Cud'n Cynthia just thinks we're all country saints up here."

"Yes, Cynthia's a pious fraud," said Hugh McGehee.

Charles and Edward had left the parlor at last and were walking along outside toward the stables.

"Yes, Mamma, every blessed thing," Lucy said, answering

some question of her mother's and gazing at the two figures on the lawn. "Mamma, what was Charles' mother like?"

"It would be hard to tell you," Agnes McGehee said, smiling and looking also out of the window, but only as if with the eyes of memory. "I used to see in her armoire. She'd always given everything to anybody that came begging. All there was ever in her armoire was her bonnet and shawl. She had one little gold pin, an ivy leaf. She always wore it, it was buried with her. We used to visit at Belle Grove sometimes when she was living. Nobody knows where half the things in the house have gone; they say now it's like a barn. I remember at the time of the funeral I asked where the silver goblets were, but nobody cared. She had a locket with Charles' miniature, painted in New Orleans, when he was a little boy. It had diamonds around it; and goodness knows where that went to; the darkies got it, I suppose."

"What a shame!" said Lucy, turning away and straightening the line of books on one of the shelves. "And now they'll never find it."

"No, I shouldn't think so, it's gone," her mother said, quietly, though she had not missed the tone in Lucy's voice. With the same thing in mind she watched Lucy during that day and the next.

"I wish we had a good miniature of Buddie," Lucy said, avoiding her mother's glance.

Later in their bedroom, Agnes put her hands on Hugh McGehee's shoulders and stood looking into his eyes, her lips quivering in spite of her. "I'm frightened for Lucy," she said, "I'm so frightened about her." She knew that Lucy was the kind who would love when she loved and would not change easily.

Without lighting the candle, for the moonlight filled the room, Agnes threw the blue cashmere shawl over her shoulders and stole down the hall to Lucy's room. In a **few** moments she was back: "You thought she'd be asleep and she was. But she made herself go to sleep, just by sheer will power."

"Now, great God, wife!" Hugh said, "how do you women know that?"

"I know it."

"No doubt ye are the people and wisdom shall die with you."

"No doubt, if you want to drag the Bible in. She's stretched out straight as a drill. Sometimes I think it's the people with the will power are the pitiful ones. They don't ask any help."

"Nobody can help Lucy except by loving her," he said. "If she knows you do that——"

"I suppose people can make themselves go to sleep. But they can't make themselves stay asleep," Agnes said. "Their will goes to sleep when they do. After a while that child will wake up, then she'll just lie there. If he were the sort ever to care anything about a girl like Lucinda——"

"Aye, that would be a horse of another color," Hugh said.

Her mother was right. Lucy had closed her eyes and forced herself scornfully to fall asleep. But after two or three hours she awoke. The moon had sunk behind the trees, and in the dark room the sweet smell of roses and pinks had followed the damp wind from the garden. She got up and shut the window, and stretched herself again on the bed. That morning two letters on green paper heavily sealed with green wax had arrived for Charles. Before he came down she had looked at them to see the postmarks. The small writing was full of flourishes and shadings. Having looked once at these two letters, she took pains to look well. They had been sent from New Orleans. One of the seals had run, on the other there showed the initials M. B. As she lay there with this picture of herself and Charles' letters in her mind, Lucy despised her-self. Green paper, green wax— "At least I never thought I'd be common," she thought dry-eyed, bitter. "Spying."

That evening she had made excuses not to sing, and from this on, while Charles was at Montrose, she would not sing.

XXIV

LUCINDA's dress from the establishment of Madame Rosière in New Orleans had arrived for the Arlington party, and been tried on, pressed and laid out on the bed in the yellow room upstairs, where nobody would be and all at once get to talking and sit on it. George McGehee had arrived from Woodville; in the stable his horse, after a long ride, stood sleek from the currycomb and brush.

"It may not be a bad idea for Lucy to go," Agnes said to Hugh McGehee, as they sat that morning on the gallery. "Just as well to see some other young men beside Charlie Taliaferro. Sometimes I think life should be so that two creatures like this—you saw this morning how they both sat their horses—could just ride away along the sky forever, while they are still young——"

"How are you, Mr. Munger?" Hugh said, partly to warn his wife that one of their invalids, hat in hand, had stepped through the library on to the gallery.

"I can't complain," Mr. Munger said, in a tone that implied that nothing short of divine aid enabled him to speak.

"I find you looking very well," Agnes said. In days like these such a long face about nothing was more than she could bear. "What we were talking about is the evening party at Arlington."

"No use repeating my opinion of the waltz," Mr. Munger said, sucking his teeth and turning to Hugh, who stood offering him a chair. "No, I guess I won't sit down, I shall take my constitutional."

"Then if you'll excuse me," Hugh took his seat again.

"Mr. McGehee, what are you thinking about now, child?" Agnes said, seeing the frown on his brow as he watched the slim, stooped figure walking briskly down the path. It was a good Anglo-Saxon type and would have been a fine head but for that cranky and self-centred look.

"I was thinking look at that. It's this sort of man will be one of the things that will ruin this country some day. This notion that you must judge everything for yourself and have it on your conscience to judge everything is a good notion, of course, the only thing the matter with it is that it requires brains. And where's the average man to get any brains? Even if we'd once had a society, some sort of idea of a civilization, this great thinking individual judge would refuse to stand on it. And what happens? If he's inspired, the result is inspired. If he's average, his opinion is average."

"And this is one of the things will ruin this country?"

"Wait, and see now. The next generation and the next may lose this conscience to judge, et cetera. But the society or idea of a civilization will have been forgotten, and so you have thousands of people thinking at random. The result of that will be public opinion, and that will mean equality of ideas. One man is as good as another——"

"That's a dream that's only natural," Agnes said, "and human."

"Yes, but it's a little too human when one idea is as good as another."

"I'm smiling because I agree with you. Thomas Jefferson has always seemed to me confused about these things. Grandmother Bedford used to say if all men were born equal, then who were those choice recipes for that her famous nephew had the envoys of this republic sending back from Europe? Here comes Mr. Munger. I'm sorry, but lately it seems to me we have enough without invalids, so I'm glad poor little

Mr. Trippler has gone back North. I wish he'd been less frail when he left; he says flannel scratches him and won't wear it."

A moment later Mr. Munger ascended the steps and crossed the gallery to the door without glancing at them. They were used to him and thought nothing of this stern look of heading somewhere worth while.

The trap could have taken them, but Charles proposed that he and Edward ride to Arlington and that George McGehee, since he had already ridden up from Woodville the day before, should share a carriage seat with Lucinda. It seemed all a simple plan to Edward, who thought nothing of it also when Charles Taliaferro, after the horses were brought round, went back upstairs for his gloves, so that they were well behind the others in starting.

For a while Charles was silent; then speaking rapidly at first, as if he were shy, and then as if arguing or defending himself, he took a letter out of his coat, held it up in the dusk, and put it back again. There was a woman in New Orleans. She knew he was going to the war and this was the third letter of hers that Charles had received at Montrose. This letter said that she would be in Natchez that night, at a tavern in the lower town. He took out the letter again, but could not see to read the tavern's name.

"You mean she's a quadroon?" Edward asked, when Charles had said that this woman was under the protection of an old man; her mother had settled her at sixteen with an old French banker.

"Yes," Charles said, the reckless quality coming into his voice. "I saw her at a Quadroon Ball, at the Orleans Theatre, last year after I left the seminary. I went with our cousin Mr. Francis Eppes and his Paris friend, that marquis. The protector, however, was in Paris for the time being, or there'd have been a duel, you know how 'tis. So he was gone two months. And just now he's at his sugar plantation in Ascension Parish, and she's slipped off up here for tonight. The Magnolia goes back to New Orleans in the morning."

"By God, man!" Edward said bluntly, as Charles went on to describe what everybody had heard of more or less: the quadroon girls, the little houses along the ramparts where for a hundred years these women had lived. They were not prostitutes, they were not slaves, they were free women of color, many of whom had come first from the West Indies; they were proverbially faithful. A few of these relationships lasted. Most of them broke off when the white man married. The women then married, to men of their own color. Many of them, when they were older, kept successful rooming houses for gentlemen. Foreign noblemen visiting New Orleans declared the women of the quadroon balls the most beautiful women in the world.

"By God, Charlie, that doesn't mean," Edward said, "that I'm glorfying you, for all the princes may say!"

"I know that. Just the same I know you're not setting yourself up."

"I'm not setting myself up. But what's the use of telling me what's been written and published? We all know the quadroons are given an education and their mothers lock them in till they pass to the protector." His own voice, breaking out in the dusk of the road, surprised him. "And so on and so on," he said, stopping abruptly as he realized that Charles was less concerned about the quadroon than he was about Edward's good opinion of himself.

"You can't claim it's my fault," said Charles, reining his horse closer to the other, "if she goes and takes it all so—the way she has."

"All I say is this: nobody can do anything for her, Charlie. But what is it you're asking me to do for you?"

"For that matter——"

"I'm not getting mad and don't you. You know I'll do what I can, damn it!"

"Look here," Charles said, "one thing, of course, they won't let her in anywhere, she'll have to go to some place down there under the hill."

They had come to the Arlington gate, overgrown with trumpet vines, flowering red; there was a lantern lighted for the carriages.

"Here 'tis—" Charles held the letter toward the lantern. "Titi Richards, I knew I couldn't remember it."

"That would have to be Natchez-under-the-Hill."

"And that's what you can do; you'll have to go with me. I couldn't just not go."

At that moment the carriages from D'Evereux and Richmond came driving in. Hands were waved from the windows to Edward and Charles, and they rode alongside to the carriage mount. Garlands of ivy and camellia leaves hung between the columns of the portico.

In the parlor at Arlington they saw her Woodville cousin, who was a famous dancer, whirling Lucy around, in her blue silk with the sleeves of pale blue tulle and little ribbon bands. George McGehee looked more than ever like a young Louis Napoleon; and Lucinda, though a trifle taller, rested her long, slender hand on his shoulder and danced well. Down by one of the windows Valette, not dancing for the moment, stood talking with Douglas Walworth.

For the next waltz Charles Taliaferro presented himself to Lucy. But he had never troubled to learn to dance beyond what was necessary. A company of people gave him less pleasure than did one or two, and so now what was only lack of skill seemed to Lucy, in her proud mood of secrecy, to be indifference on his part toward herself. Before the end of the waltz she broke it off and led him to where her father and four or five other guests stood with the host, Judge Boyd, talking of the patrols that were being established for public safety.

Hugh McGehee was saying that his two plantations south of Baton Rouge were suffering for want of his oversight. He had not spent a night away from home since the autumn, for it was considered unsafe to leave women alone. The negroes had got an impression that Lincoln's election was the symbol for their freedom.

"I should have no fear of negroes," he said, "it's the baser sort of white man scattered over this country and ready to scatter firearms, revolt, death."

"Precisely," said Judge Boyd, and went on speaking of the man who had come last month to Woodville as a Presbyterian preacher, bringing with him a very large unmarked trunk. This trunk looked so suspicious that the negro carrying it had been ordered to drop it accidentally. It was filled with pistols and bowie knives. "And in every Northern newspaper we get," the judge said, "and the quotations in our press, it appears that the North regards the idea of black insurrections, cutting the levees, and so on, with unmixed delight."

When a little colonel from Baton Rouge began to speak of the war as if the South could win with one eye open, Hugh McGehee drifted away and joined Malcolm Bedford and Mrs. Quitman at the punch table.

"You were the last man of us to hold out for the Union," Malcolm said, "but now the die is cast——"

"Aye," said Hugh gravely, "my choice is made."

Mrs. Quitman held out her cup to the punch bowl. "We might have known all along you'd be above reproach, my dear."

Lucy, after the one waltz, kept away from Charles Taliaferro and the dancing. But Valette, before they were half round the room, told him to forget compliments and remember that the time was one, two, three. Her words were sharp, but she said them in a voice that seemed only an invitation to happiness.

All the fine houses of Natchez had come to Arlington that night. The trace of sadness underneath the scene gave a certain romance to everything. Valette, when the last strains of the waltz died, sent Charles to join the hostess' court; and she, half waltzing still, came up and kissed Mrs. Bedford lightly on the cheek.

"You little rascal, and you want my Duncan to believe you are his inamorata!"

"Why, My Dumplin'!"

"But tell me who 'tis you're in love with here," Mrs. Bedford said, putting up her lace fan over Valette's face as if to blockade a kitten.

"How sweet those voices are out there on the gallery," Valette told herself. "The flame of the candles is like a heart, heart shaped. How beautiful that is!" "Please forgive me, My Dumplin'," she said, suddenly turning the same gaze on Mrs. Bedford.

"I'll settle it. I'll answer it for you. You're in love with everybody and everything." The long strain of the violins came swelling into yet another dance, and she sighed as she relinquished Valette to one of the sons of the house. "Go on, I'd as soon try to chaperone a skylark."

"Yes, ma'am," the young man said, making her a courtly bow at the same time that the hand behind his back waved off three other young men who had come up to beg the same dance of Valette. One of these, a red-haired youth who stammered, tried to call out something witty, but before he could say it the white dress and its partner were off into the swirling billows of tarleton and lace.

"If you will be so heartless," Mrs. Boyd said, when Agnes and Lucinda came to bid their hostess adieu. "And Lucy has declined my invitation to spend the night at Arlington."

"Be careful what you say," Agnes replied. "We are plain Montrose country people. We might stay on and live with you forever."

"Exactly what I'm plotting. Even Mr. George McGehee would have none of us. He too favors Montrose. So I've told him it's the very last time I ever say he's as handsome as his father. How lovely your Lucy is, Agnes, what a patrician! I said to her, I said, 'Child, before we know it you'll be wafted away and standing on that bridge of Canaletto's.'" She waved her sandalwood fan toward the painting on the wall near them. "But I'm sure she'd rather be our Carlo Dolci, with the eyes. All young girls would rather be sad than eat."

These things and things like them were being said all over the room. Such compliments were very Southern, presented like a bouquet, not so much to penetrate as to give pleasure; they had a perfume but not intrusive depth, touching the vanity rather than the ego.

"And here we have the full moon for you," Mrs. Boyd went on. "Yon 'tis, above the water oaks. How we do laugh sometimes over that little mot Colonel Harrod made about them!"

Colonel Harrod made a deprecating gesture of putting the crown from him, and straightened his black stock as she went on:

"You may remember that old Monsieur Pierre Surget, who built this house for his daughter, continued, at least for a while after he got here from Bordeaux, to live on his vessel. And so, as you see, the colonel said, when M. Surget did come to live on the land, he planted right off water-oaks.'" Mrs. Boyd said this in her clear, friendly voice, and—whatever she may have thought of Colonel Harrod's wit—laughing, and at the same time straightening her cameo bracelet so that the central goddess came on top of the wrist.

"The moon is not the sole surprise," said Judge Boyd. "But

I shall only reveal this much: another swan from D'Evereux."

Nobody understood what this meant, but they had all seen the swans floating on the mill pond at D'Evereux.

It was going on midnight when Edward and Charles were both at the same moment disengaged and able to make their adieux. They found their hostess outside, standing by the round pool in the centre of the rose parterre, where a harp had been brought out under the swinging lanterns and the moon, and some visitor at D'Evereux, a cousin of theirs on the Bolivian hero's side, was going to play. Judge Boyd, leading forward a dark-eyed young lady in white lace, extravagantly flounced, presented her to the guests around:

"Another swan has joined the swans of D'Evereux."

He had been repeating this phrase to one guest after another all evening, but everybody applauded just the same; and Edward would have liked to stay on to hear the music. But he had given his promise. In fact, when he considered his promise, he said to himself that if Charles had changed his mind about going, he would make him go. Mrs. Boyd, smiling, with one finger held prettily before her lips, nodded graciously a good-night; the first chords had already struck, the clear notes could be heard far out over the garden.

XXV

Below the town bluffs and down nearer the river, ran the long winding road, one side of which was precipice; along the other were the shops, bar-rooms, taverns, gambling houses, slave dealers' sheds, and brothels. Sometimes the river carried off pieces of the ground where they stood. The streets, sunken and rough, were crowded with sailors from all parts of the world, with young men, with women loudly rouged, thieves, soldiers in uniform on leave, children, Indians, negroes, mulattoes, quadroons, dogs and straying pigs. There were the cries from the wharves where ships landed, the roar of the bar-rooms, street bawling, music, noisy traffic up and down the hill. At night some of the uproar moved indoors where it went on long after the streets were darker and almost empty.

Bargemen from up the Mississippi stopped here to barter fur, lumber, merchandise, or to squander and to drink. Travellers on the steamboats saw the wharves running a mile along the coast of the broad river, bounded with green walls of forest, the streets full of all nations, heard the clamor of these, and took home with them stories of vice, strangeness, and romance.

Charles and Edward rode into John Lum's stable to leave their horses. When he saw who they were, he took off his cap and tossed it on to a peg where bridles were hanging. He had a bald head and an honest face, his nose was stubby and tilted but whiskey red.

"Where's Titi Richard's?" they asked John Lum.

"Richard's, that's in river town."

"We know that," Charles said. "But where?"

"You goin' to Titi Richard's this hour of night?"

Charles began to swear and started for the street.

"Ah, you are!" Lum said, with an obscene grin. "In that case, gentlemen, Titi Richard's is the second house at the far end, near the old dock. The coast ain't no place to be careless. Have you got your pistols?"

"No."

" 'Twon't do like that, gentlemen. I'll lend you this."

Charles put the small pistol, which smelled of sweat, in his pocket.

"Sorry I can't let you have one," the liveryman said to Edward, "obliged to keep something on hand myself. Besides I might be goin' down the street myself before mornin'.'"

"Be careful, Mr. Lum," Edward said; the red nose pulsing in the lantern light made him laugh, "hide your light if you go."

"Ef I don't up and enlist," Lum said, with a single movement turning back into the stable and sitting down on a box. "Otherwise I mought go down the line myself tonight. Yes, sirree, I mought at that."

As they went down the three winding streets spotted with lights and darkness, Edward and Charles did not stop for the noise of orgies, music, and dancing. Here and there they saw a mustang pony tied in front of a house, Texas pinto ponies with white spots. The orange shops were closed at this time of night, the glare of them gone, but here and there the lights from the liquor shops streamed out against the shadow. Out over the river spread the flatboats and barges with lanterns twinkling among them. At last almost at the wharf was the sign with Titi Richard's name in gold letters, two of them smudged out.

"Would you gentlemen kindly go to the side there," the barkeeper in charge at the moment said, speaking through a sliding shutter in the door. "And on upstairs. The south corner door, sir. Thank you, sir, sholy that's too much money, but I'm much obliged, sir. Not the south corner, the other door, sir, please."

A little way down the street four or five bargemen coming up the hill began shouting at them; to stay outside would mean a fight.

"There'll be a room upstairs where you can wait for me," Charles said to Edward.

But when they reached the hall above, all the rooms had people in them; and before he could decide what to do, one of the farther doors opened and Edward saw standing just inside it a young woman in a green silk dress. She was slender, almost thin, with a full bosom, pale gold-colored skin, and long dark eyes. In her shining black hair, to the left, she had pinned gardenias. Behind her the candlelight of the room was glowing and dingy at the same time. She moved backward till she stood in front of the old oilcloth table in the middle of the room. As they entered she made a movement as if to speak to Charles, but with a timid look at him, turned her gaze to Edward and, from then on until he left the room, did not take her eyes off his face.

"What can I do?" she said to that face, in a low, tense voice, moving away from the table and coming nearer Edward, "what can I do? He's going away and I know."

He could think of nothing to say. His eyes shifted to the locket that hung around her neck. A little boy with black hair, in a green velvet jacket, the miniature was set in an oval of diamonds.

"I see you know who it is," she said, following Edward's eyes. "When he was a little boy. He doesn't feel about anybody the way he feels about you, and now I see you I see how that is. But he's going to the war. And now I know I'll never see him again."

"Nobody knows that, the way it is in war," Edward said.

"People tell me that old Madame Olivette said things from her cards, but how would she know? But I know."

"Nobody can know," he said, clasping his hands behind his back to stop their trembling.

The movement gave him the effect of drawing himself up straighter. And so her voice changed as she asked, "Does he hate me for coming up here like this?"

"I think he's glad you came," Edward said, blushing. He could no longer meet her eyes. At the same time he noticed that the perfume she used had spread through the musty air of the room. Charles at the window remained with his back to them, and for a few moments all three waited. Then Edward heard the quadroon come a step nearer him, and her low, passionate voice. Under his foot the floor creaked; afterward when he remembered this scene he would hear that creaking floor.

"I know you are good," she said. "I can tell from men's faces; if I can't, where's the woman could? Would you leave us here by ourselves?"

Edward nodded his head. "Charlie, I'll wait in the big room down below," he said, and without looking either at her or Charles, went out, closing the door after him. The latch did not catch at once, and as he stood turning it again, he could hear a low, terrible, reckless cry.

Edward walked past the other rooms. He was so absorbed in his own thoughts that he scarcely heard the sounds that came from them. At the end of the hall the narrow stair led down to Titi's main room.

"Hey, brother," a tall young man with thick yellow hair, his eyes red from drinking, shouted as he saw Edward pausing for a minute on the bottom step. *"Salutamus."* Edward raised his hand to salute, as if they were both of the military.

"He's got a gal up there, eh? Got a gal up there'n that room! And you've got one too, may I inquire?"

"No," Edward said, coming forward and smiling.

The drunken man smiled back. "No gal?"

"No gal," Edward said. *"Salutamus."*

In front of the man stood a bottle of claret with two large duelling pistols, one on each side of the bottle, and a bowie knife lying across between them. The man opposite, whom the landlord called Cap'n, kept watching him as if he wanted to leave but was afraid of giving offense. The young man slapped his palm on the table and ordered the landlord to bring a rum punch. "For this gentleman. Your wine's nothin' at all, not worth a tinker's damn," he said, and turning to

Edward, "Pray sit down, trash we meet constantly, but a gentleman—*rara avis*. I've not the pleasure of your name."

Edward shook hands, introduced himself, and sat down at the end of the table.

"Ah, Edward McGehee? My name's McClung, nephew of Colonel McClung, Colonel A. K. McClung, know who he was? Don't know who he was? Here's your rum punch. I'll tell you."

McClung now turned to the old man on his left, whispering loudly, "This is a gentleman. I'll tell him about my uncle." The old man, slapping his mug down, began to sing—

"The miller's big dog lay on the barn floor,
And Bango was his name."

"Shut up," McClung said. "You've cracked your mug and your damned old voice is cracked too. 'The man that hath no music in his soul'—but I don't call that music."

"Damn nigh true," said the old man. He leaned over the liquor that seeped from his mug and was starting to run along the table. McClung pointed to it.

"That's the way my uncle's blood did. Mr. McGehee, you listen now, and I'll tell you."

"And Bango was his name," the old man began again, in a higher key.

"Lend me your ears, Bango," McClung said fiercely. "See this knife. Everybody knows who invented it, it was Reese Fitzpatrick, right here in Natchez. Called a bowie knife. And here it is, my man."

"Go on, you can tell me about it," Edward said, gently.

There were, besides the old man, two others at the long deal table, which smelled reeking and sour. Over by the way, on puncheon seats that were split halves of young oaks set on four peg legs, more men were throwing dice; they were hard customers from the barges. Every little while the door from the kitchen opened a crack so that the landlord, whose name was John Monsanto, could keep an eye on them.

"Stop your Cajun talkin'," one of them would say to two Creoles who now and then spoke to each other in French. They were talking about the seizure of the United States arsenal at Baton Rouge by the Louisiana troops. It was useless to resist, and so the New Orleans militia got the stores and arms. Now and then two negro boys with dirty aprons came in with bottles or plates of ham and river shrimps, peppered over with cayenne; but they got out of the room as soon as they could. When there were rowdy voices outside in the street and a knock at the door, one of the negroes went and whispered to them, and nobody came in. It was better to lose trade than to have a killing in the tavern.

"Tell you about Uncle"—said McClung.

Edward, as the young man went on, speaking quietly and tenderly, his voice full of sadness and affection, forgot that he, like everybody else, had heard of this United States marshal who fought so many duels that a Kentuckian, hearing too often of the duellist, came all the way to Mississippi to make his acquaintance and pick a quarrel. It was said that the ghosts of the men McClung had killed followed him; he walked the floor all night or slept sitting up in a chair fully clothed. Earlier in his life he had been an officer in the Mexican War; he was also an orator, his eulogy on Henry Clay was read even in the schools.

"But indeed, my uncle had a heart of gold," the young man said, in his polished speech. Upstairs in one of the rooms an accordion was playing. The sound swelled and grew fainter and swelled again, and Edward in his mind saw again the quadroon's eyes and heard her voice.

The old man who had tried to sing "Bango," began to cry.

"Hey?" said McClung.

"I believe it," said the old man, no longer crying.

"You keep quiet. You're not fit to speak his name."

"All right, Mister."

McClung pushed the golden hair back from his brow, as he turned to Edward:

"Mr. McGehee," he said, "it was at the old Eagle Hotel over there in Jackson. My uncle dressed himself spotlessly and had his boots polished. Then he poured a cup of water on the floor to see which way it ran, placed himself so that the blood would not stain his clothes, and shot himself in the temple, here, right here in the temple. Was the 23d of March, five years ago, 1855. Beware the Ides of March!"

"I'm sorry," Edward said, pushing his glass of rum away.

"I know you are. But your eyes were sad when you came in here. Am I right, your eyes were sad?"

"Maybe."

"Yes, sad. I find your eyes sad. You must forgive me. That's what makes me want to tell you about one night." He began to describe a fight he had had on the river. "On your steamboat," he said, turning contemptuously to the captain. His lips curled contemptuously, but the fine eyes and golden hair, and the air of ruined splendor and elegance could not be ignored. "On your steamboat," he repeated, "before you blew her up in a race with the *Magnolia* and went to the dogs, like you are now, nothing but bilge, by God!"

The captain made no reply, and McClung, standing up to show how three men had attacked him, rushed along the table. He lunged at the air with the bowie knife, and then, coming back to his seat, took up the pistols, waving them about as he went on describing the fight. No one in the room spoke, their eyes were on the pistols, which were hair-trigger and loaded.

McClung paid no attention to them. Suddenly he finished his story, and turned courteously to Edward.

"So you understand how it was?"

"Yes, I've seen fights."

"But not like this one I tell you."

"No, I reckon not," Edward said. "May I order you a drink?"

"No, much obliged. I drink my own wine."

The frightened negro boy came in and told Edward that a white gentleman was waiting for him outside. The men who had been playing dice at the table by the wall had stolen out. Save for those at the long table, McClung had emptied the room. As Edward rose, the captain and his friend next the old man, who had put his head back and fallen asleep for a while, got up with him. Both of them were careful to bow to McClung, and to say good-evening, again bowing with formal and effuse politeness. They stuck as close to Edward as they could.

As they reached the door McClung jumped up from the table.

"Stop," he shouted, with a pistol in each hand. He spoke first to Edward:

"Now, Mr. McGehee, you don't believe one word of that story. You are the kind of man can't believe anything you don't see with your own eyes. But I don't care. That's the way you're made and you can't help how you are made. I like you, and I won't try to make you say you believe anything. You may go. But these two are different, and they've got to say they believe every word I've said or I'll shoot them where they stand."

He pointed both the pistols at the captain.

"You believe what I said?"

"No gentleman, sir, could doubt any word of yours," the captain said, solemnly.

McClung looked at him with a scowl of contempt, and turned to the other.

"Why, of course, mister, no person could doubt a word of yours," the man quickly repeated.

"All right, you two may go."

"Good-night," Edward said, "I wish you good-night." The stale smell of the room was more sickening than ever.

"Good-night, Mr. McGehee," McClung said, in his polished speech. "I am honored to have had the pleasure of your company. Should there be a gentleman waiting for you—as I infer there is—I am sorry to have detained you. Au revoir."

Edward saw that Charlie, as they walked along, wished to avoid talking, and understood that it was not so much because he was sorry for the woman or for what had happened as because he wanted to get the whole thing out of his mind. In that case, if all Charlie wanted was to get it out of his mind, there was no use discussing it. He glanced at that pallor and look of exhaustion on Charlie's face as they walked along in silence, keeping the middle of the road, to the top of the hill.

At Montrose the same night Hugh McGehee awoke an hour or so before dawn. He was a man of great refinement and restraint, not reserve; and though he liked those he loved to be with him and near him as constantly as possible, he was a solitary man, with the special qualities of solitary men, which are candor, clarity, and feeling. His son·was going off to the war, and he lay there thinking of what he would say to him when the time came.

XXVI

THAT last morning of Edward's at home, Lucy came upon him alone in the hall upstairs. There had been visitors the day before and some earlier this morning, to say good-bye; so many of them with flowers that the vases spread beyond the parlors into the dining-room. But now the morning was well on, and only the family was left.

Charles was in Woodville, to join Edward there: and Abner, who was to go with Edward as his body servant, had ridden ahead and would wait for him in town. The governor of Mississippi had already called for enlistments, and by the middle of May the number of men responding was to be so great that he was compelled to announce that no more companies would be received for the present. A few weeks after this day when Edward left, the troops from Natchez were to assemble for the steamboat that would carry them northward; among them the Adams troops, for whom a citizen had bought $15,000 worth of arms from the Ames Company of Massachusetts; they presented him with a sabre in appreciation of the order. There would be bands of music, flowers, flags, all the troops together, all Natchez there to wave good-bye. But Edward was going away differently. He was impatient to be gone and have it over, and around his heart he felt a hush of tenderness, as he walked back and forth up and down the carpet. But at the sight of Lucy he turned to a bookcase there as if he were looking for some title.

Without meeting his eyes she said that she knew his father was in the cabinet room. "I don't suppose he'll say much, he just wants you with him. He told me to ask you if you knew where"—her lips began to tremble—"oh, some book, but, of course—" She hurried on past him.

The door of the study was half open, but his father sat in an armchair with his back to it. He looked up as Edward shut the door.

"Son?"

"Yes, sir."

"So you've got a little time to sit in here, have you? I'm just not doing anything. I reckon you're all packed."

"There's no use taking much with me, Father, I'll have to be fitted out anyway when I enlist."

"I don't know if you said money enough, I wish you'd carry enough."

For some reason he could not have explained, Edward did not take the armchair opposite his father's, but sat down beside the desk, resting his elbow on it.

"I was thinking the other night when I couldn't sleep," Hugh McGehee said, presently, "about this day, about when the time came for you to leave. A man's mind is a strange thing, son." Edward was silent. He was looking at his father, whose eyes as he spoke were on the floor. "Yes, sir, a man's mind is a strange thing. I was wondering about my father's grandfather when he came over here to Virginia. There was his father, the MacGregor, and his mother's father, the Mac-Donald; and the great Montrose was dead—the MacGregors outlawed, losing their name; there were two sons, this was the younger one. He was leaving Scotland forever—I was wondering if it broke his heart—just broke his heart." He added quickly, "Not, of course, Edward, that you are going away from us forever."

"You want me to go, don't you, Father?" Edward said.

His father disregarded the question.

"You know how 'tis in our family. It's something to know that you were loved before you were born."

Edward was too young to have any answer, he began to finger the pages of a book lying on the desk, noticing as he did so how the gold edges glimmered from the trembling of his fingers.

"The way I've been obliged to see it is this: our ideas and instincts work upon our memory of these people who have lived before us, and so they take on some clarity of outline. It's not to our credit to think we began today, and it's not to our glory to think we end today. All through time we keep coming in to the shore like waves—like waves. You stick to your blood, son; there's a certain fierceness in blood that can bind you up with a long community of life."

"I never forget you, Father," Edward said.

"Your father wouldn't know what the world was without that. And think with passion, it's the only kind of thought that's worth anything." He settled back in his chair. "But I don't want to monopolize you, son, you'd better go now. I'm going to say good-bye, son. Your mother'll be wanting to see you at the last."

"So I'm going to say good-bye," he repeated, as Edward rose and came over to him. "Yes." He took Edward's hand and drew him down and kissed him.

"Good-bye, sir."

"Your mother'll be seein' you."

"Yes, sir."

"So you'd better go, son."

"Kiss me again for when I was a little boy."

The door did not catch and swung open again a few inches; and Edward, without turning his head, reached back and pulled it to. It banged louder than he meant.

A little later Hugh McGehee, watching at one of the windows, saw his wife and son going slowly down the drive to the road gate. Edward was on his horse, his mother walking along beside him. He seemed to be looking across the fields ahead. Her hand rested on the stirrup of his saddle. They did not seem to be talking.

Hugh McGehee watched Edward and his mother along down the drive where it turned across the open lawn. She was walking with God, he believed that. At the gate from the lawn into the road that led to the public highway, Agnes and Edward talked a little while. Then Agnes took her hand from the stirrup and Edward leaned down and kissed her. Then he rode off, and she was standing by the gate watching him.

Hugh rang the bell for a servant, and Paralee came. "I wouldn't let um others come, Marse Hugh," she said, her face puckering as she held back the tears, "yes, sir?" He wanted to know where Miss Lucy was, and Paralee said she had taken the shears off the hook and gone down to the rose garden.

Lucy started at the sound of footsteps; the shears clipped off the whole branch of a rose. "Now wouldn't you know I'd do that, Papa," she said, kicking the branch away from her. "If I saw Aleck do that, I'd snap his head off, wouldn't I?"

"They need cutting back anyhow," he said. "But you've done enough. Here, I'm going back to the house; give me the shears, I'll take them."

"Papa, there's one thing—don't worry about me," Lucy said, holding the shears out behind her for him to take, as she stooped to gather up the rose cuttings and carry them off.

On the steps into the house Paralee was standing in his way with her broom and he shouted at her, "Great God A'mighty, what do you women find to be always sweeping?"

"Lord Jesus, Lord Jesus!" the old woman moaned.

"Throw your fool broom down and go on out there to Miss Lucy."

XXVII

On April 29 President Davis called for 100,000 volunteers and 366,000 responded. But it was almost May before a letter came from Duncan. Malcolm Bedford said nothing of his worry but went off hunting with Dock, the Indian. The wild hogs, multiplied from those that escaped from De Soto's camps in 1543, were no longer plentiful, but there were wild turkeys in abundance. Malcolm, tramping through the woods, had his son on his mind more than the turkeys.

One morning Mrs. Bedford came in from the garden, where she had been directing Uncle Thornton and the two young negroes under him. They were planting garden peas: the two marrowfats, Royal Dwarf and Peruvian Black Eye, the new Tom Thumb, and the Champion of England, which required sticking. Large butter beans, the seeds from Landreth's in Philadelphia, had been planted, and Tilden tomatoes, curled India and white Cos lettuces, eggplant—every one but the gardeners called it by its other name, the melongona—and broccoli, which she was trying for the second crop from seeds imported by Frères Duval in New Orleans. Squashes, beets, snapbeans, and other vegetables were already on the table; but with the cool season the garden was behind for the last week in April, and Uncle Thornton had been prodding up what he could. The citron and casaba melon vines had benefited from the heavy showers; and she had sent a basket of green pears to the kitchen that morning to be poached.

On the gallery by the guest wing Mrs. Bedford found Valette sitting by the little iron garden-table, where a letter seemed to lie waiting. Valette sat, with a solemn fixed look, like a little animal that will not stir until his master comes.

"My Dumplin', are you ever coming!"

"What on earth, why, honey? Why 'twon't bite you," she

said, as Valette pointed to the writing. "Of course I know that hand as well as I do the Lord's Prayer. And so do you. Whyn't you call me and tell me there's a letter from Duncan? Where's Darlin'?"

"Dock came and put it here just a little while ago, and I just waited." Valette's lips quivered as she watched Mrs. Bedford break the seal and open Duncan's letter. A second letter, also sealed, fell out and on to the floor. Either she stooped to pick it up and saw her name on it, or else had seen her name on it already, for she skipped to the end of the gallery laughing, then back to Mrs. Bedford, and began kissing first the seal and then the other's shoulder, contriving in the meantime to get the letter open.

"Dear Valette, I have written Father and Mother that I have enlisted for the South but I want to write you too, and tell you I am thinking of you, just as I am always thinking of you. I will write more soon. Your own Duncan."

Mrs. Bedford sent her to fetch Duncan's father, and Valette, whirling him out of his chair in the library, flew to tell Mammy Tildy, who was in the kitchen, that Duncan had gone to the War. Four or five of the house servants came out with Mammy and stood in the court at the feet of Sallie Bedford and Malcolm and Valette while he read the letter aloud. It was only at the last, when she caught the look in his mother's eyes, that Valette thought of the sad part of the news. It had seemed to her perfect happiness to have Duncan's letter.

"But, My Dumplin', why do you cry?" she said suddenly, her eyes full of tears as she saw Duncan's mother receive the letter from Malcolm's hands and fold it gravely.

"I'm not crying." The small white hands were clasped before her breast, with the letter in them. "The little rascal! But Duncan oughtn't to've done that."

"Why, My Dumplin? Why not?"

"I wish he'd waited."

"Don't you believe in the South's cause?" Valette went on, taking one of the small hands into hers and noticing that it was cold.

"I love the South."

"But Secession, My Dumplin'."

"If the war comes here, I reckon I'll get through it as well as anybody." And Valette, as she felt the hand withdrawn from hers, understood that it would be strong character, pride and anger that would sustain her beloved foster-mother. She gazed in silence for a moment into the gray, direct eyes, and then leaned over to kiss the wrinkling brow.

On the first of the month Malcolm had sent $4000, part of it for books to be added to a library of Duncan's own, part of it for two of Duncan's friends, Mr. Hubert's sons of Plaquemine Parish, cousins of the Natchez family who called themselves Hubbard. From the letter they now learned that Duncan took the money and bought a beach-wagon and a team of mules, loaded it with the Southern boys who wished to join the war, and rode off to the battle of Manassas. Etienne and Jacques Hubert had been among the first. At the top of the letter in pencil was written "Victory is ours," and at the end Duncan promised to write the very first chance he had.

By the magic of these things and perhaps through the negroes, before that afternoon was spent, all Natchez society knew of Duncan's putting the money his father had sent him for books and friends into a wagon-load of students from the university to fight in the Army of Virginia. Etienne and Jacques Hubert were just as bad, they said, and that afternoon the Surgets drove over from Clifton, the Oaklands' carriage arrived, and Mrs. Quitman driving with Mrs. Wilson, who had stopped by Monmouth to pick her up. In the evening, which was cool and starry, nobody sat on the gallery; every one gath-

ered in the parlor. Hugh and Agnes McGehee and Lucinda
came and Colonel Harrod, driving a new trap. There would
be more people next day. Duncan's letter was read aloud over
and over by his father, who every time, when he came to the
end, said that nothing could conquer the Southern spirit and
that the war would be over in three months. Very few of the
guests during these conversations seemed interested in any of
the political questions of the moment, in the proclamations
of the two Presidents, North and South, in the news from
Europe; nothing was talked of but the leaders of the Southern
army, the unheard of Federal generals, and the men who had
gone from Natchez or were about to go. A hundred messages were sent to Duncan. "Be sure you tell Duncan for
me—" and his father beamed and drank too often with one
guest and then another. Sallie Bedford showed them the picture Duncan had sent last month, with that air of a young
man of fashion, very quick on the trigger; and repeated to
nobody what she had said about Duncan's waiting until later.
Nearly every one had already seen the picture, but all looked
at it now smiling, as if to say that Duncan had always been
a captain. It was just as true, nevertheless, that Valette and
Malcolm, when either of them was a moment alone, grew still
and grave, thinking, or would go to a window and stand
looking out at the world, where spring was green everywhere
and birds were singing, and the sky overhead clear and soft.
And it was true that Valette just before supper-time went
down to the quarters, where she sharply ordered the two
laundresses to mind what they did with her petticoats, the
Valenciennes had been ironed yellow that week, and then
went to Aunt Tildy's cabin and sat down, leaning her head
against the old woman's shoulder, sobbing.

"Go way from here, honey, ain' nothin' go hurt Marse
Duncan!" Aunt Tildy said ten times.

"Do you think so, Mammy?"

"What you talkin' bout? 'Tain't in dem Yankees to whip him. Marse Duncan can whip de whole passel of 'em wid a cornstalk."

That night when Malcolm had settled himself in bed, his wife, putting the white cashmere shawl over her nightgown, took the candle and went into her dressing-room, where a bundle of letters lay on the toilet table. It was like Duncan to write letters daily when he first got to a place, and then let weeks pass without writing a line. That was because at first he felt the strangeness and was lonely and homesick. But if such was his nature, what was there to be said? The first of these letters was already faded with age, it was written from his Connecticut school. "If you can spare an hour from your many duties to write a letter for me I would receive it so thankfully," it said. "I love every Southern thing with ten-fold fervor. There is a pair of Southern mock-birds—rara avis——"

"Yes," she said to herself, "and I've always wondered if that were only a flowery passage. Are there mocking-birds in Connecticut really?"

"Rara avis—that have built their nest in a neighboring orchard and every evening and morning bring their songs fraught with the recollection of home and all I love. If you ever find time please write in return."

Duncan had written thus piously from the college at Middleton; though, nevertheless, he had stayed but two months and then taken the cars home. That's how that turned out.

"Wife, what are you up to, it's late?" Malcolm called to her from the bed in the dark room. He frequently talked from one room to another in the house, as if you sat conversing with him on a sofa. Sometimes he even conversed from the hall to some one upstairs.

"There are things women have to do, Darlin', you go to sleep," she answered.

"I hear paper rustling but when you're putting up your curls you tear it. You're not tearing it. Don't you know Duncan's letter by heart now? You surely do."

She got up and went into the bedroom. "You're waking up the whole house, Darlin'."

"Well, let them hear me."

"Do you know, I was thinking: we ought to send Duncan money, there must be plenty of things he's in want of. And your silk scarf would be a good thing, and some of those Paris gloves. You bought New Orleans out of gloves, I always say."

"Duncan can have anything he wants. You decide."

She chuckled when she kissed his brow.

"Is that for me or for Duncan?"

"I'll just read you the next letter, the second he wrote from Middleton." From her dressing-room he heard her read:

"Since my long & memorable vacation I find that close continued study is not as pleasant as while at Portobello. When I think of years of unremitted labor, love of ease makes me shrink back almost with despair. I find there is a great difference between reading what I please, when I please, and closely tied down to one pursuit for hours day after day. But when I think on the ultimate object to be attained I blush at my supineness & want of energy. I have made few acquaintances and as yet can speak but little of the character of the people. I expect there are as many unmarried ladies in this town as in half our home country. Frequently walking in the evening I have met twenty. The misery of it is they are all young or wish to be."

There was the essay "Moral Philosophy," from the University of Virginia, marked *Read before the Society, February 16, 1861.* She would read that again tonight, or at least the last paragraph, where Duncan made his conclusion:

"Theology and Psychology have frequently gone hand in

hand, sometimes towards intelligibility, but more frequently towards mazy obscurity. Among those who advanced highest in these confounding but entrancing speculations, Plato's name will forever stand first; & it is probable that if he had not so imbued all his thoughts with the spirit of theological inquiry, he would have produced a clearer exposition of the anomalies & intricacies of the soul than has yet seen the light."

"He's no fool, now," she said to herself, and then, "Darlin', he's no fool, Duncan."

"No," said Malcolm, "and I'll say the same for Plato."

"That boy's sho got sense." She smiled when this last came into her mind out of long ago. One day when Duncan could barely talk she stood with him in her arms watching old Aunt Tildy's Thornton pruning a rose-bush. "Son, don't you like Uncle Thornton?" she said. "I love Uncle Thornton!" said Duncan in his baby voice. "Dat boy's sho got sense," Thornton chuckled. Even then how sweet Duncan was!

"Sallie," her husband's voice called, "whyn't you come to bed?"

"Darlin', I'm coming. It's not going to kill me reading my child's letter."

Valette in her high bed with its blue silk curtains lay awake a long time. And so Duncan had ridden off to the war! It seemed to her that the family did not understand properly how noble Duncan, with his quick ways, really was; and she tried to think of what she could do from now on to make them understand.

XXVIII

There is a type of people, often reared by cities, whose one idea of life is doing what everybody else does. Without any clear desires of their own, they have, nevertheless, a steady movement toward what by imitation and envy they have come to want. They are sometimes even avaricious and greedy about this; and often, in a sterile way, they get their ends. The McGehees had cousins like that in New Orleans: Francis Scott Eppes and his mother Mrs. Cynthia Marigny Eppes. In her youth Cynthia had had a very fine voice which she used as an excuse for spending most of her time in the city, and her talent was so great that both her parents and her singing master were persuaded that she practised many hours more than she really did. Her husband, Francis Collier Eppes, was kin to the Montrose McGehees and Edward McGehee at Woodville through their grandmother Collier, at Portobello in Virginia. The first Eppes in Virginia had been Colonel Francis, gentleman of the bedchamber to King Charles I, who, after the Royalist defeat, emigrated to the colonies. Sir Francis Eppes was celebrated as fighting duels on every possible pretext, and Francis Collier Eppes, Cynthia's husband, had inherited an over-amount of this talent. In the course of the duelling fever that struck New Orleans, he had fallen in a duel with Pepe Lulla, the famous *maître d'armes,* whom he should have known better than to call out, even in the cause of a slandered prima donna.

Up to that time the family had divided the years among three places: their sugar plantation (Beaux Anges on the Bayou des Glaises), Paris, and New Orleans. They kept a box at the opera in both New Orleans and in Paris. After her husband's death Cynthia lived entirely in the two cities, with her one child Francis Scott, whom all the McGehee kin called Scott and she called François. She left Beaux Anges to a manager and overseers, and in bad years raised money by mortgages. A great deal of the money was spent, partly on cards, for which François inherited a taste that his mother (from whom he got it) considered excessive. They had been obliged to give up Paris, but they clung to New Orleans, passing never more than six or eight weeks on the plantation. Cynthia's family was Catholic, and the conditions of the marriage had required the children to be so. Francis, if in late years intermittently, had gone all his life to confession in the shadowed chapels of St. Louis Cathedral. Father Palissy, their priest, had come straight from St. Cloud, a tall, rosy man with charming manners, who explained the mysteries of religion so that any sensible person could grasp them easily.

"Nobody can assert," Cynthia said, "that I neglect my duties." She would open the case that her jeweller had made for her, with her opera glasses on one side and her prayer book on the other. "Though I once said to my confessor when he got too finicky, 'Father, I may as well tell you, I get my hats and my absolutions in Paris.'"

In the early autumn of 1861 President Davis, after some urging, at last appointed Mr. Slidell of New Orleans to go, together with Mason, as resident Commissioner for the Confederate States in Paris and London. Slidell had come many years before from New York, fleeing the consequences of a duel, to Louisiana; where in time he had married one of the Deslondes; and where in time, by fair means and foul, with none too good a reputation, he had succeeded in making himself a man of wealth and political influence. Mr. and Mrs. Slidell with their son and two daughters had made the journey overland to Charleston, avoiding the perils of the Federal blockade, and from Charleston had gone first to Nassau and then Havana, where he joined Mason and waited for a vessel to Europe.

When Cynthia heard of this it seemed to her that with her son as an attaché of the Confederate Commissioner, they had found an excellent means of getting abroad. She had absorbed both the New Orleans and then the French attitude that each of these cities was the only place in the world where one could possibly exist. They had spoken of this that same night to their cousin Miles McGehee, with whom they were dining at the St. Charles Hotel. He was one of those men who eat well, drink well, and think almost any proposal that any person desires to execute is a good idea. Since he was taking the *Magnolia* up the river that evening on his way to his home on Lake St. Joseph, he had invited them to accompany him. They would stop over at Natchez for a visit to Montrose, which he had not seen for ten months. He told them of having been engaged with a commission from the governor of Louisiana for cloth to be made at the Woodville factory, which, he went on, belonged to his brother Edward, and was the first factory of its kind run by slave labor to be built in the South. To Cynthia, drawing out the fingers of her gloves, this was only another assurance of the South's victory; and Francis Scott remembered that he had not been up the river in a long time and then thought of those two card sharpers who had got on at Baton Rouge dressed like parsons. His mother recalled also that the Edward McGehees, at Woodville, would know Mr. Jefferson Davis, whose parents lived only two or three miles away.

Miles McGehee kept a special chair for himself on every boat that went up the river. They were large and easy, for he weighed 400 pounds. Cynthia and Francis were sitting with him on deck when they came in sight of the Natchez bluffs. "Yes, yes, of course, my brothers know Jeff Davis. But they don't think he's any great shakes. When Brother Edward heard Davis was elected President of the Confederacy, he walked the floor all night."

"Fancy!" said Cynthia, who took walking the floor all night as a mere operatic phrase.

"For that matter Jeff Davis' brother's the one made him what he is. Clever man, lives next to us at St. Joseph's. You know President Zachary Taylor, who was a great friend of our family, was Jeff Davis' father-in-law."

She knew that. Mr. Davis' first wife, the one who died singing that pet of a song, yes, it was "Fairy Bells"; and he himself was lying desperately sick of the fever and couldn't go to her. If President Taylor hadn't died from eating too much iced cherries and milk, he'd have lived to be proud of his son-in-law surely.

"No doubt," Miles said, and began to tell them the story of the time he bribed the captain to let him ring the bell as much as he liked. $500. He kept ringing and the boat kept having to back to shore; the captain cursed so loud the ladies had to withdraw to the dining-saloon; "Ah," said Miles, with a wheezy sigh, "the good old days are gone, Cud'n Cynthia!"

"*C'est la vie, c'est la vie.* Was that our captain, St. Clair Thompson?"

"No, no, God A'mighty, 'twarn't the *Magnolia,* 'twas the *Southern Belle.*"

Her cousin's manners were cut to suit himself, but Cynthia had been in sophisticated society long enough to relish characters with some go to them. Two of the plantations that Miles had pointed out first on the east, then on the west side of the river, as they came upstream, belonged to him, some of the rest to his brothers. She had long since observed how much more fitting it was when oddities, characters, and independents were rich. Like everybody with any kin in Panola or Natchez, Cynthia knew all about Mary Cherry, and she was delighted when Miles spoke of the old woman's being at Montrose now. Miss Mary had no plantations and said the world owed her a living, but Miss Mary was a character with a vengeance.

Francis Scott had left them to stroll among the passengers, who had increased with every landing. Even on deck you could smell the bouquets that had been sent aboard for the captain.

At Montrose, after their first flourish of greeting the cousins,

Cynthia and Francis Scott could not say enough of the steamboat, the staterooms with four-poster beds, mosquito bars and toilet tables, the walls in pale yellow and gilt. Said Cynthia, stretching her dark eyes, "Indeed, while we were on the river everything, everything for this earth, seemed perfect. *Au minuit tous les chats sont gris.*"

"But, *Maman,*" Francis said, "but——"

"Go on, young man," Miss Mary said, chuckling hoarsely. Francis, for some reason, had already won her good graces.

"I was only going to say to *Maman* that when Gautier said that he meant something else, ah, yes, Miss Mary, Gautier meant something else."

"Well, now, I studied the French language when I was a gal; at midnight all cats are black, is what that saying means. My old uncle, who lost a kidney at the Battle of New Orleans, used to say he'd seen a cherry-colored cat. You were supposed to exclaim, and it turned out he meant a black cat. 'Ain't there black cherries?' Uncle Pelham said."

"The pun is," said Francis, bowing to Miss Mary, "*gris* also means tipsy, at midnight everybody's tight."

Mrs. Bedford and Valette arrived with Judge Winchester, Doctor and Mrs. Martin for supper, and when the greetings were over, Cynthia left her son with them and turned to Lucy.

"And how does the singing go, chérie? Ah, to sing!" She threw a kiss with the tips of her fingers with a sigh deep enough for opera, and began to tell them about singing at Compiègne for the Empress Eugenie. "I had a mauve gown of Worth's. Naturally I had spoken good French all my life, could I forget my father's old friend General Humbert, who had the San Domingo affair with Pauline Bonaparte and died drunk in New Orleans reciting Corneille? But I was careful to sing with a strong Creole accent. It reminded the Emperor of his grandmother, the Empress Josephine from Martinique, and it brought back the rich careless warmth of her

Andalusia to Eugenie—what chic Her Majesty had!" She did not say that among other plantations belonging to other Louisiana ladies, M. Worth had a mortgage on one of hers.

But in her rooms as her maid changed her into the gown of purple velvet with its full hoop and its ripples of Valenciennes at the neck and wrists, Cynthia knew that the tone of their conversation at Montrose so far had not been quite right—François had known it too. She had seen him glancing at her.

"And it's not at all because"—she thought.—"Here, Elise," she said to the maid, "for goodness' sake, don't make me tell you every time, the brooch." It was the one the Empress Eugenie had given her, a round cluster of garnets. Yes, the tone of the conversation had been not quite right. It was not because the McGehee cousins were stupid. That serene-looking Cousin Agnes McGehee, for one, was capable of poking you under the ribs. And everybody had made François and herself feel as welcome as the May. No, it was Cynthia who felt the compunctions herself. How easy it is, she thought, to be a little flighty! Descending the stair into the parlor she went on with these thoughts. No, no. Admiring for so long the library, the painted Bohemian glass with the fine medallions let into the white, the long concert Steinway piano that Hugh had gone to New York to choose, was not the right note at Montrose; though why should one not expatiate on the collection of 10,000 books chosen with such pains and abundance, and the glass bought by François' young and headlong cousin, George McGehee from Woodville, travelling abroad? No reason. "No reason in the world," she said to herself, as Hugh offered her his arm to go in to supper. "But here 'tis, yes, it's the fortissimo where I go wrong. Running on so. Too much plumage. Spreading your tail, that's it. Among these dear people. Makes me feel vulgar. *Mais non alors par example,*" and immediately on top of these thoughts, she exclaimed to her cousins, as they entered the dining-room. "But I must adore such silver!"

"Ah, then, if you like plate we must take you to Routhlands where they're really superb. For one thing there are to the service fifteen great silver platters," said Agnes.

The idea of her condescension one way or another would never have occurred to anybody at Montrose. Cynthia knew it; knew she would be only a fool if she felt condescending; she wanted to push in her ribs, which seemed to be swelling out. "There's something in me that's like a brass band," she thought; and looking at Hugh with gentle melancholy, she asked if he remembered the opera ball where she had presented to him her fiancé?

He nodded. "And the same bloom on your cheeks today."

"I put it on even then."

"But she's not as red as she's painted, Cousin Hugh," Francis said, sitting between Mrs. Bedford and Lucinda. This *mot,* not so ancient at Montrose as in the Bois de Boulogne, set everybody laughing.

"*Maman,* do you hear?" Francis said, with his flattering voice. "This is the Judge Winchester who educated the first lady of the Confederacy."

"Impossible, my darling, that would be an old man."

"This is he, *Maman.*"

"Then, my dear judge, is it true that Mrs. Davis reads Latin as well as the President?"

"As Doctor Johnson said of Queen Elizabeth, Miss Varina had learning enough to be a bishop," the judge replied. "I say she had, not has; after marriage the ladies often desert the classic groves, Mrs. Eppes."

"Dear Cousin Hugh, you answer Judge Winchester for I can't. In Paris Garcia, Malibran's brother, gave me lessons. If I'd only had any sense—but now even if I had studied well I should only squawk. Rossini took the piano for me one evening. How bad I was! I was behind. 'Dear lady,' he said, 'shall we make a rendezvous at the bottom of the page?' "

She drew out her lace handkerchief and passed it lightly over her lips. The scent she used was not of flowers, such scents as were preferred by the Natchez ladies; it was heavy, exotic, and reminded Hugh of the chromo upstairs called "Moonlight on the Nile."

"Or, at least," Cynthia went on, looking at him now with a downright, disarming twinkle, "I daresay he said it. Every woman that ever sang for him says Rossini told her that. So why not me, eh, Cousin Hugh?"

"Indeed, why not, Cousin Cinthy?"

Mary Cherry, beside Mrs. Martin on the sofa, was watching Francis and the two girls leaning over the music-stand. His figure in the blue coat with its tall velvet collar had great elegance, she thought.

'Sister," she said to Mrs. Martin, "what do you make of him?"

"Sheep's eyes at the girls maybe?" Mrs. Martin said.

"Oh, just that French Paris."

"Maybe. What a patrician Lucy appears! I don't call her tall."

"Animation would help her, I say."

"Nobody could say she looks insipid. She's reserved," Mrs. Martin said.

"There's something makes Lucinda sad, yes, of that I'm positive. But I've never heard tell what. My conscience, the McGehees are clannish!"

"She may be in love," said Mrs Martin.

"Then why don't she say so?"

At once, Valette, when she was asked, sat down at the piano. She liked to sing, and it seemed to her that you gave people a song as you might give them a flower, what was there unusual about that? The accompaniment began.

"Ah," said Francis, "listen, *Maman,* we shall have 'I Dreamt I Dwelt in Marble Halls.'"

His mother sighed, and leaving her chair she came up to the piano and stood listening, absorbed.

Everybody applauded, Francis most loudly and most gracefully of all; but Valette, instead of waiting to begin another song, turned at once to Cynthia and asked her if she liked her voice, blushing with delight when she heard the praise.

"But one song's enough from just me," she said, catching Lucy by the hand and drawing her nearer the piano.

"Go on, honey, let Valette play," Mrs. Bedford called to Lucy, "I tell the little rascal she sings better perched on a stool, like a wren on a bough. Let her play and you sing us 'Kathleen Mavourneen.' The last time I saw your brother Ed he was talking about your singing that."

Valette began the music before Lucy could reply, and suddenly the mezzo voice took up the air. It was a low voice and Lucy sang the words and the thought as if they were all of it, and the music her own feeling. As the voice grew proud and full, the feeling seemed more veiled. It was not easy singing to compliment, however one liked it; and Doctor Martin, who could not tell one tune from another, served the graces most easily. He had one compliment for every singer and every song. "Mockbird could not have been sweeter," he said, and Valette, springing up laughing and seizing the singer's hand, made Lucy bow with herself like two prima donnas.

Old Cynthia surpassed them both. Without having started with any notion of singing, for she had given it up long ago, she found herself seated at the piano.

"*Una voce poco fa, una voce poco fa*—" "Ah, Cyndy," she said, having launched thus far into this aria from "The Barber of Seville," "that was off, madam. Basta!" and so had them all laughing and listening at once. Then they heard Cynthia beginning a Louisiana song, *Les Deux Oiseaux du Lac*. By some miracle of taste she seemed to be perfect; whatever voice was left seemed to be enough. Hugh McGehee looked at that sagging face so full of vanity and folly, and never having thought much about a theory of art, felt humbled and perplexed, and turning to his wife, saw that she had forgotten everybody in the room. The song had ended. Francis, without any of his fine manners at all, went up to his mother and kissed her hand covered with rings; and for the moment he was all one might have fancied him to be. The miracle too had ended, which nobody but Francis, in his sharp and exotic perception, had understood, though they had been carried away by it. Something had been in the room, like a presence; and now Cynthia again looked merely fashionable.

Judge Winchester rose and escorted her to a place beside him on the sofa, and she launched into how Garcia would beat on the piano when a student sang flat. "He'd look at you," she said, crossing her eyes and going into a gale of laughter, "look and bleat. Bah! I kept the poor man bleating every other note I tried to sing. Do re mi—bah! bah! la fa la si—bah! If I hadn't married so early, I'd have turned Garcia into mutton!"

"An old male sheep," said Valette, laughing. There were tears in her eyes, nevertheless, old Cynthia saw that; Cynthia was one of those people who are moved by youth, not only from vanity and a sense of what they have lost, but because they feel only in youth the tears of things.

"Were you so flat, Cousin? I can't believe it," said Agnes. "And the Empress giving you the brooch."

"Exactly. There you are."

"I'll tell you, Sis Cynthia," Mary Cherry said. "I had some singing lessons once when I was a gal. From the choir master at our church. During choir practice he stopped, 'Please, please,' says he, 'you're off the key,' stopped me four or five times, 'you're off the key.' But I got him. Next time he stopped me and said off the key, I said, here, if you'll hush your mouth, sir, and listen a minute, I'll give you my A."

Both Cynthia and Francis went into peals of laughter over that, and Miss Mary sat looking at one and then the other, very much delighted.

It was still not late in the evening when the servant brought in two visitors' cards and Mr. Dix, the mayor of Natchez, came in. There were usually guests with the Dix family at Kenilworth, and this time it was an officer from Colonel Wheat's regiment, Captain Derosse, who was in Natchez on a military matter. Captain Derosse was a dapper little man of forty, with cotton in one ear, but he heard well enough; and soon after he had been presented, a discussion started about the war in Virginia. The western slopes of Virginia had refused to secede and had been recognized by President Lincoln as a new State. After the Confederate victory at Bull Run in June, the war had moved across the State in the struggle for these slopes with their outlet toward the West and the Mississippi Valley. The campaign had been a failure and public opinion turned on General Lee. He had just been removed from his command and put in charge of coast defenses from South Carolina to Florida.

"Nevertheless," Captain Derosse said to Hugh, "though the public is right—vox populi—in a sense, the trouble behind it all is the politicians. What's more, General Lee suffers from lack of authority and the power to enforce discipline, and President Davis is bound and determined to remain our military chief if the army were camped a thousand miles away. General Wise demanding to be detached from General Floyd's command—and so on—General Lee obliged to use tact with them instead of ordering them shot."

"You are right," said Hugh.

"You mean to tell me our victory at Bull Run did not establish the South's supremacy, Captain Derosse," said Cynthia, pushing down her flounces and then standing with her hands clasped as if about to sing an aria.

"I mean to say the loss of West Virginia is an inconceivable calamity."

"Never believe it."

The captain only bowed.

"One thing, Captain," Hugh said, looking gravely at the officer's lively face, "more people are beginning to see now that the war will not be a matter of a few months."

"Most statesmen thought it would be only a matter of ninety days or so," said the captain, vaguely; he had just noticed that his feet fitted exactly into a wreath in the velvet carpet. "It is a fact, however," he went on, now lively again, "that General Lee knew better, and even better the United States Commander-in-chief, 300,000 men, plus an able general, might carry off the business, he said, I mean General Winfield Scott."

Nobody replied at once to this remark of the captain's.

"I don't fancy my brother Edward at Woodville will be flattered to hear so, but he has held to the same opinion—he and General Scott are the same age. This war we are in may last a long time."

"By the way, sir," the captain said, "that reminds me. One of the pleasures of this visit was to deliver a message from my mother. She used to know General Scott very well, when he was stationed down here at Washington, a young man, fifty years ago."

"Our Montrose Arabians," said Hugh politely, "all go back to one brought down from Kentucky for a present to General Scott when he should pass through after the war in Mexico."

The captain went on to say that his mother had received a letter from General Scott. As a friend not unmindful of the past, he deplored the tragic chances of war in this country and could only regret that his decision was in favor of the Union, against Secession, and contrary to some of his kinsmen. "And so my mother asked me to tell you this," said the captain.

"Thank you."

"Valette, child," Mrs. Bedford said quickly, trying to rush into the breach, "it's nigh the moment we set out for home. No use trying to do anything about General Scott, I suppose." She went on impishly. "Not a bit of use. *Nisi Dominus, frustra,* as Pa used to tell us, which means 'unless God did it, you're wasting your time.' Pa would say it when we tried to bleach or make ourselves pretty, *Nisi Dominus, frustra!* Honestly, if Latin phrases left a bruise when they hit you, by the time Pa was through with us we'd all been black and blue."

Captain Derosse was lost again in his feet on the carpet pattern when he heard Lucy saying, "I'll tell you, Captain——"

"Do, please," he said.

"Papa is mild as cream when he gives an opinion, but I think I know mighty well what he'd at least like to say."

"And what would that be?"

"To send his compliments to your mother. But otherwise as for General Winfield Scott to tell her that it's all very well what General Scott says about war and that it might be known to her already that General Scott's Papa's cousin."

"But certainly," said the captain, blushing very red, "that's why she sent the message."

"Papa's mother having been Nancy Scott of Portobello, eight miles out from Williamsburg, Virginia, and that General Scott can go to the devil."

"Lucy, my dear!" her mother cried, reprovingly.

"Was I the one or was it Papa ordered the old fool's portrait down off the wall there?" said Lucy.

The captain had gone into uncontrollable laughter. To tell

the truth, it was exactly what his mother thought, too, he said; he would give her the message.

XXIX

To all the rooms at Montrose black coffee was carried before you rose, but for breakfast itself the Eppes took chocolate. They professed great delight that the chocolate was supplied by their own Limong, whom every one in New Orleans knew to be supreme; and they ate nothing of the Southern breakfast but slices of bread. As they sat dipping their bread into their chocolate in the foreign fashion instead of drinking from the cup, they discussed the news. Twenty-four hours out from Havana, a Federal officer had boarded the *Trent,* flying the British flag, and had seized the two Confederate Commissioners, Messrs. Mason and Slidell, and their secretaries, one of whom, young George Eustis, was a schoolmate of Francis'. Over the protests of the English captain the Confederates were ordered into the boats. When Slidell, who was a man almost seventy, did not move fast enough, a young subaltern took him by the shoulder, at which Matilda Slidell, recognizing the young man thus rude to her father as one she had danced with the spring before, slapped his face. The marines with fixed bayonets advanced a step toward her, the commander who represented the British Admiralty on board, ordered, "Back, you damned cowardly poltroons!"

If the English Government should resent such a high-handed affront as this boarding and seizure, and should therefore break off relations with the Federal Government, it would mean European recognition of the Confederacy and the end of the war.

In the North the Federal commander was being fêted. The Secretary of the Navy had officially endorsed the seizure, along with Congress voting the officer a sword; and the President and Cabinet at Washington declared that the prisoners should never be surrendered.

"It's well known where the emperor's own preference lies," Cynthia said, as they discussed this crisis in the international situation. "François, you can tell Cousin Hugh something about that."

Francis, who was able enough when he chose to trouble himself, told of the position taken by Napoleon III. The French Emperor, he said, had once been in New York for a short while; but it was from study and curiosity that he had gained his vast information about America. He doubted the effort of any union between, as he saw it, the landed aristocracy of the South and the industrial democracy of the North. He opposed slavery, but thought the Southern form of it as humane as could be hoped for till economic reasons led to its abandonment.

" 'The braggart democracy of the North' are his words for it," Francis said. "He would be glad to see them taught a lesson. The upper classes in France lean toward the South."

"*Nos frères de Louisiane—*" said Cynthia.

"Exactly, *Maman,* they call Southerners that, I hear, France needs our cotton and tobacco, we her silks. The Emperor has ambitions in Mexico, next door to the Southern States. And how droll history can be! Once the *noblesse* wanted America democratic, now time has made them sick of chaotic democracy. They are either Republicans with their illusions shattered, or they are Imperialists. The government is careful. But not the press. Oh, yes, *Maman* and I have had copies of *Le Moniteur, Le Pays, La Patrie.* Whatever else, they always say it is quite impossible, any American reunion."

Mary Cherry wiped her lips and folded her napkin.

"I don't bank on this *frères* business particularly," she said, "what I trust is England."

"After all, Miss Mary," said Francis, bowing deferentially in her direction, and with a gesture of his plump white hand, "you know what the French say to that. Historically treacherous, *Perfide Albion.*"

"The thing I'd like to know is what Brother Miles and Brother Hugh say. It's no fancy diplomacy with'them, they've got cotton to sell—I reckon you know we are one of the largest cotton planters in the South."

On the console in the hall after breakfast was over, two Dresden vases and a basket of camellias were waiting for Agnes to arrange. As she stood there she could hear parts of what was being said in the drawing-room, the talk about cotton that had been repeated over and over up and down this plantation country for two years.

She heard her husband telling his cousins that he had been one of those who had urged the Confederate Government at the very start to store millions of bales of cotton in European parts, before a blockade could begin. There would thus have been resources free to draw upon, in the purchase of war materials abroad. But it was argued, against this proposal, that if England lacked cotton she would favor the Southern States against the North in order to get it.

"Mr. Davis was deaf to our argument."

"Not so fast. I champion Mr. Davis," Agnes heard Miss Mary saying.

It turned out that since their plans had now to wait upon the Slidell and Mason news, the Eppes need feel no hurry. Their cousin Miles was to proceed without them northward on the evening boat, and they would remain at Montrose for some days. From there they would pay a visit to the Edward McGehees in Woodville. The fine weather reminded Cynthia of autumn in Touraine.

"It reminds me," Mary Cherry said, firmly, "of autumn in Natchez, Mississippi."

From her sitting-room window upstairs that afternoon Cynthia could see Lucinda mounted on a prancing roan, which she sat perfectly, riding off with Francis. Both of them, in her eyes, rode superbly.

An idea had been coming into Cynthia's head. With the nations going to pieces on the high seas and the hemispheres promising to cut each other's throats, one must remember that there are other things. Little Cousin Lucinda—sixth cousin, of course—put one off a trifle, perhaps; but she was a well-born, well-bred young girl, a lady and looked it. In the right clothes she might pass for a young princess, not beautiful but a young princess. Cynthia had a feeling that if this McGehee girl once loved a man it would mean her whole soul. "Her whole soul," Cynthia said to herself, quite touched by the phrase that she found on her tongue. God knows as a mother she had not, as it were, increased Francis' estate: he would need somebody's whole soul.

She pointed her slipper into the fuchsia color of the carpet, velvet, and French. *C'est la vie.* She rang for her maid, Elise, to bring the green silk gown that she had taken to press; voices were already gathering in the parlor downstairs.

That night by the time Elise had put up her curls and helped her into the cambric nightcap and the dressing-gown of challis, cream color sprigged with roses, with bowknots of cherry ribbon, and a Watteau pleat running down the back into the short train, Cynthia had said her prayers. One way or another she had edged them in, so that now when Elise had been dismissed and she was alone, her thoughts should be free to dwell not on her own but her son's likelihood of blessings. "Amen. Good-night, Elise," she said. Francis, she knew, fell asleep as soon as his head touched the pillow, but at the moment for some reason it seemed clear to her that if she was thinking he was thinking.

"The ceiling might fall, it wouldn't wake him," she thought as she stood at the foot of his bed looking at her son and not troubling to shield the candle. Francis lay on his back with only the sheet over him, drawn up to his chin, his blond hair still as brushed and shining as a portrait.

"Doubtless," Cynthia said to herself, "there are those who take him for a young *élégant* and nothing else. *Boulevardier. Boulevardier?* Fiddlesticks. Lucinda—Lucy, *chère,* I wish you could see him now, more perennial and male."

A moment later she caught up her train with one hand and, holding the candlestick up in the other, lightly waltzed three steps to the door, which she closed softly but definitely as one might seal a letter.

XXX

The war, though heavy battles were fought, was still far away to the North and the surface of Natchez life had not greatly changed. The shadow of absence lay on the family houses, from which so many of the young men had gone away, and men like Hugh McGehee and his brother Edward at Woodville felt an inner sense of disaster; but the visiting went on and the planter society left in Natchez kept up a show of proud hopes, defiance, and practical affairs. With the Woodville invitation to Cynthia Eppes and her son, came a letter from Mrs. Edward McGehee to Agnes, which she read aloud. "You and brother Hugh," it said, "must accompany our cousin to Bowling Green and share with us the pleasure of their visit. You know it is one of my infirmities never to be satisfied to enjoy a thing alone. Nor have I seen you for a long time, and being in your company for these few days will put me in possession of a little bit of yourself."

"My stars, she writes like poetry!" Mary Cherry said, in a tone as if poetry were something that spoiled overnight.

"Mary lives like poetry," Hugh said, bluntly. He could have a short way sometimes with Miss Mary, who wore him out acting as if she were Judgment Day.

Next day the carriage set off for Woodville, leaving Miss Mary in charge at Montrose, with the invalid Mr. Munger, who was in bed with a chill, Miss Whipple, and Lucy. No sooner, however, had the carriage vanished into the road south than Lucy, with one look at Miss Mary turning her head like an owl and about to express her opinion on some topic, decided that it would be a good time to keep her promise to Mrs. Bedford and go to stay with Valette at Portobello. "What's more," as Valette had told her, Monsieur La Tour, the singing master, was coming to Natchez that week, and Lucy herself might have a lesson in these flowery airs that Valette knew. Perhaps Lucy was wrong and perhaps not, but these airs always seemed to her as if your heart were asked to go on like a bird. William Veal drove her over in the trap to Portobello.

The absence of the family from Montrose led to a comical occasion that would last for a long time among the kin and lose nothing in the telling.

His mother had spoken at last to Francis about Lucinda. "*François, cher—*" she said, and put her slender old hand, with its diamonds, on his plump one. She had asked that he promenade a little with his old mother, and had ended in the rose arbor, whose fragrance she had hopes of in its effect on her son; in her estimation Francis—who romanced only his appetites—was an incurable romantic. "*François, cher,* I can see you appreciate that child's quality." She repeated the word as *qualité*. "Such breeding! I myself can see the *ton* when Lontiec in Paris has done with her. Her waist is a little high, but he'll know how to dispose of that. She has great tenderness, and the McGehee loyalty, my precious. Tell your *maman* you'll let Lucinda see your true worth. What motives could I have but the desire for your good fortune?"

Francis had the sincerity of reckless people, who would as soon lose as not. He wanted to say, "*Maman,* why don't you say 'marry a fortune' and be done with it?" and as for his true worth there was a lady with red hair in the Rue du Quay who, all unknown to his mother, would be a judge of that. *On ne badine pas avec l'amour.* Nevertheless Lucinda had an air, as his mother said; and, it must be confessed, the Arabian he rode that morning and the ten others he and Lucy left behind in the stables, had contrived to give him something of his *maman's* perspective—he changed for himself the word—dream. He said, with a grave smile, trying to remember who the deuce he had seen do it in Paris once, "*Chérie,* I give you my promise."

Cynthia embraced her son, with tears of what amounted to salvation in her old eyes. "I know your father's happy now." She loved to bring in religion like that, it was like the curtain rising at the theatre. She always assumed when speaking of her dead husband that he was now living in heaven.

So tinged was Francis with his mother's vision and the fact that he missed Lucinda's company, which baffled and engaged him by its animation, force, and distance, that he had not been twenty-four hours at Bowling Green before a longing to return to Montrose possessed him and the idea of a serenade seemed the happiest of resolutions. Riding up to Montrose was easy enough; he had only to mention a horse at Bowling Green to have his choice; and any Natchez tavern could supply the negro players at a pin-drop. As it turned out, they told him in Natchez of a band of travelling musicians passing through town. He found them at a dance hall, paid the bill himself, and took a conveyance for them with their instruments out to Montrose.

From the parterres beneath the south gallery Miss Mary heard music. She got up and dressed herself, went to the pantry for the wine glasses and decanter, cut a cake, and took the refreshments out to the gallery, where she thanked Francis and the musicians profusely.

"It's lovely of you to come way out here and play for me when you know Lucy is not at home," she began, and so profuse were her thanks that he could not tell her better.

When Lucinda returned to Montrose, Francis could never after that see her again without Miss Mary's joining them and monopolizing the conversation, to his chagrin and doubly so when she insisted on referring to her favorite pieces in the serenade.

Throughout the connection it was the wives who did most in Miss Mary's direction. The McGehees themselves remembered her share in the elopement of Caroline, one of the McGehee nieces, in Panola County. Caroline herself was thirty at the time and Mr. Stark, who belonged to the Vermont family, had come South to preach, and was soon, everybody said, to be made a bishop. Caroline's father, nevertheless, had packed her off for a season of New Orleans society, chaperoned as far as Memphis, where she was to take the boat, by Mary Cherry. Instead of chaperoning, Miss Mary presided at the elopement. When the first baby came, there was a reconciliation; but Miss Mary's part in the affair remained.

One afternoon in the arbor—the same arbor that Cynthia had chosen for opening up to Francis the matter of his suit for Lucy's hand—Agnes McGehee found her husband chuckling to himself, the open book on his knees forgotten.

"I'm thinking of how Mary Cherry sits with them," he said, laughing out loud.

"Lucy and Francis?"

"Aye. I was thinking that what Mary Cherry treacherously helped to happen in one McGehee house," he said, "she credulously helps to prevent in another!"

Agnes, who had a knack of mimicry that not half a dozen people ever guessed, made a face like Miss Mary listening to the serenade; and they sat there a long time amusing themselves over the comedy going on at Montrose.

Meantime, during these days at Richmond, Windy Manor, Arlington, and one or two other houses where Cynthia and her son had been entertained, the impression got about, nobody could have told exactly how, that Francis and Lucy were betrothed. It may have come from the charming things that Cynthia was always saying of her young cousin—*"ma petite cousine,* though she's only a sixth cousin to my son." It may have been, also, partly due to certain people like Mrs. Boyd, with her bright eyes, or Judge Winchester, who often said that, barring his pupil of years ago, now Mrs. Jefferson Davis, Lucinda was the finest young woman ever born in Natchez. They both noted Cynthia's gracefully put queries about Montrose and "all the so many dreadful plantations that my cousin Hugh has to direct, what Herculean labor!" In an off moment once, when Mrs. Boyd presented a great bouquet of the Arlington amaryllises, Cynthia exclaimed, "Ah, who would not choose these over all the McGehee fortune!"

It was after the Arlington visit that Agnes, seeing how things were going, felt her conscience hurt her.

"I think I should tell you, Cud'n Cynthy," she said, when there was a chance to draw Francis' mother aside, "that, though nothing definite has been arranged, my daughter's affections are otherwise engaged." She was surprised to hear herself thus using the old phrase from melodrama, or the opera in New Orleans, but went on. "I trust I don't seem indelicate speaking in this matter; it seems better."

"Exquisite girl, but these things happen, my dear, ah, yes, you must not think of it," Cynthia said, with a smile that was almost too glittering.

The Trent seizure had unsettled the Paris question. There remained nothing to do but wait. It seemed, however, advisable to post a letter to the President of the Confederacy before leaving; and Cynthia found the book of quotations in the library and carried it up to her room for a suitable Latin quotation; Francis would then copy the letter. And since political items and news could be better studied in New Orleans, the Eppes decided to postpone the visit to their Cousin Miles McGehee at St. Joseph's, and go directly home. Then Miles himself arrived at Montrose unexpectedly to confer with his brother on some business of cotton and the blockade. They accepted with the same readiness as before his invitation for the river journey, this time on the *Southern Belle.* Cousin Miles took out his pocketbook and put ten new $100 notes into Francis' hand.

"You'll find them useful in that enterprise of yours," he said.

"We shall regard it as a loan?" Francis said, bowing with a smile. "$1000 at eight per cent. But thank you, sir."

"I know when to kiss money good-bye. One good time is when a handsome young man gets his fingers on it."

"Very well. But how kind, how very kind, isn't it, *Maman?*"

"Very, very," Cynthia said, as she deftly took the bills out of his hand and put them in her bag, "but before we see Bayou Sara, there won't be a sou left."

"Maybe not, if we should get in a race," Miles said, laughing. "There's as many as nineteen boats a day pass now sometimes. It's only natural they race each other. On the Pearl No. 2 last year, racing the Princess, one wager ran as high as $16,000. Passengers got so het they threw their valises into the furnace. And bacon in. And then, by God A'mighty, she blew up, after all."

"But, *Maman,*" Francis was saying, staring at her purse and without listening to any of that about the races, *"C'est incroyable, ma mère.* I'll die of embarrassment."

"Tant pis. How smooth, *mon cher,* the river is!" said his mother, coldly.

At Montrose that night the house, without their city guests, seemed deserted, only Miss Mary kept the conversation going. All must agree, she said, that here was one young man at least who was preparing himself to serve his country.

XXXI

It could not have been said that Edward wrote home to Montrose very often; he was not the kind of man that writes letters. But nobody at Montrose ever expressed any criticism of that.

And all the time, nearly a year ago now, since Charles Taliaferro had ridden away with her brother from Natchez, Lucinda had kept him in her mind. Sometimes she saw the picture of his glowing, handsome head, sometimes she saw him only as echoes within her.

Lucy was one of those people who hold themselves up to what they believe, and expect other people to do so. She did many kind things, had a hidden tact all her own, and was very popular in Natchez, among young people and older people, though to hear her talk you could have thought her a bore in any company. Several young men would have liked to come oftener to Montrose; she merely left it so that they could come if they chose and go if they chose. In those last

months before the war—how far away they seemed now!—
the young preacher, just moved into the parsonage and much
admired by the ladies in his flock, had, after numerous calls,
managed to fall on his knees when Lucinda was not looking
in his direction, and to make a proposal. "I wish you'd get
up," she said. "You look like a jockey to me."

"My stars, child," Mrs. Wilson said to Lucy, one day over at
Rosalie, "men feel foolish enough as 'tis, getting down on
their knees, without your adding to it! They know they've
got to pop the question somehow. The trouble with you is
you kick them before they can come to the point."

"And I don't see the point," said Lucy, laughing not at this
but at something else in her mind. She looked into those open
Irish eyes and began a story that their tutor, Monsieur Olivier
Humbert, had recounted for her and Edward once. Old
General Humbert, Monsieur's father's cousin, was stopped
one morning at the Cabildo door by a beggar. "Only a *sou*,"
the beggar said, "only a *sou* to save my life." "I'm sorry, I
don't see the point," said the general.

"So that's the way you feel for your swains; you're as cold
as Dian. And for the love of grace, couldn't General Humbert
remember how he himself, being Pauline Bonaparte's lover,
escaped Napoleon and got over here to Chartres Street?
Yes, Lucy dear, what you do is before the men get to the
point you cut them off."

"They might as well know, and be done with it, Auntie
Wilson, that this foolishness of theirs is not to my taste. I
like to see men standing on their feet."

"Ah, indeed! And then look at her, sweet as a lily, walking
like a princess. And could sing, too, if she'd let herself go."

"Go where? Now, Auntie Wilson, go where?"

The old face shone with fresh wrinkles. "Where to go, my
dear? Where you choose. What else is a voice but a chance
to choose?"

"That's pretty. But the other side is: or else don't sing."

"In that case you'll choose anyhow but may not be chosen. No," she added quickly, glancing at Lucy, "I retract that last. It's only my blathering, it is."

At home Lucy had not sung in a twelvemonth. She knew that Charlie Taliaferro did not love her, and she had spoken of none of this to anybody. At first when she wrote her brother, who was with the army in Virginia, she would send Charles her compliments. Then she grew self-conscious even at that.

"Dear Buddie,

"I fancy in this winter weather you all are—" No, that would be for Charles too. She tore the letter up and began again. That letter too she might tear up. Lucy was no fool, and tones might be found in it that her pride would not have there.

"My own dearest Buddie, it's almost October, and I wish you could smell the air around this house. Sweet-olive like orange blossoms, roses— Papa, Mamma, and I speak of you. Aunt Paralee sent you a funny message. She says tell you to take 'your time whippin' them Yankees, the race is not always to de swif's.' At least, that's what she says. . . ."

Now that was better. Nobody could think— She got up and threw herself across the bed, burying her face in the pillow. Yes, that was better—nobody could think— She turned on her back and lay with set eyes and her lips together, looking at the ceiling.

She would sit for hours in the armchair in her room, but if any one came in, would take up her knitting and make an appearance of being busy.

"Are some of those socks for Charlie Taliaferro, too?" her mother asked one morning.

"Mamma, of course not. They're too small. I'm making them for Buddie."

"Are Charlie's feet so big? All I thought was that he hasn't any sister, nor any mother."

"You know Buddie's feet, Mamma. The McGehee men's feet," Lucy said, in a tone of indifference.

What letters Edward wrote brought some news of his cousin, but, beyond a graceful remembrance now and then, there were none from Charles himself. One day when a message came like that, Lucy said to herself, "He's honorable at least, no flowery pretensions, no gallantry." Why walk in shadows? Where was her proper pride? She would go down to the quarters where there were two old people sick. She could build her own character.

"Got eyes lak glass," old Aunt Viney said, looking up shrewdly from her pillow. "Fines' lookin' eyes of ev'ybody. But what you been thinkin' about, little miss?"

"How are you today, Aunt Viney?"

"Jes' got dat misery roun' here'n my jints."

"What joints?"

"Ev'y bone in my body seemed lak hit's achin'."

"And what does Daddy Felix say's the matter with him?"

"I'o know'm, lessen he ate de skin off a ten-pound ham and made um sick."

"Aunt Viney, have you taken the quinine?"

"Yas'm, I spec I has."

"Yes'm, my foot! You get right up and take it."

"Yas'm. I always puts what tas'es bad on the shelf outside de window. Let the yar git to it."

"Let the air blow it away, you mean. You'll laugh on the other side of your face when you find yourself as stiff as a board."

At Portobello Mrs. Bedford had long been surprised at the affection that she saw between Valette and Lucy.

"What is it—" she said one evening, as the last touches went on Valette's toilette for a party at Magnolia Vale. "Celie, you can go now, and don't you listen at the door— What it is you and Lucinda McGehee find so much to talk about I can't for the life of me understand."

"But, My Dumplin'—" A pin squeaked as she drove it into her belt.

Valette's dress was white, garlanded with tulle, which was caught at intervals over the whole skirt with triple loops of narrow blue ribbon. She knew that Mrs. Bedford believed a young girl should be lovely and beset with suitors, and should have the fineries for such happiness, and have them when the time was ripe. "Gather ye roses buds while ye may," she would say. But, as Valette knew also, Mrs. Bedford had better eyes for roses than for any dress; and so now, in front of the glass, she was studying the effect for herself

"You couldn't better it one iota," Mrs. Bedford said, "so— What did you two talk about the other day, for example, when you rode to your Uncle Hugh's nigger hospital off in the woods? The way any darkey of Hugh's can enjoy an illness surpasses everything. I suppose you saw the sufferers?"

"Four of them," said Valette, laughing, "were stretched out on the porch, and one was playing the banjo and two or three were dancing."

"Cut the Buck, was it? Or the Pigeon Wing? They're both terrible diseases."

"Of course, the poor darkies who were very sick were in the house."

"No doubt."

"We just rode up; we didn't go in."

"May I inquire on what did you and Lucy converse?"

"You have to understand Lucy, My Dumplin'," said Valette, turning a serious face to the mirror.

"I know, child, of course, I know. But Lucy's shut up in a knot, she's her own worst enemy, whereas a certain other young person is open, blest by the Gods, to be open like a rose."

"You mean?"

"I mean take those pins out of your mouth and give me a kiss."

"I love you, My Dumplin'," Valette said.

"Get out! You don't know what love is. Do you want to wear the onyx bracelets? You'll be tellin' me next that every young man at Mrs. Brown's soiree tonight will be at Lucinda McGehee's little feet and she herself passionately enamored."

"There are not any young men left she'd look at. They've all gone to the war."

"I see. Well, now that I understand everything so perfectly. I'd advise your putting a flower in your hair—what with the bracelets. Or am I wrong? At any rate, Duncan always likes you to."

Valette leaned over to the vase on her dressing-table and with both hands took up the white camellia tenderly as if it were a heart.

XXXII

Not long after the news of the fight in the early part of March between the *Monitor* and the *Merrimac* reached Natchez, a letter arrived for Valette from Duncan. It was for her alone and a long letter.

The one-time United States steam frigate *Merrimac* burned by the Federals had been raised by the Confederates and covered with the first armorplate yet seen in America. At Hampton Roads she steamed into the Federal squadron, sank U.S.S. *Cumberland* and U.S.S. *Congress* and fought the *Monitor*. In the meantime McClelland advanced on York-town and Stuart's cavalry was harrying his outposts and patrols. In the company, Duncan wrote, was a Leipzig professor, who, when he heard some of his students speak of going home to fight for the Confederacy, had resigned his chair in the university and came along with them. He brought a Latin grammar, and sometimes by the campfire gave them lessons, which would be useful in the professions afterward; and he knew the history of military strategy and tactics. Duncan and the professor often talked of this war and the place it would have in military history. The letter was about that.

This was to be a war of rifle bullets, trenches, abbatis, wire entanglements, hand grenades, winged grenades, rockets, and many types of booby traps, Duncan said in his letter. Magazine rifles and Requa's machine gun were invented. Gas bombs were ordered, balloons used, armored ships were now made, and armored trains, torpedoes, land mines, flag and lamp signalling, and the field telegraph. At Mobile had been built an under-sea boat. But the great tactical revolution had come with the rifle. And because of the rifle the wind went out of the bayonet as arms; it was descended from the pike of older times, and Schultz thought it almost as out of date. Professor Schultz had examined many corpses and found very few bayonet wounds; what had come into war now was the rifle and its mates: the spade and the axe for earthworks.

Because of the rifle the defense had become the stronger form of war. Stonewall Jackson had said that his men sometimes failed to drive the enemy from his position, but to hold one, never! Professor Schultz took for a good example the Battle of New Orleans in 1815. Out of 7000 British taking part in the attacks, 3300 were killed and wounded, and 500 prisoners; the Americans out of 4500 men had eight killed and thirteen wounded. The Americans were armed with the long Tennessee flintlock rifle, the British with Brown Bess muskets, and they attacked in rigid formation. "The Herr Professor says," Duncan went on, "he was once in the war in Bavaria but never battles like ours. A plain with the lines advancing, the generals leading in gold braid and cocked hats, colors flying, bands playing, is not seen in our army, not when we make an attack. All the Yankees see of us is bushes and smoke, every man to himself, running forward, kneeling to load, running forward again. So we talk late at night sometimes about tactics and the rifle.

"I will write you again as I have occasion to know more. How is my Greenwich rifle? Please make them keep it cleaned. Your own Duncan."

This was all the letter was about and all of it was to her. Valette reread it several times, stopping to kiss the writing. She finished it walking about the room. It was the sweetest letter Duncan had written her. It was the most beautiful letter ever written.

"But My Dumplin's gone calling and is not back from Magnolia Vale!" she said, "I'll go see——"

She flew up to the dressing-room where Duncan had his guncase, and took out the rifle. His father had ordered it from Greenwich, England, for Duncan's eighteenth birthday; he had paid $325 for it, the barrel was Damascus, the mountings were gold.

"Of course, of course, of course," Valette said to herself, "My Dumplin' watches Duncan's guns. But there must be a spot left or something. She took the rifle and stood looking at it as if it had been a flower, and then turned to a drawer for the cleaning rags and grease, and at the same moment decided to take everything down to Mammy Tildy's cabin. "It's just as well Mammy should know what Duncan's discussing with me. She's just a little too certain I'm not good enough for Duncan, that's what I think of it."

While both of them worked at the unnecessary polishing, Valette explained to Mammy Tildy the new tactics, about the bayonet, the march formations.

"So Mr. Duncan says this is a war of the rifle."

"I see it is," said the old woman, "Yes, m'am, and da's whar my lil Marse Duncan gwi' shoot de b'ar. We gwi' rub dis here bar'l off efn we don't stop, Miss Valette."

"I'll read you all these things," said Valette, leaving the gun to Mammy, who stood there holding it lightly across her arms as if it were a baby, "you'll see. She took the letter from her bosom: "trenches, abbatis, traps, hand grenades, winged grenades, bombs, rockets, wire entanglements."

"Jesus, hep yo'sef!"

When Mrs. Bedford returned, Valette was waiting to give her the letter to read. She was going upstairs to dress; after dinner she would ride over to Lucy's.

The rifle was back in the guncase, but now that she had seen it better she remembered Duncan's explaining to her once how barrels like this were made, she said. They were made by welding together narrow thin strips of three metals, fine-wrought iron, steel, and another harder steel, and while that was hot they twisted it around a rod to make the bore in it. "Which," Valette said—for love of Duncan she remembered these details quite rightly, though Mrs. Bedford was not herself informed enough to know it, "makes a spiral, My Dumplin', which is welded solid later."

"Precious, if I were you I don't believe I'd explain it too fully, you might blow your head off."

Later, on her way to Duncan's room, Mrs. Bedford stopped to give back the letter.

"So you think there never was such—Would anything but a man ever have written it? Do you know, precious, at the battle of Salamis there was a lady admiral and they say when she got her blood up and laid about her, she sank as many Greek ships as she did Persian. Don't glare at me. And now, don't choke me—kiss me though. So you think this letter—well, I suppose 'tis."

There were callers at Montrose when Valette arrived. Their voices came out to her on the gallery as she stood for a moment watching the shadows of the columns. The shadows were cast strangely together in the afternoon sun; and where there were none, the walls in this light were softer, waiting for the rich sundown. She heard some one among the callers saying what a good story about Monsieur Humbert that was. "But it's five years ago, it's ages," they were saying as Valette entered.

"But it's forever true of that type of young man," said a lady whom Valette had never seen before, some visitor at Monmouth, a friend of Mrs. Quitman's. "We have scores it could be true of." She went on to describe the type as a tall, slender, young man with full dark eyes and long hands, the dark eyes quiet and easy enough until you looked at them twice.

"And no good can come of that type." Mrs. Quitman said. "It's one Southern type that no good comes of."

"I don't see why we have to say that," said Lucy, who so far had been listening in silence.

Mrs. Quitman, hearing something unexpected in Lucy's voice, turned toward her in surprise. "Say what?"

"I just don't see why tall and dark and eyes have so much to do with it."

"Lucy, Mrs. Quitman doesn't mean just that," her mother said, glancing from her daughter to the old lady, who got nothing except the tone in Lucy's voice.

"You don't? Well, mark my words, at bottom that sort of men are reckless, they are arrogant."

"But, Mrs. Quitman, what if they are——?"

"Often enough they are most agreeable, fine manners, insinuating. Just you follow them up, you find some devilment or other. You don't understand yet, my dear."

"I imagine I don't. I'm sorry." Lucy rose and excused herself from the company.

"Since Edward's left, the child's been keeping too much to herself," Agnes said, in a tone with which, unconsciously, we speak to older people when we think they are stupid.

Valette followed Lucy on to the gallery. "I remember Monsieur Humbert's eyes," she said, putting her arm around Lucy's waist. "I remember how——"

"I've almost forgotten him."

"For goodness' sake, you have?" Valette understood and yet was astonished at the blunt way Lucy had said that.

"Do you see all that fluttering about down by one of the pigeonnières?" said Lucy, using the Creole form of the word. "I'm going down there. If it's Paralee's old tomcat I'll wring his neck."

On their way down the path, Valette avoided looking at her

friend. They could find nothing wrong, though there was a great stir of the pigeons going on, in and out of the openings and above the pretty cupola. The shadows of their wings flecked over Lucy's white dress.

"Has Eddie written since I saw you?" Valette asked.

"Only a line—let's go round by the pond, I don't want to hear any more from old ladies about dark-eyes,-mark-my-word. Do you? Buddie wrote, always busy with General Beauregard, said nothing about himself or anybody or anything else."

"Smell how sweet!" Valette plucked two roses from a trellis and was giving one to Lucy. "They say General Beauregard's the best for military tactics, and Eddie was good in that at the seminary, you remember? So that's what keeps him so busy."

Unconsciously Valette put her hand to her bosom and felt there the crackle of Duncan's new letter. She thought, "I'm happy, happy, happy! Lucy must be happy, too, and if she's not I can't help it. Why shouldn't I go on being happy?" Then a catch took her generous heart. She left Duncan's letter, which she had hurried over from Portobello to read Lucy, unmentioned, lying against her young bosom. She did not mention the letter, but caught her friend's hand and kissed it so hard that Lucy turned, looking at her with that clear gaze:

"Now don't you be worrying over me, Valette. I can take care of myself."

"Oh, yes, I know you can."

They strolled along in silence. "Not one word of Charlie Taliaferro, oh, Lucy!" Valette said to herself. "Not a word, and you won't speak it." Glancing sidewise at the proud, white face with its delicate mouth, she resolved that as for herself she would cry and howl whenever she was unhappy; it was better to have it out. Was it wicked to go along as Lucy was doing, so alone from every one? It was like Valette to feel that half of life consists in what you hide and what you do not hide from people, and especially people who love you.

As they passed the camellia bushes the rain of petals underneath, now white, now pink like a shell, seemed to be laid at the feet of love and happiness? Did she not know that Duncan would come again? What else was love? When their elbows brushed the camellias, the petals fell in showers.

"Tell me, Valette," Lucy said, "did it seem mighty strange to you at first, not knowing where people were, I mean having them off there in the war?"

"Yes. But time passes, the end of February will be here before we know it."

"Yes," said Lucy, and then suddenly, "so don't be worrying about me. People tell me Valette Somerville's a butterfly, mighty pretty and attractive, of course, Cud'n Abe McGehee saying to me, Valette's about as serious as a bird; but I said, now look here, Cud'n Abe, you can't tell me, for I know better: you go choose yourself a raincrow—if that's what you admire, there must be plenty. You know Cud'n Abe a year or so ago was in love with a young plump widow in Clinton, but she went up a tree with a lamp looking for her cat, and he was disenchanted or something, we never found out exactly what."

"But, Lucy——"

"You're just smarter than these people, Valette, that's what's the matter. I reckon you're about the best friend I have."

"Lucy——"

"Yes, the best friend."

During the rest of the visit they told each other names of those who had gone to the war. John Lyle, Henry St. Ange, Victor Fleming, George McGehee from Woodville, Urban Wagner, and Victor Dunbar, Ike Campman, Francis Carroll, boys away in the Confederate armies.

XXXIII

At Montrose those very first days in April there was a strange air of suspense, even of commotion. Nothing was being moved, the house was the same, Aleck and his assistants were busy in the south garden with the second planting of peas and lettuces sown already in February. Hugh McGehee was to be absent from home for some days at one of his plantations near Bayou Sara, which for months he had neglected because he had thought the times too unsafe to be away from home overnight. But all over this river country the air was full of strain. People had known from the newspapers of the march of the Union Army across Tennessee. General Albert Sidney Johnston retired before it, gathering recruits as he went. General Grant, as the *Natchez Gazette* reported it, had halted at Pittsburg Landing on the Tennessee River with 33,000 men, 5000 more some miles away, and 20,000 marching down from Nashville. General Albert Sidney Johnston, General Beauregard second in command, with 40,000 men was at Corinth. People in the Natchez country knew only too well what was at stake. Unless the Federal movement was checked the cotton states would be invaded.

Every day for some time when Dave came back from his trip to town, Agnes had waited for a letter, but none came. Edward was too busy to write, she would say, knowing that he was on the march. But on April 6 there came a letter. Edward was at Corinth, with General Beauregard, under General Johnston. Governors of the nearby states were sending in recruits. On the Confederate side, and the Yankee side, from what Edward heard, they called for a battle. Some trial must be made. In three days General Johnston would be at

Pittsburg Landing for a surprise attack, or so it was hoped. A battle had to be, the letter said and ended:

"When I write my mother again I hope it will be a victory to tell you of.   Your loving son,   EDWARD."

Agnes McGehee read the letter twice and, holding it still open in her hand, rang for a maid to send Lucy to her.

"Darling," she said, "you know Dave has brought the mail, and there's a letter from Buddie. He was at Corinth. That was the third, this is the sixth of the month. He says here, there would be a battle in three days." She held out the open letter and Lucy read it. The end of it said that Charlie Taliaferro and General Beauregard talked sometimes about the old days in Louisiana, for General Beauregard followed the French practice of mingling with his men, he would stroll sometimes from one camp fire to another, smoking a cigar, talking with them, as Napoleon used to do.

Her mother had said only that there was going to be a battle. Now she heard her saying, "Lucy, I know what it means, Edward's dead. I'm going and bring him home."

"Do you think you can see him, Mamma?"

"Not alive, I know."

"No, no, Mamma precious! I don't see how you feel so sure of this."

"Lucy, I know it."

Arguments would get nowhere, Lucy knew; and if her father had been there, it would have been the same. There was something you could not discuss; and without comment, she heard her mother say that she would set out in two hours, in the wagon with William Veal. They would leave the wagon to wait at Jackson, where they would take the train north.

"You are so sure, Mamma?"

"Yes."

With trembling lips and half closed eyes Lucy turned away and left the room.

A telegram was to be sent off to Hugh McGehee and Dave went to town with it. On the street he met Dock, and so it was that Sallie Bedford learned at Portobello of Agnes' intention. She was at Montrose within a hour. Miss Whipple, the seamstress, was on the gallery walking up and down, and Sallie, who could never bear the sight of her, stopped only to say, "Why, Miss Whipple, I thought you were always sewing like forty." She went on into the hall without waiting to hear a reply from Miss Whipple, who was already making her familiar motion of swallowing, but had not her reply ready.

"Sister Agnes," Mrs. Bedford said, when Lucy had shown her the letter and they stood watching the small travelling box which Edna was packing for the journey. "Are you really goin'? Of course you are going, but don't go. It's not given to human beings to know these things."

"Given or not given, I know," said Agnes.

"Mamma," said Lucy, "do you think we know what Papa would think?"

"He would ask me if I must go. That would be all. If I said I must, he would know."

The tears filled Lucy's eyes as she heard her mother say this beautiful thing; it would have been beautiful if said about any one.

Mrs. Bedford stuck to the point: "I don't propose to believe Duncan is killed, oh, no."

" 'Loved thee with an everlasting love,' " said Agnes simply.

Sallie Bedford folded her hands and was silent. "She will go. It's exactly like her," she said to herself.

In her own way she knew women and the tragic nature of their desires, wise or foolish. Her own spirit, downright mind and loyal impulses could not comprehend the fact that in Agnes it was a certain deep power of feeling, almost a monotony of passionate devotion, that gave those who loved her the sense of judging her tenderly. It was a preposterous thing for Agnes to set out like this on a sheer whim or foreboding. Why should Edward any more than anybody else be killed, even if there was a battle now being fought? And to come out with that line from the Bible: "Love thee with an everlasting love." As she thought these things, she heard Agnes' voice saying:

"Sis Sallie, you're mighty good to me."

"No, honey, the very idea."

"You are, and thank you," said Agnes.

"Thank me your foot, you just hush up, Agnes McGehee."

Agnes only smiled, as if at a naughty child.

"But dear Sister Agnes, let me say to you, nothing could make me believe my son was dead; I'd have to know it. And I don't believe there's anything inside me would know— know something had happened to Duncan—they'd have to tell me."

She got no reply, and all at once, as if there were some choir heard singing when a door is opened, she heard the birds outside in the trees; it would soon be spring; life was new, not ended. Then she saw those arms unclasp from Agnes McGehee's lap and rest on the chair arms; and, though she could not have told why, the idea came to her that in life always are both the beginning and the end, Alpha and Omega, as the Bible says. Going over to Agnes, she dropped down kneeling and buried her face in the other's lap. For a moment Agnes gazed with surprise at this, then she began to pass her fingers gently over the little round head, with its smooth hair.

There was an early dinner and Agnes set off with William Veal, on the spring seat to the wagon. Work on the fields near the house had stopped, and a crowd of negroes gathered at the entrance gate to watch the departure; they were silent and stood with their heads bare as William Veal drove out. He wore an old pair of riding gloves that Lucy had brought to him, and looked straight ahead down the road. Mrs. Bedford had stayed on, and she and Lucy when they had said good-bye and the wagon had started, went back from the lawn up the gallery steps and stood watching. Everywhere was green. The trees and shrubs, the garden, the orchard, stood under a bright sky, with soft clouds like summer drifting round its rim. For a time you could hear the sound of the wagon as it went along the road, then suddenly it was the doves calling. In some field, some wood or grove, the doves called. The soft wind from the south stirred the foliage.

And so her mother was gone, where Edward and Charles were; and Lucy, with her temple resting against one of the columns, stood gazing at the stir among the leaves, as she heard them, and beyond them the doves calling, and then again at the green lawn.

XXXIV

When Valette, with the two children, reached Montrose in the morning, they saw three coffins on the front gallery. The stench had made that necessary. On the floor stood saucers of charcoal. The ends of the coffins rested on chairs. Mrs. Bedford had left Portobello soon after daylight and Valette saw her with Mrs. Quitman, Mr. Balfour and another gentleman who had his back turned her way as she came up to the steps. They were watchers with the dead.

The two children at the sight of the coffins clung to Valette's skirts. "Lette, which is Cousin Edward?" Middleton whispered, drawing her down to his little ears.

"Hush, precious, you must keep quiet. Lette doesn't know. Cousin Edward's not there—that's only—. Come, let's sit over here." She led them to a seat at the far end of the gallery, partly to keep them from seeing the men standing inside the graveyard wall. There were three men, two of them negroes, and Black Dave was waiting outside the gate with a spade on his shoulder. The children on each side of her put their arms through Valette's, shutting their lips tight, and sat looking around them, and then into each other's eyes. Their mother left the other watchers and tiptoed over to that end of the gallery with her finger on her lips.

"You must be good chillun," she said, "do what Valette tells you."

Middleton slid off the bench and put up his arms to embrace her. "Aunt Sallie, which is Cousin Edward?" he whispered, "which is Cousin Edward, Aunt Sallie?"

"Sh! He's the one at this side. You mustn't talk——"

"No, m'am." He took away his arms and sat down on the bench again, never taking his eyes off the coffin that she had spoken of. She watched him a moment and then, brushing her hand across her cheek, leaned down and kissed his brow.

"Yes, my darlin'."

Valette learned that the second coffin was the Hammond boy from West Feliciana Parish, the other was from that parish also and of the same company; but there was no trace of his name on the coffin. Charlie Taliaferro had never been found; in the confusion, the tents being destroyed, the retreat, nobody knew what had happened to him.

When Valette heard that, tears sprang into her eyes and began to run down her cheeks. She caught Mrs. Bedford's hand.

"Charlie Taliaferro, My Dumplin'?"

"Yes, poor thing! But you hardly knew him, honey. It's just the way war is."

"But if he were alive they would know it."

"We're talking about your cousin Charlie Taliaferro, honey," Valette said to Middleton. She laid her hand on his.

"I know you are," said the little boy, looking at her strangely, as if to say that he knew more than she thought.

"Valette, you haven't heard how 'twas, I reckon," Mrs. Bedford said. "Well, they wouldn't let Agnes go on the field, 'twas night already. But old William Veal stole out there. And he went over the field, feeling all the hair of all the dead till he found Edward, he knew him by his hair. You know how fine it was. Yes, so that's it. And then, after they left Jackson last night, it was so dark that they stopped at a house and got one of those piney woods people to ride ahead of them on a white horse. So they could follow along the road. That's how dark it was. So the man rode ahead on those blind roads and they followed."

Mary Hartwell, hearing this and seeing the expression on Valette's face, began to sob, making almost no sound; and Valette took her on her knees, pressing the child to her bosom and whispering to her: and then looking up at Mrs. Bedford as if to say they should not have brought the children.

"If Mary Hartwell cries," her mother said, patting the little shoulder, "we'll have to take her home, do you hear, Hartie, hear what Mamma says? But I think 'twas right to bring them. They ought to be here and see— They ought to see it with us."

"My Dumplin', do you know where Lucy is?"

"No, I haven't seen her. But I'm going in now, I ought to."

"If you see her—everybody'll be with Aunt Agnes and Uncle John. My Dumplin', if you see Lucy, you talk to her."

A number of people arrived in carriages or on horseback, and came up the steps and indoors. A few remained on the lawn and presently went down to wait at the cemetery. After a few minutes some one opened a window, and Valette could see into the parlor where Agnes and Hugh McGehee were with their friends. Valette gazed into the room and thought. it seemed older and sadder there than it was on the gallery, where the dead men lay in their coffins, heaped with flowers. The air stirred the leaves, the sun shone bright over the lawns and fields.

The two children leaned against Valette, talking in low tones about their Cousin Edward. She could feel their little heads pressed against her, like birds. But she did not hear quite what they were saying. She sat looking vaguely in front of her. "Blessed are they that die in the Lord—" she had heard that often, but now for the first time, she said to herself, she understood it. To die in the Lord meant to die young, tender, beautiful, all that love is.

XXXV

On the way to her room, Lucy saw her uncle, Miles Mc-Gehee, on the upper gallery walking back and forth. He had arrived the night before and looked now old and troubled; at Montrose he was reminded every moment of his own sons, who were with the army in Tennessee, and it seemed to him that the low voices and people moving about so quietly in the house were more than he could bear. When she saw him, Lucy gave up her thought of being alone.

Miles took his chair over to a north window, away from the morning sun in Lucy's room, and sat there for a long time, now looking out, now resting his elbows on his knees, his fat shoulders rolled up against the back of his head, his brow in the palms of his hands.

"Dear Uncle Miles! Dear Uncle!" Lucy thought. She could

hear again his voice long ago on the gallery some morning, offering a reward for every gray hair they could find in his head. The McGehee children and Buddie and herself, when they visited River Orchards. Now that she was older, Lucy knew that this had been only a way of keeping them around him. "Plenty money," Miles used to say, "and right here in this wallet 'tis, too; and the one that gets the most gray hyars I'll give the first silver dollar I find in a pig track." She could see him now with a pair of tongs bending over to pick up walnuts from the tree at the gate. Sometimes on the gallery in the summer evenings, in the full perfume of the dusk, Uncle Miles would tell them stories he had heard as a child about the family. Lucy could hear his voice again telling how Mary Queen of Scots restored to one of their ancestors a title that her father, King James V, had deprived him of: Lord of the Isles.

"Lucy, you and Ed were like my own children, even Blanche," he said now, "you know that, don't you?"

"Uncle Miles, of course,"she said, unconsciously imitating the sob in his voice. At the same moment she remembered that he had ten children and her cousin Blanche's golden hair.

"I never felt an iota of difference between Edward and my boys."

"I know." She laid her hand tenderly on his shoulder, feeling some blunt annoyance at the pain he caused in her own breast, so much greater it seemed to her young mind than any he could have. "Men go on like babies," she thought.

"Eh?"

"We feel the same about you, Uncle Miles."

"Eh?" he raised his head, and wiped his eyes. "Well, there's no accountin' for tastes, as the old woman said when she kissed the cow. And, see here, have you heard about your Cud'n Abe? Ed would have laughed at that. You know your Cud'n Abe can't sleep, so t'other night down at Woodville they tell me Abe got up at three o'clock in the morning and went out and started walking around the house. Round and round. 'Anybody here want to buy a piano? Anybody here want to buy a piano?' You know Abe's always said Edward was the pick of the lot."

"I know," said Lucy. "Cud'n Abe would always say, yes, sir, he would tell you Buddie was the flower of the family."

"So he did. Can't you hear Ed laugh about such moonshine as this of Abe's? About the piano."

"Oh, Uncle, if I could only speak to Buddie—just say—" she looked at Miles timidly.

"It's always just the same," he said. "Always. If we just could—just once——"

As she lowered her beautiful eyes, now more beautiful for that loving pain of memory and regret for what she imagined had never been expressed, Miles said to himself how like his mother's eyes they were. He reached out and set a chair for her beside his.

"I was thinkin' your eyes are like my mother's And now we have this war on our hands!" He spread out first Lucy's fingers and then her palm. "And who knows?"

Lucy gazed first at her palm and then at Miles' face, the round cheeks crowding the eyes, the rolls of fat under the chin, the clear, fine lips from which came that arrogant, teasing voice, as proud and as kind as his heart. His black velvet waistcoat bowed far out in front. She thought of him filling his private chairs on the steamboats.

"At Shiloh, Uncle Miles—" Lucy said, avoiding his gaze.

"Eh?"

"Nothing. I forget what I was going to say."

" 'Tain't worth the pains bothering your head, sweetness, what we were goin' to say."

"Mamma and Papa are down there with people in the parlor, I imagine. And that's right, I know, but I just can't do it. I imagine what I was going to say was the spring's coming in the same as ever."

"Yes, it's a fair season this year."

"All the jasmines, all the roses. When Charlie Taliaferro was here he liked a rose in his lapel. But what Buddie liked was the orchards and the land, just as he did our horses."

She thought, "Those calacanthus buds down there by the oval beds, they are just the color of Buddie's hair, aren't they?" But by some strange jealousy at the bottom of love, she did not let her Uncle Miles share her thoughts.

He would not have heard her, for on the gallery he had seen, from where his chair was placed, that people were assembling, and down at the graveyard the Montrose negroes were arranging themselves respectfully on each side the gate. Every one understood the burial had to be hurried because of the time that had elapsed.

Lucy did not notice that he had shifted his chair more in front of the window to hide from her the sight of the two coffins being put into William Veal's wagon out there in the stable yard to be carried to St. Francisville. By what strange thing was she about to tell Uncle Miles, with his fat, proud face and the diamond cluster in his cravat, tell Uncle Miles what she knew she would never tell her father, nor tell her mother, nor anybody else? "No, not a single solitary person," she thought. "And you know how I am with people; stiff as a buckboard." Yet she had the feeling that if she could tell some one all that was in her mind, she would be saved. Saved from what? she asked herself, and thought, "From the rest, from what's going to happen to me the rest of my life. If I've lost—if I never have again—if I——"

She reached down for one of the plump hands and laid her cheek along it, catching in her breath like a sob.

"Uncle," she began, and was about to tell him when Miles, drawing away his hand, rose with a sudden effort from the chair where he was sitting. He had seen people gathering in the walk at the foot of the steps, ready to start.

"We'd better go on down, Lucindy," he said.

She started and her face turned white.

"Now, Uncle Miles?" With a moan she closed her eyes and pressed her quivering lips together. Not herself, not Charlie, only Buddie now she thought of.

"We'd better go on down now. And you take my arm. Yes, it's time."

XXXVI

"DON'T put no flowers on the table lak we does," Paralee said to one of the servants, as they prepared for the dinner that day. She knew that Mrs. Quitman, Mrs. Wilson, Judge Winchester, the family from Portobello, and two or three friends would stay until late afternoon. "No roses nor nothin'."

Fanny was surprised. "How come?"

"Don't you know, you fool nigger, my missus ain't go want to see flowers again today? Git dem roses and dem other blossoms outin' de dinin-room."

"Yes'm."

Hugh McGehee sat at the foot of the table, Agnes at the head, and their guests around. Many of them ate with that sharp appetite that has often been claimed for people after funerals; and the conversation, if always in low tones, was animated. The children sat at a little round table by the window. The talk was of the neighborhood, and here and there about the war. They spoke of General Albert Sidney Johnston's death, which was one of the few details of the battle of Shiloh that had so far reached them.

"And I can tell you one thing," Mrs. Wilson said, "Sir Walter Scott will be the ruin of the South, so much so I'd take my oath on it."

"You mean?" Hugh asked, but he knew what she meant. General Johnston had reproved his men for looting the Yankee tents, then thinking he had been too harsh, he got down himself and took a little tin cup, which he held from then on, riding with it in his hand. Later he saw a petty officer of the Federals lying wounded on the ground, and insisted that his own surgeon remain to care for him. A few minutes later a minie ball struck an artery in Johnston's leg. His staff did what they could, trying to stop the blood. It would have been simple enough for any one with experience; but they could do nothing, and in a short time he was dead. The attack ceased, and for two hours there was a pause. The victory from then on was lost.

Hugh McGehee glanced at his wife, and seeing that she had not lifted her eyes, did not repeat the question; but Mrs. Wilson went on, "I mean this chivalry obsession. Sometimes I think it's only male vanity. Then I know I'm wrong, so then I think, no, it's the male soul."

"Men always have and always will make war to suit themselves," said Mrs. Bedford. She disliked Mrs. Wilson, and back of her mind was the thought that you must give birth to a son before you judge men; and this old woman was childless. And this was not the time or the place for such a subject. She had noticed that Hugh McGehee's eyelids were red from crying, but no one had seen him do it.

"I don't know about that, but what I mean is, chivalry's dead, and we'll have to learn that fact in the South, or we won't stand a dog's chance. If General Johnston had let that little pish of Yankee officer go on and die—and a good riddance, too, I imagine—he wouldn't have been without his surgeon, and we'd have won the battle. That's certain, Mrs. Bedford."

Instead of saying more, Sallie turned to Miles McGehee. "Have some sweet pickle," she said, in a tone as if he lived for nothing but to eat.

"I heard what was just said about General Johnston, Brother Hugh," Miles said, simply. "I heard about it all. And I thought——"

"Yes?"

"You can never tell which kind of death is worth the most."

Hugh heard that from his brother without surprise, but said nothing. The fatness and the crowded plate led some of the other guests to think that either Miles meant nothing, or was quoting something his wife had read to him.

That evening about dusk, Hugh McGehee went out on the gallery alone. He stood by the rail at one end looking down past the garden to the graveyard, seeing in his mind the grave there, the heaped-up flowers, and thinking of Edward's mother at this time of day. Then he turned and walked down the gallery toward the far end opposite. Here and there he saw the negroes, some drifting around alone, some in groups talking; they were taking advantage of this chance to spend the day idling about. Hugh stood leaning against a column, and without thinking about it very much, watched them. With his mind so concerned for his wife, the thought of her relation to their negroes came to him. Most of her Natchez friends said that Agnes spoiled every negro she laid her eyes on, and nobody could have denied that the Montrose negroes drifted through many things as they chose. Sallie Bedford with any and all negroes regarded them as animals. "You needn't try to tell me, I know my niggers." About them she was without imagination and dismissed their feelings and traits as those of monkeys. "Can the leopard change his spots?

Can the Ethiopian change his skin?" she said. "Are we going to improve on the Bible? Not that I ever read it much, but Ma did. There may be some place in Scripture about equality, but Ma never found it."

Down in the court beside the kitchen door, Hugh saw two little negroes with their arms on each other's shoulders watching with Middleton, who went up and down squeezing the touch-me-not buds in the pots there. The three children watched for a flower to pop when Middleton squeezed it between his fingers, laughing and talking. A cur puppy from the cabins ran back and forth among the children, jumping up against their legs, wagging his tail, but none of them noticed him, and after biting at the little negroes' toes, he stood gazing at their feet for a moment and then quietly lay down across them.

In the vast silence you saw the sky deep and open, the trees drew away from it and came near, dark and still in the shadowless air. It was so quiet an evening that the movement of the trees seemed to have no sound, as if that were lost in space; and then there was the sound of a dried leaf against the ground, brief and final.

The children's voices now and then, the voices of people, things they have said, come into the mind and are gone; and you stand waiting, Hugh said to himself, waiting and looking on this quiet and sky as if nothing passed or was ever forgotten. A hush, a pause, and with the falling of a leaf, you might hear the secrecy of your deep tenderness asking what you have done to bring between yourself and others the simplicity of affection and—in the old phrase—the communion of saints. He suddenly felt old; he was seventy, and he had lived a long time.

XXXVII

Letters came from the Bedfords' friends and cousins in the northern corner of the state, telling of the invasion by General Grant's army. On the road to Corinth Malcolm Bedford's friends, the Whitbys, lived. Some one had fired from ambush into the Union army, and General Grant gave orders in reprisal that the next house in sight of the road should be burnt. The Whitbys were roused from their beds and given ten minutes to get out. It was at night in the sleet and snow, snipers would be taught a lesson. There were many other stories of ruin and suffering, such as wars and invasions always afford. Valette and Mrs. Bedford also read in the *Natchez Gazette* various accounts and hearsay that came through. In Natchez parlors little else was talked about.

Sitting on the north gallery, waiting for Valette to bring the secretary and start a letter to Duncan, Sallie Bedford gazed at the sunset rising at that hour through the trees and spreading over the fields, and thought of the garden at Clifton an hour ago, in its full flower of spring. They had walked through the arches in the hedge of evergreen, within whose privacy was the great flower bed in the shape of a heart. The white pinks and mignonette, amaryllis and tuberoses were in blossom, and the mimosa trees above the hedge were as sweet as they. How green and lush the spring fields were!

"Too fast for you?" she said to Valette, after five or six words.

Valette shook her head: "We've just been to Clifton——"

"Where, like everywhere else, people are talking of the devilment old Grant's army is doing up toward the state line. It's hard to sleep at night after hearing what some of our friends have suffered; I get up and sit by the window, or go in your room a minute sometimes and see if everything is all right there. All your guns are polished like a looking-glass, son; they'll be as good when you get home as they ever were. But you know how we all chatter; and I couldn't help thinking this evening at Clifton that some of our friends seemed to console themselves too much maybe by the chance they get to show pity and resentment."

"Now, now," Valette stopped, passing the tip of the feather pen back and forth across her lips, "My Dumplin', how can you say so?"

"Why, all on earth 'tis is that I'm sensible. Nobody hesitates to praise his heart, but nobody dares to praise his brains."

Valette made no comment on the maxim, for fear of having to put it in the letter. She dipped her pen into the inkwell with its gold top standing open, and sighed. "From what," Mrs. Bedford dictated, "we see reported from the North with regard to Shiloh that they first beat the drums for General Grant, and now they are skinning his hide off for allowing his troops to be taken by surprise. He seems to have been eating his breakfast in some house off somewhere from his army, when he heard the guns, and did not reach the scene till toward eleven o'clock, and thus General Halleck from Washington is now in command. General Beauregard, sick with fever, led the Confederate retreat to Corinth. They say that only something like 10,000 out of his 40,000 men are properly armed, while General Halleck has over 120,000. Miss Mary Cherry has written us that figure also, but she is not afraid for a moment, she says. I enclose the page she wrote about the women of the South, though before this Yankee invasion she always said women were fools. But now we are not fools, we are noble womanhood."

"Can't we tell him about the bird, My Dumplin'?" said Valette; but seeing Mrs. Bedford's eyes turned away toward the garden, she added quickly, "No, forgive, me, I don't suppose that's very historical of me. I just thought——"

"It most certainly is historical, what I was thinkin' of is you're My Dumplin's little darlin', that's all, and all I ask the good Lord is that my own children—. So there, don't be jumping about with ink." She began the letter again. "Oh, yes. It seems General Beauregard, who had a fever all this time, had a bird brought him by a soldier who had found it in the grass stunned, I reckon. It was a pheasant, which would please a sick man's palate. So General Beauregard sat on his horse as he gave orders, stroking the bird. He brought it back to Corinth with him for a friend's child."

"There, that's enough for today," she said, rising and scanning over the letter, as Valette closed up her writing desk, "tomorrow we can put in a little more. Tell him everything here at Portobello is going well. He'll be knocking somebody's teeth out for no reason at all but just because he's worrying about us here at home."

"I'm afraid so," Valette said.

Besides there was enough gloomy in the last letter we had to write him."

"Duncan loved Ed, My Dumplin'."

"Yes. Then tomorrow the chillun must write him, what with writing or printing it out. Silas says the mare's likely to foal any time now. Duncan would give his eye teeth to hear of a colt of hers. And now what are you thinkin'?"

"I'm thinkin' we'll have to ask Silas exactly what to say, not be mixing a horse all up the way Duncan says I do."

They walked slowly down to the carriage gate and back, over the green moss underfoot, on one side the statues rising from the dark wall of the hedge, on the other the trunks of the live-oaks. The early stars were coming into the sky. Sallie Bedford was talking of the work at Portobello, the Concordia and Tensas plantations would have to drift for themselves.

"I vow she's not listening to a word I utter," Mrs. Bedford said, cutting their walk suddenly short. She peered quizzically into the young face.

"No, My Dumplin', and I agree with all you've said."

"Agree? How can you agree if you don't know what I said?"

"I always agree when you use that tone of voice; I know you are right."

"I know who's a monkey."

"You see I heard that, but your voice changed."

Mrs. Bedford chuckled at this way of saying she was wrong, but made no reply, and slipped back into her own thoughts. For Valette it was as if she were still writing the letter to Duncan. Words said to love, any words, anybody's! She could not have expressed it, but it seemed to her that in life you take every moment for a marvel, as the light opens a flower and draws up sweetness. When, a little further on, Mrs. Bedford put an arm around Valette's shoulder, she felt a suppressed sob shaking them.

"No, My Dumplin'," said the low voice, "no, I'm really very happy."

Silas, coming round from the stables, met them at the steps and said that Mr. Duncan's mare had foaled some time ago, mighty fine everything; and Valette, beaming and ready to clap her hands, sent him off to fetch a lantern so that they could see for themselves. The little colt, a dark roan, was standing close to his mother.

"Colts walk and suck in twenty minutes after birth," Sallie Bedford said, holding the lantern higher. "And are dry in an hour. But the mare's anxious about them for several days."

"I certainly hope his mother's got his ears and spots and everything right," Valette said, "because I wouldn't know how they ought to be."

"So?" Mrs. Bedford smiled.

"You can just imagine what Duncan would say."

"Oh, no, Miss Valette, da's a fine colt, yas, m'am" Silas said. "Ain't it, Miss Sallie?"

"Yes, and, Silas, you don't go naming Mr. Duncan's mare's colt till he sends us word."

"No, m'am, no, m'am."

"What do you call him already?"

"I calls him Prince."

"Well, you just uncall him till we get word."

XXXVIII

For some days after Edward's burial, Lucy did her part at Montrose. Her sister Annie did not return at once to Baton Rouge and the older sister, Mrs. Bowdoin, had come as soon as possible from New Orleans. All day long they sat talking; the memory of Edward and of years now gone was not hurried past; death had put on the house an air of quiet purification, like an old symbol. Of them all Mrs. Bowdoin, the most fluent, was tinged with the theatrical in her expressions, though her emotions were none the less genuine for being set in a certain imaginative nonsense. There was no one in the family who did not know how to listen to her flowery effects, and at the same time to listen for the sincerity at the bottom of it all.

Lucy was of the family, but she could not talk of these things as her sister and the others could together. This oneness of theirs was something where the soul is suddenly aged and must speak itself. Simple words were spoken that seemed to share among the others all that was in the person speaking. Whatever part there was of it that might be forgotten afterward, it remained as something in the family, in the blood, and constituted an inexplicable force among them which they never thought of explaining.

Except when she went about some small duty or other, Lucy sat with them, listening. In the midst of the conversation one day, her father, whose eyes she had seen more than once resting on her, said,

"Are you all right, daughter?"

"Now listen here, Papa," she replied, "don't worry about me. Of course. I'm tough as whit-leather. You know how 'tis with me."

How 'twas with her— But meanwhile no news had come about Charles Taliaferro. She had lived all these years so close to Buddie that his death was enough to fill her thoughts—to break what heart she seemed to feel breaking. But as the days passed, she was thinking: where was Charlie, what had happened to Charlie?

Belle Bowdoin, the oldest daughter, a little faded, but with small red lips and very eloquent, kept on talking: Annie Randolph had slipped back into the family like a fish to water. Of the three women their mother said least; but she spoke at times of her journey to Corinth, of people's kindness to her. They were details which everybody understood for what they implied. She gave Lucy some of the letters to read that she had written; leaving always room for a postscript.

Lucy took up first that to her uncle, Malcolm Bedford, in General Joseph E. Johnston's army. She read,

"Dear Brother, I write to tell you—" and so on, and then: "I have been too earth prone. I have suffered the *cares* of life to eat the heart out of my enjoyment, never fulfilled the injunction to 'cast my care on the Lord, who careth for me,' "——

How could her mother go on like that? She gave back the

sheaf of letters, "Mamma, I just can't," she said, looking off anywhere, "not even a postscript."

Finally one day at the end of breakfast, when Agnes Mc-Gehee had excused herself and gone upstairs, a letter arrived from Shelton Taliaferro.

Belle looked at the letter before she opened it and began to read.

"My Saviour, look at this magnificent stationery it's written on, with the Shelton crest! I'd wager it's as old as I am—he fished it out of some old secretary—all Belle Grove's full of these scraps of old grandeur, I imagine. Poor old Cud'n Shelton!"

Shelton Taliaferro began with an expression of sympathy for his cousin's loss, but her father stopped Belle in the midst of it.

" 'Tain't worthwhile reading all that, not aloud, child, we know."

She stopped.

"But go on, look, is there something about Shelt's boy?"

"Yes, here 'tis, Papa. 'They have reported to me that my son was never found. He is thought to have been burnt in his tent. Pray God for me so that I can bear——' "

"All right, all right—," Hugh said, "Let it be, Belle."

Lucy taking her workbasket along as if she were only some machine, passed out of the room. Her sister looked after her and then at her father, inquiringly, before she picked up the fichu that Lucy had left where it had fallen on the floor.

"Listen here," their father said, in a low voice, frowning at his two daughters, "the child feels something special about—I mean—when Charles was here nothing came of it—he went off so soon to the army. Your mother and I both have an idea —but don't you speak a word about it to Lucinda, you hear me? You hear me?"

"Of course not," both the sisters said, quickly, nodding their heads. Belle Bowdoin added,

"In New Orleans, when he was there, people liked him."

"That's not what I'm thinking of, Belle, I'm thinking of her."

"One thing," Belle said, "wild as Charlie Taliaferro was, one thing we've got to grant him, he loved his old father."

"Aye."

"What poor old Cud'n Shelt will do without him I don't know. Whether he ever saw him much or not, since Charlie got grown."

Slowly there had spread into Lucy's whole soul the feeling of withdrawal from them all. This had happened even before word came from Charlie's father, but the morning after that letter, she rang for the servant. "Ask my mother to excuse me," she said. "I have a headache."

When first Annie and then the older sister knocked that morning at Lucy's door, she snatched a book and looked up vaguely at them, fingering the leaves. When they did not repeat these visits, she knew that her mother had managed that too, along with her father's not coming. "Buddie's dead, and now Charlie's dead, I knew it," she thought, "I knew it all along. And here I am, everybody else in the family with something in life ahead of them. Well, why should I have?" she went on, in the way she had of dismissing herself as good for nothing.

She got up and went to sit on the edge of the bed. "If Valette had been in my place— Now don't be saying anything against Valette— If she'd loved him—you say that and I'll say if he'd loved her too, why not? Somebody ought to take a stick and kill me. As if Valette were not good as gold."

She caught sight of her face in the dressing-table opposite. She saw those lips so tight, but did not notice the wonderful wide eyes.

"Yes, and you go on screwing up your lips like that, somebody'll wring your neck. And just about right too."

There was a knock at the door into her sitting-room and

she caught up the book out of her chair and sat down.

"Good evenin', Miss Lucy. Dis here's a letter," the maid Fanny said, and went softly out of the room. It was a note from her mother.

"My dear Lucy,

Pardon this intrusion—this interruption—& at the same time that I crave pardon—I feel that I should have better liked to intrude *in person,* if I had not feared that the effort to admit me would have cost more than it would have availed —I have been with you in thought often today—wished to go to your room & sit this afternoon; but I had no reasonable pretext. More than this, no key to the present state of your feelings & might have wounded where I meant to bind up. On this day I would ask 'Why seek the living, the immortal, among the dead, he is not there.' May God comfort you. I fear for your health, that you will shatter your body, by the agitation of your mind. If I could do you any good, how gladly I would, but rather than make a false step, I stand still, & so it has ever been with me, during your days of affliction.

Your affectionate mother,

April 16, 1862.   AGNES McGEHEE.

"I will send Fanny presently to bring you a cup of tea. I think you had better."

Lucy held the letter flat between her palms and pressed the back of one hand to her cheek.

"My darling mother, saint on earth, writing me this, because—But I can't even throw my arms around her neck, or say—All I can say is, Mamma, how are you?—Mamma, can I do anything?—that's all."

"Don't let anybody do anything against my mother, or they'll have me to deal with," and with that thought she smiled, imperceptibly. It was only a twist of the lower lip, as she remembered that day when she was six and Belle had flown out at her mother over something about Mr. Thomas Bowdoin's calling so late, and Lucy had given her such a butt in the back that Belle went to bed for all one day and talked for weeks about her pains.

When Fanny returned Lucy had her wait for the tray while she drank a cup standing. Dusk began to fill the room as she sat there alone.

Tomorrow she would make herself go down. The same as every day. But they couldn't just believe she could never forgive them. One thing you had to grant—he loved his old father—Sister had said that loud enough, goodness knows, to hear from the hall upstairs. Not one single soul of them thought anything of him at all. "And I who did—" she said to herself, "I who did—and what came of that?"

There was a noise at the stableyard gate, and in the late twilight she could see Willian Veal there, giving some order to the boy who was bringing in the horses, sitting bareback on one and leading the two others. The boy with the horses disappeared within the gate, and she saw William going slowly down the walk to the quarters. She thought of him at Shiloh among the dead, that night, going over the dark field, stooping to feel every head till he found his young master; knowing Buddie's hair.

She closed her eyes with a convulsive sob, and when she opened them and sat looking, for no reason, toward the stableyard, leaning her chin on one of her hands, her elbow on the window sill, her whole body quiet, thinking of the old negro and of Edward lying there in the dark field among all those dead—at least not lost forever in some tent burned over him—can some one die like that, wounded and not able to move, die and nobody ever know anything about what happened, what he felt and wanted to say?—she saw Charles come through the gate. She saw even in the dusk that it was the roan, she knew well that step of the Arabian. Charlie sat a horse that way, as if nothing concerned him until the time came when he would ride like the wind. Then he was at the window, sitting there in the Spanish saddle with its high pommel; his long hands rested on it indifferently, one above the other, his eyes warm and indifferent, his mouth with those fine lines of dissipation to the sides of it. She knew that he was only riding off again, as he had done that night she saw him from this same window of her room.

"You think I don't know about you and women, Charlie Taliaferro? I'm not a fool," she said. No, she could not have said that, it was only in her thoughts. To say that sort of thing, she would have to be the sort of woman who appears at her worst when she is in love, and therefore cursed. "I may be that sort, I may be," she said to herself. "Charlie, you're so pale," she said, "white as wax. You loved Buddie, so you know they all want you to come on in the house. But I love you. You knew it. I believe Buddy knew it, too, when he went away. Yes—knew I loved you. I'll always love you." She huddled forward with a groan when she saw him put his hand to his side. "That night at Shiloh, lying in my blood, I remembered how you sang," he said, gazing sadly at her. No, she was saying that to herself; he had never cared about songs, not from her. Not from her at least, perhaps in New Orleans, in those houses down near the riverfront that young ladies were not supposed to hear about. But yet he must have spoken, for now he went on: "Then," said he, "what was it I cared about?" "You don't have to talk foolishness to me, Charlie, just because you hate to see my feelings hurt. In general you are cruel, but face to face, in little things, so tender—all the more dangerous!" He closed his eyes and seemed whispering to himself; all she made out was, "—Even if the tent had not been burnt, where, where even then, with that bullet through me, would I have gone to?"

So, here he was, to whom women had given everything, and then he died alone.

But she said to him quickly, "You could have come back to me. I'll never leave you."

"One thing you'll have to grant Charlie Taliaferro," he said, "he loved his old father."

His eyes looked up at her, insolent and faint, as he turned his head away, and she knew he was gone forever.

Lucy got up and went over to the door, opening it wide, and then suddenly, leaning her hands on the frame, let herself be half choked with sobs. Presently the sobs checked: and as she still remained there in the door, she heard her two sisters talking in her mother's room. Her mother was saying little, but Anne and Belle addressed her every now and then as they talked. She heard Mrs. Quitman then, brought up by the servant to join them. Mrs. Quitman, cheerily and meaning to divert them, was telling them fresh war news. Belle and Annie began to make inquiries. For example, what was this about the threat to Memphis, if Memphis fell?——

"But Papa, where's he?" Lucy asked herself, "my father?"

She went back to the washstand and felt the water cool and startling over her eyes.

"I was just thinking about you, daughter," Hugh McGehee said, looking up at her but not raising his chin from his breast, as Lucy, having discovered him in the library, closed the door softly behind her. "Yes, sir, just thinkin' in here by myself. We've lost Edward, my son, and—in case I never mention it again—I know for you, daughter, there's been also —also— Perhaps we'll all know some day. Sit down here by me."

She leaned forward and pressed her cheek to his brow. As

she noticed the handkerchief crumpled in his hand, she felt
tears blinding her eyes.

"Must take up your singin' again now, Lucy."

"I will."

"So sit down here by me for a while."

XXXIX

"I AM writing," Duncan's letter began, "on a sheet of General Stuart's own letter paper with the monogram at the top; it is run through the blockade for him from London. You look at this and see that it goes with the plume he wears in his hat, the white gauntlets, the gold spurs and the banjo player. And at that he's the greatest cavalry leader in the world." Duncan went on to say that General Stuart had seen him writing home on a newspaper margin and had made him take a piece of his own stationery. "I do this," he said, "because your buttons are so bright," and laughed that laugh that everybody in the cavalry knew, even those who thought him high-handed, ordering gentlemen's sons about.

From then on Duncan's letter told about the S. S. *Marblehead* and Stuart; it was the first time in history anybody ever heard of cavalry whipping a gunboat. The S. S. *Marblehead* started two cutters ashore to fight the skirmishers they saw firing at them. Major Pelham, hidden in the wood, opened up with his little horse-howitzer; the cutters turned back, and the S. S. *Marblehead* steamed away with one of them upset. The stores had been only partly burnt and, beside 10,000 rifles, there had been such luxuries as nobody had ever seen with an army: champagne, ice, cigars, and a great box of white-kid gloves, which a private found and sent off to Richmond, to be sold for all those weddings of Confederate officers. And they found a carload of blue overcoats, which Martin's Mississippians had on next day when the U. S. S. *Monitor* saw them and thought nothing of it, and so sent some of the crew ashore. The crew was bagged.

This news Middleton went flying down to the quarters to tell Duncan's mammy.

Mrs. Carroll, whose son was also in the Virginia Cavalry, drove out soon afterward with a letter that spoke of the effect that General Lee had made after this on the morale of the Northern generals sent against him; though it was true, as Francis' mother said, that from what he wrote, you would never guess the Confederates had lost a man since the war began. How different, too, her son's letters were from this of Duncan's that Mrs. Bedford read to her! Let Duncan tell it, it was all as if they were on a big hunt or running horse-races. Which was true, Mrs. Bedford said, even with the hot summer weather raging; in a July like this even your hair was hot on your head. And it was true in spite of this war of hatred that everybody knew had arisen throughout the South because of General Pope's having started a new kind of campaign. Up to this time on both sides there had been humanity and even a certain chivalry in the Virginia fighting. But Pope's army began to live off the country, to arrest people, insult, and take citizens for hostages. The news of it had gone over the South and everywhere new recruits sprang up. Of course, if Duncan wrote at all—the rascal—it was apt to clap your ears with things like this of the cavalry with the gunboat, or the blue overcoats, or how General Stuart picked Duncan out to send off on some chase as wild as an Indian. "I declare, sometimes I think General Stuart's about as bad as Duncan is," she said.

"The proof of the pudding is in the eating, which is what Francis thinks," said Mrs. Carroll. "Jeb Stuart wins victories, look at everything you hear! Otherwise, I daresay Stuart would seem reckless. Francis writes me he sings and goes on as they march, that Sweeny of his playing the banjo, and then holds you up to scratch, you've got to be a bold rider and keep discipline or you are in disgrace, and so 'tis."

"I expect General Stuart knows what he's doing," said Mrs. Bedford.

"So Francis writes, you judge by the fruits, Mamma, he says."

"The feathers on his riders are gone, the gold braid, the jackboots and finery. They've just got their blooded horses left, Duncan says, and they are thin as rails, and bellies blown out, I imagine."

"Tell about the oats," Middleton said, looking from his aunt to Mrs. Carroll with such shining eyes that even such a stiff lady bent over and kissed his little brow. He had got back from Tildy's cabin. "Will you, please, Aunt Sallie?"

"I don't know anything about any oats, you tell Mrs. Carroll yourself, Captain."

"Duncan had a fight with a farmer because the farmer wouldn't sell him any oats for his Arabian. So Duncan knocked his head off. Because Prince has to have oats." Middleton glanced at his aunt.

"Now, there's a Homeric account of a battle, surely," she said. "Yes, oats, just as little boys have to have sweet-milk. But tell Mrs. Carroll Duncan had offered the farmer double for his oats, it was in the Bull Run Mountains."

"Duncan offered double for the oats," said the little boy, gravely, "in the Bull Run Mountains."

"That's the way it was," Mrs. Bedford said, and began to tell Mrs. Carroll how the soldiers went on when they raided General Pope's stores. They had been living on corn and green apples, so no wonder they ate like mad and rode off with hams stuck on their bayonets. In the midst of the account she paused. It was all true, Duncan had written in that brief style of his about it; and their cousin Charles Marshall, General Lee's aide-de-camp, who was reliable and plain as an old shoe, had told of it in a letter. But life entertained her so much that she often felt, as she told things, that she was lying.

At that time Malcolm Bedford had been gone from home three months. He was in the army of General Joseph E.

Johnston. His letters had dealt with two things. He had his doubts about General Pemberton, who had been given too much command in Mississippi and would cost the South dear yet. He gave his wife accounts of conversations with General Johnston, whose scholarship and elegance of address often reminded Malcolm of what he had once pursued and then later done nothing about. "I sometimes think," he wrote, "that in our class, planters' sons, like me, we have got into the habit of thinking life was just to entertain us, riding around looking for pleasure, rounds of visits, rounds of conversation. And yet these are wise things. But sometimes I think of all this. When you send the shirts mark the name on the tails and may I trouble you to put in the bundle the Reverend Lawrence Sterne's *Sentimental Journey,* the passage about the goat reminded me of a certain generalissimo; and also enclose the copy of Lucretius. We have been talking of it, but I couldn't recall the passage about the battle wounds, and I did myself and my family very little credit when I referred to what Lucretius says of our father the sky casting the rain drops into the earth, & the bright crops arising, & the trees growing, & heavy with fruit. There was a time when I had my Latin, long ago at the university, but I believe now I shall be very sorry at it."

She knew what the Sterne would be. There was the place where Tristram met the idiot tending the goat, and the poor idiot sat looking at him and the goat, back and forth from one to the other, and Tristram says, with the tears running down his face, "Do you see any resemblance?" Some way or other this passage was going to apply to General Pemberton.

She looked in the Lucretius and very easily found the passage about the wounds, for the page was turned down, Malcolm treated all books any which way. It was where Lucretius says that a man usually falls toward a wound, and the blood jets out in the direction of the blow, and if he is close by drenches the enemy. What Latin she had left from her father's tutoring was enough to make out this simple place. The other, however, was too much and she let it go.

> Postremo, pereunt imbres: ubi eos pater æther
> In gremium matris terrai praecipitavit.
> At nitidæ surgunt fruges. ramique vivescunt
> Arboribus; crescunt ipsæ faetuque gravantur.

What the meaning was she had not Latin enough to know, only a hint of it. But the style of it, the music—or however you wanted to put that—seemed to her to be Malcolm's. Yes, if you knew Darlin' well.

XL

At Portobello during this first half of the year 1863 life went on very much as it had always done. Two or three of the negroes had run away from the quarters and those with children had been sent to the plantation farther away in Concordia Parish. Twelve of the house servants, all women, remained. In much of the country that had fallen into Federal hands, slaves that had run away or been seized either were with the army companies or were collected into camps or in plantation houses under guard. But in Natchez itself, down by the lower town the runaway negroes were established in a kind of stockade, under the eye of a Federal gunboat; Natchez itself was as yet not occupied. The stockades were near the edge of the river, and those who died of the crowding and the epidemics breaking out among them were buried in the sand of the river bars. On the Portobello plantations, with negroes leaving and uncertain management, the working of the land had dropped to a third.

Over this whole part of the country the unrest among the

negroes was growing. On January 2nd President Lincoln
had made the Emancipation Proclamation. Since then agents
had been travelling among the plantation hands, who now
heard of Lincoln's plan to enlist 100,000 negroes in the
Northern Army. It was during the siege of Vicksburg that
the first negroes were enlisted in the Federal Army. The
agents did not spread the information that General Sherman
had done this against his will and had declared that as soldiers
the negroes were a joke, nor that General Sherman sent out
to corral negroes all over the country and held them prisoners,
to prevent their being used in trench digging or felling trees
in the Confederate blockade of creeks and rivers.

There had always been a sharp division, however, between
domestic slaves and slaves under plantation overseers, and
Mrs. Bedford handled her servants as if affairs were the
same as always. She saw the look in their eyes sometimes,
and knew that they were thinking and saying things among
themselves, things they did not tell her of. She even suspected
that they might have some plot hatching. But she let one day
after another run its course nevertheless.

She went about her life, keeping the garden planted, with
the help of Uncle Thornton, Mammy's husband. In the garden
the Tom Thumb peas, the corn, okra, potatoes still flourished,
and the melon patch was as large as ever. To keep the
negroes from stealing the melons and to protect them from
foraging soldiers who might come by, Sallie Bedford went
out herself early in the mornings and sprinkled flour on the
gashes she cut in the melons. She did the same with the meat
in the smokehouse. The negroes were afraid to touch anything, and to the soldiers who asked if the meat was poisoned
she said, "You can judge for yourselves, gentlemen."

Up to this time so far as concerned the Federal soldiers
that appeared around Natchez, it was only a beginning. At
Portobello a panel had been kicked out of a door that some-

body forgot to leave open; Silas had led the way to the stables and the horses, all but the Arabian mare hidden in the woods, had been taken, leaving only a mule that the Indian owned. The rest of the molestation had been for food and supplies. The family could still buy tea and coffee and medicines in the town, though at blockade prices, tea $30 the pound, a barrel of flour $300. Mrs. Bedford tore up old silk dresses, carded them, spun that into thread and knitted stockings for herself. She had resolved, whatever else, that she would not give up silk stockings.

The children were now without the governess and in Aunt Sophie's charge. They had no lessons save those Valette gave them, mostly a song on the piano now and hugs and kisses.

Sophie ran things her own way. She slept in the room with the children, gave them milk and mush before they went to sleep, woke them up before it was light, put on their dressing-sacks, set them by the fire and gave each a sweet potato roasted in the ashes. In the ceiling was a trap door to the loft under the roof. She told them that up there lived old Raw Head and Bloody Bones. If one of them nodded around sleepy in the morning or stayed awake after being put to bed, Aunt Sophie would say that Raw Head or Bloody Bones was coming. Sometimes she turned her eyelids back and looked in the door from the next room with a gray blanket over her head, and Frances, whose imagination was very literal, hid herself under the covers, her teeth chattering. Sometimes, during the day, the children in their turn put on sheets and went down as ghosts to Aunt Sophie's cabin and she pretended to be terrified. She would moan and groan and cry out, "Look at them hants! Go 'way from here, ghos'es!"

There were visitors to Portobello as of old, but not so many. And on Easter Sunday Valette had sung divinely at St. Mary's. They drove home in the carriage from Montrose, where there were still horses to be had.

"What are you smiling at, My Dumplin'?" Valette asked, not taking her hand.

"Was My Dumplin' smiling?"

"You know you were. You chuckled is what you did."

"Well, honey, I was thinking of Agnes McGehee. I reckon she thinks it's for the saints that lovely voice rose with such sweet tones of passion. 'Twould be just like your Aunt Agnes to think you were singing of the Resurrection."

The kind, clear eyes twinkled as they looked at the young face. The sacred history meant very little to her; she would have liked Valette to speak of Duncan, so that they could praise him. Valette did not look at her; she said only, "Maybe Aunt Agnes would." To herself she said, "You don't know everything, My Dumplin'." She felt a wave of resentment pass over her, and that between the two of them, Agnes McGehee in this case might be the wiser; for she herself, with her lover in her soul and her soul arising unto him, believed too that she was singing of the Redeemer arising from the dark grave.

In July of that year Mr. Frank Surget at Clifton gave the first of those ill-fated parties for Federal officers which in the end destroyed him.

He sent his barouche to Portobello, since Mrs. Bedford and Valette could not both ride the mule, and since, also, he and Mrs. Bedford were old friends on grounds more than commonly agreeable to him, which was flowers and shrubs. The gardens at Clifton were so famous that tourists from the North as far as Boston knew that the boat stopped at Natchez long enough for Clifton to be seen.

The Federal colonel, an Indiana gentleman with rings under his eyes, cared as little for the portraits by the great Benjamin West as did Mrs. Bedford. She hated them because of their pompous air, a quality that she had trained herself to endure, since she was obliged to, in her father, but nowhere else. They were soon out of the house and Mr. Surget was speaking of his experiments with the land, circular plowing and horizontal furrows. He promised to show the colonel the manuscripts he had of Sir William Dunbar's, the friend of Jefferson's, who had commissioned geological surveys of the Natchez country from him. The colonel praised the Egyptian lotuses, which stood high up from the water in full flower, with their curious heavy fragrance, and beneath them in the water of the pool, the stars were reflected.

"There's a story for you," the host said, as the colonel leaned over to see into the centre of a lotus flower. The lotus seed had been sent from Africa to his father by an ex-slave named Prince. He told the colonel the story of a man who, after years as a slave, wrote a letter in Arabic to the consul at Tangier, speaking of his rank among the Timboo tribe, his capture in battle and his sale. The consul sent the letter to President Adams, who, in turn, had Henry Clay inquire for what he could be bought. The owner presented the slave with his freedom; diverse Natchez citizens raised a sum to purchase his wife and a Moorish costume, and the two set off by way of Washington for Morocco.

"Where the sun teems life teems, my father used to say; he was a traveller. And your father?" said the colonel, turning to Mrs. Bedford.

"My father was something of a continent in himself," she said, laughing, "six foot eight." She would have liked to say more about her father to this man who was by contrast so restless and agreeable; but she could think up very little besides Latin phrases and stately principles from physics and chemistry.

"Meanwhile, here we are," Mr. Surget said, as they reached the steps. "We must be gay, if you'll help us."

"*Dulce est desipere in loco*," she said, suddenly remembering the Horace quotation that her father never tired of quoting when he was tired of himself. "My father, sir," she added in a mischievous tone that made the sharp little colonel chuckle, "translated that: 'it is pleasant to relax when a suitable occasion arises.'"

At Portobello, it was all changed when Malcolm Bedford unexpectedly came back. Then the war was brought home to them.

By the close of the year 1862 the Vicksburg Campaign was well under way; Malcolm was transferred from his Jackson battalion to Vicksburg, where he was one of the officers in charge of the Yazoo River blockades. He directed the felling of trees and the placing of batteries at points where the invaders might pass. There was rain, the creeks and rivers rose. Even the Yankees, contending with the overflows and mud, made jests about it, calling themselves beavers. At the end of May he wrote that he was suffering from a dysentery ravaging the camp, and hoped for a leave of absence.

When Malcolm Bedford came home one morning, riding out from Natchez on the mule with Dock, the Indian, walking alongside, Frances, running out at the front door to meet him, threw her little arms about his neck and burst into tears. Her mother and every one of the others had to kiss him with the child in his arms. She would not look again at his gray, hollow face, and whenever they tried to take her away she shrieked and buried her face closer in his shoulder, sobbing.

XLI

As is always true in wars, the people who pay the cost know little of the issues behind a war. The long stretch of its general meaning, the roots of its emotions people know. They wage the battles around their own loves and passions and interests. As for the South and this war in which it found itself engaged, it would be true that in the end, when there had been time enough for this to happen, the loves and dreams behind the war would emerge in the figures of men like Lee and Jeb Stuart and Benjamin Hill and others. In the meantime, the war's fortunes would be directed by its leaders, by politicians, by movements of cause and event, such as European recognition of the Confederacy, the demand for cotton, and unity among the single States.

Near to the war it was natural, therefore, that the family at Portobello should think of it in terms of people; they read the newspapers which shrilled and declaimed, but got their best notion of events north of them from letters that their friend, Doctor Gholson, sent from Holly Springs. He wrote of the occupation of Memphis under General Sherman's governorship, and of the cavalry raid on Holly Springs, when Grant's military stores were taken or destroyed. After his base of supplies was captured, Grant learned the business of foraging. In this rich Mississippi country he found that his army could live twenty days on five days' rations issued. This changed the whole face of the campaign in that region, along the Mississippi.

From Doctor Gholson and from letters the McGehees wrote, came stories of Mary Cherry's exploits around the seat of war; and Mrs. Bedford, trying to entertain Malcolm during the long hours on the porch, told him stories of them.

"Miss Mary has commandeered the Boones' horse and buggy from Hernando, and goes in and out of the Yankee lines constantly with boots and shoes and Lord knows what supplies tied under her hoops. And they let her pass, Darlin'."

"Napoleon said the fear of the Cossacks kept dead battalions on their feet." He laughed outright at the thought; Miss Mary had always amused him more than she did his wife.

"And another time she carried stores of quinine under her hoops."

"Good, and nothing is more needed in our camps than quinine."

"But the pickets let her pass."

"Now that shows one of two things: either their lack of courage or her lack of fascination."

But Malcolm was already too tired to listen to the story of how they had stuffed a dead mule with medical supplies and got permission to drag him out of the city. Mrs. Bedford tried to get up some queries as to how the stuffing was managed, but he did not open his eyes to hear any more or to answer.

On another day Mrs. Bedford tried the subject again and brought out a letter Miss Mary had written some months before from Oxford. She had gone just before the time General Grant took up his headquarters there in the late autumn.

Mrs. Bedford began reading the letter.

"'After Grant had made himself master of Oxford, he endeavored to oblige the citizens to—' But we can skip that, eh?"

"I should say so. It's that trick of Mary Cherry's trying to begin like Plutarch, or like some orator she heard trying to begin like Plutarch."

"Then here 'tis," said Mrs. Bedford, with a chuckle. 'I have not spoken with the Grants, of course, but everybody has seen them. They are at Colonel Josiah Brown's big house. At Holly Springs there is a house already called the house where Grant took the piano, and here Mrs. Grant goes about looking for finery. But there is a young lady here, who lives not far away from Colonel Brown's, who was about to plight her troth to a certain young Holloway when the war began, and had her trousseau ready. One day recently she heard such a hubbub upstairs that she went up to see, and there was Mrs. Grant quarrelling with a private bluecoat about the trousseau linen and embroidery in a dresser drawer. She was on her knees before the drawer and the soldier was standing by her. He claimed he had a right to the things because he had been the one who found them, and she said she had a right to them because she was the general's wife.

" 'Says she doesn't know how they settled it between them.

" 'I possess a friend here in Nancy Thompson, a most spirited young miss of sixteen. In her home some of Grant's men ordered her to play "Yankee Doodle," and she scorned to comply, they tore up an Aeolian harp and a piano. I was there at the first when they startled the town by pouring in in large numbers. Their first target was a little negro boy who was perched in a big apple tree at the Neilson place, the Neilsons say he dropped to the ground like an apple falling. And Quit Wilkins, son of Captain Wilkins, standing at a woodpile watching them pass was shot in the leg, and will be a cripple for life; he is fifteen. There is a good deal of smashing, but I tell my Oxford friend just to wait, we shall have worse later on. Was it not Shakespeare who wrote, "Cry havoc and let loose the dogs of war"? God willing, I hope to join you as soon as possible.

Your most obedient servant in the Lord,

MARY CHERRY.' "

Mrs. Bedford folded the letter. "Well, here it is some months gone and the Lord hasn't willed it so far. But we're bound to admit Miss Mary is a fiery one. You remember, Darlin', what they say your mother told that old circuit rider who stopped and said the Lord had revealed to him that he should stay in her house? She said when did the Lord tell you this? And he said last night, in a dream, and she said, 'Well, this morning the Lord told me he'd changed his mind, and for you to go somewhere else.'"

One day late in June the porch was wet from showers and Malcolm had been brought into the small parlor, with the red damask. He lay on the sofa sometimes dozing, sometimes watching the parrot on the gallery outside the window, smiling at the way the bird leaned about on her perch. The parrot kept turning her head this way and that. If there was a gust of wind or leaves, she would call Mrs. Shaw. "Mrs. Shaw!" Then the parrot would put her head in the window and peer around the room.

"Old Billy's bird is lonesome," said Malcolm.

"It's more than likely it's the chillun Polly misses, but not more than we do."

"So Bill McChidrick just lay down and died?"

She nodded her head without getting on that subject. Uncle Billy had been dead for months. They had found him lying doubled up on his side on the cabin floor. The negroes were afraid to go near him, and only peered in at the door. There were conjure bags under the steps. When Mrs. Bedford leaned over and called to him he did not open his eyes or speak. He did not take the medicine, or pay any attention when she asked if he would like to be put on his bed, but lay there like a dumb animal, with now and then a moan. He was like that for three days and then one morning was found dead. Sam and Ernest, the carpenters, made a coffin

of boards from an old shed, and Mrs. Bedford sent some of
the negroes along for a burial at Mingo Church.

After Billy McChidrick's death they gave the parrot to
old French Nancy to care for. The parrot's cage hung outside
her door, from a crêpe myrtle; and Big Dave, the colored
overseer, threatened to kill it because it had learned to call
him in a voice he could not tell from Ole Miss calling, "Here,
Dave, come back here! Dave!" The children when they liked
brought the parrot on to the gallery.

"My stars, look yonder!" cried Mrs. Bedford, and sprang
up so suddenly that the parrot hunched down between her
wings. "There's a carriage and there's Miss Mary Cherry
shakin' herself out." She hurried into the library and out by
the south porch.

"Dear Brother Malcolm," Mary Cherry said, as she came
into the room first. "Well, sir, well, sir!" Malcolm could
hear already Dock taking the trunks up the back stairs. "I say,
well, we're not goin' to let the bluebellies take Vicksburg, eh?
Ah now, Sister Sarah's pinchin' my arm, but I'm a woman
speaks her mind."

Malcolm was half way through a glass of toddy and took
more interest in what was going on around him than he
would have done an hour before.

"Welcome, Miss Mary," he said, holding up his hand a
little, while she glanced at him sternly as if he should know
better than exert himself. "I see Mrs. Bedford looking at me
to see if I'm strong enough to be receiving company. I am.
I'm tolerable enough today, in fact. Pray sit down."

Miss Mary took the armchair near the head of his sofa. As
he and Sallie Bedford looked at Mary Cherry, Miss Mary
looked at them.

"I'm damned," thought Malcolm. "Yes, sir, I'm damned."

Mary Cherry had always been a veteran from a cause,
however vague. Now she seemed truly one. "She looks more

battle-scarred than ever," he thought, "and there's more of that air of gunpowder clinging about her nostrils than ever."

"Well," said Miss Mary, "it's a good thing the Lord sent the shower, laid the dust for me. Colonel Harrod sent me out in his carriage. He's been in Panola on government affairs, he accompanied me on the cars. Here, Dock—" she called to the Indian, who was crossing the gallery outside—after so much managing of blockades, bandages, and other matters, she was bossier than ever—"Dock, come take this glass for your marster."

"But I'm not through," said Malcolm. "I want the rest of it."

"Well, then drink it, Malcolm, and let's get through with it."

Malcolm winked at his wife. "By God, if she hasn't absorbed some of the quinine."

"Very well," Mary Cherry turned to Dock, who had come to the door. "Get out. He wants to keep it."

"While we're on the subject of buryin' us all," said Malcolm, "I'd as lief agree, when it comes to you, we'll have to bury you deep, Miss Mary. I remember my father use to tell—he knew General Sam Houston when he was here recruiting in the '30's—that years later in a letter, Houston said that after the battle of San Jacinto an old lady threatened to sue him because some Mexicans were left unburied in her field, and her cows gnawing at the bones made the milk taste like red pepper."

At the moment Miss Mary did not feel like losing her temper, so she gave a sort of husky titter and started to match the story: "Aye, on one occasion—" The loud voice stopped. On the gallery, behind Miss Mary, the parrot, who had been silent ever since she entered and unnoticed by her, began to make the sound of somebody seasick.

"Great Scott!" Miss Mary cried, squaring in one jerk around in her chair, with her good eye on the bird; while the parrot in turn, now quite recovered, twisted her head silently to eye

Miss Mary. "Don't tell me you've got that abomination still!"

Malcolm lay there chuckling, but Mrs. Bedford hastened to soothe the old woman. The bird was a fool and since Billy McChidrick died, the cage hangs in the crêpe myrtle by French Nancy's cabin. "And every time the wind blows the parrot remembers the sound she must have heard on the boat they brought her in: people seasick."

The parrot began more seasick noises and Mrs. Bedford called to Dock to take her away.

"Now, Darlin', she said, "you try to sleep a little bit. Shall we go up, Miss Mary?"

"Aye. I'll see after my trunks. Whyn't you drink up your toddy, Brother Bedford?"

"Tout de suite, madame." He emptied the glass and felt it warm him, and smiled to see the look of encouragement in his wife's eyes. Then he looked tauntingly at the craggy figure standing above him.

"If a man drinks not his sack,
What becomes of the Zodiac?"

"Now, Malcolm Bedford, you just imagine for yourself the sky full of twins and fish and so forth, and a goat and a bull."

"The poet says the bull opens the year with golden horns, Miss Mary, and fine Latin it is."

"I take that to mean like some stuffed dude opening a cotillion. I'll wager I could get it open for them."

"Get what open?"

"Why—I disremember—something they had to get a bull to open for them. What was it?"" She peered at Malcolm, folding her arms again.

"The year, Miss Mary."

"Aye, of course, of course. I was thinking of those detestable Yankees."

That night when Sallie Bedford was leaning over him, Malcolm held tight to her hand, murmuring, "Get her out."

She did not hear him distinctly. "Get who?"

"Old Mary Cherry."

"You want her to go?"

"Yes. Ask Hugh McGehee to take her there. I won't have her with her big bossy mouth of hate."

"We can do that easily. I'll send Dock over early tomorrow with a note and Agnes will write to invite her there. Can't you imagine, Darlin', that pale grey note paper of Agnes', with the faint scent of geranium, and Miss Mary sniffing at this fancy business! But I'll have her off before sundown, that I promise you."

"All I say is get her out," Malcolm said, not answering her smile. "With her mouth full of hate, hate."

She took hold of his hands, which were twisted convulsively together. "Of course, Darlin'. You won't have to have her here."

"It's not what it's about."

"What's about what?"

He gazed at her with a hurt look in his eyes for not understanding. "You understand when you want to—and yet you say what's about what. What else could I mean but what this war's about. What the war's about. It's about——"

"I know, I know," she said.

"Then read me the poem we cut out of *The Gazette;* that will tell you. Will tell you what the war's about."

She got the clipping and holding it in her right hand, the candle in her left, read it to him.

> Oh, my dear land that I have loved so well,
> With your rich fruit and blessed rain,
> If for your sake I have died
> I shall not have died in vain.

My own country, my own dear land,
From you I was born and you were born of me,—
I shall not have died in vain.—

The voice broke and stopped reading.

"Darlin', that's enough. Ain't that enough for now?"

Without opening his eyes he nodded his head.

"I don't think it's such a good poem," she went on in her honest voice. "It just makes you sad."

He took the paper out of her trembling hand and thrust it under his pillow, frowning and not looking at her. She rose and went blindly over to the window. "So tomorrow we'll be much better, Darlin'."

XLII

WHEN Malcolm Bedford first came home to Portobello the children made little vows to take good care of him. They would bring him water, they said, they would be his messengers. They would be quiet, show him what they were playing, everything indeed that he asked of them. His wife put him in the hickory rocking-chair on the north porch where the sun spared him: and Middleton, the little nephew, kept bringing him cold water from the two cisterns in the court with the granite tops. The little girls put on their dolls' finest dresses and a hat on each and brought them to visit their father. He whittled a doll for them out of cedar wood and they made a wig of red yarn and called him General Sherman. They could hardly wait to duck this doll in a pan of water.

"Shot cannon balls at your old father," Malcolm said to them, "hurry and drown him. I must see that; I'm all in a swivet."

"What's a swivet?" Frances asked.

"Can't say, I'm sure, never having seen one."

Hearing his tone she asked no more. He himself had said he was in a swivet. "But he's all in a swivet," she thought gently, stroking the thin hand, "I believe he just shuts his eyes and gets in."

This cheerful mood did not outlast the first three or four days at home. The June heat spread everywhere, with dull air, heavy and sickening from moisture. The nights were hot, and toward morning rain would fall, after which the sun rising brought only smothering days. Malcolm began to forget this new comfort of his home and the fresh linen next his skin, his clean bed, and the refreshment he had felt at the change. He began to brood on what the men he had left at Vicksburg were going through. He heard the silence at the stable-lot, where the saddle horses and the carriage horses had been and Duncan's colts. When his wife or the children were out of his sight, he thought of them with nothing but sadness; and tears, partly from weakness, would come into his eyes. But when the children came out on the gallery with him, he found them noisy and tiring. He saw that they too were tired of attending him so many hours out of the day. He was quickly vexed with them, and noticed the look of surprise in their eyes when he spoke sharply. His wife saw it all and said nothing; she felt heavy in her heart; she knew there was nothing to say; she had to wait. One day when he saw Middleton stealing off to the peach trees, where his aunt had forbidden him to go for fear he would founder himself, like a little colt with green corn, Malcolm set the collie, Flora, on the boy, meaning only to frighten him out of it. But Frances, seeing the dog nosing Middleton and nipping at his heels, began to scream at her father, "Mean, mean, letting that dog eat a poor little orphan!" Once Malcolm would have laughed or would have soothed her; but now he only looked at Frances with raised eyebrows, and shutting his eyes indifferently, leaned back against the headrest on his chair. His wife, making one of her rounds, saw the whole thing. She gave instructions to Aunt Sophie to keep the children as much as possible away from the north porch. Mr. Bedford was not well enough, she said, sadly, as if it were fate, to enjoy having them.

Malcolm had spoken little to the children about the war where he had been. Only in the morning when he felt fresher he would tell them some story. But now at night when his wife had put him to bed, he began to talk more and more to her, and she began to see more fully what the war meant to him. It had brought him back to something he had been when she first knew him, and perhaps before she knew him. She saw that the suspense of the Vicksburg siege was always at the back of Malcolm's mind. She herself had been busy with the children and with the managing of the place. Somebody had to do that, for children must eat—and now, talking with her husband in the solitude of the bedroom sometimes past midnight, she understood more profoundly what it meant if Vicksburg fell. Vicksburg was the last Confederate stronghold on the Mississippi. Its fall meant that the North would possess the river from St. Louis to New Orleans; that the Confederate territory would be cut in half, the eastern and western; that the Northern army now in this country would be freed to be used elsewhere in the war against the South. If the Southern leaders were not mad, Malcolm Bedford said over and over, they would know that the fall of Vicksburg would mean defeat and the end of the war. "No use trying to speak of the ruin that would follow," he said to his wife. "Oh, no use speaking of it."

"Darlin', don't put your hands up to your head like that," she said, and turned away to find something she could do about the room.

The famous Vicksburg Campaign had begun hastily and

half on the impulse. McClernand, once a congressman and now a major-general, had visited President Lincoln in October of the year before, and had come away with a paper that granted him the authority for a Vicksburg expedition. To be ahead of this new rival, Grant and Sherman, with the help of the admiral's gunboats, hurried up their plans to be the first on the ground. Grant had to be present in person, because, through being in command of the Army of Tennessee, he was the one officer of higher rank than McClernand. In late December the troops in Memphis and north Mississippi started south. Before the end of spring in 1863 the Vicksburg bluffs showed fortifications that were complete, two hundred feet above the river, difficult for guns to reach. On the north of the town lay the Yazoo, the creeks and swamps spreading out for miles. To the east there were hills and gullies, and farther on, Jackson, the State capital. This approach was first tried, Sherman with 3200 men up the Yazoo River, Grant from the land. It was poor strategy, for the two forces were not able to combine. The raid of Van Dorn on Holly Springs, with its Federal supply base, caused Grant to retreat northward and Sherman lost two thousand men at the Vicksburg bluffs. McClernand arrived at New Year's, and hastened down to take over the command. Gunboats might run past the Confederate cannon on the bluffs above, but it was clear that the cost in men made transports impractical. The army was set to digging canals and building bridges. Grant held on with the tenacity and bludgeoning that, as all agreed, was the core of his military gift. They cut the levee to channel the Mississipi waters into the Yazoo for the gunboats. Trees felled to block passage were at the crucial points, sharpshooters hidden on the banks pursued them; the gunboats in the hard streams were battered, smokestacks knocked off. The admiral tried retreat, but found trees felled now to the rear of him. He would have blown up his boats had not Sherman appeared on the banks against the Confederates. The second canal, cutting across the curve in the Mississippi, was drowned by the rising water. The campaign narrowed down to the problem of transportation.

It was at this time that Malcolm Bedford was transferred to Vicksburg, to direct work on the creeks and bayous. On the night of April 16 he stood on the bluffs and saw the passage of the seven gunboats, three steamers and the barge fleet. The night was dark, but the houses set afire along the shore lighted the whole river. He heard the guns from the fortifications and saw their flashes across the sky, and spurts from the cannon. On the river, columns and spouts of water went up when shots missed their aim. The transports kept to the far side of the river. One of them took fire and was sunk. In the sharp light from the burning houses Malcolm saw the small black shadow on the water where the crew was putting off: then he looked down and saw the dark shadow of his feet on the ground. Once past the batteries the business of the fleet had been to transport the Northern armies to a landing south of Vicksburg, and from there for the first time to begin the actual siege.

The morning of June 20, a week after his coming home on leave, Malcolm did not get out of bed to go downstairs to the porch. He had tossed about all night; and when his wife asked how he was, he opened his eyes only to look at her and say that his throat was dry. She put her hand in the collar of his nightshirt and saw that he had fever; and Doctor Martin later the same day pronounced it typhoid. She watched the doctor's strong square fingers pressing on the sick man's pulse, then saw him lean down to listen to the heart. "Well," he said, standing up and drawing the sheet back to cover Malcolm's chest, "you are, naturally, in a very weak condition. But we'll have you up in no time"; and by the tone of his voice Sallie knew he meant that whatever was most agreeable might as well be said, since the case was hopeless.

Malcolm began to curse at the heat of the bed, and begged for the trundle bed that could be hung from the hooks set for it in the ceiling. It would be near the window and could be swung to and fro like a hammock. When Dock and Uncle Thornton had brought the bed and Malcolm was settled on it, with the sheet pulled up only to cover his feet, because he hated the sight of naked feet, the doctor laughed. "Camp life teaches us makeshifts, eh, Mac? I'd never thought of trundle-bed breezes." He was stacking the powders that he had been putting into squares of paper cut with the gold knife on his watch chain. "And you'll be back in Vicksburg and standing by General Pemberton's side before you know it."

Malcolm struck the mattress with his clenched fist. "General Pemberton!" he said in a weak and petulant voice like a child's.

She began to fan him. "That's all right, Darlin', of course Pemberton's not fit to command Vicksburg. Of course, of course. Doctor Martin knows that too."

Malcolm scowled at the doctor. "He's a cursed fool is what General Pemberton is—with his liverish skin and black, flat eyes like a dumb beast's. Mark my word!" The scowl stayed but the eyes wrinkled shut and a slight convulsion like a chill shook the lean body.

"No need to call me unless something special turns up," Doctor Martin said, and then, pulling himself together, "Unless, that is to say, you want to look at a handsome man."

The children and Valette were sent over to Monmouth where only Mrs. Quitman, Sallie Bedford's most loyal friend in all Natchez, was left and there was plenty of room. At Portobello full summer was on everything: the apricots and figs dropped ripe to the ground with a squash and thud; the white lilies and the lemon lilies were in bloom, the roses, verbenas and heliotrope. All day in the warm sun the blue jays and blackbirds were singing, and day or night the mocking birds, sometimes harshly, sometimes like flute notes.

During the days that followed, Malcolm, when he was awake, kept talking to his wife of the siege. He told her of the marches and deployings, the assault on the parapets. General Joseph E. Johnston was at Jackson and that fellow Pemberton was left to hold Vicksburg. "And there's nothin' to him," he swore. "Don't I know him! You just reach out and put your hand through him." Johnston sent Pemberton word not under any circumstances to allow himself to be shut up in Vicksburg. Come out and strike Grant. But Pemberton was one of Jefferson Davis' favorites, and it was Jefferson Davis who had ruined the South. Nevertheless notwithstanding, Malcolm said, the general assault had not amounted yet to a row of pins; and Grant had settled down to a siege, to starve them out if he could. That was three weeks ago at the beginning of June. Grant turned his men loose to forage the country.

"The damned lot of them are living like lords, I tell you, Sarah Bedford, on the fat of the land."

"Oh, Darlin', don't fret and go on, the South's not ruined yet."

"If Vicksburg falls 'tis. General Johnston is a Greek scholar and a French scholar, and I used to sit with him sometimes and figure astronomical equations. It brought back to me my old studies at Virginia. Even through camp he'd ride at a gallop, said his father had taught to ride that way. Fine gentleman, great soldier. But that man of Jeff Davis's, I mean that damned General Pemberton, with his yellow face!"

His wife sat by him and listened, laughing when she could. Sometimes to side with Malcolm she too swore, as she begged him to take a little of the cordial mixed with cold water that Dock had brought from the cistern. It was the *Parfait Amour* that Rose had always made. "Drink it, Darlin', for my sake. You know what 'tis. Rose petals, full blown, for the perfume, and syrup poured over, and stand a day and night and then strain and then twelve tablespoonfuls of alcohol, but before you bottle it, toss in two handfuls dark red petals, to——"

He beckoned feebly and she leaned her head down. "Let's look at you. When I'm dead don't cry this way. I know you're crying. So now you see."

"Two handfuls of dark red rose petals to give the color. Now, Darlin', drink it for me. You know I'd do anything for you."

"Then you drink it," he said.

He tried to smile, but the cracked lips only showed the front upper teeth, yellow from the iron tonic they gave him. She saw his lips move to say, "Pray excuse me," but knew that he had forgotten the liqueur and was sinking into an exhausted sleep. Nevertheless, taking care of Malcolm gave her strength, though once when she caught sight of herself in a mirror she thought, "My hair is the same, it's my face is turning gray."

He obliged her to send daily into town for *The Gazette* and to read to him the reports telegraphed from Vicksburg. The siege advanced. The Confederate trenches and the Yankee trenches were five feet from one another, the men talking. The people of Vicksburg and the Confederate soldiers were living on mule meat. They ate rats. With the reinforcements, Grant had almost 80,000 men. Mrs. Bedford could not always tell how much Malcolm heard of what she read. Sometimes he broke in with an observation, sometimes with a curse, or he lay looking beyond her at the wall. She herself was so worn out with the nursing that the words often meant nothing to her as she read them out.

It might have been easier if guests had broken the monotony

of her watching. But on the very first day after his return, when Doctor Martin drove over with a bottle of Otard Cognac, 1820, and two or three ladies had come, she saw that Malcolm was ill at ease and unhappy. When they asked questions about the siege he replied timidly. She understood at length what it was: his pride was hurt.

"Darlin', you don't owe us an apology for Vicksburg," she said to him, when their visitors had gone.

She was relieved at the thought of being spared the sight of his poor, anxious gaze that searched one face after another, as if to ask their approval or forgiveness. But she said, "Go way from here, Darlin', you know they want to see you. You're a popular gentleman."

"Just the same you tell them."

"I'm positive you want to see Hugh McGehee," she said later that afternoon, when Celie came to tell them that the carriage from Montrose was driving in.

"Hugh, yes, this one time. But not Agnes."

Not after Shiloh: his mind filled with the scene at Vicksburg between the lines, where the dead Union soldiers had swollen in the sun and the stench was so great that a truce had to be arranged while dirt was spaded over them. Mrs. Bedford saw from Malcolm's eyes something of what he was thinking. She said nothing more of Agnes, but merely stopped to arrange his necktie before she went to greet the guests.

Gradually she realized that she was trying not to meet his questioning gaze.

When she understood this she began to believe that she did not want him to live.

If Mrs. Bedford was out of the room, Dock sat with Malcolm and swung the trundle-bed for coolness. One day when Malcolm was sleeping, Dock came downstairs to tell her that from the upper windows he had seen soldiers in blue. They were coming up the avenue on foot. She sent the Indian back to the sick room, went into the library, took out a pistol from the secretary and met the soldiers at the door. They could make up their minds, she told them, that the first one to cross the threshold she'd shoot.

"All right, you heard what I said."

They looked at her and grinned, and she kept the pistol on them. But they were friendly fellows; it was plain they cared very little about the business. The soldier who had remained at the foot of the steps tipped his hat and turned away; and the others, tipping their hats also, followed, laughing and talking. She saw one of them, the one who had first tipped his hat, stop, pluck a rose and stick it in his lapel, then seeing a rose he liked better, throw the other away and put in the second, as he began to sing, and then to bawl, in a tenor voice that deserved better treatment, the song, "Juanita." She and Rose had sung that when they were girls. When they got to the gate, the soldiers stood a while lounging against it, looking and pointing back down the avenue, where the light fell on the marble figures, raining down on them from the trees overhead and the draped moss. Then she saw them waving their hats in the air and cheering, "Hurrah for Secesh! Secesh!" With a yell they turned, crowding through the gate, and disappeared toward town; and she remained, leaning her slight body against the door-post. Malcolm's first wife, she thought, before her marriage day had planted these trees, Mary Hartwell McGehee then, before she was Bedford. She looked at her own hand, which for all her incessant work these days was still white and delicate, and thought of the Sully portrait of Malcolm's first wife, in the dining-room. The hands in the portrait were larger; yes, that was one thing, the other woman's hands were quite larger.

"When in the world was all that," she said to herself, "when was it, this first marriage, Malcolm then, and so forth?"

Dock had come to tell her, in his usual word or two, that the sick man was awake.

"Dock," she asked, "how about you and the war?"

"If shoot, kill," he said.

"That's about right too, Dock."

XLIII

MONMOUTH, whose mistress was the friend that Mrs. Bedford had felt most free to send Valette and the children to during Malcolm's fever, had been the home of the famous General Quitman, hero of the Mexican War and idol of the nation. But at the banquet given to President Buchanan in 1859, the general along with many of the guests had partaken of the poison thought to have been put into the food. He returned to Natchez but never rallied from that illness and so died.

On the June day the carriage with Valette and the three children drove over from Portobello, only Mrs. Quitman was at Monmouth. She was delighted to see them and stood smiling at the strange team hitched to the carriage.

"I understand Sallie Bedford," she said to Valette, looking at the old plough horse and mule that had been drafted into a more elegant service than they had ever known. Having thus explained the equipage and expressed her friendship, she turned and kissed each of the children again, as she led the way indoors. An old woman called Aunt Tankie, for Thankful, which was her name, was sent for and given charge of them.

The three Monmouth gardeners had all run off, the hedges and flowers showed neglect here and there, and all the peacocks were stolen. Only the dovecot was left; and since the dinners and hunt balls had ceased, the pigeons numbered more and more.

"So that you'll just be good company for me, and it's a big place, plenty of room for all my birdies," said Mrs. Quitman, giving Valette a little kiss and pointing to a flock of white pigeons that had fluttered onto the gallery outside, cooing as they moved over the floor, and flying up here and there before alighting again. Their wings gave to the sunlight an air of glittering.

"At home we hear so many doves lately—in the evenings," Valette said, wistfully. "All out in the fields."

"And you like to think of our pigeons as doves, too? I remember I used to, I was romance itself in my day."

When Mrs. Quitman asked for Duncan, such a look of gloom came over the lovely young face that she pressed for the whole story and Valette presently, on an impulse, drew a letter from her breast and gave it to her friend to read. It was Duncan's last, and had come around by Atlanta. They were in Maryland on their march north, General Stuart's tent was full of flowers the ladies sent all day long. General Lee was on his way to Pennsylvania. And Duncan relied on Valette to see that everything at Portobello went well.

"Ah so, so?" Mrs. Quitman said more than once, bobbing her fine old head as she read the letter. "What a splendid young man! Sallie Bedford brought Duncan over with her one day and I remember General Quitman saying he should have liked a son exactly like that. 'Yes, my dear friend,' my husband said to Sallie, 'had I the choice of such a son I would not change him one iota.' You realize this compliment came from a national genius and a famous general."

Valette, instead of showing her pleasure, burst into tears, and Mrs. Quitman scowled at her in astonishment and then ran her eye down the letter again.

"Come here," she said, and drew Valette down to sit on

her lap, "you're not heavy, you're too thin as it is. So you hate Duncan Bedford?"

Valette shook her head without taking it from the motherly old shoulder.

"Can't you see all he says is that if you fail him the bottom drops out of the universe? When the general was courting me and we were betrothed, the whole town tiraded us for having a marriage contract; he was a stranger and my father was rich. It was a great romance and they all lived to see they were geese. 'Yes,' General Quitman said, 'if I had had the choice of such a son as Duncan, I would not have changed him one iota.' But the young lady, it appears, wants to change him."

Nevertheless, in spite of the strength she felt herself drawing from her old friend, Valette abandoned herself more to sadness than she would have done at Portobello. Torn from her life there and the things she found to be done, she had less to divert her thoughts and take up her time; and she needed the feeling that her own courage played a part in the family fortunes. At Monmouth she neglected the children, who were well enough, she told herself, with Aunt Tankie; they played in the garden all day long. At times she liked to think of herself as a coquette with a soul as black as sin. At other times she saw herself as a woman passionately devoted to a soldier who had ridden off to the wars. The second morning at Monmouth she rose before dawn and went to the window where the morning star was shining. In the half dusk, so fresh, so quiet, with only a few birds and, far-off, some dog barking, she looked out and felt a calmness in her breast, and perceived by that that she was saying a prayer. She listened to her own little words as she had just listened to the sounds of the world at this moment before dawn; the words did not seem to be her own and seemed to her beautiful and never spoken before by any one. She remained at the window a long time, and all the images of the fading stars, the lost galaxies, the dying night passing from the sky in a mysterious flight, meant nothing in her mind, to which the dawn's image in the east, the nearing of glory and brightness there, came like a full and divine promise.

"Tell about the swords," Middleton begged Mrs. Quitman, as they stood for the twentieth time in front of the portrait of the general in full military dress, his brow crowned by a laurel wreath. They went into the hall where the two swords hung crossed on the wall. She was obliged to tell how Mr. Reese Fitzpatrick himself made one of the swords right there in Natchez, he knew how to temper steel as well as any man in the world.

"I know," the little boy interrupted. "And tell what else he made too."

He made the first bowie knife, and now they were found from Gath to Bathsheba, Mrs. Quitman said.

"The general got the other sword in Mexico," said Middleton, jerking his little elbows in close to his ribs and about to laugh.

"Not in Mexico, and you know it, you plotter! The United States gave him that sword in 1847, for the victory at Belan Gate. Mr. Jefferson Davis was an officer, the President of our Confederate States, and General Zack Taylor was there who became the President of the United States. But it was General Quitman who stormed Belan Gate and Chapultepec Castle. His men marched victoriously through the city and Frederick Macrery from Natchez raised the flag over the castle, and he was one of my husband's men. Now."

"Great Scott, you chillun come on!" Aunt Tankie said. "Ole Miss ain' go fight de Mexican War for y'all ev'y minute."

"General Scott's an old devil," Frances observed coolly and without looking round, as she studied another portrait of General Quitman when a young man.

"Mercy!"

"Papa told me so."

"General Scott's your uncle Hugh McGehee's cousin, Fannie," said Valette.

"I don't care. Why has General Quitman left his swords off in this picture of him?"

"Hartie," Valette said, turning to the oldest child, "it's another Scott Aunt Tankee meant, not General Winfield Scott."

"And Papa said Uncle Hugh said General Winfield Scott was an old devil," Frances repeated, going up to stand by her taller sister and putting her arm through hers and looking in her eyes with a confidential air.

"He's a traitor to the South where he was born," Hartie said, "but that's not Great Scott. Great Scott is Gee Whiz."

"Well," Mrs. Quitman laughed, "however that is, we'd better go and sit in the summerhouse by the fountain where the pigeons come to drink. I can see no General Scott would ever have a triumph like my husband. Ladies all in white strewed flowers before Quitman and sang 'Hail to the Chief,' and he rode a white charger."

"I suppose," Frances said, "the flowers the ladies strewed were white too."

"I suppose they were," the old lady said, laughing gayly and leaning down to give a kiss to Fannie, who was her favorite. "And I suppose you're just a plain monkey, you're as downright as the general."

At the summerhouse near the fountain, Tankie took some corn from her skirt pocket, and the pigeons fluttered over the children, pecking the grains out of the little open hands and alighting on their shoulders and wrists. Each child discovered that the pigeons had pink eyes and made a sound like keeping your mouth shut tight and whirring your tongue in your throat.

"He won't let you, he won't let you," Middleton shrieked, as Frances tried to put her cheek against the sleek head of a pigeon, which flew up, to be followed by half the others. "He will."

"He won't." Middleton jumped up and down.

But this time one of the pigeons, finding so much in Frances' palm, kept on eating and did not seem to mind the little lips passing over his head and down his snowy neck.

The July morning passed with Mrs. Quitman mending gloves and Valette beside her. A writing case of black, inlaid with mother of pearl flowers, the pad of blue velvet, was open on her knees; but she had given up trying to write a letter. "My dearest Duncan," she had written but could get no further. He was in an army, fighting in a war, and she sat here waiting for him, watching children playing with pigeons beside a fountain and an old lady, whose life was in the past, mending gloves. "My dearest Duncan—" She watched Mrs. Quitman cutting off the top of an old glove ten years out of fashion and stitching down the edges. The conversation went on, for Mrs. Quitman liked to talk:

"When Duncan comes home from the war you must marry at once," she said. "No matter how things are, marry. This postponing we hear about people's doing is silly nonsense, my dear. I can tell you the strains of that minuet were not out of our ears when Captain Quitman and I were engaged, and off to the church soon after. And we never repented it."

By now it was well past noon. The shade, which had shrunk when the sun was overhead, began to stretch out in a new direction. The low jet of the fountain threw a trembling line of shadow on the water of the basin and across the marble ledge. The scent of the honey locusts in flower grew heavier in the heat of afternoon, and Mrs. Quitman drew a full breath of them.

"When my daughter was here, before she was married of course, she used to say we ought to cut down some of the locusts. But her father always said no perfume could be too sweet for him. When he was a young man, he said, he couldn't spark any young lady unless she had a sweet smell. There was one man for you who always knew his mind, thank the Lord! I hate nammy-pammies. One reason I was always Duncan Bedford's champion."

Valette laughed, looking up at the locust blossoms as if they had answered for her.

Mary Hartwell came politely over to the summer house bench and sat down by Mrs. Quitman to ask for the story of General Lafayette. She was growing daily prettier, the gray eyes were open and seemed waiting for nothing but kind thoughts from every one.

"It's right to be a little lady, darling," Mrs. Quitman said, glancing from Hartie to Valette with a smile. "But you've already known every word I could say; you'll have too much of a muchness."

But Mary Hartwell insisted, and called to the other children that they were going to hear the story about the ball.

"Well, when Lafayette had helped George Washington to whip the British, he went back to France, because that was his country, and years afterwards—" She told of the great ball they gave Lafayette in her father's house, which once upon a time some Spanish grandee had built, in Washington Street. There were hundreds of candles lighted, the ladies wore flowers and jewels, and some of the gentlemen were in uniforms. In that gown of red satin embroidered with golden wheat that you could see in the portrait over the parlor mantel, she had led the grand promenade with Lafayette himself. And one of the gentlemen in uniform, of course, was Captain John Quitman of the Fencibles. They wore French-blue broadcloth with braid and silver lace and silver buttons.

Middleton and Frances, when they heard again about the silver finery, looked at each other and burst out laughing, as if they knew something very funny. But at that moment a boom and then a rumble came through the air, and as they looked quickly up at the sky another sound came, closer at hand, the windows of the house rattled, and they saw the servants crowding at the kitchen door.

"Cannon," Mrs. Quitman said. "What is it?" The guns had begun in earnest from the river, "Valette, they're bombarding the town."

The old lady threw aside the gloves she was mending and stood up. The noise and the guns increased.

"That's it, child, they're bombarding Natchez."

Valette sprang from the bench and knelt down by the two smaller children, putting her arms about them.

"What shall we do?" she asked. "Listen!" A crash came from some street in the town where a ball had struck. They saw smoke rising and filling the sky over Natchez. The sound of the guns kept up, the smoke rose. Then smoke and flame together, a fire had broken out.

"Do? There's nothing to do," Mrs. Quitman said. "Stay here, out here in the open. I'll go speak to the servants."

Valette heard distant cries and shouts. Tankie came running out to them, the whites of her eyes showing far off. Valette pointed to the children and put her finger to her lips; and the old woman, without saying anything, crouched down beside the summerhouse and sat listening to the cannon.

Frances had pulled her little skirt around sideways so that it covered Middleton's knees. Another roll of smoke arose over Natchez, where fresh fires had started. From the direction of the river, columns and twists of white smoke were going up toward a dingy canopy that filled the sky. Suddenly Vallette herself buried her head in her hands: She heard a child screaming, one terrible cry after another, only to be drowned by the guns again. Tankie began to whine and call louder on Jesus, glancing at Valette as if asking to speak. "Oh, dar dey is, oh, my sweet Marster!" she groaned.

"Dry up, Aunt Tankie, I told you."

The smoke of the cannonade had spread out toward Monmouth, the air darkened, roosters crowed down beyond the stable. The noise like drums kept up. Then at the end of half an hour they saw people coming down the roads, buggies and carts loaded with household objects, trunks, some furniture, but no carriages. The negro woman stood up, shading her eyes with her hand, to see the road and who the people were passing on it. "Jes' trash," she said, and sat down again on her heels.

Besides the guns there came the sound of explosions. More carts and wagons could be seen along the road, only half visible beyond the bridge. The people in them were talking. "Like to got us," Valette heard a man say.

"A miss is good as a mile," said a woman's voice.

"One shell went as far out as Ashburn. But didn't go off, naw, sir."

"Rooted up the ground lak a hog," a negro voice said.

A file of slaves passed crowding close together, some of them praying in loud voices, some crying, many of them dumb, and there were cries, moans, and laughter, with wheels creaking and shouting to horses. Valette and Tankie saw Mrs. Quitman go down the steps of the portico and to the gate and stand watching the people fleeing on the road. Two servants left the crowd of negroes huddled against the wall of the house and followed her. They crouched down by the gate near their mistress.

The Federal guns from the river now came less often; and Frances and Middleton were looking about them at the sky and the strange world and at Mary Hartwell, who stood pressed into an angle of the summerhouse lattice, her eyes wide and solemn. Aunt Tankie saw her too and giggled, "Tain't judgmen' day, Miss Hartie." Then she shrieked, "Oh, oh, my God A'mighty!" A sound like a big beetle flying close to their ears came through the air, then a whistle. Then they heard a thud and across the lawn saw the dirt fly and a ball rolling. The bomb had not exploded. It crashed along through a bed of pinks and then on to the lawn, and rolled slower and slower over the grass till it seemed to stop. Pigeons seeing where something had been thrown, fluttered down to it, but the ball was not spent. The children saw one of the pigeons lying on the ground, flapping its wings, then quite still, and the others scared off.

Mrs. Quitman, turning from the gate, saw Valette running after the three children and heard their cries as they came to the pigeon. She saw the children kneeling on the ground; Frances was wiping the smudge and tears from her face with one hand, and holding the dead bird to her breast, sobbing that the Yankees had killed her little pigeon. She took the child in her arms and carried her over to the fountain where the pigeon could lie on the ledge; they would bury it that evening. "And look, Fannie Bedford, at my flower bed, what that old cannon ball's done to it. Don't you think we'd better go tell Aunt Liddy to have dinner? People are hungry, *n'est-ce pas?*" She kissed each little eyelid, "Of course people are hungry. And smell the pinks now; polly vous français?" But the little girl only put her arms tighter around Mrs. Quitman's neck and it was a long time before she stopped sobbing. The two other children walked along beside Mrs. Quitman, frightened and silent.

The guns were firing less and less. Overhead the sun was now as bright as it had ever been, though the fires at the farther end of town blazed and sent up fresh clouds of smoke. The voices and hubbub down there in the streets kept up, but the sound was different, excited but not so full of horror and cries. Within an hour of the first gun from the river the bombardment had ended. Some of the negroes came to look at the bomb, but stood at a safe distance.

XLIV

THE laudanum prescribed by his doctor had put Malcolm into a sleep that the far-off noise of the guns on the river did not disturb; but Mrs. Quitman's note a few hours after the bombardment was welcome. Mrs. Bedford learned from it that the children and Valette were safe, and callers told her what had happened in Natchez. The Federal armored gunboat, the *Essex,* anchored in the river, had started two small boats ashore. In Natchez the town guard, the Silver Grays, was largely old men and boys. Some of these, when they saw the boats on the river, ran to consult young Major Douglas Walworth; he was at home on sick leave, and for the moment at the dinner table. In spite of his protest they went to the landing and opened fire on the boat crews. The *Essex* retaliated by shelling the town. The shells fell everywhere, plenty of houses were hit; fires broke out. The fires were worst in the town under the bluff, houses were burning there right and left.

But somebody up North had sold the government shells that would not explode, and after an hour the bombardment was obliged to stop.

Commander Porter of the *Essex* stated that he had sent ashore to get ice for the sick on board, and that two hundred citizens had attacked them scandalously, wounded the officers and killed one man. He therefore shelled the town, shooting, he said, at those who shot at him. In Natchez, besides the fires, a little girl had been killed by a flying piece of shell, Rosalie Berkman. When they came out of the house into the street, her father saw her fall. "Get up," he said, and she said, "I'm killed." He took her in his arms to the carriage, the blood running down over his clothes. The child's screams could never be forgotten.

On the second day of July Malcolm Bedford merely said that they would leave the newspaper where it lay on the table, and his wife was glad, for it announced a truce between the Vicksburg armies to discuss the terms of the surrender. Lately the sick man's mind had turned away from the military to the more human side of that siege, and he spoke of how, during his days at Vicksburg, the two lines would declare a truce and come out to eat the blackberries, which were good for their dysentery. At night, sometimes, men from the two armies would come out of the trenches, shake hands and sit talking together. They spoke to each other of their homes and of their troubles. They judged their leaders, the jealousy between McClernand, who was a good talker and not a bad officer, and Grant, who was kind and simple-minded but could stick at it, plus Sherman, who blustered, stood by Grant, was red-headed and hasty, but pretty straight at that. None of these three generals, the soldiers used to say, was a fine strategist like that chilly Johnston, who had to carry the burden of Pemberton on his shoulders. They told stories on these leaders.

"Darlin'," Sallie Bedford said, drying his forehead of the cold sweat that broke out now at any time. "You know as well as I do it's the ordinary mortal that gets driven to the shambles. Nothing new about that. Why don't you try and go to sleep?"

"I don't care about Grant's whisky and I don't care about his military skill, or Pemberton's being a fool. What I care about—" He began to speak of the soldiers who had to bear the brunt of what these men did and of the officials in Richmond and Washington. At other times that day he rambled on about the pillaging and burning and what his people had to suffer from the Yankees. He had heard the bluecoats tell of their feasts, the ducks, guineas, hams, cordials, the whisky and wine, the molasses, and of the houses burnt. For thirty miles around, the Jackson country was a nightmare to look at. Peering furiously about the room, Malcolm would begin accounts of horrors he had seen with his own eyes, but often the story broke off, his lips moved for a moment and then stopped, and he lay with his mouth open and his nostrils quivering.

Sallie Bedford, sitting by him, keeping the trundle-bed slightly swinging, heard all this in agony. Once she laid her finger on his lips. If only Duncan were at home! But how could that be? Malcolm brushed the finger aside, and found a loud voice.

"Yes, and what's war to you? It's like a woman, everything's personal. Everything's the same importance. The moon or a button, all's the same."

"Oh, Darlin', very well, lay on, MacDuff! Go on, give it to the women!"

Her pitiful air of laughing away the hate he felt toward her only provoked him further. He half sat up on the bed but sank quickly back, speaking between his teeth. "Why in hell's name are you so busy? Always running an infernal house! If you'd sit still a minute and think—" He shut his eyes, and the tears ran down over his cheeks to the pillow. His hand, when she raised it to her face, left hers and tried to caress her head, but there was no other sign from him; and for the first time since she had been nursing him she broke down into loud sobbing.

The next morning Malcolm made a gesture for his wife to come to him, drew her down and kissed her, and when she asked how he felt, pretended he was much better. He forced the hand that clasped hers to show a strong grip. She was so far persuaded of this that she changed her mind and decided that Dock on his trips to town should wait till tomorrow or next day to call Doctor Martin. But when the newspaper came with the brief despatch of the fall of Vicksburg, she did not take it upstairs. The stronghold of the Confederacy in the west had fallen, 31,600 prisoners, 172 cannon, 60,000 muskets.

At eleven o'clock, when he had drunk a little of the rose cordial in water, Malcolm asked for the children and was told again that the doctor had sent them away until his fever was past. When his wife told him this he shook his head, refusing to look at her. He knew that he was dying, but it seemed farther and farther from his thoughts in the midst of the death struggle between the South and the North. Some time later she was standing by the window counting the number of powders left to be given him, when she thought she heard him speak.

"Mary Hartwell," he said, in a low, passionate voice.

With a passionate tenderness of her own she accepted it. "Yes, Darlin'."

She was no longer jealous. He had loved this other woman, but he loved her, too; he loved her, too, and she would not be such a fool as to refuse to know that he must have loved her.

He was reaching now for her hand. "Wife?"

"Yes, my darlin'."

"Sallie, I couldn't have lived without you, dearest."

"Well, if you'll just sleep—just go to sleep."

He frowned, smacking his shrunken lips as if to moisten them. Then he tried to say something to her but only mumbled.

"Darlin'—dearest—tell me, what is it?"

He gazed steadily into her eyes, mumbling a few more words. Then he suddenly spoke quite distinctly.

"Where's your breastpin?"

She looked over toward the dressing-table, where the old brooch with its leaves twisting around a column, must be.

"You always wear it," he said. "Where is it?"

"Yon 'tis, precious, I'll get it."

"Now that's better," he said, fixing his eyes on the brooch

that she had pinned at her throat. "You always wear it."

She sat down quietly, hoping to calm him, but was astonished at his strength when he began to speak of Vicksburg, cursing at Pemberton and Grant, until suddenly his voice gave out and he closed his eyes, the tears trickling down his cheeks. Then his eyes opened and he looked at her, angrily trying to move his lips. She understood that he meant for her to wipe away the tears.

"Thank you," he said, in a hoarse whisper. "Thank you for everything."

"Oh, Darlin', I haven't done anything," she murmured, leaning down to put her cheek against his. He only turned away his face, shutting his eyes, and then a moment later turned to look up at her, as if to say, "What is there more to say? Before I can close my eyes at last? Do you want me to say anything else?"

A long while after that, it seemed to him, he must have asked again for the children; he heard his wife's voice saying, as the air from the gently swinging trundle-bed passed over him, "Now that you're so much better this morning, just wait a teenie bit longer, and you'll be up, and the chillun playin' with you."

"Sallie, if I should die," he began slowly, "what do you think?"

She knew he meant to ask what she thought of the soul after death, and that, counting on the change in herself since Rosa's death, he wanted her to say that all those who love each other will meet again. But he must not be excited. She was startled by his shining eyes, looking as if they saw the very depths of her. Long ago his eyes had shone like that—and yet not quite. She felt his hand stroking hers.

"Darlin', why think you're goin' to die? But, since you ask what I think, I say I'd ask you to find Pa in heaven. I'd ask you to tell him to be good to my Abner." Abner Francis was the little boy she had lost, two years younger than Duncan. "You could just tell Pa," she added.

A twinkle came into the dilated eyes: he remembered the obituaries he had written of her father: "Whereas of stature lofty and splendid intellect, Colonel Lucius Quintus Cassius Tate—" It was all he could remember now. His brain felt tired out with the effort. He had known his wife's pompous father, whom her mother beheld as a god, and had finally decided that women admire in their own way, nothing else to be said. He would not mention the old colonel's obituaries now—yes, at one place or another he had put, "Canst thou draw leviathan out with an hook?" Yes, that was it to a T. What a thought it was, drawing out old Colonel Leviathan with a hook!

Then he thought drolly, "I've never got an obituary written for myself after all."

"You rascal," his wife said, so happy at seeing him smile that she forgot everything else, "here you are talking away about dyin' and you are so much better you can laugh. You certainly are a case, Malcolm Bedford! So you've got to entertain us now, or we'll just leave you, yes, sir, and where'd you be in no time?"

"Then listen here," he said, refreshed by the happy sound in her voice and noticing at that moment Dock, who had come to relieve her, "You let Dock take care of me and you go get *The Gazette* and we'll see what's happened."

When she was gone, he turned to the Indian: "See here, Dock, you're worth a thousand dead Chickasaws—" he used the old saying from the days he and Dock had hunted together, but his eyes were fixed intently on the Indian—"do me a favor. Go look on that window pane, the left, the top. And spell me what you see there."

The Indian, shading his eyes against the afternoon glare, spelt out the name on the pane: Mary Hartwell.

"There's a date, Dock."

"1832," Dock read.

"I'm obliged to you. Come sit down here."

When his wife entered the door she saw his eyes watching for her. He kept them on her face, with a look of love and trust. He said nothing, but raised his index finger as if to warn her she should read him the news. She read only the line that said Vicksburg had fallen; then she paused to look at him. The fact seemed slowly taking hold on his mind. She heard him give a moan and then a sort of whimper, as he turned his face away.

From that time on for eleven days Malcolm's eyes were closed. "Darlin', General Lee is back in Virginia, I'm glad to know," Mrs. Bedford said one morning after the newspaper had come. But she did not mention that Natchez had been occupied, not to speak of ten thousand bales of cotton having been captured that day by a Federal garrison. He opened his eyes but made no reply.

"There's no use in my coming," the doctor said. "It's just that way, no use at all."

Just before sundown on the day when Malcolm lay dying, Sallie Bedford saw from the window their negroes going across the garden. They were making their way from the quarters to the carriage gate. She knew what it was; there had been, what little time she had had downstairs, a curious air of whispering and insolence lately about the place. They were leaving. That was why when she went down for the newspaper the kitchen part of the house had been so still. She stood at the window and watched the negroes, recognizing one and then another. She saw, also, two or three strangers among them, negro men, that she had never seen before. They were on their way to the stockades that had been established on the river flats below the town, for slaves fleeing from their masters to the protection offered by the Union. Reports had come from Jackson of the ten miles of negroes deserting the plantations to follow General Sherman toward Vicksburg, when it should surrender. In the Natchez stockade crowds of runaways were already huddled together, under the protection of a Federal gunboat. Once in, it was not easy to leave; permission had to be secured from Washington and that took time. Already, in the heat, disease had broken out and the negroes were dying, sometimes at the rate of a hundred a day.

As Mrs. Bedford heard Dock in the hall downstairs shutting and bolting the doors to the house, she reminded herself that old Mary and French Nancy and some of the darkey children would be left behind at the quarters and she found herself thinking that one or another of their negroes would not be found among those leaving. Then she saw Mammy among those in the rear.

The figure on the trundle-bed had scarcely stirred. Now and then his wife saw a quick spasm pass over his body. She was only waiting for the end.

Shortly after midnight, she saw that it was death and no longer the motionless silence, and that the eyelids were only half open in a glazed stare at the candlelight. So Darlin' was gone, and the world had changed. It was all over. Everything was changed. The hour would strike and there were things for her to do, since nobody else was left at Portobello to help with anything. She washed and dressed him, took a linen handkerchief from a box to tie up the chin, and pressed down the eyelids till they were set. She put a clean sheet on the bed, and called Dock, who lifted the body on it. She told him then to take away the trundle-bed and to wait downstairs in the library. When that was done she sat down at the bed's head, where Malcolm lay under the high red satin tester, looking taller than in life.

"If I was proud I asked no more of others than I did of myself," said the proud, white, dead face.

She took a seat beside him and the great bed, sitting there small and frail like a child. "I couldn't cry to save my life," she thought, "I just haven't any tears, I reckon."

She did not touch the body.

"Where could Darlin' be now?"

At daylight she went downstairs to the kitchen to get breakfast for Dock, who would have to saddle the mule and go to town. She took him in to the dining-room table, paying no attention to the surprise and awe on his face at being seated there, and stood watching him eat, and went to fill his cup again with coffee, but did not sit down with him. Valette and the children must come home now; and all day friends and Malcolm's kin would be driving out to Portobello.

XLV

WITH things as they were a will, and almost any other legal document, was little better than a literary exercise. Nevertheless, on the Monday after his death, Malcolm Bedford's will was opened and read.

After bounding the land——

"In the name of God, amen! I, Malcolm Stewart Bedford of said Portobello of said city of Natchez, aforesaid planter, being of sound mind and memory do ordain this my last will and testament.

"First I recommend my soul to God, etc."

"I know Darlin', just let the lawyers run that in," Mrs. Bedford said, smiling. Malcolm had already become to her a mere youth, all freedom and spirit—"but go on, Judge Winchester; Doctor Johnson, you know, said no man's on his honor in a lapidary inscription."

They were in the library at Portobello. She had always referred to this judge as "very plausible," which coming from
her was not a compliment.

The entire estate Malcolm left to his wife until her death,
the income to be used as she saw fit. On her death the Portobello plantation would go to Duncan. But she had always
known that. The other two plantations, at Lake St. Joseph's
and in Concordia Parish, went to the other children, Valette to
share equally. He left $5000 to the library of the University of
Virginia "to be spent on philosophical and liberal books," together with a cornelian seal that had belonged to Thomas Jefferson, his mother's cousin, and $1000 to General Robert E.
Lee if he should be still living at the time the will was read.
"The portrait by Sully of my first wife Mary Hartwell Mc-
Gehee is to go to my eldest daughter by my second marriage,
her namesake. Provided said daughter dies without an heir
begotten of her body this portrait to go to Lucinda Mc-
Gehee, of Montrose."

After that point they went on through the pages only as
some fantastic irony. All that detail of the slaves meant no
longer anything. "Those several old and faithful servants who
have been good, dutiful, and obedient to me through life and
whom I am extremely anxious shall not serve as slaves after
my death—" the will read. "My negro man Thornton and
his wife Tildy, who came out when I moved from Georgia
in 1808, are to be freed, my son Duncan shall act as their
guardian and protector, and see that they are paid a reasonable
compensation for their services in whatever capacity they may
see proper to serve. The four children of Nancy are to live with
her until the youngest is fifteen. Blind Mary is to be no longer
a slave but is to live at Portobello, her daughter Ellen to live
with her and wait on her till death. Old Lucy no longer a
slave, she is to live with Duncan, the son Jesse to remain a slave
two years to support Lucy, and then be freed to serve whom

he wills. My stable man Silas is to be freed and given owner-
ship of the field called the Louisa field, in Concordia Parish.
I give——"

The reading went on but Sallie Bedford did not hear it.
Mere scratch paper was all it now amounted to. When the
lawyer finished, cleared his throat and folded the document, he
saw her eyes gazing at the wall beyond him.

"But Uncle Thornton and Mammy ran off to the Yankees,"
she said.

The eyes in the handsome old face were full of pity for her
and of shame and humiliation. He was not naturally as foolish
as she thought him. "Any of the niggers that ran off and want
to come back," he said, as he rose, "are free to come: I figure
this will of your husband's amounts to about that now."

It was true that the position of the negro was still vague.
January 8, 1863, Lincoln had decreed Emancipation, but it
applied only to states that had seceded; nearly three years were
still to pass before slavery was abolished in the entire United
States. General Sherman was an Anti-Abolitionist but saw in
the removal of slaves a means of weakening Southern owners.
Mrs. Grant visiting her husband brought along with her their
slave maid Julia. "We free your slaves to ruin you and win the
war," made sense to everybody; but the people found it confusing when they heard that the slaves were freed because
slavery was a sin and then recalled even such a trio of facts
as that Mrs. Grant had her slave with her at Vicksburg; that
Lincoln's announcement of the emancipation of slaves in seceding states as a part of his platform in December 1862 caused
Ohio, New York and Pennsylvania (no state west of the Hud-
son, in fact, thought much of it) to fail to support him with the
vote, that negroes in states that had not seceded from the Union
were still slaves; and that General Sherman had announced
that loyal masters could recover their slaves who had fled to

Union lines, plus, even, the wages they have earned by their temporary use under the military authorities. Thousands of negroes were in the Union lines or following the army.

Whatever the judge might say, he could tell Mrs. Bedford little that she did not know already.

"At the stockades down there by the river, I hear they are dying like flies," he said, in a harassed and weary voice, as if he was too old to bother over negroes any longer. "Look, my dear lady," he went on, drawing his purse from his breast pocket and taking out a small faded paper, with the red wax still left on it. "Nowadays I must go through all my papers. I came across this my mother wrote me, I was in Princeton— she had a romantic touch. I'll read you just this. 'Oh, we do groan, in this tabernacle, being burdened, we in this *Southern region,* of roses and sunshine—not in my day, not in the life-time of my children, perhaps not in that of my children's children, shall we be free from this burden of care and responsibility and toil and vexation! How long, how long?' That's what she says. I've four of her letters here. What would she say now? *Errare est humanum?*"

"I don't know that she's so far wrong, Judge," Mrs. Bedford said, wishing that Captain Ruffin were there to talk this old man down and let her go away to her room. "And here we are," she said to herself, "Darlin's in his grave for them, and the soldiers having tea parties up at Vicksburg with the Yan-kees!"

The judge paid no attention but went on silently reading his mother's letter, bobbing his fine head with professional politeness to whatever his client was saying.

She waited until he had put the letters back into his pocket before she gave him the sheet of paper with the design for the tombstone. "I should be obliged, Judge, if you would send this right off to old Marini."

On the paper was written:

East Side.

Thus Died
The Saint
July 15, 1863
To us, who loved him
He is not dead, but ever lives
To
warn, to encourage, to instruct.
"Then shall we also know, if we follow
on to know the Lord."
For
"Weeping may endure for a night,
but joy cometh in the morning."
Psalm XXX, 5.

North Side.

one Line in Greek characters,
Mark X, 49.

"But what is that line from St. Mark?" the judge asked.

" 'Be of good comfort, rise. He calleth thee.' He said once, long time ago, when we were talking he wanted that line put. But he wants it in Greek; it's there at the bottom of the paper. Marini can just copy it off."

While the judge was folding this paper among his others, she rang the bell for the field hand whom Dock had found to help about the house. A plate of supper from the kitchen was to be taken out to old Blind Mary.

"And find Middleton and tell him for him and his little darkey to stand there while she eats it, so French Nancy will keep her hands to herself, or I'll break her legs and throw her over the fence. But no matter—'twon't do any good. Just tell Middleton."

XLVI

THE late summer crowded up to the walls of Montrose, the flowers full and heavy with their fragrances, the air warm, the sky shining. Some of the orchard leaves had turned with the ripening of the fruit, and in the pine grove to the east of the orchard the sweet dry odor was like autumn already.

As the war progressed and the Southern cause grew more uncertain, Hugh McGehee had less and less patience with the newspapers. The tone of sensational events, flowery oratory, and shrill abuse in the accounts annoyed him. "Reporters and editors licking their chops!" he said to himself as Lucy read *The Natchez Whig* aloud to him. They were on the gallery and he let her go on, though he scarcely took in a word. "The altheas are full of spider webs," he said to himself, but he was thinking of other things. What would come after Vicksburg, and the defeat at Gettysburg? General Beauregard had seen that the decisive point for the South in the war lay in the West, not in the East. He had advised a campaign in Tennessee and Kentucky that would relieve the Mississippi Valley and Vicksburg, and that temporarily forces be drawn from the Army of Northern Virginia to this end. But the Davis Government would not accept the proposal; nor did General Lee agree to it; he feared, perhaps, too much for Virginia's safety. And yet, only last week, a letter had come to the Bedfords from their cousin, Charles Marshall, who was aide-de-camp to General Lee. Beauregard, he said, was making his proposal again, and General Longstreet had advised concentrating to recover Tennessee and Kentucky. General Lee had replied that the enemy's great effort would be in the West and the Confederacy must concentrate its strength there to meet them. But Lee deferred completely to the President of the Confederacy. He would say to Mr. Davis, Marshall wrote in the letter, when there was a campaign question to decide, "The expedience of this measure you can judge better than I can."

Hugh thought,

"Better than I can—Jeff Davis! In that case all I can say is, General Lee, you'd better give your place to another sort of man, one who would say to Davis, 'Mr. President, you imagine yourself a military genius, because of that V formation at Buena Vista, under our cousin General Winfield Scott, who has sided against his own State. You should have asked Zachary Taylor, asked Governor Quitman; they'd have told you what a military genius you are! Unwilling either to do anything yourself or to let go the directing of the war!' "

These thoughts and Lucy's voice reading were broken off by the clattering hoofs in the court beneath. In a moment Yellow Dave brought the carriage up at the foot of the steps. He drove a span of old plough horses not worth commandeering by the Federals.

"Who's going to town, Lucy? Is your mother?" her father asked.

"I am," Mary Cherry said, as she appeared in the door, wearing her black silk dolman with the bead fringes partly gone from it. She had her bonnet in her hand.

Miss Mary had been for weeks now at Montrose, and had seen more people than would have been possible that summer at the Bedfords'. Her blunt declarations and rudenesses had already made many in Natchez respect and fear her.

Hugh said nothing but, without meaning anything, he looked at her so quietly that Miss Mary was almost offended.

"I'm going into town for a pair of shoes. Besides, I need the airing. Besides, I haven't done anything for the Confederacy for weeks." She whacked her bonnet with its sprays of heads like flies down on her head and jerked the strings into a bow-knot. "I hear the ladies are very piert, plaiting bonnets out of palmetto leaves. I'll just tell you, long ere a Yankee soldier set foot in the South, I got this bonnet and still have it, thank God! Lord knows it's carried enough blue mass and nux vomica through the blockade."

For a while Lucy and her father strolled up and down the box walks and amused themselves trying to picture Miss Mary shopping in Natchez, where at that time a pair of shoes might be $300, and at that you were lucky. Miss Mary had begun her shopping practice the year before in Memphis. She would walk into a store and say to the clerk, "Young man, I'm Mary Cherry. I want a good pair of shoes." "Young man, I'm Mary Cherry, I want a dolman."

"You know," Lucy said, "that's where the dolman came from, Papa. She got it in Holly Springs. Don't you reckon the little clerks are so taken by surprise—or the poor old thing makes them think of their mothers."

"I expect they think she's a little cracked."

When Mary Cherry reached the Federal lines she found that it took longer than usual to pass, and learned from the pickets that General Grant had arrived the day before from Vicksburg, on his way to New Orleans. He was staying at General Ransome's headquarters at Rosalie. In the town more soldiers were abroad in the streets, where Federal flags were out, and more houses had their shutters closed. It was not like Vicksburg, where since the fall, they said, the town was on a holiday. Congressmen and their wives, prospectors, auditors, adventurers poured down from the North; the shop windows were full of goods for sale, the balls and gatherings were crowded, everything was like a picnic. Miss Mary saw soldiers standing about the old Spanish theatre with its galleries and brick arches, but the doors were shut.

No longer did you see the carriages with ladies, and accompanying them the gentlemen on horseback with their planters' whitecoats, white hats, and riding whips in their hands.

In the opinion of many it was General Sherman who had won Shiloh and even Vicksburg, but in the North General Grant got the glory and then the blame for Shiloh, and the credit for Vicksburg; and Miss Mary was glad of it. She despised that little red-headed Sherman, whom she had encountered at College Hill and in Memphis. She gave the driver a poke in the back with her fan.

"Where are you goin'? This is not how you go to Rosalie!"

"Miss Mary, you ain' said nothing 'bout Rosalie, tha's Miss Wilson's house, you said Mr. Carradine's stow."

"Aye, you're a smart darkey, ain't you! Smart where the skin's off. Dave, you heard those Yankees say General Grant was at Rosalie. We might as well go down Orleans Street and come round by that side."

This was true, though Rosalie could hardly be said to be on their way. It was down overlooking the river, on the site of Fort Rosalie, where the Indian Massacre had been, a hundred and thirty years before.

"Go slow, go slow, Dave," Miss Mary said as they came abreast of the house, set not very far back in its garden. "But not stop, fool! Meander along like."

There were only the two guards, however, at the head of the steps. An orderly came out on the gallery, stopped to smell the flowers of the Madeira vine on a column, broke off a sprig and sauntered into the house again by one of the tall windows.

But farther on, to one side of the river road, by the parade ground, Miss Mary saw half a dozen officers on horseback in their blue coats; they were drawn up in the shade of an oak. She knew General Grant from the pictures of him in Memphis.

The hot sun allowed Dave's horses to go at a walk, and Miss Mary's good eye was on that side, so that she could look without seeming to.

So that was General Ulysses S. Grant! She had expected, and hoped— But what she saw was a short, stocky man around forty, with a face—the bright sunlight showed that torpid look that was well known, but the features were delicately made. He sat carelessly and slumped on his horse like a farmer at a market, and held an unlighted cigar in his mouth, as he rested his hands on the pommel of the saddle. His hands were lazily spread out, so that you saw the fine, slender fingers, like a woman's.

But as Mary Cherry came along opposite the spot in the road, the figure that stood out was not General Grant but the young man who had squared his horse about to confront him. A swarthy man with straight black hair like an Indian's, his voice went up and down like an orator's, his black eyes flashed, and now and again he shook his finger in the general's face and paused.

Miss Mary saw General Grant take the cigar from his mouth.

"All right, Rawlins," he said, "give the order."

At that moment the flashing eyes turned on the carriage and Dave set the horses off.

Who didn't know about Rawlins? Lawyer from Grant's village in Ohio, a nobody; but when Grant was made brigadier-general the first thing he did was to make Rawlins adjutant in his brigade. He was called Grant's conscience. His business was to stick at Grant's elbow, swear him on his honor not to drink whiskey again, curse and revile him, supply ideas, sting him out of torpor into action. If you hit Rawlins on the head, the saying was, you'd knock out General Grant's brains.

"We'll go back home, Dave," said Mary Cherry. "Sufficient the day. Turn here."

'Yas'm," said Dave; the sight of the officers had scared him.

"He's not the beast I'd a said. It's a good face."

" 'A's right, Miss Ma'y."

"I don't mean that snappin' turtle Jeremiah, who gave these plugs we are drivin' such a fiery look, I mean General Grant. Hush your mouth."

"Yas, m'am."

At Montrose Miss Mary found visitors. Colonel Harrod had driven Mrs. Wilson out, since her carriage had been taken over by the Yankees. They sat in the blue parlor, and silver goblets of scuppernong wine and a silver cake basket were on the table. The mistress of Rosalie was an old lady, grown fat; she wore a dark dress over a high tilter and a shovel bonnet of heliotrope silk. Long ago she had escaped with her husband from the siege of Derry and settled in Natchez. She was now a widow.

"Every word I've told you is true," she was saying, in her pretty Irish voice. "General Grant may have given orders that everything should be done to make a good impression on the people of this country, so peace will come sooner, avoid arousing hate, and so forth, and who'd say it was not a good policy. Eh?"

"That's wise," said Hugh, "a farsighted course."

Miss Mary remained standing by the mantel listening in silence to the conversation.

"It's me that saw the Yankees coming up the hill,'" Mrs. Wilson continued, "and run I did. Go home, my dears, go back, I said to the mayor's wife and daughters in their carriage. Why? they said. The devils have come to town, said I. So I was punished. The first shot out of the box, they chose my house for General Ransome, his headquarters. So this, said I to the Yankees, is how you win as far as possible the people back to the Union!"

Colonel Harrod emptied his second glass of wine. "It will not help," he said and touched his finger tips lightly on his napkin to dry the frost from the ice in the goblet, "not help one scintilla this pacific impression when people learn that

General Wade Hampton has ordered 47,000 bales of cotton worth $1,200,000 gold on his plantation south of here, to be burnt, to keep it from falling into Grant's hands. No, sir." He looked at Hugh McGehee who avoided his eye.

"Somebody ought to tell General Grant about Mr. Hyde," said Mrs. Wilson. "Anybody in the State could tell you, an old man burnt up in his house by the soldiers." She paused to loosen her bonnet strings.

"So is war always, I reckon," Hugh said, quietly, as he saw his wife's listening in silence.

"Don't tell me. As if I'd been at Derry siege for nothing, my dear."

Rawlins must have worked him up to it, Mrs. Wilson said, for General Grant had flown into a rage to find that certain families had been left inside the lines; he had ordered them removed, even the orphanage. " 'What a storm! Will you just recollect, General,' I told him, 'your own wife and four children and your two slaves will be in Vicksburg when you get back, to spend the summer with you, and here you drive these poor orphans out, you do,' said I. He's past forty and has never sworn an oath in his life, they say, ah, but he looked at me! I put the slaves in for love of the devil. 'Your two slaves, General,' I said. 'In the South, Mr. Lincoln set our slaves free. But up North you still own them.' "

Mary Cherry coughed.

"But, Miss Mary," said Agnes. "Won't you sit down, do forgive me! Tell us, my goodness, we ought to have asked you long ago—did you, by any chance, see General Grant?"

"I did," said Miss Mary, still standing.

Mrs. Wilson looked up eagerly, Colonel Harrod said. "Indeed, indeed, m'am. Hear, hear!"

"General Grant was holding a conference with his staff."

There was a commotion, but this was all she chose to say in spite of questions. She gave only the impression of having been present at something of importance, about which she chose to keep her own counsel. Lucy could hardly keep from laughing out, at that expression on her face, which seemed to be saying, "to be opened a hundred years after my death." Miss Mary merely stood there with her good eye turned away from them.

Afterwards she would always act like that.

She listened in silence next day when the McGehees drove over to Kenilworth for a morning call and their host spoke of General Grant. As mayor of Natchez, Mr. Dix had gone to confer with the general. The mayor was to be replaced by a provost marshal as the civil government gave place to the military. Grant received him with every courtesy, heard his request, granted it, and then went on talking of other matters. At last he went outside with Mr. Dix, and held the stirrup for him to mount, then stepping back he gave the military salute.

Sometime later when the news came up from New Orleans that General Grant had fallen off his horse drunk and been laid up for a week at the St. Charles Hotel with a broken leg, and later been carried on a stretcher to the Vicksburg boat, Miss Mary heard it without comment.

She left the others to talk of events, while she went to her room, from which there came no sound of the hymns but only her chair rocking back and forth.

XLVII

DURING the siege of Vicksburg General Grant lost his false teeth. He put them into the washbowl for the night and a negro steward threw them out with the water next morning into the river. His dentist at home, Doctor Hamlen, was sent for, and very soon afterward he was "authorized to practice his profession anywhere within this military command." In due time this brought him to a visit among the Federals stationed at Natchez. So that when one hot August night Miss Whipple, the little Iowa seamstress, had knocked her front teeth out against a closet door, she went straight off to her countrymen's headquarters and asked for the dentist. The set of teeth turned out not to fit very well, perhaps, or it may have been too large; however that was, from then on her expression was changed. What had been a bitten-in and cautious mouth was now always on the point of a smile.

It very likely altered Miss Whipple's sense of herself, seeing herself both in her mirror and from the eyes of other people with that pleasing readiness about the lips. At any rate she began to be agreeable. She even gave up saying Mac Gee Hee on cloudy mornings or when she felt annoyed. The upshot was that a mature German sergeant named Bonn, billeted at Weymouth Hall, whom she had met in town during a military parade, began to call on her at Montrose, and asked her to marry him, which she did, with an army chaplain performing the ceremony, and then returned to announce her news, in the course of the evening, to the McGehees. If, according to any social code they had ever heard of, the information was to come like that, it was about on the level with the darkies' little affairs, and so they took it. And Sergeant Bonn's enlistment period being presently up, Miss Whipple went away with him North. During the decade of 1850 more than a million Germans had emigrated to the United States and he had many friends settled around Lake Michigan.

And so with Miss Whipple gone, there were no longer any of their outsiders at Montrose. Mr. Munger, his health greatly restored, had joined the army at Vicksburg as a chaplain or preacher. Little Mr. Trippler had written several letters since his return to Providence. He had learned that a letter—unsealed, of course, ten cents—could be enclosed in an envelope directed to General Benjamin Hager, Commander of Confederates, Norfolk, Virginia, enclosed in another envelope directed to General Wood, Fortress Monroe. But Mr. Munger had not communicated at all with Montrose; he had only sent a tract of his own writing and evidently meant to be distributed among the soldiers in camp. The envelope with the tract was addressed to Hugh McGehee, Esquire. It began, "Unsaved friend"; and asked him to pause in his hasty course and take one honest look into the future. He should put his finger on his pulse, count his heartbeats for a little while, and meditate on the fact that every heart throb is one more measure of the time before he has to meet with God. If he was under any delusion that God was going to be lenient, wake up; God would settle yet for the murder of Jesus Christ, and Hell was yawning to swallow up the wicked. Have you thought of salvation? the tract asked.

These were the questions put to Hugh by his two-years' guest. "Do you know," he said, when the servants were out of earshot and he had read the tract aloud to Agnes and Lucy, "I thought of one thing; how Mac Bedford would have enjoyed it. It reminds me of that day we were at Portobello and Malcolm had taken a notion——"

"He'd taken a toddy is what Uncle Mac had taken," said Lucy, "and you know it, Papa."

"Well, both. A toddy and a notion, then, to quote Gibbon's saying that all religions are equally true to a believer, equally useful to a ruler, equally interesting to a philosopher."

"Poor Brother," Agnes said. "It's not for us to know, I know; but I believe he is in heaven, bless his soul! At any rate, the difference is Mr. Munger hasn't got any soul."

"What are you perusing, Lucinda?" said her father, glancing from the tract, which he was reading again and chuckling over.

"It's Cud'n Cynthia Eppes' Creole recipe for eggplant. I'm

tired of it plain. You take thick slices with a little water till
they are cooked done. Then you make a thick sauce of
tomatoes with bayleaf, majoram, eschallots, and butter, and
pour it over, then let it bake slowly in the oven awhile."

"Have you thought of salvation, Lucy?" said her father.

"What I've thought," she said, mischievously and elaborately
turning down the page where the recipe was, as if she were
laying a plot, "is we made a mistake not having more cooking
like this for Mr. Munger. It might have killed him. Cud'n
Abe would be good for Brother Munger; you know the time
they said Cud'n Abe drank so much peach brandy that he
tried to pull his hat off with a boot-jack."

"Lucy, Lucy," her mother cried, "what a mind you have,
child!"

"You're laughing yourself, Mamma."

"Well, of course."

Meanwhile the scandal of General Butler's New Orleans'
administration had spread up the river country, over the South
and into Europe. In April the year before the Federal gunboats had passed the forts at the Mississippi's mouth and taken
that city hidden in the smoke of cotton bales set fire to on the
wharves. Benjamin F. Butler, a Massachusetts lawyer and
political schemer, had pulled wires to such effect that the
Lincoln government had appointed him major-general; he
was now military governor of New Orleans. He studied certain of the great contractors who were cheating the Union at
Washington out of millions, and the generals who were stealing Southern cotton in their own behalf; and before long his
brother joined him and sold contraband supplies to the Confederates for cotton and sugar in exchange, with immense
profits. The general himself was robbing banks, robbing
houses, shipping out his booty—Silver Spoons Butler, Beast
Butler, they said in New Orleans and all the way up the
river. It was well known that Mr. Lincoln, at least until after

the coming presidential election, was afraid to tamper with him.

Agnes McGehee liked sometimes to go and sit on the bench in the Montrose graveyard. She would put on a white dress and go sit there alone. There was nothing morbid about it, she merely liked to be there, quietly among those she had loved. It was a kind of celebration of their memories.

One day as Agnes came along the path from the graveyard and had stopped to look at the amaryllis beds, she saw a young soldier standing at the gate, half hidden among the laurels, as if he tried both to watch the house and at the same time not be spied by any one coming from the highway. She remembered having seen the figure before like this, but was too used to soldiers and strangers nowadays to have thought much about it. However, she said to the soldier that she had seen him before.

"Yes, Mrs., this is three times I've been here," he said, touching his cap, on which she saw he had lately shined up the buttons, "but couldn't find the coast clear. Mrs., don't ask me anything." The soldier told her then that he had lately come up on a troop steamboat from New Orleans and had brought a small packet for her, he had given his promise to someone. He put the packet into Agnes' hand and turned quickly away, cutting through the bushes and off through the grove; the packet was wrapped in green paper tied with a cord, heavily sealed.

Agnes went directly to her room, locked the door and opened the parcel. It was Charlie Taliaferro's picture. The miniature of a little boy with black hair, in a green velvet jacket. Two of the diamonds in the oval of the frame had been pried out, the settings were scratched as if with a jack-knife and the back of the miniature had a dent in it.

"Poor Charlie!" Agnes said to herself. Then she thought of his father and Lucy. "If I sent it to Cud'n Shelt he'd just break his heart over it, or right now he would, poor old thing, and the darkies would steal it. If I show it to Lucy—no—some day—" To Lucy it might mean— To Edward's mother——

She stood there so long, leaning over the miniature where it lay on her table, that the light was fading from the windows. The little boy's face in the frame had gone from the midst of the diamonds, which still sparkled in the sultry light. It could have been any child's face. "In the gloaming, O my darling—" but that was only a song people sang. She took the miniature over to her desk, sprung the secret drawer, laid the green wrapping in and put the locket on top, scarcely even wondering who it was that had sent it, and when she had locked the desk, turning directly to go downstairs to the others.

XLVIII

That autumn of 1863, there was no party at Montrose for Hugh McGehee's birthday, but the two married daughters came home with their children. The three Bowdoin children, Linda, Helen Louise, and Abner, were too pretty not to have learned to want their own way; but any time they saw their grandfather or grandmother, they would run up to be caressed, so that nobody could resist them. The two Randolph children, Huella and Abner, whom they called Annie's Abner, had been taught to obey their elders; but when they escaped to the gallery outside or the hall upstairs, there was always a burst of healthy noise. With grandparents in the parlor or Paralee in the kitchen it was one thing, with Lucy it was another. The children did not crawl over Lucy, hugging her, or kissing her eyelids, or wriggling about; they sat near her or stood at her side whenever they could, trying to hear anything she might say. What she said to them had a curious matter-of-fact coquetry about it.

"Now, look here, Aunt Lucy won't have the curtains torn down. We like ladies and gentlemen in this house. If you want some cake and pickle or a drumstick, all right, that is different, go to the kitchen and ask Aunt Paralee. If you don't, then remember other people might want to talk some. Abner, what's the matter with you, old man, that sweet little face looks a mile long to me. You haven't got the cramp, have you? You know I say for you all to cram all the sweet pickle you want, and then when you're ready to curl up and die, I imagine you'll know it. Perhaps I'm wrong, of course." She would have said cake but flour was now $700 a barrel.

The birthday dinner was at noon, and Mrs. Bedford stayed on with Hartie, Frances, and Middleton. Valette was to go to Clifton, where the Surgets were giving a dinner for some of the Federal officers, and there was to be music later in the afternoon. The air for two or three days had been sharp, the skies gray; and to celebrate the birthday occasion the sofa had been drawn in front of the fire for Hugh McGehee and as many children as it would hold. The rest had ottomans. The two Abners and Middleton, while the hickory logs were freshly on, kept half an eye on the fire, hoping one of the sparks would pop so far that it fell in somebody's lap. Lucy, who had declined the Surgets' invitation, was popping corn. "I'll tell you, what you young people ought to do," she said, "make your grandmother tell about the commencement at the convent where she went to school."

"*The Gypsy Countess*," cried Middleton, springing up to stand beside Agnes. She was obliged to tell about the entertainment that the sisters at the Sacred Heart had drilled the young ladies to present for the graduating exercises. "But first, of course," Agnes said, "the sisters worked their fingers off for months getting everything perfect." She knew how to be with children. They listened to the quiet voice, saw that expression in the eyes and around the mouth as if any minute everybody would laugh together, and you could have heard a pin drop.

In *The Gypsy Countess* they had borrowed an anvil from the blacksmith. The gypsy lover sang:

"Fly with me now!
Can I trust thy vow?"

The dresses were yellow tarleton ruffled with string after string of yellow beads.

"Aunt Agnes, there was Cousin Carrie and—you know," Middleton said, putting his fingers to his lips.

"Yes, your Cousin Carrie, who lives in Panola now, sang

Come, birdie, come and live with me,
You shall be happy, gay and free.

The sisters had trained five or six months. Cousin Carrie with her golden hair and a white dress. When she sang that, a little bird flew out and lit on her shoulder. She had seafoam beads sewn on her stockings, and the other young ladies were dressed in white with diamond dust."

The little girls' eyes were popping out of their heads at what seemed so beautiful a thing. There had also, Agnes went on, been a play with the school children of the same size dressed as cobblers, with boots and shoes of every color, and they sang "Blow Away." Then there was *The Ten Commandments*.

"Now it seems to me, if we're going to hear about that," Lucy said, "I'd better go get the diploma; and this basket ought to be enough popcorn to kill you."

In the play called *The Ten Commandments* each girl carried a stick wrapped with white tissue paper and fluffed out like feathers or angel's wings; the paper had been curled with scissors. The girls stood in a line, the tallest down to the smallest, and carried also banners made of a square of paper, the number of the commandment on each banner. In some way which Agnes could not quite remember they had advanced to the front of the stage. The chorus was, "With all thy heart love God above. As thyself thy neighbor love." The banners were transparent.

Her father had to read aloud the diploma, which Lucy had brought in its little frame from the wall of Agnes' dressing-room.

"Now Linda and everybody," said Lucy, "this is what your mamma got when she went to school, which wasn't a convent, though."

Her father, forcing a serious expression on his face, read,

"Twine round your brow the unfading breath of intelligence and virtue.

"This testimonial of approbation is awarded to Miss Elizabeth McGehee certifying her attendance at the Worthington Female Seminary during four sessions, or two academical years. Her progress in the following branches, viz. Reading, Arithmetic, English Grammar, Geography of the Earth, History, First and Second Book, United States History, Child's Astronomy, Botany and Theology, Natural Philosophy, Human Physiology, and Composition, with her attention to study and amiable deportment have given much satisfaction to her teachers and merit affectionate approbation. French also included.   S. Marsh, Principal."

Worthington 8 May, 1848.

"Well," said Lucinda, "French also included—S. March had written nicely and didn't want to copy it over again."

Linda's mother listened to the reading with a smile half forced; she had no sense of humor about herself, not even herself twenty years ago. But the children were both awed and laughing. Miss Bedford pretended to be astonished to know that a McGehee had been on the stage. "If it comes to that," Lucy said, "what of the play with the young ladies in brown calico with crinkled paper tails? They sat under trees—squirrels—nodding and knitting. And tell what you all sang, Mamma?"

"If these creatures will stop choking me to death, I will," said Agnes laughing and trying to hold Annie's Abner down. "It was,

> "We won't go home till morning
> Till daylight doth appear."

The time to laugh at anything and everything had arrived for the children, so now they roared and shrieked in a whirl among the grown-ups, who too were laughing at the picture of the convent young ladies with paper tails singing these words.

Later on, visitors began to arrive at Montrose. There was one carriage and an old rockaway drawn by plough mules, but for the most part there were only old buggies that had not been worth the Union's while to commandeer.

"It looks like a nigger funeral," Sally Bedford said, regarding grimly the array of vehicles and animals to be seen from the window.

The visitors who had to pass through the Federal lines to reach Montrose had been obliged to secure permits from General Ransome. Two or three times, one of the ladies when she arrived withdrew, before she was seated, to the library, closed the door after her, and emerged with a gift that she had taken from beneath her hoop. Mrs. Quitman brought two bottles of cordial. Mrs. Balfour brought from some closet at Homewood a good, strong pair of boots that was to be called for by Confederate soldiers hiding about in the woods; word had been sent to them already. "But you, my dear, have learned your lesson," she said, turning to a beautiful girl who had driven out with her. Every one knew what she meant. It was Ellen Scully. Not long before, as she passed the Tremont Hotel she had been ordered to salute the United States flag and had refused in such temper that she was arrested and sent to prison.

"I've learned my lessons you should say, Mrs. Balfour," she said. "The first is what would we do without General Ransome to order us freed? The second is carry nothing in my tilter." She gave her hoop a push that set it swinging lightly. "However—" she reached up and deftly took from inside her bonnet a box of quinine, "who wouldn't have chills, sleeping on the ground these nights, even a Johnny Reb?"

The Tremont soon after her arrest had been burnt by a company of negro troops that had gotten out of hand.

Mrs. Wilson, mistress of Rosalie, had fared worse than Ellen; she had been banished to Atlanta for as long as the war should last.

At length, when the parlor was empty for a little, Sally Bedford stole back to an armchair by the fire. As the dusk came on the white camellias in the two silver urns on the mantel near her looked faint and dreamlike against the darkening leaves. There had been only seven or eight visitors, but they both seemed more and seemed less; they seemed indeed only one, for the war and the state of things in Natchez bore down on all of them and bound them together.

Judge Winchester was staying on to supper. He was talking with Hugh McGehee in the library. Hugh kept up with every sort of news and reports that could be got at. His natural disposition was gentle, with a suggestion of violent feeling; but his mind was accurate. His mind was bold and high, though the expression of it was so often softened by humanity or tenderness. Few people knew what scorn he had for what he sometimes called trash mindedness, opinions based on straw.

Hugh was speaking of General Sherman's operations in Tennessee. Iuka, Chickamauga, Lookout Mountain. Headquarters were necessary to the plan for a march to the sea, through Georgia, and finally South Carolina, to Charleston, where the secession began, but where Sherman himself had been stationed when he was a young man. General Sherman had all but fallen in love with Southern life. What that fact would mean in the end remained to be seen. What was intended in Georgia was clearly a terrible lesson to the Southern people. To put the fear of God in the Southern people. And the one man who might stop Sherman, the man he was afraid of, was General Forrest; and Jeff Davis slighted Forrest, General Bragg was the Davis favorite, and General Bragg meant ruin. Hugh McGehee cited the main points in Bragg's career, with deadly precision.

The library door stood open and Sallie Bedford listened to what was said. They were talking about the discussion going on in Washington of an invasion of Mexico. An armistice should be declared, during which the Federal and Confederate forces should unite and drive the French out of Mexico. From the start Secretary Seward had thought a foreign war would cure all the national dissensions. And now a common enemy, it was said, would reconcile North and South; perhaps a dominion over Mexico would be established, as far as the Isthmus of Panama. Thus peace might come, between two countries, North and South."

"But President Lincoln," said Hugh McGehee, "always calls it peace between the people of our common country. And it's well known that Lincoln favors an appropriation to pay us for our slaves, four hundred million dollars and he knows that is only fair. Indemnify the South and thus bring the war to a close. In the end 'twould be cheaper than war, but you'll see they'll never let him do it, not that Cabinet of his, and not that Congress in Washington. But why the Mexicans should have to pay for our peace is a horse of another color."

"I presume, then, if we took their country the poor Mexicans would have to be part of the Union, and rebels if they tried to leave it," said the Judge, in a bitter voice.

Mrs. Bedford opened her reticule, took out her handkerchief, folded it tidily on her knee, put it carefully back and drew the string, and listened.

And was the Confederate cause lost, after two years of the war? We must not believe so. Judge Winchester was eloquent; but Hugh McGehee was gentle, he was pure in heart, he was without debating ambition, he was intelligent like destiny. He was the best man she had ever known.

The best man——

She thought of that evening on the gallery at Portobello, when Malcolm had been writing the obituary—President Zachary Taylor had said Edward McGehee of Woodville was the best man he had ever known, but Hugh McGehee——

On the gallery at Portobello.

"Wring these Yankees' plagued necks," she thought, as she touched her handkerchief to the corners of her eyes. "Eh, Darlin'? Where are you now, Darlin'?"

Presently she heard them looking for her, and went out into the hall. The barouche with its crackled leather sides was ready and the children were waiting for her. There had been a candy-pulling in the kitchen. Middleton stood clasping Annie's Abner by the hand. His mother had given the little boy permission to spend the night at Portobello.

"What is it, precious?" Mrs. Bedford said, as Middleton tried to draw her down to him. "What, precious?" He whispered in her ear.

"Aunt Sallie, what is it? Aunt Sallie, somethin' today makes my feelin's feel bad."

"No, darlin'."

"Tell us somethin' funny."

She told them about Francis Carroll's horse, who was in General Stuart's Cavalry along with Duncan. "You know how Francis acts, strutting like a turkey gobbler. And he sent home for his finest horse. Then first thing you know one morning the horse hasn't got any tail, just a stub. Now, what on earth? Of course, Duncan and General Jeb Stuart knew what was the matter. Some old army mule, tied up with Francis' horse, had chewed the hairs off his tail. So Mr. Carroll had to ride out to drill with this stub-tailed horse."

As she told the story, Middleton stood holding his breath with fear lest Abner would not laugh.

On the way home Mrs. Bedford ordered Dock to stop the carriage at the Clifton gate, and instead of Dock, she sent Middleton in to tell Valette they had come for her. She wanted the little boy to see the gardens, the lanterns already lighted along the drive, the glimpse of pavilions where walks ended, the gleaming columns of the house. He stepped to the ground and crept forward, his hands held slightly ahead, as if into a secret, fairy place.

"Go on, son," Sallie Bedford called, trying to keep her voice practical, "the roses are not going to bite you."

The party that Valette saw was the last at Clifton. Soon afterward, by order of Captain Peter B. Hays—at that time captain, he was soon to be promoted to brigadier-general—chief engineer of the Natchez fortifications, it was announced that the line of a new fort would cut through the house. The need for the fort was not clear, since the able-bodied men of the country were off at the war. The Surgets were given time to gather up their clothing and the silver plate; then the house was blown to pieces and the remaining walls pulled down with ropes and horses. Mr. Surget, in giving the dinner for the Federal officers had forgotten to invite Captain Hays. Not only the house; the garden was torn up, the lotus pond and fountains exploded, the grottoes and summerhouses were blown to bits, and all the ornaments and hedges left in piles of rubbish.

XLIX

On the first of March, 1864, on his way to New Orleans to confer with General Banks, General Sherman stopped at Natchez for a brief inspection. A strong division under Brigadier-General Davidson was stationed there. He had found, also, in his Vicksburg mail, a letter from his old colleague Captain Boyd, once Professor of Ancient Languages at the Louisiana Seminary of Learning, under Sherman's administration. Captain Boyd had been picked up by Federal scouts, and from the jail in Natchez wrote, as a prisoner of war, asking Sherman's assistance. At that time a certain poise and confidence had come at last to Sherman from his successes; but he was still harassed.

He had hoped to be made governor of Vicksburg, where he could set about the administration, as he had done so successfully at Memphis. He himself knew that his gifts were not military in the sense of battles and strategy; they were suited best to marching armies and executive discipline. He enjoyed management, and had been proud of his Memphis proclamation to Southern civilians with regard to pillaging and depredations. But he had been denied the governorship of Vicksburg.

He was upset and complicated emotionally by his relations with Grant, whom he had spoken of as his second self, and to whom he had written that all he wanted was "to serve near you and under you till the dawn of that peace for which we are contending." He had wanted Grant to take the army back to Memphis and then come down by rail to the rear of Vicksburg. Every military reason showed this to be the proper plan, but Grant was already committed to the river attack and could not face the Northern criticism that would follow its abandonment. And when the siege triumphed at last, Sherman had worked to give Grant the whole credit. The rivalry and claims of McClernand, Lincoln's favorite, had drawn Sherman closer to Grant. There had been a controversy between Sherman and the reporters, whom he held to be no better than spies scattering false news and scandals in the Northern press, about Grant especially. Lincoln, in order to mollify *The New York Herald,* had sided against Sherman. Grant had stood by him, and in doing so bound Sherman to him forever.

This was only one of Sherman's irritations with Lincoln. Lincoln called for 300,000 recruits, but only a third of these were to be scattered among older companies. Two hundred thousand were to form new regiments so that there might be jobs and honors to reward civilians and to placate politicians made into officers. For the young men in the army that would mean thousands of deaths from disease, taking more toll than bullets; since the recruits would have no veterans to teach them how to endure and care for themselves. There was even an order from the government to combine regiments that had dropped below 300, which meant the dismissal of their trained officers and more new political jobs and commissions.

"Might as well turn the whole war over to the niggers," Sherman said, "they would do as well as Lincoln and his advisers."

Thank God there was no president near to thwart the Vicksburg plan. And he was enraged that the Washington Administration made so poor a use of Vicksburg's fall.

Meanwhile among his own men in the Federal Army of the Southwest discipline relaxed after the victory. The men wished to escape the hard drudgery of camps, the officers sought leaves of absence, and the new draft slowed up.

Sherman found Boyd dirty but in good health. "I will receipt for you," he said to his old friend, who stood looking at him, divided between affection and annoyance at the military intricacies. "I'll receipt for you and get you exchanged. You go along with me to New Orleans." He offered the prisoner money, but it was declined. They went to the Burn where, in July last year, the Walworths on a half hour's notice had vacated the ground floor for the Federal officers' headquarters.

"See here, Professor," Sherman said, refusing to see him as an officer——

Captain Boyd had caught sight of himself in the Venetian mirror with its flowery frame, and was already trying to better his dismantled appearance.

"Yes," he said, "and what?"

"Natchez is the place one of our cadets came from. Edward McGehee. I remember that odd spelling for McGee, and his saying his ancestor when he left Scotland made it up so as nobody else would have it. Odd lot, these aristocrats, granted their point of view."

"I remember McGehee," Boyd said, passing by the last remark and knowing very well how Sherman had never forgotten the taste he had had in Carolina and Louisiana of Southern life. "I've inquired about him. He was killed at Shiloh."

"His parents are in Natchez, I should judge."

"Their place is called Montrose," Captain Boyd said, thinking more of being out of prison, "why?"

Sherman looked at him and said nothing; the sardonic twinkle of his smile was gone, and a sad quiet expression showed on his face. He had resolved to go and see the cadet's family.

His feelings as he made this decision were not unmixed. One day in June, during the Vicksburg campaign of the year

before, he had heard that General Wilkinson's family from
New Orleans, whose son had been one of his cadets, was
refugeeing in the country nearby. He had found Mrs. Wilkinson sitting on the porch with a number of ladies, and had
asked if she was from Plaquemine Parish. He had asked her
about her son and learned that he was inside Vicksburg, an
artillery lieutenant. But when he inquired of her husband,
she had burst into tears and cried out in agony, "You killed
him at Bull Run, when he was fighting for his country." He
said he had killed nobody at Bull Run, but when all the
women burst into lamentations, he had felt so uncomfortable
that he mounted his horse and rode away. But the day before
the Vicksburg surrender he saw from his roadside bivouac a
poor, miserable horse, carrying a lady, and led by a little negro
boy, coming across a cotton field, and as they approached he
recognized Mrs. Wilkinson. She knew Vicksburg was going
to surrender and she wanted to go right away to see her boy.
From there she had ridden on, twenty miles to the town.

Nevertheless, General Sherman knew that he would go to
see Edward's parents; afterward he would join Boyd on the
Diana.

"He was their only son," Captain Boyd said, seeing the
curious look, eager yet touching, on his friend's face.

When William Veal, eyeing the Yankee costume with quiet
insolence, showed their visitor into the drawing-room at
Montrose, Agnes and Hugh McGehee saw a calmer face than
they would have seen when Sherman set off from the Burn.
The ride out, through the deep-sunk roads with their green
arches of the trees, had rested him. It was spring by then,
and he could hear birds everywhere in the trees, and from the
cleared ground the field larks went up like ripples of sunlight
toward the blue sky of afternoon. He had ridden ahead of his
escort and now left them at the road where the entrance to
Montrose plantation began, as he rode with his aide toward

the gate. On either side were hedges of Christmas roses, white; and finally azaleas in full blossom began and the green camellia bushes. Roses, mignonette, verbenas, and phlox were in the garden. The scene at the house struck him for its air of solitude, spaciousness, and sad dignity. He sighed: to his mind it was only the headstrong perversity of these Southern planters in a wilful effort to destroy the Union that had brought this on themselves. From his former life there and his stand as regards secession, the South both fascinated and enraged him.

It was Hugh McGehee who first greeted General Sherman. As he presented Sherman to his wife, he noted the tall and slender figure, the large head with its red hair—and its beard already grizzled, the thin, high nose, the gray eyes. Both Agnes and Hugh noted the air of cynical indifference that was habitual, and that showed now despite the evident nervousness and the twitching about the mouth as he bowed, looking at them. They did not realize that they themselves were standing side by side to receive him.

"I have called," Sherman said, "your son was one of my cadets."

"Edward—" Agnes began, but did not go on; she stood with her hands pressed into the folds of her skirt, glancing at the visitor and then at the armchairs.

For some time after they were seated Sherman addressed his conversation only to Hugh. Voluble and smiling, talking all over when he talked, he spoke of the Louisiana seminary and his former friends, of the fine young fellows who were enrolled there, and then of Edward. His voice was sincere and kind. Suddenly he paused and was silent; and Agnes leaned forward, gazing at him a moment before she spoke.

"General Sherman—" she said.

"Yes, Madam."

"I think I know what you would like to ask. So many were

never found after Shiloh. We brought Edward home afterward, and buried him here at Montrose."

General Sherman jerked himself out of his chair and walked the length of the room; and they were touched by this more than by anything he might have said—there was nothing to say. Then they saw him after a moment direct his eyes toward the walls, where numerous paintings hung.

"And this?" he said at length, angrily clearing his throat and going to stand with his finger tips resting on the mantelpiece as he studied the portrait by Audubon.

Both the McGehees were relieved by this tact of his; he sensed their gratitude as they rose and joined him.

"That belongs to my wife," Hugh McGehee said. "I myself am inclined to architecture but painting I'm no judge of. The Vernet over by the sofa, General Sherman, she commissioned a cousin to buy for us in Paris. On one of our plantations Audubon made many of his studies. It was just out of Baton Rouge, my sister, she's dead now but was Malcolm Bedford's first wife, got the Elephant Edition of the birds, it's over at Portobello; but we are not so fortunate. The portrait of me is by Fontaine, a Frenchman who came to this country via Panola. They said he couldn't paint unless it was a McGehee. At any rate, my brother, up there in Panola, had nine copies done of his likeness, one for each of his children, so you can see, Sir, why they said it."

Sherman laughed out like a boy and then as suddenly grew still as he looked at the portrait. It showed a lady in white satin, with a spray of camellias at her breast, in her hair two moss-roses, shell-pink. In spite of the French academic coldness, Audubon's subject had compelled him to her romance.

"My sister's name, General, was Mary Hartwell. Mary Hartwell McGehee."

A flush spread over that boyish, lined face. "I tell you," he said, his voice rising as he felt in the picture the beauty of a kind of living that was closer to him than his Union thesis allowed, "I tell you, sir, it's a shame this whole secession from the Union. 'Twas absolutely unnecessary."

"In that," Agnes said, "we once agreed with you. But now——"

"Meaning I'm your guest."

"And that, naturally, when Secession came we cast in our lot with our own."

They took their seats again and Hugh turned to the general, smiling. "Every time I think of this Fontaine picture I recollect how they said for one whole winter that Brother's house smelled like nothing but turpentine and varnish, you could air it as much as you would and burn sugar."

"There was a time I wanted to be a painter," Sherman said. "Long ago that was, it seems long ago. Who knows where life will take us?"

Under the tan of his face the signs of exasperation and strain were evident.

"I know that Audubon went to Paris to study under David," this strange man went on, jerking his hands about but seeming to look with pleasure at the blue brocade of the curtains and the dark carpet with its wreaths. "Painting, painting—but in a mad world, who knows? That's it, who knows?" He looked mad himself with those wild eyes, focussed into the scowl of some heroic boyishness. Indeed the newspapers of the North, often copied in the Southern press, had reported General Sherman insane. Presently he grew calmer, and Agnes saw him examining the room again, glancing at it and then at them. She saw his manner becoming more formal and gracious. What this added manner did was to confuse all the more the thought uppermost in their minds from the start. Anybody in this part of the country would have felt the same: could this man in their parlor at Montrose be the

Sherman with the looting, burning, and wreck behind him—around Jackson for twenty miles the country stripped and burnt to a cinder?

Agnes watched Sherman and listened. She could see as he went on that he was convincing himself of something; she decided that he knew he had entered on a new stage or policy toward the invaded territory, that he went back and forth between his first attitude and this later harsher one, that this conflict of policy had become a conflict in his own nature, and that the story that was building up of him as a ruthless monster did at the same time both serve him and his purposes as a picture of war, and antagonize, grieve, and enrage him as a picture of himself. Her intuitions saw him, then, as tormented and wilful.

General Sherman got up and went to look at the mosaic of a table top, colored marbles and semiprecious stones, that stood near a window. "There was some of this," he said, leaning over to look well at the table, "at Hard Times Plantation, Mrs. Reverdy Johnson's, on Lake St. Joseph. It was on the front porch, with the grand piano, and satin chairs and mirrors and books and two portraits, full length, of Mr. Johnson and his wife—one of the most beautiful women I saw in Washington—well—" his voice rose shrilly as he turned and began pacing up and down. "Well, I found some of their niggers and ordered them to put the house in order, and I made some of them take back furniture they were stealing! And I sent a wagon back from camp for the portraits. But by then the house was already burnt—by the niggers or by soldiers, I don't know! And as I have said a thousand times, if the Southern people don't like what they are getting, all they have to do is to declare their loyalty and come back into the Union, and that's the long and the short of it."

"You make it very simple, General Sherman," Hugh said,

rising and going to lean against the mantelpiece. He looked
at his wife, who had grown very white; they would not have
believed it if they had been told so yesterday, but neither of them
was angry. His motive for coming to Montrose had touched
them profoundly, and in General Sherman's reckless stream
and gift of words there was even something persuasive. They
saw in him a kind of rough cleanness of soul. His remarks
had the authority of impetuous people who feel with the
clarity, if not the finality, of logic.

The truth was, a liking had sprung up among the three
people there which none of them would have been apt to speak
of.

"In lieu of that subject, General Sherman," Agnes McGehee
said, when he had paused and was looking at the Audubon
again, "I mean our going back into the Union, which you
speak of as if it were as easy as painting out a tree in a picture——"

General Sherman got up and sat down again.

"—which," Agnes continued, "Mr. Audubon has tried, and
now it's come through again—that dark spot that you see—in
lieu of the Union I might say you would find some paintings
you'd like in Natchez—" She was going to mention the Gilbert
Stuarts at Gloucester, or Doctor Martin's Benjamin Wests,
certain Sullys or Carlo Dolcis but—he read her thoughts.

"As a matter of fact," he said, in a low, tense voice, "I'm
ashamed of my army for the amount of plundering and stealing." He turned to Hugh. "I tried at Jackson to show by
restoring horses, paying for supplies and friendly exchange,
how lenient the government would be once the people in the
South saw they were defeated and would return to their
loyalty."

General Sherman looked into those fine, sad eyes as he
spoke of this, but Hugh saw something besides enthusiasm
for an idea.

"A policy of weaning them from the Confederacy, we can say that, General Sherman?"

Sherman nodded, smiling, as he rose to go.

"Have you done it, General?"

"Well, at Jackson they gave us a beautiful supper. We lost a brigadier, but found him safe under the table with two other generals next morning."

"This is when Edward was seven," Agnes said, taking up a small photograph from the mantel and handing it to General Sherman. "That's his sister Lucy with him."

The picture showed a little boy with long trousers of some light, finely-striped cloth, a black silk jacket, and a linen collar turned down and tied with cord and tassels. He rested his arm on a table with a flowered cloth. Standing beside him was a little girl in a white dress to her ankles, with short, puffed sleeves and a sash of Roman silk. His eyes were large and looked straight at you with a sweet childish regard; her hair was parted in the middle and brushed smooth on her head; her eyes looked away, and the hands hung down at the sides against the little skirt.

General Sherman held the picture, looking at it.

"Yes, when he was seven," she repeated.

"I always saw in Edward McGehee," he said, "hope for a gentleman and for a gallant soldier—in my mind's eye."

The hand with the photograph trembled as General Sherman returned it to Agnes, then reached for it again. After a glance at it, instead of returning it to her or meeting her gaze, he set it back in place on the mantel. Last October his own little boy, the apple of his eye, had died in Memphis. After Vicksburg Mrs. Sherman with the four children had joined him at his camp on the Big Black. Willy was nine, and used to ride with him on horseback at the drills. He was called a sergeant and thought he was a member of the Thirteenth. On the boat up he was stricken with fever and the evening after they reached Memphis he was dead. Later Sherman had written his wife, "Sleeping, waking, everywhere I see poor Willy," and that he would try and make the memory of his little son the cure for the defects which had sullied his character, all that was captious, eccentric, and wrong. He thought of this now and at the sight of the picture. But Agnes McGehee did not know of that, and it was just as well.

L

"WHAT in the wide world has he been talking about?" Agnes said to her husband, when he returned from the gate. He and General Sherman had stood there for a long time, while William Veal held the horses.

"He's got it all worked out," said Hugh. He told her how Sherman, now that Mississippi was in Federal hands, believed it was the time to think of what should be done when peace returned. Having lived in the South, he ought, he believed, to have a right to an opinion. He had written, therefore, a letter this past September, which was intended to reach Mr. Lincoln's hands and had done so.

General Sherman doubted if for years to come there should be any civil government in Louisiana or Mississippi or Arkansas; a military government would be best to rule them, to control the new labor problems that would arise now that slavery was abolished, and to teach the States and territories, both North and South, that no State was endowed with such sovereignty that it could defeat the policy of the whole nation. Whatever the cost of the war, it would have been well spent if it settled forever this question of the Union.

"He likes to talk," said Agnes, "and he probably likes to write."

"The worst thing about war," Hugh said, "is what it does to men's minds. All our family were Union men, but the Union is not a religion; it's a mutual agreement. However, I suppose if General Sherman didn't take it so singly, he might not have been the man to——"

"To come out here to see us."

"Yes, and just now it was I who asked his opinion. To rule the Southerners who make up these States along the river, so he tells me he said in his letter, we must recognize the classes into which they've divided themselves. I'm afraid there's something to 'divided ourselves.' First the large planters, slave owners, the ruling class. In some places bitter as gall; they have given up everything for the Confederacy. In some they are more conservative. If the United States were crowded like Europe, it would be easier, in his opinion, to replace this planter class than to try and reconstruct them, to subordinate them to the national policy."

"Replace us!" said Agnes, in astonishment. "Now that's going pretty far."

"But since they can't replace us, they should establish a military rule."

"I'm sorry he said that 'replace' us, I am really. It's not a good sign."

"Then there's the class of small farmers, mechanics, merchants, laborers, three-quarters of the whole Southern population. Tired of war, he thinks. Used to obeying leaders; they follow blindly the lead of the planters. Then the Union men, with sons off fighting against the Union, General Sherman despises these Union men and the position they take. And finally, the young bloods, sons of planters, sportsmen, never did any work and never will. War suits them, splendid riders, first-rate shots, they hate Yankees *per se*. The most dangerous set of men this war has turned loose upon the world. Stuart, Morgan, Forrest are the leaders of men like these—the best cavalry in the world."

"I declare you'd think it was Duncan Bedford he was talking about," Agnes said. "No, you wouldn't either; the one it fits would have been poor Charlie, Charlie Taliaferro, no matter."

"Aye, it's true what General Sherman said, part of the truth. But what makes them riders and shots and hate Yankees *per se?* What makes them not afraid of the devil? It's Duncan, but it's not Duncan, ah, no, General Sherman's kind of talk makes things too simple. Yes, sir, makes things much too simple."

Agnes said, like a woman (for whatever men may say to the contrary, what is, is): "The fact remains so much has happened, so much outrage, and everybody knows that as well as you know your name. The fact remains."

"Yes," Hugh said. "He's good. I can't understand it."

Human nature is a mystery. War is a mystery, he said to himself. But he made no reply and turned away his eyes to conceal the moment's tears that arose; for he knew that she was thinking then of Edward; and she was right to be thinking of that, even at this moment, for the great and divine and near mystery is love.

Dusk drew on, and William Veal, coming in with the candles, asked if they would wait supper for Miss Lucy, who was not in her room upstairs. But before anything else was said they heard light steps in the hall outside and Lucy came in. She was in her riding habit and carried her hat and crop in her hand.

"I know, Mamma," she said, as she stood with her hands on the back of a chair, "you and Papa'll tell me it's not a time to be riding around the country these days. Now let me tell you all something. If you want to you can, but I won't be caught entertaining any Yankee general."

"Lucy, where on earth— You know better than to go out on the roads with things as they are," said her mother. "Where have you been?"

"I've been to see General Sherman. I went right down there."

"Where?"

"I've been down to the Burn to see General Sherman."

"My conscience!"

"I just took him a sheet of paper. He was on his horse by the porch just starting. 'General Sherman,' I said, 'you might read this.' 'Read what?' he said, and looked at the paper. All it was was General Butler's New Orleans proclamation. But I made a better copy than this one. It's two years old, but all that means is it's a year worse." She drew a folded sheet of letter paper from the bosom of her dress, opened it and began to read. Her mother's eyes rested on her without moving; but Hugh McGehee sat looking at the floor.

General Butler's Order 28.
Headquarters Department of
New Orleans,
May 15th, 1862.

As officers and soldiers of the United States have been subjected to repeated insults from women calling themselves ladies of New Orleans, in return for the most scrupulous non-interference and courtesy on our part, it is ordered hereafter, when any female shall by mere gesture or movement insult or show contempt for any officer or soldier of the United States, she shall be regarded and held liable to be treated as a woman about town plying her vocation.

By command of MAJOR GENERAL BUTLER.
George A. Strong, A. A. G.

Lucy stopped reading and, looking straight into her mother's eyes, sat with the paper clenched in her hand.

"I wanted to tell him about Lord Caernarvon rising in the House of Lords, when the news of this got to London, and saying that in the history of modern war there had never been so barbarous an act. And about that island—" Lucy meant the incident in which a New Orleans lady playing with a child on an upstairs gallery had been arrested for laughing in mockery of a soldier's funeral passing in the street below. She had explained that she did not even know the funeral was passing; but, notwithstanding, had been condemned to two years on an island in the Gulf, garrisoned entirely by negro troops. "I had that to tell him," said Lucy, "if there'd been time. But——"

"What did General Sherman say?"

"I used the last decent paper in the house. It's scented. Well, the old thing took it, he could smell the violet, and turned and smiled at the young lady, me! Then he opened it and read it. He sat still and read it, then gave his horse a kick of the spur and rode off down the drive, didn't look back, kept the paper like that in his hand."

There was a silence for a moment.

"How old is General Sherman, do you think, Mamma?"

"Oh, I should think forty-three or four."

"He seems older and he seems younger."

"That's because he goes through so much. I mean within him."

"Besides," her father said, "fortune has laid a great responsibility on him, and power. If Fortune were actually a woman what she'd know about Sherman is this: he has the blind gift of thinking everybody else can stand what he can stand."

"Yes, and so everybody's got to be explaining him instead of knocking his head off."

"He'll listen to them, Lucy," said her mother. "But he'll pretend he didn't. And that in itself's a torment."

"Well, let him be in a torment is what I say. I can't help what I am."

"Nobody wants you to," Agnes said, rising and going toward Lucy.

"You'd think at least he'd brush that hair."

"Yes, you would," her mother said, gently.

"I was in the library," Lucy said, harshly, drawing back from her mother's touch. "I heard the whole conversation, and heard what Father said Sherman said down there at the gate, all that. How could you all, how could you, when they killed——?"

"I know, I know," her mother said, no longer trying to caress the girl, and going back helplessly to sit by Hugh.

"Daughter," he said, "it's all different when you remember why General Sherman came out here at all, aye, that puts a different face on it."

"Don't you think I heard what he said about the kinds of men—that about the young bloods? What does he know about them? And you listening to it, Papa! She gave the sofa cushion a whack with her riding whip. "From his blab mouth!"

"Lucy, this is not doing any good, not doing any good at all."

Lucy stood in the door, the tears running down her cheeks. She would not allow herself to brush them away, but let them show for a moment as an answer, then she turned and went quickly down the hall.

"You see how 'tis," said Hugh, when she was gone, "you know what all this is. It's not Edward, it's Charlie Taliaferro she thinks we've betrayed."

"She thinks we misjudge him," said Agnes.

"In my opinion it's the last time she'll show us anything she feels about him—we've got to be careful about that."

"And try not to talk about her even just between ourselves. And not even think of it. It doesn't do a particle of good. And it's more loyal not to."

Without looking to choose, she took up one of the books from the table and opened it, then began to read; and Hugh went to sit by the window, from which, far away he could see the cornfields and the pale green of the sky, almost gone. Then he turned to gaze at his wife. Sitting there looking at Agnes with the open book in her hands and the whole posture of her body given to it, he wondered what he might have been without her. With the wealth, the clan pride, and the persuasion of such ease and advantage, he had been invited in this and that direction of life. She had never suggested or urged him toward anything, she had only some knowledge that wished him to be what at bottom he most wanted. She had even known at times how to make herself appear to be the fruits of his own nature; and then what she did seemed to be what he must have done already. Sometimes now in these vexing and confusing times, with the war going on, and all that Hugh saw ahead of him, he would set himself to recall one of those instances of hers, for the sake of its serene energy and its intangible common-sense.

Agnes, sitting there with her book, appeared to be more absorbed than usual, because she was forcing herself to read. Though she would have died for Lucy, she was, unconsciously, impatient at this moment. What she wanted to think of was Edward. Without ever knowing women very much, Edward believed in them, and he had died with the glory in him of what women might be.

As she gazed out of the window, the thought came to her that the stars or beautiful heavens might have something to do with man's conception of women; who are the stars of masculine desire. It is hard on women to be placed thus, but beautiful, too. But Edward was just a boy, almost a child, no, that was only something in her that was possessive and negating; he was one stage of a man. She saw Edward looking at her out of the eyes of a son and of a man; the eyes did not ask to explain or absorb her for his sake, but were asking only that she be divine. And he had gone when he was just at the flower. He had lived by splendor.

Without saying to Hugh, as she had intended to do, that she had no idea of what she had been reading, so that he would not think her cold and indifferent, Agnes rose and put her arm through his and they went out to supper.

LI

On the fifth of October Hugh and Agnes McGehee were
sitting in the cabinet room at Montrose, next to the library
and looking south beyond the beeches on that side and toward
the cotton fields. The day had been warm and bright, without clouds, the roads dusty for lack of rain. It was time for
planting and they had been in the vegetable garden with
Aleck, the mulatto, directing the arrangement of the beds. At
the end of it Agnes had amused herself speaking French with
him, which he had learned as a boy in the Bayou Teche
country. Sometimes in the midst of the conversation he would
slyly lapse into Spanish, his eyes twinkling when his mistress,
not quite following, went on with her remarks, pretending
it was still French. Though but ten years at Montrose, he was
a valuable hand, could do cooperage, locksmithing, and had
been well trained as a gardner, and seldom got drunk. With
his three assistants Aleck was sharp-eyed and severe. With his
master and mistress he was perpetually smiling and knew how
to say very pretty things about this flower or that. Hugh
McGehee trusted him with many things, but his wife thought
Aleck would bear watching, though it was she would talk
with him and smile at his sayings.

In the small cabinet room, its walls filled with their finest
books under glass and hung with framed impressions of
classic gems that Agnes' father had collected in Italy long
ago, they had finished their cups of tea, and Agnes ordered a
tray sent to her daughter's room. Belle was in bed, her child
was to be born in a few weeks. The Audubon portrait had
been moved to hang in this room, and its place in the parlor taken by a Holy Family of Parmigiano's, all curves and
whirling postures, which nobody at Montrose liked. Hugh's

nephew George had sent it from his travels in Piedmont. They had changed the Audubon to this new spot because the light was better here and because General Sherman on his visit had admired it.

When they looked at the portrait they thought of Sherman and his visit to Montrose; and the more time passed the more they were touched by his coming. Otherwise their sense of General Sherman took two forms: first, that he was a straight, impetuous, high-toned, and honest nature, clean, if confused; second, that he depended emotionally on other people, at the moment on Grant—his tone when he spoke of Grant had shown that. And since Grant, for all his natural kindness, understood in war only the smash and stubborn devastation of it, Sherman was likely to become a brutal factor in the fate of the South. Nevertheless, they had been touched by him when he was there. Agnes, especially, thought him a pathetic, strong child, full of impetuous integrity.

When General Sherman was attacked, after some fresh news of his troops' outrages, Agnes tried to shift the blame, asking how any man could keep an eye on everything that was done. And many of his troops were mere hired Irish and Germans. Toward the end of August Miss Mary Cherry's friends sent her a copy of *The Oxford Falcon* in which the burning of Oxford was described. General A. J. Smith had arrived in Oxford very well disposed toward the town; he had appointed a provost marshal and put guards at private houses. But an hour after his arrival a courier had arrived bringing the news that General Forrest, with 4000 men, had outmanœuvred him, with 16,000, and instead of being about to be captured had, in fact, taken Memphis. In his rage General Smith ordered the town burned. He himself, with turns at the bottle, directed the operations. At the house of Jacob Thompson, a former member of President Buchanan's Cabinet, General Smith superintended in person the burning.

Mrs. Thompson was allowed to take some of the clothing and furniture from her room; General Smith had what he chose from the house loaded into a wagon he had caused to be brought up for the purpose, and everything else had been burnt. The soldiers rang the church bells, the courthouse was burnt, even the negroes were pillaged for what little they might have. And yet it was a fact that General Sherman was at this time miles away, and that he reprimanded General Smith, though not for Oxford, for the several days in which his superiors had lost sight of him entirely.

A carriage drove up to the house, coming to a stop as if from a race, the horses snorting and striking their hoofs on the stone court, and Mrs. Fleming rushed into the library and then to the room where were Agnes and Hugh, without waiting to be announced. She told them that a large force of Yankees were at Windy Hill Manor on their way into Natchez. She had been dining at Gloucester when a servant of the Farrars had come over with the news.

"It's three miles home to The Towers," she said, "and I hardly dare to try the road. I'm going by the back road through your fields. I've only a minute."

"It's out of my cup but drink it," Agnes said, pouring tea, "it's better than waiting for a fresh one." She put the cup in the shaking hands.

Hugh went out to give the order for the carriage and horses to be driven across the pasture and then around to the creek swamps for safety.

Before sunset Lucinda came in from Portobello, riding the mare, Fancy, with William Veal on Mario. The road was full of fugitives. She did not recognize the people, they must be working people from town. They were also overseers and their families from the plantations, she thought, with frightened negroes among them, some of them dragging children along by the hand. She was trembling and rushed to her father; and as soon as his arms were around her, burst into tears. The woods near the house were full of Confederates, many of them without coats, hats or shoes, who had told her the Yankees were in close pursuit of them.

Before it was dark the house was closed, every door and window fastened, and when supper was served they sat down to it and tried to eat. Five times during the meal there were sounds of feet on the front gallery and knocks at the door. Men came to ask what they knew of the enemy.

"How many do you figure they are, sir," they asked.

Two of them, from the way they spoke and the sharp look around that they gave, were plainly spies. The rest of supper was left untouched, every one prepared for the night in his own way. There was an unfamiliar silence in the house, only the sound of speaking now and then in low tones and of footsteps in the rooms, back and forth.

Agnes, after looking in their room for her husband and not finding him, went to the library. He was standing beside the walnut armoire with a book open, a scrapbook bound in leather, warped and frayed.

He turned and looked sadly into her eyes, as he laid the book down on the table, muttering something of which she seemed to make out only the words "my father and his father." She reached up, and putting both her hands on his gray head, drew him down to kiss his forehead.

"Choose Thou for me, our Father," she whispered, the tears running down her cheeks.

"Is that Lucy I hear crying?" Hugh asked.

"Yes, poor little thing, she's just a child. I was looking at her eyes just now and seeing what a child she is, in spite of all that strong character she has. You go and see her."

Agnes knew the book that her husband had taken from the armoire and then left there on the table. It was a ledger of recipes, cures for one thing and another, that had been in the family for generations. The first recipes were written down in the time of James V, father of Mary Stuart. When she took it up, the page where it opened told how wounds should be bound with the leaves of bergamot.

"Bergamot—" she began to laugh. It seemed to her ironic that wounds could be healed. "God forgive me," she thought; she would try to school herself in God's will.

She found her husband and Lucy in Belle's room where she herself intended to pass the night. She had wood placed on the hearth, for the air had grown chillier; saw that the windows were fastened; and dismissed all the servants. Then she fastened the doors of the room, and with her candle and book sat down in her daughter's room. She had studiously kept word of everything from Belle who lay sleeping quietly. Once or twice she opened her eyes to ask, "Why don't you go to bed, Mother?" and fell asleep again.

The book was "The Philosophy of the Plan of Salvation," by a Mr. Walker, a lawyer in New York. She had read it before. The clock, faintly in its alabaster case like bells far off, struck eleven; the stillness in the house was profound. She read; she tried to pray and to stay her mind on God, trying to feel that nothing could befall without his permission. At half past three she lay down in her dress, on the day bed at the foot of Belle's.

She had not been on the bed a quarter of an hour when she was startled by horses' hoofs and then the loud jangle of spurs and sabres, and immediately a heavy knock on the door that opened on the gallery, and a voice calling "Mrs. McGehee." Without opening the door, she asked who it was and what did he want.

"I am Lieutenant Poole," was the reply.

"And who is Lieutenant Poole?"

"One of Colonel Gobel's scouts, and we want to know if you have seen or heard anything of the Yankees tonight."

She went out to the hall door and opened it, told them what little she could, gave them water to drink, and saw them ride off. The night was now past and it was going on toward five o'clock. She called in the servants, and giving up the charge of the sick room, where her daughter had slept quietly, she went upstairs to her own chamber and lay down. But she could not sleep and rose and began to bathe. While she stood thus she heard cannon very near the house. Again and again the cannon shots came, shaking the house, then the rattle of the sharper musketry and shouts mingled with these sounds. Lucy rushed in the room, her features convulsed with terror and crying.

"Oh, Mother, I can't stand it! Oh, Mother. Oh, Mother!"

"My dear little girl," she said, surprised at her voice and the ordinary words, for she felt as if she would faint, "you must be calm and brave. You must control yourself. We may have a great deal to do today and we must seek strength and help from God. Kneel down and ask God to give us strength."

Lucy, who had started with every fresh report of the cannon, grew quiet as she knelt by the armchair and buried her face in her arms. She was on her knees quiet thus for some minutes and from that time on was calm and helpful.

Before Agnes had finished dressing, William Veal knocked on the door; the whole place was full of Yankees, he said.

"Where?" she called, taking the garments Lucy held out to her and hurrying to dress herself.

"The house is surrounded by Yankees," William said. "Nigger Yankees."

By the time she got to the front gallery, cavalry in their dusty blue uniforms were riding through the gate. She ran down the stairs and to the kitchens. There was not a servant male or female in the whole court or in the cellars or servants' rooms. A skirmish was going on in the wood beyond the gate. Servants were running to the scene of the fight, risking bullets through their brains. Then after a few minutes the firing in the wood ceased; the cook and housemaids returned. Agnes ordered breakfast immediately. She went to Belle's room, ordered a tray brought to her, went through the dining-room and upstairs. Edna, the maid, brought tea and buttered bread on a small silver platter to her room. And after taking it, for she was weak from the long night, Agnes went again below stairs.

Over the grounds there was a great confusion. They were cooking in the back court for Colonel Gobel's Confederates, with Paralee standing over the fire. But in the dining-room no breakfast had been brought. A little mulatto girl, Bessie, ran to Agnes from Belle's room.

"Oh, Missis," she said, pulling at her collar, "them Yankee niggers is in Miss Belle's room and they ain' nobody wid her 'tall."

Agnes darted along the back gallery into the room, seeing on her way that the whole grounds were full of negroes. They were at the smokehouse and over the kitchen court, on foot and on horseback. She could hear them tramping in the parlors and the rattle of their sabres and spurs. She rushed in to her daughter. There they were. Lucy was in the bedroom and the negroes were tramping through the sitting-room, threatening, cursing.

"Get out," Agnes ordered. "Get out of my house. Get out of my sight!"

A big black who seemed to be in command gave a guffaw, and the other negroes, watching him evidently, followed. One of them came up to her and with his open hand boxed her on the cheek. At once another negro put a pistol against her breast; she could smell his sweat. Then the big negro who had struck her said, "Don't shoot her, Mose, slap her. Slap the old slut." He broke into a stream of abuse.

Trying to keep them out of her daughter's room, she stood

between the negroes and the door until Belle called to her from her bed and begged her to let them come in. She saw her daughter raise herself in bed, push the mosquito bar aside and, calling them to come in, bid them look all through the room.

"You'll find nothing here but a sick woman," Belle said.

The negro soldiers made a show of searching the rooms, chattering all the while.

"I'se gwine obey mah orders. I'se gwine to search dis here house," they said. But they did not open one closet door or look into one shaded recess, for fear of meeting Confederate soldiers. They squatted about in the middle of the two rooms, feigning to look under beds, where the coverlids were never raised. Two or three of them rushed up the staircase leading from the sitting-room to the attic above, and finding the door locked to a room there which had been Aunt Tildy's—when Belle was a baby—they bawled for the key. Lester, one of the house negroes, was with them. He came to Mrs. McGehee for the key.

"Tell them to break the door down if they want to get in," she said.

Other Montrose negroes were going up the stairs with them. She pleaded with Belle to remain where she was in bed, fearing for her life if in her condition she got up and tried to walk about, and thinking she would be safe there if anywhere. Lucy stayed with Belle, and Agnes went out to the back gallery. A crowd of negroes on horseback, and fully armed, filled the space around the smokehouse, mingled with negroes from the plantation, who swarmed over the grounds.

There was one white man. He was sitting on a horse, between the smokehouse and the columns of the gallery. Agnes called to him, but either in the din he did not hear or he pretended not to. She sent the little mulatto girl, Bessie, who kept hanging on to her skirts, to the officer, "if the gentleman would permit her to speak to him."

The officer turned and rode up to the gallery on which she stood—she was above him as he sat on his horse and he scowled as he raised his eyes to her. As a gentleman and as a man of humanity, she said, she asked him to compel these negroes to leave this house. One of her daughters was ill and in danger of her life. She showed where she had had a blow on the head.

"I ask your authority to protect us from these drunken negroes," she said.

He hardly heard her through. "Hear that, boys? Drunk niggers! Drunk niggers, you shan't talk so to me! There ain't a drunk nigger here—not one of these men has had a drink of whiskey in a month. You shan't talk to me of drunk niggers."

He turned and rode back to the smokehouse. They had broken open the doors and there was a rush up the steps. Negroes on the plantation who had never been able to work she saw rushing about. Women filled their laps and aprons with meat, lard, sugar, beef. One young woman, whose husband had run off to the Union army, filled her apron with pork piled up as high as her head. Agnes from the gallery could see it all. The throng thickened, they swarmed everywhere. The dairy, which was in the basement of the house, was crowded. She could hear cries and oaths as they drank off the milk or smashed the basins on the flagstones. The preserves and the store room for meats adjoined the dairy. They too had been broken open. Hams, brown sugar, soap, loaf sugar, flour, candles, dried fruits, dried vegetables were being carried off or scattered. As she went indoors she heard shots fired at the door of the library.

"Damned old scoundrel, what did you shut that door against us for," a soldier shouted as the door opened and Hugh McGehee appeared. Blows from a cavalry pistol and a sabre struck his head. As Agnes put herself between her husband

and the negroes, a pistol was held against her temple and they began to curse her. A negro drew his sabre and slashed the air, threatening to cut her throat; but seeing her looking him in the eyes, stopped slashing about, and then all of a sudden brought it down, though flat, upon her head. She staggered back to the gallery where she could again speak to the white officer on horseback.

"Take him off," the officer was saying. "Take the old scoundrel to the colonel and tell him they are cooking rations for a hundred Rebels here this morning."

At this point two officers coming in at the gate saw Hugh McGehee among the negro soldiers and ordered him back into the house. Meantime the cotton ginhouse across the pasture from the house had been set afire and was burning. Hugh found his wife in the hall, with her back against a door. The house was going to be burnt in twenty minutes, he said. They could save what they could. She appealed again to one of the officers who had just arrived, a major.

"Madam," the officer replied, with some embarrassment on his handsome face, and she noticed a bullet scratch on his check. "I wish you to understand that I'm not acting on my own discretion. I am only obeying orders."

"What have I done to be—?" Hugh began.

But the officer said that they were only losing time. If the family was not out in twenty minutes the house would be burned over their heads.

The destruction had already begun. The table in the dining-room, which had been laid for breakfast, was overturned and smashed for kindling a fire in the middle of the floor. The china closet was crashed up. They could hear axes smashing over the house, splitting up banisters and furniture for the fire. The pictures on the walls were being slashed or cut down. When he came to Henry Clay's portrait a negro corporal, for some reason, shouted a new volley of filth, as he lunged into the face. In the meantime other negro soldiers were pouring turpentine over the library and a sheet of flame spread there. Before the flame was lighted, Hugh could see the officer standing with the ancient recipe book in his hand, which he had picked up from the table. He would scan a page, then tear it and crumple the paper in his hand, scan another page and do the same thing; and then as the flames began in one corner of the room, he hurled the book into them. More than any of the rest this angered Hugh; his wife laid her hand on his arm.

The black soldiers were in the attic and were running through the house from room to room, searching into closets and drawers, and carrying out silks, objects, painted window-shades, damask curtains, linen, blankets, and men's clothing. They threw scarfs and mantles over their shoulders, and filled their haversacks. The officer came out of a door stuffing his pocket with lace handkerchiefs. The flames had started up the stair to the floor above, and a fire roared in the rooms where the consumptives from the North had lived. From Mr. Munger's door smoke was pouring into the halls. When William Veal and two young negroes carried Belle from her room to the gallery, the major himself appeared. Seeing that face, so drawn and white, he stepped back against the wall, touching his hat; so that, without knowing what she did, Belle smiled at him, holding out her fragile hands for him to come to her. She begged him to save her piano and music; if not, she said, she would die; and he, very much confused, bowed stiffly as they passed on with her into the garden. He ordered his men to bring out the piano, the music rack and a part of the music. A sofa and four chairs had also somehow found their way out of the house.

Not long after, flames poured from windows, and down the

long hall a torrent of smoke and flame rushed out through the door. Timbers crashed and then the roof fell in. The columns of the front portico remained standing.

The family stood together watching the scene and trying to form a protection around Belle who lay on the ground on the pallet made for her. Only now and then she looked around, then she relaxed into exhaustion again. In the outdoor light the blue tint under her eyes showed more distinctively and the transparency of the ears characteristic of pregnant women. A number of negroes were with them. They saw Bessie, the mulatto girl, dash out and lay hold on a little black boy who stole along the box hedges, looking about him as he went and rubbing the whites of his eyes. As Bessie dragged the little negro forward, he screamed loudly, pulling away from her and hiding one hand behind his back.

"What you got in yo' han', boy. Show me what you got in yo' hand!" the girl was saying, as she jerked his elbow and shook him. She snatched his arm from behind him and pried open the little black fingers, which were clutching a red silk handkerchief. Hugh McGehee, who liked anything that was alive, stood watching the little negro's eyes, from which the tears ran down to make a worse smudge of his sooty face. He was Aleck the gardener's child. It eased Hugh to see the destruction and pillage reduced to this level, when a piece of red cloth gave the feeling of excitement and booty. He looked down at his daughter with her drawn features and shut eyes, and at the green grass around her pallet.

"Let him have it, Bessie," he said. "Let him have it," and the little black boy, darting first to the camellia bushes, ran along the walls of box on his way to the quarters.

Four or five trunks had been brought out, into which the scant clothing saved had been put. The young major came striding over the lawn to them. He had assigned them, he said, a negro guard for their property. On one sleeve some

falling cinders from Montrose had burnt a large hole in the
blue cloth; he kept looking at that.

LII

By autumn most of the house negroes returned to Portobello. One way or another they had been able to leave the
stockades, where the crowding, and the feeding question, the
epidemics, like smallpox, measles, and fever, and the number
of deaths made the Federals there glad to loose them. Some
of the negroes escaped, some were allowed to go. At various
times the Portobello servants came straggling in, old Tildy
among the first. Her husband, Uncle Thornton, had died and
been buried in the sandbar.

Sallie Bedford did her duty by the Portobello negroes and
wanted them not to suffer; but she had little sentiment about
them, and so looked over the old woman at the foot of the
back steps coldly.

"Go on to your cabin, Aunt Tildy. You've been an old fool
and I hope you know it. I had a board nailed on the door to
keep the other niggers out."

Plantation negroes had moved into a few of the other
cabins. The lane along the quarters had grown up with dog-
fennel and crab-grass. What she most resented in Tildy's
case was the fact that it was Duncan's mammy who had been
one of the negroes to desert.

"Go on now out of my sight," she said, as the fat old hands
were raised to thank her, and Tildy began mumbling and
rubbing her eyes. "Your clothes are all down there. If you
haven't got any castor oil, send Feeny up to get it. You need
it, I'm positive. If 't hadn't been for you, madam, Uncle
Thornton would be here. You can't tell me it was in Uncle

Thornton to leave us. So, you can just keep your mouth shut now."

Tildy broke into loud lamentations. "Oh, Miss Sallie——"

"Didn't I tell you to hush your black mouth!"

The old woman turned and started for her cabin.

Valette, however, did not take these matters as Mrs. Bedford did. That day after sunset she went down to the cabin and read the riot act to Aunt Tildy, who felt better after it. Valette had done the same with the other negroes when they came back, first scolding and then giving them orders what to do.

"Have Miss Valette been give you one o' dem tongue lashin's?" Feeny asked.

"Oh, my Jesus!"

"Lak she give we all?"

"I ain' say she didn'."

"Aun' Tildy, Miss Valette can sho' raise de blisters," Feeny went on, in the tone of some one who has just been listening to a fine orator.

"I ain' say she can't."

The next morning Tildy, in a dress she had washed the night before and ironed at daylight, went up to the children's room and sat down as if she had never been away at all. Middleton climbed into her lap and Frances stood leaning her little head on the fat shoulder. Only Mary Hartwell understood that Mammy had gone away and deserted them; the others, seeing her back again, accepted the situation.

"Did you know Duncan had been in a battle?" Middleton said. "Did you, Mammy?"

"I hyerd Marse Duncan go be a colonel soon," Mammy said, opening the little boy's mouth to look at his teeth, "and you got yo' new eye teeth, ain't you, son?"

"We haven't hyerd Brother go be a colonel," Frances said.

"Dar you is still, who ast you to be talkin' like a nigger?"

"Say *heard*," Mary Hartwell told her little sister, firmly.

"Fannie's got to say *heard*," Middleton chuckled, standing on his knees, with his arms around Mammy's neck.

"De truth too, y'all can' be talkin' lak a passel o' white trash."

One night in November when only herself was awake in the house, Mrs. Bedford heard the dogs at the quarters barking. At all the front windows of the house blankets had been nailed up, which a Federal officer, riding in one day to find some of his men looting the smoke-house, had told her to do. Many of his company were hired and scum out of the big cities, Germans, he said, and he could not control them; any night passing along the roads, if they saw a lighted window, they might take a shot at it. On the south side of her chamber, however, toward the rose garden and away from the road, Sallie had left the windows free, merely closing the shutters when her candle was lit; and that night, instead of undressing and going to bed, she had blown out the candle and sat down in a low chair by the sill. It was a clear night and she could see the starlight over the garden and the trees, and could smell the red roses blooming near the porch. The soldiers had finally looted the smoke-house; one of the negroes had told them that the white powder sprinkled on them was only flour. Keeping house grew even harder. When night came she was tired.

Sallie Bedford was too proud and bitter to pity herself, and could scarcely have told you what she was thinking of as she sat there that night by the window. She leaned out listening to the dogs, one of them a shrill little fice that had belonged to Uncle Thornton, you would have known that bark anywhere. Then she seemed to hear swishing noises and a sound of heavy breathing somewhere beyond the box hedges, then only the dogs. The dogs barked less and grew quiet again. Then she heard voices and horses' feet and presently, off beyond the garden and in a direction opposite that of the quarters, she saw lights, now twinkling, now lost in the trees. She felt her way across the unlighted room to the bed-table where her pistol lay every night, loaded, on top of the books. Valette also heard the noises beyond the lot and came into the hall. She had put a long dark wrapper over her nightgown.

"My Dumplin', you certainly can't go downstairs by yourself," she said.

The two women, Valette following and holding on to the other's hand, who kept it behind her back and clasped tight the young fingers, stole out into the garden, bending down and keeping to the box-walks till they came to one of the pavilions. Here the one leading stopped and turned to the startled girl.

"No. You stay at the pavilion till I get back."

"But, My Dumplin'—" Valette begged.

"No use arguing, or we'll just pack right to the house again, and no knowing what will happen." Valette said no more but stood close against the pavilion, and saw the other's form moving away.

From the pavilion the walks led through the camellia bushes; then came open ground, now full of weeds, along the bordering shrubbery. Mrs. Bedford could follow this shadow till she reached the heavy clumps of bay bushes, and from there could see what was going on in the wood beyond. The horsemen, whoever they were and whatever they were after, had halted there and she could hear their voices, the stamping of the horses, and a stir of activity. Her own small body in its black dress was tense; she was not afraid of the devil. But she went as noiselessly as she could, and found a place where the leaves were thick as a wall and she could watch. They were not fifty feet away.

There were twelve or fifteen men with their horses, and at that moment three others rode up and dismounted. In the

light on a pine-knot that a negro held up she could see that
they were Confederate cavalry. Some of them had gray uniforms, some no coats. On two horses and on an old mule she
saw men, and at the same moment saw that their uniforms
were blue. The clothes of all three were dirty and torn, two of
them wore caps. They were not astride but, with the men
cursing at them, were trying to stand up in the saddles. A
soldier who was trying to throw ropes over the boughs of a
post-oak swore at the negro for not holding the torch higher.
The flare of the pine-knot struck all around, and even from
that distance she could hear where birds flew upward from
the trees around. Meanwhile the officer who directed the
hanging was stepping back and forth, giving orders and
cursing at the prisoners. He was a middle-aged man in a better uniform than the rest, and wore a black felt hat with the
wide brim turned straight up in front. He looked in a fury,
and then, as the preparations neared completion, grew quieter,
until finally he stood motionless, watching relentlessly what
went on. The officer's silence affected his men, who were
now silent, looking at him, at the men on the horses, and at the
tree limbs above where the ropes were being thrown. In the
moment of stillness Sallie Bedford heard the little noises in
the grass near her, the small innocent life going on, and faintly a bird calling, far down toward the end of the avenue.

When the three soldiers who held on to the bridle-bits of
the mule and two horses were standing them on the spots
where the nooses could be put around the prisoners' necks,
Sallie Bedford saw that the one standing up on the first horse,
balancing himself with his hands now and then—none of
their hands had been tied—was a young man, a foolish-look-
ing Swede, some farmhand who had doubtless enlisted for the
pay. His face was greedy and coarse, with a shock of blond
hair under his dirty cap. Next to him was a short, lean man
of fifty. She could see him screwing up his eyes and trying to

grin at his captors. He was already hysterical and kept glancing at the mule and up at the face of the soldier standing on it, a thin, consumptive youth scarcely of age, who held his lips tight together and shut his eyes. The soldier in charge of this prisoner she could see. He stood in front of the horse's head, holding both reins in one hand and the bridle end in the other like a whip. He was even younger than the youth on the horse. This young soldier had clothes almost as new as the officer's and a black felt hat. His face, fresh as a child's and delicately molded, wore a look of severe control, as he stood ready to do as he was commanded.

The faces of the onlookers had now, after some talking among themselves, again grown quiet. Some of them pretended to be busy with their belts or rifles; and one who had sat down on a log to take off his shoe held up a sock full of holes.

"Just look at that," he said, "by God, nine tomcats couldn't keep a mouse in it."

He threw the sock away, put back on the shoe and came to stand among the others. Unconsciously, perhaps, the company took a position; they fell into a kind of semicircle, watching the soldiers who held the horses by the bit. The presence of death, even under circumstances so hasty and so rough, imposed a certain formality.

"Go on, go on, we've got to get to Port Gibson," the officer said coldly. "Stand up, God damn you!" One of the men on the horses had half stumbled.

Sallie Bedford turned her head away. "Leaves on their boughs," she thought vaguely; they had always meant coolness and shade in the garden at Portobello—Duncan in Virginia—they well ought to hang, the thieves—if she'd caught them like this, she'd——

The thin-faced youth uttered a short scream, and at the same time she heard the officer's voice give the order, the sound of a lash and of a horse rearing. When she looked, the young boy in gray with the black hat was holding down the horse, and the thin youth's body, the legs jerking up and down in a spasm, the arms bent, swung back in the air.

The officer swore at his two other men, who struck out wildly. The mule did not budge, but the short man, pulling at the noose and his cravat, had slipped and lost his footing and then jumped. The cravat ends flipped into the air, the hand shot convulsively forward as if scattering something.

"By God, he'll hang himself, mule, if you won't hang him," the officer shouted, giving the mule a kick in the flank.

"He wants to shake hands with you, Captain," a high voice said.

The officer ordered the negro to trample out the pine torch. "Come on, Alexander."

The young soldier who had held himself so rigidly and had struck the first lash got up from where he had sat down against a tree, forced his hands down to his sides, and without looking at the others, mounted his horse. A few minutes later they had ridden off.

Sallie Bedford put up one hand and moved a branch of leaves out of her way. It was dark now under the post-oak, but she could see dimly the shapes swinging above the ground. She clenched her fists to stop her hands shaking. The soldiers had done what the officer commanded. The negro had held the torchlight, the three Yankees were dead. Except for the officer, whose tense excitement she could not understand, none of the men had seemed to be in a hurry to kill the prisoners, and they had gone through with it like the parts of a machine. So she had seen this. It confirmed her feeling that we are all animals and fight for our existence, that all love is fierce and watchful, and that pride and scorn must be in the nature of passions. "What did I always tell Darlin'?" she said to herself. "I always told Darlin'."

And at the same moment she was thinking of Agnes McGehee. Agnes was not a McGehee born, but she had married a McGehee and was like one. As she stood there, all the McGehees seemed to her at this moment soft and tedious. With Darlin' gone she was farther from them and less patient. These war times——

With the pistol still in her right hand, she hurried back toward the house. It was all dark, and she saw that the quarters were dark; the negroes would have heard the noise and some of them would have peeped through chinks or cracks in the door, but had not made a sound.

"The child's gone out of her head," was her first thought when she heard Valette's voice talking. "I oughtn't have left her by herself. Lord knows what anybody ought to do in these times!"

"But try to stand up," she heard Valette whisper. "We can get you in, Sir. Try to stand up."

"What on earth?" she called. "Valette?"

On the ground and propped against the lattice wall she saw dimly a man's form and Valette kneeling beside him.

"Eh, My Dumplin', it's a Yankee soldier. He got away from them. They shot him." She was almost sobbing.

"How'd he get here?"

"He came crawling through the hedge, nearly scared me to death."

"They ought to've killed him."

Valette caught hold of Mrs. Bedford's skirt.

"I could understand him better just now, My Dumplin', but not now, the way he's muttering."

"We'll see. Get up, Valette," Mrs. Bedford said. She stood Valette to one side and put the pistol against the soldier's forehead. "Are you dying or just playin' possum?"

The soldier jerked his head back from the pistol. The

fright and the cold steel perhaps revived him. "I'll tell you," he said, quite distinctly.

"What were they after you for?"

"They caught us on the road with some jewelry," the soldier said.

"That you dirty dogs had stolen like this child's mother's watch. The soldier that got that she followed all the way to the gate crying and wringing her hands, but he just dangled it in his hand and rode off laughing at her."

"Three of us," the soldier went on, under his breath and trying to turn his head to peer into the shadows around him. "Not the short old man. He wasn't in the army. An agent. They caught him at a nigger cabin, trying to get the niggers to tell where the cotton was hid, that's what that was."

"Yes, gathering up our cotton," she said.

"He said they pay for it."

"So General Sherman says. The officer out there tonight glowered like a crazy man."

"He said he'd hang all four for the way somewhere they'd treated his mother. But it wasn't us did that." He began to whimper, leaning over first on his all-fours; and then slowly, with his fingers hooked through the lattice, getting on his feet, while they stood thinking what to do.

"All for a damned gold chain, Mrs. Oh, Jesus, hanging men!" he muttered.

"You dry up, you stinkin' little thief." At the same moment she was putting her arm through his at the shoulder to support him. "Here, does that hurt you, does it?"

He gave a groan.

"Once you're in bed, boy," she said quietly.

Valette, holding the other shoulder, was telling him it didn't hurt so much, afraid meanwhile that she would retch at the smell of the blood.

"Poor thing," Mrs. Bedford said, "I'm a good doctor. You're thin as a rail."

They drew the curtains close in the room and lit a candle. The soldier had already collapsed on the bed.

"Bolt the door," Mrs. Bedford said.

Valette ran to bolt the door and came back to the bed where the other stood with the candle looking down at the soldier.

"'Twon't do to let the niggers find out he's here. There's no knowing them now, what they'd tell. Mammy Tildy especially. You know what she's feeling. She's likely to get us in trouble yet. I don't know what we're going to do about Tildy. I've told her ten times, if she didn't stop talking about getting even with the Yankees I'd tell them to go out there and get her."

Thornton had been buried without a coffin. Before Tildy had left the stockade, down on the sand bar, where the river had washed over last year's graves, the bleached bones were sticking out.

Valette could do nothing with the clenched teeth. "I can't make him do it," she said, putting the glass of water on the floor. "Is he asleep, My Dumplin'?"

"I can't tell." She rubbed her bruised forearm and screwed up her eyes, as she held the candle closer to the soldier's face. "I don't know whether he's fainted or just dropped asleep from weakness, losing blood."

The blood from the wound at the back of the head had come round the neck and soaked up in the collar. The room had filled with the stench of sweat and dirt.

"I declare," she said, setting down the candle near the bed's head, "you'd think with General Sherman capturing the whole Mississippi River they might at least wash their men. Oh, no, honey, don't mind me; I've just seen too much this night."

Valette threw her arms around her neck and kissed her. "You're a saint, My Dumplin', you're just a saint!"

"That's as it may be, no need to weep over that. But look at the clothes on the poor little wretch." She had an arm around the girl's waist, and they stood looking again at the soldier; he was as young as the consumptive youth they had hanged. "Look how it wasn't worth a shuck. That's that shoddy, honey, that's the famous shoddy some smart Yankees made and sold their government. It looked mighty fine till the rain struck it. And now see what it's like. You want to ask me some more about what I saw out yonder by the lot, but you've heard enough tonight. You go put your dress on and come back here to me."

It would soon be daylight, and at daylight she must go down to the quarters and tell Enoch to take Ross, one of the plantation negroes whom she trusted, and go bury the three Yankees off in the woods. If some of the Yankees should come and find out what had happened, they would burn the house down as sure's you're born.

"But, My Dumplin'—" Valette exclaimed, when she returned and was let through the door—"You'll wear yourself out, you're not iron any more'n anybody else is."

"Bolt that door again," Mrs. Bedford said, sitting down again on the chair by the soldier's bed. "He's been delirious, and kept calling for his mother. Then he must have thought she was here. 'Kiss me, Mother,' he said, 'Kiss me, Mother.' I passed my fingers over his lips. 'Kiss me, Mother,' he'd say, and when I did that it seemed to comfort him."

The tears came to Valette's eyes. "It's a good thing he's dying, I reckon. Isn't it, My Dumplin'?"

"Precious, how should I know? Though we ought to know something; we've seen death enough lately."

"I know you think I'm young and don't know anything—" Valette began.

Mrs. Bedford rose from her chair as she said, "I've never thought there was any connection between age and knowledge. You know what Hamlet said about old men. Said they had most weak hams and plumtree gum in their eyes. My papa used to make us read that Cicero piece on old age, De Senectute. I always said, 'Papa, he's an old fraud, I don't believe he means a word of it,' 'Then he stole it from some Greek writer who did mean it,' Pa said. Deliver me from sages. But it's better for you to think about Shakespeare and Cicero than crying over this poor wretch, so that's why I'm going on about them. In the morning if he's dead, I'll send in town for the officer who warned me about the blankets over the windows. From Springfield, Ohio, Captain Laffer— by way of a name! There was a sergeant, too, from the same town in Ohio, who said his name was Sam Silt. Miss Mary Cherry, when she heard his name, just said, 'Well, young man, I presume it was just your father's name.' Do you hear me, honey? No, you don't. Then I'm only wasting breath."

When she was gone Valette took sole charge. She had heard Mrs. Bedford talk of Florence Nightingale, who nursed English soldiers in the wars. Though she had no such flowery name, and though she was nursing a Yankee soldier, not some handsome Confederate, she felt that the moment was romantic. The soldier lay quiet now, there was nothing harrowing; for his face was tranquil and as pale as marble. The thin hands even were crossed on his breast as he lay there.

But youth prevailed, and after a while, in that perfect stillness and exhausted by this night, of which the older woman had seemed to make nothing, Valette fell asleep. She dreamed that Duncan came and asked her to put on her blue silk, and said to her that all strong natures loved only one.

Toward six o'clock in the morning she was awakened by the soldier asking for water. Coming out of that dream with

Duncan, she bent so tenderly over him that the young soldier blushed, looking away from those beautiful eyes.

LIII

"You think he'd sashay in there like a Marmaduke; a Yankee soldier in my house?" Mrs. Bedford said to the row of Confederates who stood in the front door next morning. It was soon after breakfast. They were a part of the cavalry she had seen the night before. The tallest of them had two old waistcoats on, one buttoned in front, one in the back; and among them she saw the youth who had held the horse under the first prisoner hanged. She saw he was not the sort to tell his feelings and, despite his worn home-made uniform, how neat he kept himself. The gray young eyes were as honest as daylight.

"How old are you, Major," she asked, her eyes twinkling.

"Seventeen."

"The whole war?"

One of the other soldiers, a lean Scotch type, answered. "He ran off to join Forrest's cavalry, when he was fourteen. But they persuaded him to come home, his father promised him a horse."

"If I'd just wait, my mother said," the young soldier explained.

"I'd take my oath whenever there's a call for volunteers you're the first one." She leaned her head to one side, studying him as she said this.

"That's a fact," the other soldier said, while the youth stood with his eyes gazing into hers.

"And all your life you'll do the same thing," she said.

"A man has to."

"I only hope you'll get some thanks for it. We must remember your name."

"Alfred Alexander."

"Bless your little heart! I hope the war spares you, for the sake of decency among us generally. And here's some advice: don't rush to volunteer. Let some of the others risk somethin'."

"We've been sent to look for a man," he said, simply.

Here Sallie Bedford turned gruffly to the soldiers. "I asked you people if you thought the Marmaduke was here in my house, didn't I?"

The soldiers laughed: "Dead in the woods somewhere, I reckon," the tall soldier said, "but no harm, ma'm, when a prisoner had escaped in the dark last night, asking you if you've seen or heard anything of him."

She learned that the agent had been bribing negroes to show him where a plantation's cotton was hid, and that this cotton then either was burned or was shipped by the river North, where it brought $400 a bale. This, as every one knew, had been going on all over the South. Sometimes the agent when he took the cotton had given a receipt for it, which was supposed to be convertible—when the time came, that is— into cash. At any rate thousands of bales were one way or another being seized In fact General Grant had complained that his soldiers were being robbed of their rations and hospitals of their supplies, because the quartermasters' teams were being employed hauling cotton to the river. He estimated that the surreptitious traffic had come to at least $200,000,000.

"The reason," the soldier went on, "our captain says he'll hang every Yankee he catches is because his old mother is paralyzed and one day a lot of soldiers, black and white, got in her room and danced round and round her bed, hoopin' and stickin' her with their bayonets. So he just vowed he'd hang every Yankee he got his hands on."

"Poor wretch," she said.

" 'Twas up in Lafayette County."

"Well, you'd better go catch some more for him," she said.

"Yes, ma'm."

They turned and descended the steps to their horses, which they had ridden up to the very door. On the way down the avenue the horseman with the two waistcoats on and no coat rode close by the statues along one side, touching his hat to each he had passed.

After this visit, Sallie Bedford saw more than ever how important it was, any way you took it, to get the escaped soldier out of the house, and was relieved when she returned to his room, to find him sitting up in an armchair. Valette was not with him.

"Let's see us," she said, in a friendly tone, and went around to look at the wound. A piece of the scalp had been torn away, with the loss of blood, but the wound was not deep. As she dressed the wound, she asked him what did he think of when they were going to hang him. He said he thought of his father and mother. The soldier said that so simply that her throat tightened.

"We thought you were dead last night," she said; and without making a reply, he followed her with his eyes around the room. She had devised a plan to get him into Natchez.

The doctor in charge with the Federals in Natchez had chosen the Gardens, her friends the Prynells' home, for his hospital. Once they adapted themselves to his arbitrary temper and authority, the old lady and her daughter had found Doctor Blackall a kind man and a gentleman. At the Gardens the fences had been torn down, brick ovens built over the grounds for baking the rations of bread, the piano had been turned into a horse trough, and the camellias and shrubs trampled or cut down. But the camellias sent to Mrs. Prynell from Portobello, where the neglected garden showed still so many, had been admired by the doctor; Mrs. Prynell had said that in her note of thanks.

Sallie Bedford rummaged the secretary for a proper sheet of note paper and sent an invitation; would Doctor Blackall, since he liked camellias, ride over at once before the petals began to fall. The note ended with a quotation from Pope. She wrote, with a twist of her mouth,

> When opening buds salute the Welcome day,
> And earth relenting feels the genial ray.

The camellias, starring the green masses of the garden so thickly, put the doctor in a good temper. He professed to have formed a most favorable impression of the Southern people and deplored the war, which, doubtless, only the haste of certain characters had brought on.

Portobello was indeed a Southern mansion; from the pavilion walk he stood looking at the house, with its white columns among the leaves. Mrs. Bedford had received him walking under the trees of the avenue, and contrived not to invite him indoors, thinking that, though some of the valued objects were wrapped in sheets and taken up to the dark attic, it was just as well he should not get a taste for what the house afforded.

"Very fine," Doctor Blackall repeated, squinting to get the picture of the house, and suddenly looking banal as he did so.

"From over here, perhaps," she said, guiding him to another spot away from the pavilion and the blood stains that might be there.

"I myself am not an abolitionist. Can the leopard change his spots, can the Ethiopian change his skin?" Doctor Blackall said, stepping lightly along and pointing with his small hand. "This is the alba plena, this camellia, but I have always been a Union man. I learn that many of the planters in this country were also Union men. Unfortunately now they are solidly against us. It may be the price of ultimate peace, we must accept it."

"That," Mrs. Bedford replied, smiling, "that's what my father said about Andrew Jackson's campaign." Doctor Blackall gave his polite social laugh, but stopped when his eye met hers, which seemed to say, "What do you know about it?"

She excused herself to go into the house for a basket and shears; and Valette, who had been keeping a lookout from between the library curtains, came darting to her. Valette should go at once and tell the Yankee soldier that he was proceeding to Natchez with the Yankee doctor; to steal out by the kitchen and through the orchard and wait at the gate for Doctor Blackall. And not to let him or anybody else know about being here in this house. To pretend he was coming along by the road. "And tell him to drink all the milk he can get for a while, what cows haven't been driven off or killed, and tell him we don't want to hear of him again, either."

The tall, high-shouldered figure of the doctor could be seen strolling up and down before the statues of the four continents. He no longer spoke of politics or sections when she joined him, but praised the quiet at Portobello. "Peace, what peace reigns out here! Like a retreat," he said, in an affected tone.

"Andrew Marvel's line, 'like a green thought in a green shade,'" she said.

She smiled because she saw for two seconds a flash of the good doctor himself standing upon a horse with a rope on his neck; and because, also, he was lauding the quiet of Portobello to a woman whose ears were still full of curses and moans and horses in the dark.

"I must confess," he went on, "that being constantly surrounded by sick and wounded men is hardly the ideal life. It's more tedious at a hospital than all the times I've been on battlefields with wounded men brought in by the score. In a hospital away from the field the men have less stoicism about pain."

From his tone he might have been asking the difference between camellias. But as he spoke he made a gesture with the left hand, and she noticed for the first time that half the palm with the little and ring fingers was shot away and a long red scar extended to the wrist. She no longer resented the tone he had used about the sick and dying at the hospital. He had won the right to speak of it as he chose. And so she merely said, "Mrs. Prynell tells me she has come to regard you as a friend."

"I should be most happy to think so," said the doctor, and again he laughed. This time it did not sound to her so much a polite society laugh, but more that of a man who, like her, felt a sense of futility and despair.

By that time twilight was drawing on, and under the trees at the end of the avenue a new moon hung lightly down the blue sky. She pointed it out. "I always think it's a pretty little thing, don't you, Doctor? My chillun love it," she said, noticing at the same time through the gate palings the shadow of the soldier waiting.

LIV

AFTER the burning of Montrose the McGehees moved into a cottage two or three hundred yards from the house. It consisted of five rooms partly of logs, and was known as Don's Retreat. Markings on some of the timbers showed that they had once been part of a ship. This house had been there as far back as any one could remember, and was thought to be of the Spanish times. It stood behind a small wood of holly trees and magnolias, invisible from the old house but touching on the garden. Into this the sofa and four chairs were put and the concert piano, with five blankets, which, after other beds and mattresses had been lent from Monmouth and Arlington, made up the furnishings.

When the negro regiment had gone, and the fire died down that day at Montrose, Confederate stragglers returned and helped Hugh when he went through the quarters to find what had been secreted there. They found Agnes' wedding dress, her embroidered purse or handkerchief bag, but not the veil, and some of Hugh's clothing. In the ashes of Montrose itself they found one chocolate cup of Dresden, the roses on it still fresh though the handle was gone.

Presently the carriage was brought back. Black Dave, the driver, had removed the taps from the wheels, and after dragging it as far as the gate the soldiers had abandoned it. The Montrose silver had been spared. William Veal told nobody where he had hidden it. On the eleventh, five days after the fire, Belle's child was born, a girl; and the day following died and was buried in the Montrose graveyard to the left of Edward; the space on his right was for his father and mother. On a small headstone brought out from Natchez, they had the words carved, "We shall not forget thee, nor shall God forsake thee, in the peace of love." Agnes wrote down these words for the stonemason in Natchez; and the old man himself, whose son had died in the Federal prison at Alton, Illinois, though the words were of love, cursed the invaders and wished the blackest hell on them.

The negro guards whom the major put over the belongings saved from the Montrose fire had broken open the trunks and distributed the contents among whatever slaves would promise to leave the plantation. The Federals had established not only the stockades by the river for such negroes, but had also had put some of them in Natchez houses. The Confederate Major-General Martin's house had been looted and turned over to scalawags and blacks. The chandeliers and mirrors were smashed, and horses were stalled in the drawing-rooms. Wagons and harness had been collected from Montrose as had been done from the surrounding plantations; and what was not wanted for Federal purposes had been burned.

During the week word came from Woodville that Edward McGehee's house had suffered almost exactly the same treatment. Bowling Green had been sacked and burned by a negro company under Colonel Osborn, commanding the Third Brigade U. S. Cavalry, Eleventh and Fourth Illinois, colored, and mostly full of grog. A letter came from Mary McGehee describing it.

On December 31, Saturday night, Agnes McGehee sat down to write in her journal. When she was a girl her Grandmother Randolph one day had taken her into the library and read aloud passages out of letters from her cousin, Thomas Jefferson, to prove what the cultivation of one's talents may do; and from this had argued for the keeping of a diary. This diary, long abandoned in the busy Montrose days, had perished in the fire. And now, confined as she was to the small house, with few duties any more, Agnes began the writing down of notes. There was no volume like the old one presented by her grandmother, bound in purple velvet with a medallion of painted Dresden set in, and gilt edges; she pasted the new pages into an old garden book from the bottom of one of the trunks. She liked at times to write. Indeed there were moments when she thought herself too pleased over some passage that she had composed, and feared lest her conscience should reproach her for vanity and pride.

Louise had been sent to one of the places belonging to the Miles McGehees, in the pine wood country; the trouble in her lungs was gone. Stella had returned to Baton Rouge. Hugh McGehee, a lonely man, moving gently among his guests when there were guests at Don's Retreat, wishing them to enjoy the moment, grave and gentle himself, sat not rarely in silence. Lately he had had a letter from Duncan and talked of him a good deal. Southern cavalrymen supplied their own horses, and Duncan's Arabian was shot under him a few weeks after Yellow Tavern. Duncan wrote in the letter of Stuart's death at Yellow Tavern and of his white plume and yellow sash and gold spurs, trying to make up in spirit for his cavalry what they lacked in resources. The dismounted men of the cavalry, unable to find horses for themselves, went into Company Q, a hash of good cavalrymen, derelicts and riff-raff. Duncan had no mind to be one of them, and for that matter he scorned, when Stuart was gone, to follow any other cavalry leader. Four or five months now he had been one of General Lee's sharpshooters. And that night he had gone to bed soon after supper.

"The last night of the old year," Agnes wrote in the journal, "and almost the last hour of that night! What thronging memories crowd upon me! And how far removed I seem to be from this night one year ago. Is it wrong this yearning for home? I stretch out my arms toward the home that was mine, with a feeling of desire and love and hopelessness. Is this sinful? I am thankful for the fire this bitter December, for the food that sustains me, for the presence of my husband. This evening I have lived over the past year. I think I can say 'I submit,' that I give up all will of my own, and do honestly and truly say 'on God's anvil to be laid.'

"From room to room I have passed—in memory—I turn to our own chamber—that sweet, bright, quiet room—whose east windows looked out on the beech woods and admitted the first ruddy glow of the winter morning, as it brightened the orchard boughs, and from which at night I always glanced up to watch for the Pleiades and Orion's constellation. How often the heavy and motionless leaves of the cucumber tree reminded me of a tree carved in stone. I see it tonight. I smell the south wind with the odors of roses and heliotrope in the garden. I see the moon too, and the clouds as they sometimes hid her from sight or sometimes formed a majestic pavilion around her. A thousand thousand times I have thrilled with pleasure as I traced the shadows of tree and shrub, blackening the grass and making brighter by contrast the silvery light beyond.

"This was Edward's room, and in the next room his books, some of them marked, some of them——"

She had not the heart to finish, but laid down the pen and pushed aside the ink-stand, the little bronze drum, which casual chance had saved from the wreck, with only a few of the gilt cards bent. She sat gazing at her fingers, as they lay on one of the other parts of the book, and beyond her fingers she saw the writing there. "November 29. We heard today of new orders in the town and that the Yankees had men on the roads coming this way. My husband was at Bayou Sara, where our plantation is falling to ruin, and we did not think it prudent to wait till he should return. We hastened to prepare for the coming soldiers. This was not easy, perched in this open field as Don's Retreat is, and the negro quarters between us and the forest. We did what we could and waited, listening to the sound of negro voices mingled with the jangling of spurs and the clatter of sabres. I pictured to myself our former gardener Aleck, inflated with pride at his new dignity of corporal, coming in with insolence and insults demanding watches and money. This perpetually recurring dread and horror makes night a terror and life a torment. Oh, if we women and helpless old men and children were only where we might feel safe from negro insults, negro violence, and from the constant fear of these things! God help us—I look at the graves of our beloved ones and think with thankfulness of the rest which is theirs."—New Year's Eve, 1864——

She closed the book, already praying, her eyes fixed on the last embers of the fire, her whole body quiet with some strong force that made life dear to her—and believed that God saw in every heart its own sorrows.

LV

AROUND New Year at Portobello, a quartette of soldiers, along with two negroes, came one day and went over the house opening all the drawers, throwing the contents on the floor. In a closet they found a demijohn of shoeblacking made of soot and elderberry juice. "Is it blackberry cordial?" they asked and Sallie Bedford said, "What's your opinion?" The soldier who turned the demijohn up for a gulp hurled it against the wall; it made a great stain. After that they piled all the children's clothes on the bed and gathering up the counterpane into a bundle took them out and burnt them. It began to look as if the dolman from M. Worth's in Paris was going to be the only cloak left in the house. A good many of the carpets upstairs had been cut up into lengths and sent off, along with a great bale from Natchez, to be used as saddle-blankets in the camps.

Then Hugh McGehee had a letter from Captain Ruffin in which he told in a simple, brief way of his wife's death. Mrs. Ruffin had asked to be dressed in red, her cheeks rouged, and her basque pinned all the way down with the ruby brooches as she had always worn them. Red flowers were to be put in her hands and in her hair, and red verbenas planted on her grave. "She was trying," Hugh thought as he read the letter and gave it to Agnes, "to take out of the world with her what the world was." Then a few days later some of General Smith's soldiers, coming on the new grave and thinking valuables had been hidden there, dug her up; they kicked open the coffin and left her lying on the ground. The brief letter stopped abruptly.

General Lee's surrender at Appomattox on April 9 was

published in the Mississippi papers on the 14th, and soon afterwards the force in Mississippi surrendered. Then came the news of Lincoln's assassination, which everyone took as the final blow to the South, for he was a Southern man and understood them, and he had planned a peaceful adjustment, once the Union was saved. He had pronounced against confiscations and against universal negro suffrage. Southern people were shocked to read in the newspapers the report of the famous Mr. Emerson's speech in which he suggested that it might be a kind Providence that had got Lincoln out of the way.

There was much talking about all this among the Natchez houses, but very little at Montrose. Meanwhile William Veal had brought in the silver from the woods where he had hidden it nobody knew where; and they had given him a black coat with a tail and satin lapels, and a gold watch and chain. "William Veal, Fidus Achates of the McGehee family" was engraved in its case.

September came; it was five months since the surrender and they had heard nothing of Duncan. There was not much mentioned about it one way or the other at Portobello; a certain omission, or reserve, had come into the household conversation, which had always seemed so open. Valette, without saying so, wore fewer bright colors, and had even made herself up a black dress from an old silk of Mrs. Bedford's, to wear to church when they went, which was not very often.

Duncan's mother got so she did not speak of him. She could see him lying dead; the picture summed itself up sharp and quick in a mind like hers. Not the pain Duncan had suffered: she despised that, just as he would despise it. What she felt was hatred for the Yankees, and passionate devotion to Duncan. Loyal memory came last. She could see him close those eyes of his, the scowl gone, the heart gentle and kind, leaving, as it ceased to beat, that pure face, its motives generous, the mind quick and just. She knew Duncan's heart, it was, or the part of it that she knew at least was, his father's heart.

She did not know that the death she saw was her own, and that thus she died two deaths. But when to herself she said, "My son is—," she stood up and threw back her head. Dying. There was nothing to hate. Only to be what you are. For some reason when that idea came to her she felt that her son was dead.

The other Bedford plantations were running themselves, so far as they ran at all. She had done nothing about them. White laborers had begun to come in, but most of them refused to work alongside black labor. Mississippi was not a State any more, the courts were whatever they happened to be. But at Portobello some work was going on, there was the garden, at any rate; a few times Sallie Bedford, in her patched wash-dress, but still in her silk stockings, had ploughed there herself, with a sort of harness made up of thongs, strings, and grapevine, strung up on the mule, and had wondered when the jerks of the ploughshare in the clods would throw her light shape over the mule's head. She despised the mule for submitting to such a harness, and whacked him oftener because of it. "If you were just anything but a mule," she said, "you'd kick out of such traces. You'd kick my head off." But she ploughed.

For the three children she had bought a bolt of gingham, at the cheap wholesale price for the cloth by the bolt, and made them clothes. It was better for them to go without fancy things now, she said, and have their teeth attended to and a chance to get an education when they were older, and not go out in the world numbskulls; people could think what they chose of how the children looked. There was no money in Natchez for governesses, and the two older children went to school in town, sitting on the mule, the two of them in the silk dolman caught around them with a big diaper pin, Dock, the Indian, walking alongside and carrying the primer and making the two of them keep still inside the one dolman.

Nevertheless, Duncan's going off to the war, her sister Rosa's death, the death of Malcolm Bedford after Vicksburg, the occupation of Natchez and her having to run the plantation alone, in the midst of danger and dread, and finally the uncertainty about Duncan these four months, had fallen, one blow after another, on Sallie Bedford's head. She was thinner than ever, more spry and more purposefully occupied. She had come to live not so much on her own nature but on her will. Except for those she loved already, the kind heart had dried somewhat, it went out less to people; but her manner had grown milder, more out of indifference than otherwise. At intervals she had begun to drop into moods where religion took possession of her mind. All the arguments by which she had debated religious doctrines with her friends and kin, half in mischief, now meant nothing to her. True to her character the turn she took was direct, practical, and devoted: her thought dwelt on the next world where she would meet those she had loved.

She began sending messages by the dying. If she heard that someone was dying she would visit them and say, "Tell Darlin' for me that he's not forgotten. I will come to him." "Tell Rosa—" or "Take my little Virginia I lost in your arms, she's just a little girl." She had begged Mr. Surget, when he lay dying, to do this for her. Such messages she asked the dying to remember when they got to heaven.

Other people heard her say these things and saw that it was only like writing notes to some one beloved who was far away. The hands that held some dying hand to ask such a favor were, for all their hard work, still fine and white. But, nevertheless, people noticed that to Duncan she sent no message, refusing to let herself believe he was dead.

One morning in September Francis Carroll and his mother drove out from Crescent Hood for a visit. He had been home since May but had not been to Portobello because he dreaded to meet Duncan's mother or Valette. The moment was saved by Mary Hartwell who, as soon as she saw the empty coat sleeve, ran to catch it in her hands, pressing it to her lips. Even Valette started to kiss Francis, but did not. Mrs. Carroll began at once to talk of the impeachment of President Andrew Johnson, which she seemed to think a good thing because, she said, "he's from Tennessee, and yet he is President of the North."

"I don't read the papers much any more," said Mrs. Bedford, "but isn't Andrew Johnson trying to carry out Lincoln's policies, and that's what makes old Thad Stevens, with that mulatto housekeeper of his, come out of his skin with rage?"

"Of course it is, Mamma," Francis said, in a tone of authority, and by some instinct he began to speak of Duncan. He spoke of his and Duncan's joining General Lee's infantry, when they had no horses left, after Jeb Stuart's death, and of seeing Duncan one day behind Lee's earthworks, eight men behind him loading rifles and handing them to him in succession. Valette brought out a Dresden basket of peach chips which had been made only a week before from the yellow-clings in the orchard, and they sat talking of Duncan as if he had only ridden away for a little stay on one of their plantations. "I notice people always like to talk about Duncan," said Valette to herself, as she listened, afraid they would stop, "yes, sir, whether they like him or not, they love to talk about him." The visit ended by their carrying off Mrs. Bedford to dinner with them to Crescent Hood, promising to send her back in their old rockaway, such as it was, at whatever o'clock she chose; and Middleton was allowed to go along.

After the siesta, which everybody took until four, they had a tray of watermelon and peaches.

It was sundown when they left Crescent Hood. "You'll have to make allowances," Mrs. Bedford said to the Carroll children, while their mother insisted that the visit had been all too short. "I've stuck so much at home, you see, I haven't got any manners left. That's it." She did not say before the children that it was not a good idea to be driving the roads so late, with so many stragglers and blacks at large in the country.

Some time later as the carriage turned the bend past D'Evereux, the horses shied, and Mrs. Bedford saw the driver slow them down and then stop. A group of negroes, three of them, standing along the road, had moved in front of the horses. The scared negro boy driving kept still, not even looking back at the lady and child in the seat behind him. One of the negroes, the oldest in the group, stepped out and came up to the carriage, putting his hand insolently through the bracket of the lamp.

"Phil, what is it you want?" said Mrs. Bedford, leaning forward toward the driver, as if to say that in a moment she would go on, but in reality suddenly feeling sick with a vague dread and fear. She had recognized the negro as one who had run away from Portobello early in the war. But before anything could be said, Middleton had recognized him, too; he put his little hand out and laid it on the black one grasping the carriage rim.

"Uncle Phil, are you mad at me?" said the little voice.

The old negro held out his arms, "Why, no, little Marse, why, no," and as Middleton stood up on the carriage floor, he put them around the little body.

"Where've you been?"

Middleton stroked the black face.

"Middleton, we've got to be gettin' home, you tell Uncle Phil to come and see us."

"Yes, m'am, come and see us, Uncle. Who are these men?"

"Jes a passel of niggers. Git back outen 'at road," he shouted.

When they got home, Mammy Tildy was standing by the carriage entrance; an old dirk as sharp as a needle was stuck in the fence planks, and she stood there with her arms crossed. But when Mrs. Bedford got to the house she found that the gate to the vegetable garden had been left open and the young turkeys were in the lettuce beds; and by the time that was attended to, the supper bell had rung.

LVI

ONE day, late in November, when they were sitting in the hall at Portobello, Duncan walked in. For months, every afternoon when she had heard the train blow for the crossing this side of Natchez, his mother had waited for him on the front gallery, but he had not come. Today she had re-entered the house and taken up her sewing as she listened to Miss Mary and the children talking. "Well," Miss Mary was saying to them, about something or other, "I've told you repeatedly—" when Duncan appeared.

There were voices raised, exclamations, sobs, the children clinging to Duncan's legs, and then Middleton running up the stair, sliding down the banisters, and up again and again down, shrieking and whistling, with Miss Mary scowling at him and then at Duncan and giving orders, while some of the negroes, who by some means had got wind of Duncan's arrival, began to crowd at the back door and on the gallery. It was such a commotion that a good deal of time had passed and still nobody knew what they wanted to know, which was where Duncan had been all this while. Four or five times he answered the question, "In jail," he said, "I've been in jail." But nobody seemed to think that this was an answer. "You rascal," his mother said, taking up his hand to examine it and tapping the knuckle bones for the thinness on them, "Eh, Miss Mary?"

"Aye. 'Tain't as if the war hadn't been over and done with for months."

Duncan himself was wondering where Valette was. Where was Valette?

"Look here, Duncan Bedford—," Miss Mary called to him, as he turned from the hug that Mammy Tildy gave him to shake hands with some of the field hands who had just come in, "when are you going to answer? Your mother wants to know where you've been all these months; it's plain as day you've been somewheres. Great Cæsar, now we'll never know," she went on, turning her good eye toward the stair landing. "Look at that."

Valette, in a white dress sprigged with yellow, came running down and threw her arms about Duncan's neck, covering his face with kisses. Duncan felt the blood rush faster into his heart. "Tell me—" he tried to say, but as he thought of what words would be most like those he had often fancied himself saying to her, Valette slipped from him and, dropping on her knees beside Middleton, pressed the little body to her bosom.

"Well, what carryin' on do you call that?" Miss Mary said. "Duncan, I don't know where yet you've been, and meanwhile all of us have been thinkin' that——"

"Well, you needn't expect Duncan now to tell you anything he's not going to tell you," his mother said.

"Lette, why did you take off the black dress," said Middleton, stroking her hair and leaning back to look at her.

"Did I?"

"Oh, shucks! I saw you runnin' in from the garden, and you had your black dress."

Mrs. Bedford saw Valette glance up timidly at Duncan and

then away as if at some one that had been betrayed; but at
the same moment she saw that Duncan meant to show no
sign that he had understood. The proud boyish scowl left his
face, into which came an expression of such tender sweetness
and joy that his mother felt blessed by it. But the words that
she would have said were, "He's handsomer than ever. You
can see how beautiful he is."

They had all of them observed Duncan well. A trifle
thinner and more sunburnt, but looking more of a man;
the same brown hair and gray eyes, with the boyish scowl,
the mouth fierce and delicate. His clothes were faded and
worn, he had pinned up the rent in his coat with two thorns,
and his boots were old. Mammy Tildy several times went
near to him, running her eye over him and shaking her head,
but so far as it seemed to concern Duncan he might as well
have been in either ermine or rags.

That night in the parlor, Middleton, sitting in Mammy
Tildy's lap, listening to Duncan tell of all the things that had
happened with him, cried and squealed so every time they tried
to take him up to bed, that they had to let him stay; he was
nodding at last when Mrs. Bedford had everybody to bed, and
Valette and Duncan were left alone. Duncan went to fetch the
dolman and put it about her shoulders, and they walked
together a long time up and down one of the walks by the
statues, under the trees. His feet were calloused from the
stretches of walking that he had done on the journey home,
and he had got the habit of long strides; but presently was
able to change that and keep step with Valette, whose arm
through his and hand in his seemed to his mind that night a
sufficient explanation of the world. When she looked up at
him in the darkness he could feel her eyes, and what she left
unsaid told everything.

"This old dolman," Valette said, "we used to think it was
very fine. It came from Paris. But pinning up two children

in it on a mule to go to school hasn't helped its style or shine. It's a good thing it's dark."

"I reckon it is dark," said Duncan. "I hadn't thought about it much."

"Are you tired as blazes comin' from so far?"

"I hadn't thought about that much, either."

"You've just given up thinkin' about everything?"

"Do you sing still?"

"Yes. You knew Clifton was blown up?"

"Mamma wrote me."

"Because Doctor Martin, when he gave a dinner for the officers, forgot to invite the chief engineer, Captain Hays."

"Why'd he give the dinner in the first place?"

"I never thought of that. Smell the sweet-olive? My Dumplin' thinks the fragrance is too heavy. But I don't. There's nothing too sweet as far as I'm concerned."

"So it's sweet-olive I smell so sweet?"

"What else could it be, Duncan?"

"If I had died in Virginia I'd have smelled this night."

But this was after Duncan had told them about himself and his mother had read the letter from their Cousin Marshall, in reply to hers begging for news of Duncan, as to whether he was dead or what?"

LVII

SUPPER had come so quickly after that moment when Duncan walked in at the hall door, and the children, who wanted to know so many things and whose bedtime would be coming soon, were given so much of the floor, that still nobody knew exactly what had happened to him all these months. "I've been in jail," he said, flatly.

"And why, for the love of God, why, pray, wasn't it prison?"

said Miss Mary Cherry. "Jail's a place for tramps and niggers, Duncan Bedford, and you know it."

"A rose by any other name would smell as sweet," he said.

"It would not. Nobody likes roses better'n I do. But you just bring me Butler's tea roses and all I think of is silver spoons and General Butler's stealin' everything in New Orleans, and that's nothin' more or less than a stench in my nostrils, though the roses were named for Bishop Butler long before Beast Butler was ever heard of. All right, young man, have it 'jail' if you like. What do you say, Sister Sarah?"

"I say that nobody's got to worry about Duncan and jail, Miss Mary."

"I fell through an iron grating and broke my leg, but that was in broad daylight in Memphis, Tennessee."

The connection of that with him, as Duncan perceived, was that no excuse could be enough for one's disappearing.

It would never have occurred to any one there to think that Duncan could have done anything dishonorable. And yet they noticed how slowly he came to what he was going to say and that he meant to tell his story exactly when he pleased and to suit himself.

Duncan, when he came to his story at length, told the beginnings of it scatteringly.

Toward the end of March, he said, they made a surprise attack on Fort Stedman. They carried the works and made the garrison prisoners. A week of fighting followed and Duncan, having been sent out with detachments to Five Forks, was captured with them there. If the supporting column had occupied the hill to the rear of Fort Stedman, Grant's army would have been cut in two. But that had not happened, and so General Lee's plan had miscarried. The day before the assault their cousin Marshall had told Duncan that in his opinion it was the most daring move planned during the whole war. General Lee had learned through his spies that

Grant was getting ready to leave only a skeleton army to hold his entrenchments while he led his main army to flank the Confederate right. The assault would open the way for a cavalry force to take City Point and capture General Grant himself, nothing less. "By George, nothing less," Duncan repeated. Though his eyes brightened at the thought of Lee's daring, every one saw that Duncan spoke as if he took little pleasure in his story. Suddenly he said, turning to his mother, "I might have written you, Mamma. The least I could have done was do that."

"Oh, no, no, don't let's go judgin' people, honey," she said, and he saw how drawn her face had grown. "I think there are times when it's just as much a mistake to judge ourselves. Nobody's blamin' you."

"I blame myself. But you see what happened, I was a prisoner of war with a number of others, only I had a sabre-cut in my leg. Nothing to speak of," he added, as Valette jumped in her chair.

"They started us north toward Pennsylvania. But soon I was among the men who were listed for an order of exchange, which was easy's falling off a log."

"Oh, Duncan!" said Valette, thinking him at the moment the most modest soldier in the world.

"All I mean is Cousin Charles Marshall got my name among the first on the list of prisoners for exchange."

"And that would have put you back in the Army of Virginia?" said Mary Cherry. "Would it not, sir?"

"What was left of it. And then I'd have written you all at home."

"It's no matter about writing us letters," his mother said, in a low voice, as she took up the sewing-basket from the floor beside her. Her hands these days were seldom idle. "What else, son?"

"What happened was—" Duncan began and told them how

he had been called up by the Union provost marshal. The two of them were alone in the marshal's office when he said to Duncan, "Well, young man, so you are one of those fine fellows who are letting General Lee lead you on to destruction. It's no longer an army of the South; it's Lee's army. And General Lee's a proud man." Duncan answered by saying that General Lee had against him a horde of hired riff-raff. He knew nothing about this, but said it in order to insult the provost marshal. "You're a liar," the provost marshal said, and was knocked down. Duncan's voice had changed as he told of this, and his face got red; the recollection of the scene brought back the anger with it. "When he said that, I knocked him down."

"Ha, ha, where'd you hit him, Duncan?" roared Mary Cherry, slapping her knees with her hands. "In the face?"

Because of this encounter Duncan was stopped on his way at Baltimore, his exchange order revoked. He was put in irons and locked up in the prison known as the Black Hole. He was so disgusted with life in general that he wouldn't write. All sorts of cases were around him in the prison, army thieves, free negroes, murderers, and political dissenters; some of them were out of those more than 36,000 citizens who, during the war, had been imprisoned in the North for their opinions. In April news leaked in of the surrender at Appomattox; but in the midst of the mass of prisoners Duncan was lost sight of for a time. For that matter he was not a prisoner of war, his offense was assault on an officer of the United States. By June came word of President Johnson's amnesty to the Confederate leaders, a limited amnesty; but in Norfolk, despite the fact that the terms of surrender had guaranteed the protection of the United States to the soldiers of the Confederacy, so long as they conformed to its conditions, the grand jury had indicted Lee, along with Jefferson Davis, for treason. General Lee sent his application for the amnesty through General

Grant, reminding him of these terms, and Grant added a note of his own to the Secretary of War, Stanton. Grant had made the note sharp. In it he maintained that the officers and men paroled at Appomattox, and since, could not be tried for treason so long as they observed the terms of their parole. Good faith would be the true policy, bad faith might have the worst consequences. General Grant added that the terms granted by him had met with the hearty approval of President Lincoln and the country generally. This incident was soon widely known; but it was known, also, that though the indictment for treason was quashed, the amnesty for Lee had been shelved, and he was never to have the right of citizenship and the vote.

Duncan, long out of irons but kept a prisoner, was at last brought up for trial. When the case was presented to the court, it happened that the judge sitting on the trial was a worshipper of General Grant. He resented the treatment accorded Lee as a slight on Grant. "This court does not consider it in the spirit of General Grant or the United States Government to offer insult to the other side, as this provost marshal took it upon himself to do," the judge said. He contrived to make short shrift of that trial, and Duncan set out on foot for Virginia, where he hoped to borrow money and get home.

His mother put her sewing-basket down on the floor by her chair.

"I declare, precious, you'd think Cud'n Mannie Randolph could have helped you out."

"Cousin Mannie's living in the overseer's house, on a plantation that got even the grass trampled off it."

"I reckon so," she said.

"But Cousin Sallie, his sister, had forty dollars she lent me, she dug it up after the surrender. We must send it to her right soon."

His mother sighed and leaned her head in her hands, but made no reply.

"We can get a mortgage, if we have to."

"We cannot, and we won't," she said, quickly sitting up. "Not while I live. But that can pass for the moment. We've some cotton in, if we can sell it, and we've got plenty of silver. They buy it in New Orleans. You'd be surprised how many candlesticks and teapots some of our friends have already eaten up. The Martins say they've eaten up a tester bed and six rosewood chairs. By the way, that reminds me, we've been celebrating about all we can afford," she added, rising and beginning to blow out the candles till only the one on the table was left. Its light glowed on the white marble of the top. "One candle will have to do. So then you did what?"

"Then I decided I'd come home by Washington College," Duncan said, "where General Lee is now president."

He told them what he had heard at the college, where people talked to him all those two days of nothing else. An English nobleman had offered Lee a mansion and an estate; the mountaineers came to offer him a farm in their country; offers of land, corporation stock and business positions for the sake of his name had poured in; but he could accept none of them. Then in August the trustees of Washington College, near the Blue Ridge in the Valley of Virginia, met and voted to offer him the presidency. One of them was chosen to represent the board, another member lent a broadcloth suit that a son living in the North had sent, and a lady who had just sold her tobacco crop lent the money for the journey. General Lee, excluded from the amnesty, feared that his connection with the college might do it harm, and might not be the best influence for the young, who above all must be taught respect for authority and the restoration of peace and harmony. But he had at last accepted, and they were putting the college in order. General Hunter's occupation of the town had left doors knocked in, the windows smashed, the fences destroyed, the laboratories nothing but broken glass. The endowment funds were gone. Fifteen hundred dollars a year was Lee's salary, and neighbors brought in pieces of furniture for the house.

"What did Robert E. Lee say to you, Duncan?" Middleton asked, coming up and laying his hand shyly on Duncan's knee. "What did he say to you?"

"They told me that after working all day in his office he took Traveller—know who Traveller is?"

"I know. Traveller was a gray horse and was General Lee's horse."

"That's it, sure's you're born. So every evening he took a ride in the country, by himself."

"Why does he go by himself?" the little boy said.

"To be by himself," said Duncan, gently.

Middleton closed his eyes and smiled.

"Well, what did General Lee say to you, Cud'n Duncan?" he repeated, his eyes still closed.

"Nothing. He didn't see me," said Duncan, kissing him on the cheek.

"Why?"

"I didn't let him. I just waited to see him. He looked grayer. They told me he had said to a young lady that he thought he was the oldest man in the world."

"Methuselah's the oldest man," Hartie said, suddenly interrupting as she left her stool and went to sit on the sofa by Valette, who whispered:

"General Lee just said that, honey, because—he's only fifty-eight, isn't he, Duncan? He just said that, darling."

"If he's just fifty-eight, what makes you cry?"

"I'm not cryin'."

Middleton stared at Valette and then into Duncan's eyes.

"You listen here," Duncan said, as he lifted him into his lap and began a story of Captain Moody's little nephew from Grand Gulf, who used to visit his uncle in the Virginia army. "He had his own pony, saddle and bridle, and the uniform of a captain of the artillery that the battalion tailor made him. But, of course, it had to leave the coattails off." But Middleton, leaning back with his head against his cousin's shoulder, paid no attention to that story, and Duncan, returning to General Lee, told how he had opposed military usages or discipline for the college: when there was a procession with the band playing he said nothing but walked along, noticeably out of step. With that Duncan caught his mother's eye and she nodded her head.

"That's what your grandfather always said; Pa used to say there's no such fool as the military mind."

"Well, I don't mean any irreverence to Almighty God," Miss Mary Cherry said, breaking the moment's silence that had fallen, "and I certainly don't mean any irreverence to General Lee. I respect God and I respect His word, everybody knows I carry my Bible every spot I go, in my trunk along with other things of mine, but it's my firm conviction and the opinion of plenty of other people, too, that if General Lee had been bolder and not paid any attention to Jeff Davis——"

"Jefferson Davis was the head of the government, Miss Mary," said Mrs. Bedford.

"I know and what if he was! Lee ought to've just done what he saw fit himself, and he'd gone on into Washington and hanged the whole batch. Sister Sarah, it's always been hard for me to see why God didn't make me a man. If I'd been at Appomattox I'd a said, 'All right, go ahead and win a victory, but you'll do it over my dead body.' And all this heroic time, me runnin' the blockade with my hoopskirt full of quinine!"

"Miss Mary," Valette said, hearing the trumpet voice and seeing the children's eyes growing wider, as the great frame seemed to rise high up out of the chair, "do me a favor. Tell Duncan about the coffin."

"Oh, that wa'nt anything," Miss Mary said, crossing her arms, "no more'n we were always doin'."

"What, Miss Mary?" said Duncan. "Mamma used to write me."

"Yes, and very likely she wrote you this, too. Besides, 'twas way back in October, '62, when Van Dorn was in Holly Springs. Well, all it was we got together a fine assortment of medicines in Memphis to run the blockade with and convey them somehow to Holly Springs, where I can tell you they were needed, all those soldiers—and whoever saw a man knows how to take care of himself? But how? was our problem, of co'se. Aye, so we got a coffin and packed it full, and hired the black hearse with pall and plumes on it, and had a big funeral out of Memphis."

"Miss Mary, tell about the widow," Middleton said. "You told it on Hartie's birthday. Didn't she, Hartie?"

Both the children laughed until Mary Cherry turned her good eye on them. At that they choked themselves down, but with a look as if later on somewhere they meant to explode.

"I don't recollect any birthday," Miss Mary said, sternly. "But all the rest was, Duncan, when they came up I had to act the widow. We had taken the hearse round by College Hill and stored it there in a farmer's barn for the night. A spring wagon was in the yard when General Sherman passed by next morning and he sent an officer in to get it. That's how they found the hearse and our carriage. As soon as I saw the Yankees I had gone out and sat myself in the carriage, so I thought I'd better be the widow and chief mourner. 'Twa'nt as if I didn't know how, either. I was raised near a family of Schmitts, Germans, a lot of tall, big-boned girls, and when the old man died the girls howled so at the funeral that Pa swore he thought at first it was somebody's hound in the woods had treed a coon. Aye. So I howled and howled. But they raised the coffin lid just the same."

They were all laughing. Valette, who had heard all this a dozen times, smiled at the gaunt old face cocking its eye around the room, "And so then you said, Miss Mary——"

"No, that's not the way it was."

"Then how was it?"

"So then I said let me get to that general of yours. I walked out of that yard and straight up to Sherman on his horse. They say I cussed him and called him 'You damned abomination!' But I never cussed him, never said 'You damned abomination.' I said 'You damned abomination, so to speak.' That's why I put on the 'so to speak.' And if you all wouldn't sit here with your eyes glued on Duncan Bedford and had listened to me, the South might have won the war."

Miss Mary said this last in so stentorian a voice, no longer looking at any one but straight ahead of her, that Duncan sat with something on his face like a child's and his eyes on the floor, not wanting to laugh because his heart was touched by the old creature. Nobody, in fact, knew anything to do until Valette rose and came over and patted the old shoulder as gaunt as a rock, and said, "It's a shame, Miss Mary."

Mary Cherry looked up at her, and the dry, wide lips cracked into a sort of grin, as she jerked down her cuffs but said nothing.

In the silence that followed, Mary Hartwell got up and went over to the table, where there was a paperweight, a glass globe with a castle in it about which when you turned the globe the snow circled and fell. She carried the globe with her and sat down on the stool again, quietly watching the falling snowflakes. Meanwhile, tightly under one arm, she kept the doll, Annabelle, so often buried from the Yankees and dug up again that she looked piebald and dappled in the face.

"Duncan," his mother said, at length, "since you're talkin'

about General Lee, here's a letter I put away you'd read and remember, I imagine. You see when we didn't hear anything I wrote Charlie Marshall. He begins here how's he made inquiries, all he could, but, with the surrender and everything, there was so much confusion. He hoped it merely meant you were just taken prisoner and we'd hear soon or be seeing you. Then he wrote a long end to the letter after that. The chillun have heard this letter already, but it won't do them any harm to hear it again. You must remember, if he is your cousin, it's a letter from the only Confederate who was with General Lee, absolutely the only one, when he met Grant and the other Yankee officers to arrange——"

"The terms of surrender?"

"Yes. Charlie Marshall was the only person at all with General Lee."

"You know we wrote you, Duncan," said Valette, seeing the gaunt old figure straightening itself up in the armchair and hoping to make her happy, "that Miss Mary saw General Grant."

"So I remember," he said.

"Yes, I was present," said Miss Mary, and without adding another word, sat stroking her chin.

Mrs. Bedford took the letter from a drawer in the secretary and went over to the table where the lighted candle was.

"Come here, son, and see it," she said, and Duncan went over and stood beside her, "like," as Valette thought, in the pride of her loving imagination, "an oak beside a little willow."

"This is where 'tis," said Mrs. Bedford, holding the letter in the candlelight down against the table, at a good distance from her eyes—she still refused to wear glasses. "We know by now," she said, "how things were managed at Richmond and what General Lee had to contend with, even there at the very last when he got to the Court House and no supplies had been

sent, though there were stores at hand to be sent, and everybody knows it. But General Lee, now it's all over, says
nothing about it, so why should we? That's not what your
Cud'n Charlie's letter is about."

She began to read.

" 'General Grant, seeing that Sheridan would soon be across
General Lee's march, wrote a note to him. He said that
General Lee must be convinced that further resistance must
be hopeless and he himself felt it his duty to shift from himself the responsibility for more effusion of blood by asking
of General Lee the surrender of the army under him. General
Lee had me write a letter in which he refused to admit such
hopelessness for the Southern cause. His reason for doing this
was that he feared General Grant would demand surrender
on unconditional terms. He had me write that before considering Grant's proposition, he must ask the terms offered.
Finally after the passage of letters between them, flags of truce
and so on, General Lee called me and told me to get ready
to go with him. I was in a dilapidated state and had to make
some preparations before I could go. Colonel Henry Young
let me have his handsome dress sword and a pair of gauntlets,
and he lent me a clean shirt collar.

" 'Again I beg of you not to despair of your son, in the vast
confusion let us pray that his record is lost only temporarily.
And now you will laugh, my dear Cousin Sarah, when I tell
you one thing that happened; for I recall what kind of things
aroused your mirth in our conversations at White Sulphur, it
seems to me that many years have passed since that agreeable
summer. I will tell you the incident.

" 'There was a man named McLean, who used to live on the
field of the first battle of Manassas. He didn't like the war,
and having seen the Manassas battle, he thought he would go
away to some place where there'd be no more fighting, so he
moved down to Appomattox Court House. When General

Lee told me to go forward and find a house where he could meet General Grant, whom of all people should I meet but McLean! I rode up to him and asked whether he knew a house where General Lee and General Grant could meet together. He took me first to a house that was half ruined and with no furniture. When I said this would not do, he offered his own house. The war had followed poor McLean. So it occurred to me you might be amused at his story.

" 'General Lee was standing at the end of the room opposite the door when General Grant, followed by his officers, walked in. He had on a sackcoat and had no side arms. He had been riding and his clothes were somewhat dusty and a little soiled. He walked up to General Lee and Lee recognized him at once. He had known him in the Mexican War. General Grant greeted him cordially, talked of the weather and other things in the most friendly way. He then brought up his officers and introduced them to General Lee. General Lee asked for General Lawrence Williams, and when General Grant had sent somebody out for him, General Lee thanked General Williams for having sent him word that very morn-ing that Custis Lee, his son, was not dead as was reported, but safe.

" 'After a very free talk, General Lee said to General Grant that he had come to meet him in accordance with the letter I had written for him, to treat about the surrender of his army, and he thought the best way would be for General Grant to put his terms in writing. General Grant said: "Yes, I believe it will." So they brought over a little table from a corner and General Grant wrote the terms and conditions of surrender on field notepaper. After he had written it he took it over to General Lee. General Lee was sitting at the side of the room; he rose and went to meet General Grant to take that paper and read it over. When he came to the part that said only public property was to be surrendered and the officers

were to retain their side arms and personal baggage, General
Lee said: "That will have a very happy effect."

" 'General Lee then explained that his cavalrymen furnished
their own horses—' " Mrs. Bedford stopped reading to turn to
Duncan.

"When my Arabian was shot I wouldn't have another," he
said, "though by that time horses were scarce. But what does
he say, Mamma?"

" '—furnished their own horses, and will want to plough
ground and plant corn. General Grant said that the terms
included only officers, but almost immediately added that he
would give orders that every man claiming a horse or mule
could take the animal home. General Lee having looked again
over the letter, told me to write a reply and General Grant
told Colonel Parker to copy his letter, so we left Generals Lee
and Grant talking together. When he got through copying
Grant's letter, I sat down to write a reply. General Grant
signed his letter and I turned over my letter to General Lee
and he signed it. Parker handed me General Grant's letter
and I handed him General Lee's reply, and the surrender was
accomplished. I myself shall put this down in a memoir
when I find leisure to do so; the whole transaction occupied
about an hour. There was no theatrical display about it. It
was in itself perhaps the greatest tragedy that ever occurred
in the history of the world, but it was the simplest, plainest,
and most thoroughly devoid of any attempt at effect, that you
can imagine.

" 'General Lee was in full uniform. He had on the hand-
somest uniform I ever saw him wear and a sword with a
gold and leather scabbard presented to him by some English
admirers. General Grant toward the close of the conversation
excused himself for his appearance and for not having his side
arms. He had thought General Lee would rather receive him
as he was than be detained while he sent back four miles for

his sword and uniform. General Lee said that he was very much obliged to him and very glad indeed he hadn't done so. After that a conversation took place of a most agreeable character. My dear cousin, I cannot describe it, nor give you any idea of the kindness and generosity and magnanimity of those men. When I think of it, it brings tears to my eyes.'"

She stopped and stood folding the letter. Duncan had listened to it without moving or saying a word, his finger tips resting on the table.

"Yes," Mrs. Bedford said, "I reckon that's about it. Charlie Marshall wanted to let us see there was something. I mean if you were dead, he wanted us to know there'd been something worth your dying for. As if anybody could take this away from us!— So that's why he wrote us all this—so you see——"

As his mother looked up at Duncan, he saw her gray eyes filled with love and quiet pride. Without moving his hands from the table, he leaned down and kissed the little brow and they stood there awhile, as if loath to leave this place where the two of them were together, apart from the rest of the room and from the world, in the small circle of the candle-light. Then taking herself in hand and tapping him lightly on the sleeve with the letter, Mrs. Bedford turned to the others.

"It's high time two little people and two old people went to sleep," she said, and opened the secretary to put the letter away.

LVIII

Long after the library conversation and the walk with Valette in the avenue, Duncan was awake. In his room, quiet as it was at that hour of the night, he knew he could not sleep yet. Another man might have gone to bed and lain there thinking, but it was like Duncan not to do so. He stood before the mantel, an elbow leaning on it.

It seemed to him that he had been surrounded by affection all his life. As he stood there he could see his mother, the slight body, the loyal voice, never very demonstrative but never far. Valette's face—it seemed to him that he saw only the eyes, then the faint figure of her in the shadow of her hair. But now that he had them again at last and was at home again, he found himself all at once seeing what was now far off. "Our men," he said to himself, and saw the ragged soldier—was that in '64, before the Wilderness campaign?— their trousers frazzled at the bottoms, many with their knees out, their elbows out—the patches, the officers were patched, but often not the men——

But spring was coming on them. Later, that next year, when there was hail and sleet, no shoes, thousands of the men bandaged, bleeding and with cut feet, two handfuls of parched corn in the haversacks and a strip of bacon, then no meat for three days, nothing for the horses——

Then all at once a banjo struck up. That was Sweeney, the banjo player of his first commander, Jeb Stuart. For Duncan was young.

He went over to the window. There, as if awaiting him, was the sombre night, with the bright star Aldeboran, whose name Miss Rosa had taught him, in the heavens. Shadows of trees planted by his father, the far-off sound of negroes singing—was that over at Mingo Baptist Church, which his father had given the land for? Duncan was surprised that this reality he had returned to faded now so quickly into the image of what he had left. He was learning the difference between memories that end in hope, and memories whose end is past, not to return. Before his mind's eye the soldiers marched again, and why did they follow when everything was lost, and who was it they followed? At the thought of Lee a boundless trust came even then into Duncan's soul and a strange peace, just as it had for those men in the army, and as if he himself were a child. At the same time with this thought of General Lee, he knew that here was one thing he could never tell his family. Not quite, not tell any one: though there was one man who would understand it, and that was Hugh McGehee.

A sound out toward the stable lot drew his attention. His dream was broken. Far down the yard he saw the little figure of his mother in her nightgown. She held up a lighted lamp in one hand and had a pistol in the other. How slight she looked moving across that open ground under the high oak trees! He knew at once what she was about; she had heard some noise from the lot and was going to see if the negroes were riding the horses at night. His mother and Valette, the house, the land, the children, the children that would come to him and Valette—it was all one thing—a man had to be like that.

Duncan waited until he saw his mother returning to the house. Then he undressed quickly and went to bed, and, as usual with him, fell asleep at once.

LIX

After his journey the day before and so late going to bed, Duncan might have slept longer; but he was awakened next morning by voices outside his door. He heard Middleton's little pipe begging in a low tone that they should go in and wake him up and then Mary Hartwell whispering something.

"But, Hartie, why can't Valette come in?" the little voice whispered.

"Because she's a young lady and's got on a wrapper and

Brother's a young man and she has her hair slicked back."

"Sh! You'll wake Brother!" Valette's voice in a whisper.

"Lette, the clock's struck," said Middleton.

"That's all right, the clock hasn't walked all the way from Virginia."

"But——"

More whispering followed and Duncan heard the sound of tiptoeing away. He sprang out of bed, threw the clothes on that his mother had had put there for him, and went downstairs by the small door to the dining-room and so out to the stable lot. He shook hands with the three or four plantation negroes who had gathered there waiting to see him, ordered the roan saddled, and delighted them by walking away as if it were the same as any morning and he had not been gone at all.

And if they knew what was good for them, Duncan called back from the gate, they'd have all that jimson weed out of the fence corners before they saw him again. "Yas, sir, yas, sir," the negroes said, scurrying into the stable shed for their hoes as if they had never noticed the weeds before.

"And pick up those barrel staves."

"Yas, sir, boss."

Under the oaks at the gate to the quarters, Duncan caught sight of his Uncle Henry plaiting a cracker to a wagon whip. At first the old man looked as if he would pretend not to see anybody, then he suddenly shambled forward, dragging the whip by the cracker behind him as he came.

"I heard you'd come," he said, not offering to shake hands with Duncan, but crossing his arms and still dragging the butt end of the whip on the ground. "Well, I can show you something, you'd like a salvo to welcome your return."

He pushed the gate open with his knee and led Duncan down the road through the quarters, walking ahead, his arms still crossed, and his long hair blowing about his neck. But nobody came out to greet Duncan; all but three or four of the cabins stood empty, the doors ajar and rubbish on the steps. In the cotton field that began here on the other side of the road Duncan saw only the last year's stalks, brown and ragged. Finally at the two end cabins women were on the little porches and children about. In the last yard, an old man was making a brushwood fire under a pot for soap. Duncan went up to him and asked how he was and if there was enough to eat in the cabin, and if Enoch, his son, took care of him. Enoch was a good son, the old man said, but this morning he had gone off early to look for a shoat that was loose over there somewhere in the piney woods.

"Old Enoch had a good coon dog, name was Music," said Henry Tate, "but he got him killed, Enoch says. Music kept wallowing in front of the door, measuring for somebody's grave; ain't that it, Uncle Pindar?"

The old man said nothing, and Duncan saw his uncle glance at him out of his sly eyes and then away.

"And what are you doing these days, Uncle?" Duncan said.

"I been dreamin' o' hellfire. I see my ole 'oman 'ere, and dat coon dog Music come in and her singing to de Lord, say git out o' here, you flop-yeared houn', Glory Hallelujah, I'll take a stick an' knock you down, Glory Hallelujah." He began to chuckle. "So 'twas. And I ain' mistook, dey was white folks dere, an' settin' down in chairs restin', an' each one wid 'e darkey holdin' him in front to keep off de fire."

"And bully for who?" said Henry Tate, leering into the childish old eyes now almost slits.

"Bully for Lincoln! Bully for Jesus! One freed de body, one freed de soul. Can y'all gimme two bits, Marse?"

Duncan, wondering where he would get it, promised to bring the money next time. "Enoch's wife cooks for you, don't she, Uncle?" he asked.

"Naw, sir, Little Marse. I tell you how 'tis, Mr. Duncan.

Her's gone cook for some white trash. And he's a beatin' her, and she been had a baby."

"Is she there now?"

"Naw, sir, she gone. One mornin' she wrapped de baby in a blanket and th'owed him behint de fire and come out and shut de doh. Wash Jackson was de one smelled de smell. I don' know whah she gone."

"You don't know?"

"Naw, sir, I don' know. She come by here, say she gwi' travel."

"Where to?"

"I don' know."

Henry Tate had already turned on his heel and was half-way to the gate.

In the parlor by the light-wood fire built especially for her against the autumn coolness, Mary Cherry stood enjoying the comfort of it. Her head was turned to one side, but the good eye was gazing at the floor. You might have wondered what she felt; she was always expressing her likes and what she despised or had her opinion of, but, perhaps, you knew even less than with most people of what went on in the soul dwelling within the harsh old body like a battered eagle perched on a crag.

"Well, so you're up," she said, glancing toward him with a frown quickly and dropping her skirt, which she had hoisted in the back to warm herself, as Duncan appeared in the door.

"Yes, m'am, and how are you this morning?"

"I reckon that clock woke you." She jerked her thumb toward the mantelpiece. "I know everlasting well how my sleep is broken with it going off hour on hour. Your mother said it's like chimes. All right, if it's like chimes, says I, the next time I hear it in the middle of the night, I'll join in with a hymn, and even that wouldn't give any idea what it feels like to be rung up from your sleep. During the war a Yankee tried to steal that clock, you know; but the alabaster's so heavy he soon got shed of it. A darkey found it in a ditch a mile from here and brought it in. But the angel off the top we never found. So Sister Bedford says, though I'd say 'twas an eagle."

"No, an angel, Miss Mary, that's right," said Duncan, as he looked at the old veteran and smiled to think what his father wrote about her once. His father had quoted Napoleon's remark about the Cossacks; Napoleon said the fear of the Cossacks kept dead battalions on their feet.

"All right, have it angel," said Miss Mary, "and come warm your bones."

"Miss Mary, it certainly is just what I wanted to find you here with us," Duncan said, shaking the old solid hand, now all veins.

"Why, thank you, Duncan. Thank you kindly." There was a rattle in her voice.

Then he heard the breakfast bell, and his mother's voice in the dining-room, and upstairs the sound of the children pounding on his door and Valette's laughter with theirs.

"Did you sleep well?" his mother asked him.

"In a bed like that!" Duncan said, going up to kiss her good morning.

"I hear young Mrs. Hugh McGehee up in Panola County," said Mary Cherry, "the first thing she did when he got married after he got back from Birmingham, where he'd been directing our powder works, was to saw down all the tester beds, though I like a four-poster myself. She's a pretty creature, face like a doll, reminds me of Valette. But she said she's had enough of the old, she wants a change. Do you agree with that?" Miss Mary turned to Duncan.

"Yes, m'am," Duncan said.

"And why?"

"No, m'am," he heard Valette on the stair.

"Yes, m'am and no, m'am, eh?" Miss Mary said, glaring at Duncan.

"Let's say the blessing, Miss Mary," Mrs. Bedford said, as Valette and the children came in. "You know what 'tis. A two-year-old ham. One of those we hid in the chimney."

"Aye," Mary Cherry said, taking her seat, and bowing her head, as she listened threateningly for the others to get quiet. "The Lord make us thankful for what we are about to receive, and bless us and keep us for Jesus' sake, Amen." She raised her head. "Don't give me any outside piece, Sister Sarah. Yes, not content with sawing the beds down, the young woman lets those orphan nieces of her husband's take their mother's things and play with them out in the yard, puttin' sand in the silver teapot. I know there was a pair of butter knives with amethyst handles; they're gone. Mark me, Duncan, you can ask God A'mighty Himself, what'll happen in the South, first no butter knives, then it'll be no butter, now watch."

"Eat your hominy, Middleton," said Mrs. Bedford, seeing him about to burst out laughing as his eyes followed Miss Mary's knife and fork on the ham, and his ears took the God A'mighty for swearing.

Neither Duncan nor Valette heard any of it. He was so much in love that he sat there eating hungrily and with one accusing thought, which was that he had never had sense enough till that minute to see how much more wonderful and beautiful and open-hearted and good Valette was than any woman a man ever saw. As he thought this he scowled and his eyes shone like a child's. And in his mind he was identifying her with his country, the morning that shone through the windows of the dining-room and with the resolution and spirit he felt in him for taking up this new life ahead in the South. Mrs. Bedford, seeing that Valette had forgotten to help herself to anything at all and only sat there sipping her coffee, buttered a biscuit while it was hot and slipped it on her plate.

"Yes, where those orphans' teapot is by now the Lord knows," Miss Mary said.

An hour after breakfast was over Duncan took the roan and set out to pay a call at Montrose.

LX

Even before the surrender there had been two situations.
Of the first, Hugh McGehee himself had written Governor
Sharkey.

He was prompted, he said, by the annoyances prevalent in
the community to make this communication. They had for
more than two years been infested with thieves, robbers, and
jayhawkers. At the time of the surrender the town had been
occupied by Federal troops, who kept order. Hearing that
they would be withdrawn, the citizens had petitioned to have
part of these left for their protection. They would now sign
a petition to have them withdrawn for a band of thieves.
Every morning came reports of cotton stolen, and other depredations. Could they not have an effective civil magistracy?
Or have a provost marshal backed by military assistance? There
had been a sheriff, but he had abandoned the office when the
Federals came, and had come back only when measures were
taken to collect taxes and was again elected. The governor
should give the citizens a military police and appoint officers
who would raise the right kind of men. He sent Governor
Sharkey a list of names of such men who might serve against
the marauders and blacks who were roaming about at large,
destroying the stock and stealing cotton. For twelve successive
nights that month passengers on the stagecoach from Vicksburg to Jackson had been robbed.

The second situation was on the more permanent side.
There had been plantations leased by Union men here and
there and business enterprises set up. People of all kinds were
now coming in. Under the circumstances they saw the
promise of a fortune in this region where so much wealth
and flush times had been. They were lending money on land

mortgages, and closing mortgages out; some seemed merely to be arriving and departing; some were in the mind to settle with their families. In Natchez and all this country many New Englanders and others from the North had settled long ago, and had become Southerners, among the most violent advocates of secession. Such men now saw these newcomers and regarded them with dismay: people who brought in a spirit of assertion, ruthless methods and greedy purposes that was new, strange, and ominous. Hugh McGehee, who was never, as they say, lost in contemplation but was constantly given to the practice of it, even in company and even when he himself was talking of other things, turned these new people and this new state of things over and over in his mind. He was not violently matching this against that, what had come against what had been. Most people he knew were doing so; but Hugh balanced these new people against the Southerners he had known, balanced them quality by quality. Both had their defects; and yet it was inevitable that he should come out at last at his own choice of life, his own preferences. Where these people parted from him, where this new development left him, was the conception of life, the society, in which we are to lead our lives. He made a point of talking with these newcomers whenever he had a chance ("talk with" was his phrase; he noticed that they always said "talk to"). The truth was these people seemed to him to have no conception at all of a civilization.

A strong and definite professor from a New Jersey foundation for girls in the handicrafts (who had struck Natchez, Agnes McGehee said, only because he had read of the Mississippi steamboats and the fantastic scene of them) was at pains one day to explain to them—he had been brought out to Montrose by Colonel Harrod—how false the reality was compared to the ideal that Southern people claimed for their way of life. "The fact is," said the professor, "it never existed, but Southerners are already busy creating a romantic Old South."

"But," Hugh said, "the point does not turn on whether some old fool of a colonel—or some scratter-brained old lady—is what we think he is—or she is. No, no. The point turns on what we believe in and desire, and want to find embodied somewhere, even in them."

"Whether it is or not," said the professor.

"That's incidental."

"It's romance," said the professor.

"Very well. Then the point is: not what the colonel is, being Southern, but what he would be if he were not Southern."

The professor regarded this remark as mere bombast. He had not been invited to Montrose, but had felt free to call because he was collecting statistics. Collecting statistics was already a new kind of entré. Nobody in the county had heard of statistics before, but the negroes were very much impressed. They welcomed investigation so heartily that what had at first seemed to the professor a gold mine of data began to irk him as excessively African detail, as communicative as it was imagined.

Among these newcomers to Natchez and West Feliciana Parish was Mr. Samuel Mack—"all the boys back home in Pittsburgh call me Sam," he said. Early in August, travelling South with various plans in his head, he had left the boat at Natchez. The fame of this rich country had impressed him, and, like thousands of other lovers of the Union, he wanted to see for himself what money prospects were there. He was a good-enough looking young man of thirty, with close-set lips and a face that seemed at once both shrewd and blank. He evidently had money, for he took up a mortgage or two the first week. And he had his own kind of romance. He frequently said in the course of a discussion that he owed everything to his mother; and the Southern girls moved him to sentimental longings. He inquired cautiously at the bank and at the hotel about many of them.

Mr. Mack's first Montrose visit concerned the factories at Woodville, in which, though Hugh McGehee's brother had built them, he had learned that Hugh had a share. These factories had been burned or wrecked during the Federal occupation of the country, but from what Mr. Mack had heard of them he judged that they had been all along too easy-going and needed speeding up. He was, in fact, free enough with his opinions, though he evidently took pains to express them drily, as if to say they were not mere products of emotion; and ten minutes were not over before he had expressed a number of them to Hugh. The smartness and energy of his approach to a subject confused Hugh. He had heard plenty of simple opinions expressed by simple people; but Mr. Mack apparently was not to be taken as simple, and seemed himself to have decided on what thoughts to think about many matters, national, social, and—or at least always generally regarded as such—abstract. Was this the eternal frontier mind, Hugh asked himself, or was it the eternal child's mind? To him it was as yet a novelty, this type of man, who seemed so competent both to think without knowing and to know without thinking, a temperament sustained by innocence, emptied by shallow choice, and run by steam.

As for the South in these new days, Mr. Mack expressed great hope. He disagreed with his celebrated townsman, Thad Stevens, who called on the Senate for confiscation, forty-acre tracts, and negro suffrage. "The proof," said Mr. Mack, sticking his thumbs into his waistcoat pockets, "that Mr. Stevens is wrong is who'd invest capital if things were like that, I ask you?"

As this new guest went on talking about tariffs, industrial progress, and the development of enterprises, Hugh was surprised to find that the state under which such men as Mr. Mack saw society was actually a state of war. Competition without social principles. This would lead to a legalistic attitude, law as the letter, the strategic game; and this meant the debasement of the social sense. It meant secretiveness. Not lies, but a system of moving secretly, which ends in being only deceit and suspicion. Hiding the hen-nests, the prudence of white trash.

Something, he could not have said what, made Hugh ask at length what became of young men under such a system; for youth has its thoughts and ideals that are not always easily fitted into the life offered to them later on.

"Yes, I know, excuse me," Mr. Mack replied. "My father sent me back East to college. We used to have great talks by the fire at nights, high ideals. But no matter what a man's talked about the night before, in the morning there are things he's got to do." He meant that what we philosophize and what we do in business are two separate things.

Such a remark would have blasted Hugh McGehee if it had come from some one he knew, but Mr. Mack had already established himself in Hugh's mind as nothing but lively self-assurance combined with being a stranger. As Mr. Mack went on talking of new developments, the name "Montrose" suddenly came into Hugh's head. He was on the gallery again and Edward, a little boy with gray eyes, was listening, his sister at his side. The Earl of Montrose had been a Presbyterian, and so was that McGehee ancestor, the Macgregor who led his clan to fight along with him; but they did not belong to the barbarous party of the Kirk. And when Charles the First was dead, Montrose had escaped to the Continent, where already his fame was so great that he was offered the highest command of the Armies of France. He did not remain but came home to fight for the second Charles, was betrayed, and hanged. He was to be walked by the bailiffs all along

Prince Street to the Mercat Cross, where the gallows was. Instead of his rags, friends had sent him a suit of fine black cloth, a black beaver hat with a silver band, a scarlet cloak richly laced to the knee; his stockings were carnation silk. He had also, with these, fine white gloves on his hands and ribbons to his shoes. The mobs had been hired to mock and howl at him, but when they saw him, he was so beautiful and grave, there was not a sound, except for their low prayers and tears. He was denied the privilege always granted, even to common criminals, of speaking to the crowd. But to those near the scaffold he spoke a moment, and a boy named Gordon took it down. "—— —— drawing near to God. If he enable me against death, and furnish me with courage and confidence to embrace it even in its most ugly shape, let God be glorified in me, though it were my damnation."

Hugh saw a little boy listening to this. "So when he walked along the street like that, Father, there wasn't a sound," Edward used to say. "No, Buddie," said Lucy, "not a sound, he was so beautiful. Papa's told you that." "And we fought for him," Edward said. "Yes, son."—On the gallery with his son. No. No, that was long ago!

Mr. Mack was talking about the backwardness in this country.

Hugh McGehee suddenly returned to him. He saw Mr. Mack's face and wished that William Veal, the family servant, would appear at the door, so that one might look at the noble, grave face of a man.

Then all at once Hugh felt ashamed of himself. Why Montrose, why his own boy Edward, if he himself was only to feel scornfully like that?

"Pray forgive me, sir," he said, turning to Mr. Mack. "Forgive me, my thoughts wandered, they do these times. I was thinking of— Pray forgive me."

Mr. Mack looked at him surprised; he had not noticed that

his host was not listening, and now merely waived the suggestion away with his hand; you could see he had no malice in him. "It's just that so many national matters such as we have mentioned are of prime importance just now," he said, and went on with his opinions.

When Mr. Mack inquired what the negroes were dawdling over out beyond the stable-lot, Hugh said that they were burning off last year's sedge. "While there's time left them: presently they'll have to get ready for statesmanship, our negroes are going to be senators, congressmen, aldermen, Mr. Mack. If we don't have a colored governor pretty soon, I'll be mighty surprised, sir, yes, if we don't have a colored governor of Mississippi. Mingo Baptist Church, on my brother-in-law's place, not long ago, had an assembly, chose a black congressman and then took up a collection to defray his expenses to Washington. He made a pleasure trip to New Orleans, however, and then came back and gave them an account of it."

But Mr. Mack's only function at Montrose—however much he would have been surprised to know it—was to serve as a distraction at a moment that would be very difficult for every one. This was when Agnes McGehee and Lucy hurried in to say that William Veal had seen Duncan coming and had gone, with his gold watch in his hand as if for some schedule, but really to show off the watch, toward the gate to meet him.

LXI

DUNCAN, on his way to Montrose, rode along the old Trace road at a canter and then as his thoughts gathered, slowed down unconsciously to a walk. Back from the war and all he had seen there, back to Valette, back to his home, to his mother and the children, and to this country, everything seemed to him a dream. He scowled, seeing the broken-down fences, and here and there among trees the chimneys standing up naked, where some house had been burnt; but his heart was happy. His mother was worn out with what she had gone through during the war and with hard work since. Two or three times yesterday and this morning at breakfast she had told him with a kind of strange, dry hate, as if it were some bitter comedy in her mind, various things that had happened in Natchez. "I imagine the Yankees thought they had never seen a woman like that before," he said to himself. Then he felt the callouses on his feet as he moved his toes in his boots, and noticed at the moment that his hair for want of a barber blew too much about his ears.

His mother had told him of the destruction of Clifton, of the looting at Lansdowne, when people said china was scattered all along the road three miles to Pine Ridge; of the night at Weymouth Hall when Mrs. Weymouth was dying and the hired German soldiers quartered in the house kept the drum beating on the upper gallery. These were only some of the items that she picked for him out of her memories, with a sort of fierce selection. As Duncan listened to them he caught from her the flash of her anger. For the moment he was as full of hate as she was; but now as he rode along he had none of the feeling. He had seen what war was; "such is war, war is always like that," he said to himself. When he saw from the road the destruction and ruin, it was the land, his country, that he thought of as wounded, as if some one he loved had suffered; but he thought of this as coming from some disease or from storms or natural disasters, rather than with resentment.

Nevertheless, for all his telling himself this, he turned his horse into the road along the river, where far down to the north, near the water, he saw the remains of the negro stockades. Some way off on the sandbars were stretches along which even at this distance he could see here and there white bones sticking through. A peach orchard had been planted on the spot. The Surgets, his mother had told him, had re-solved when Clifton was demolished to go to France. Mrs. Surget had gone, but Mr. Surget had died before the boat sailed. Duncan passed The Towers with its grove all cut down, and saw what had happened in other places.

And yet it was true that something sustained him that was larger and more lasting than this; and the sight of the weeds by the road, in the shadow and sun, and the moss hanging down, the birds, the rich earth, and something else that seemed to belong to it and was not it, were more to him than any change or ruin that was so in evidence. From some farmhouse he heard dogs barking far off, and saw his horse's ears prick up. The thrushes and mocking-birds were singing all alongside in the woods.

Duncan was a good example of what General Lee with his Southern troops had been obliged to meet. There was some instinct of freedom, some *amour propre,* individual reliance on himself, even arrogance, that would have made him stand up and even be shot before it would be ruled, if something happened to strike him wrong. So that for him, General Lee's method of tact and the private splendor on Lee's own part was the only one. Whatever ifs and doubts may have come to Duncan on this battle or that, or one or another strategy, Lee had sunk in. Duncan did not know how this feeling was to spread itself and grow and perfect itself in him, but he knew it was there. An ethos, a sense of being undefeated, of pas-sionate love of their country, had taken hold in the South; it underlay the bitterness, hatred, humiliation, and ruin; it was to vary acording to the nature of every man in whom it wrought. Of this spirit, felt by so many, Lee had become the chief image and the most noble and tangible source.

But when Duncan had passed through the gate and saw ahead of him the chimneys standing among the trees and then the columns washed white by the rains, he drew his bridle and sat for a moment gazing at this spot where Montrose had been. Then his eye fell on the tips of the graveyard marbles.

A flight of birds caught his eye, and he deliberately set himself to watch them. From a wide line at the rear they made a triangle to a point, in the clear autumn sky, flying eastward. Smoothly they streamed down the sky to the far horizon. Duncan laid his hands quietly on the pommel of his saddle, as he watched them fade away from sight, then touched his horse and set off at a quick trot by a bridle path through the grove.

The tenderness, the loyalty, the sense of fatality in the thoughts that occupied him brought to his face its finest quality, so that every one at Montrose, when he entered the parlor, felt it and greeted him from the heart.

"Well," Lucy said, when the first welcomes and exclamations of surprise were over at Montrose, "nobody'd think these were back from the war." She fingered the velvet lapel of the suit of his university days, smiling with her beautiful lips, which now seemed to Duncan too thin.

"You must recognize this haberdashery," he said. "Mammy Tildy had it hidden in her loft, which is a blessing."

"Yes," said Lucy, turning away to stand at the window.

He was confused at the sudden thought of their seeing him when Edward would never come again, and was glad that this Mr. Mack was there. At the same time he understood that Agnes McGehee, as if to say it was no fault of his what had happened to them at Montrose, had begun to ask him questions about the long journey home.

"In these of all times!" she said.

It was not long before Mr. Mack, who took himself for a peacebearer or prophet of forgiveness, inquired what the state

of mind had been in the parts of the country Duncan had
passed through. He did not wait for Duncan to answer, but
himself described how matters stood, in one place or another,
lamenting the continued resentment. Things, he said, were
speedily improving. "I've just read, for instance," he said,
"in a New York paper, where some member of the government who's been in Georgia says the glass is back in the
train windows."

"I suppose, Duncan, the cool weather made your journey
easier," said Agnes.

Without hearing her or glancing at Duncan, Mr. Mack
said, "Yes, we're all one country now. Miss McGehee, you
saw the Virginian's will reprinted in *The Gazette*. Most re-
grettable, not the wise spirit."

Everybody at Montrose had, of course, seen it. It was the
will that some man dying had just left, in which he "be-
queathed to my children and grandchildren and their descend-
ants the bitter hatred and everlasting malignity of my heart
and soul against the Yankees, including all the people north
of Mason and Dixon's line," and did exhort and entreat his
children and grandchildren to instil into the hearts of their
children and grandchildren from their childhood this hatred
throughout all future time and generations.

In a low, gentle voice Agnes interrupted to explain this to
Duncan rather than have Mr. Mack do it. For a moment,
as she spoke, Duncan responded to the excitement of the
words in the will. He felt the contagion of the hate there,
his face reddened. Then he saw Hugh McGehee gazing at
him; and in the midst of Mr. Mack's chattering about peace
and the return to the Union, Duncan heard himself say,
"That's what General Lee has been working for since the
hour he surrendered at Appomattox."

Agnes rose and went quickly to take Duncan's hand in her
own, standing there beside him.

"Mr. Davis' influence is gone," he said, turning to her and speaking quietly, as he felt her hands laid so tenderly on his. "But General Lee is giving his whole life now for——"

"I know, Duncan," Agnes said, "we all know." She left him and went to stand by the mantel.

"Well, Duncan, here's one doesn't know," said Lucy, sharply. "And I'd make exactly that will. I know your mother says putting Jeff Davis in prison will make a martyr out of him."

"Lucy," said her father, "don't you know that from Centenary College, where Jefferson Davis went, the entire graduating class was killed to a man?"

"Yes, but Mr. Davis wasn't killed. And General Lee's alive and a hero. Yes, we've had God but now we've got General Lee!"

"Lucinda!" her mother said, frowning and letting go Duncan's hands. "But never mind," she added, with a glance at Mr. Mack and Duncan, as if to say can't you see, you men, this child's torture?

Agnes was immediately sorry for that, and as soon as Hugh had left the room with Mr. Mack, she turned to Duncan.

"You had to come some time, Duncan. And we're all glad." Will you come again the first day you can?" she said. But she did not touch him.

Without looking back at her, Duncan followed the others into the hall.

Afterwards Hugh led Duncan down to the stables, which had been renovated on the old spot and so were at some distance from the present house. In the stalls were six Arabians that had escaped seizure through being on Hugh's more inland plantations of Monclova, First Lick, and China Grove.

They stood beside the roan, Duncan's arm through the bridle loop, for a long time talking.

"What's this Mr. Mack?" Duncan asked bluntly, scowling and reaching up to grip the pommel on his saddle. "Who's he?"

"Mr. Mack?" Hugh said. "Well, I reckon the size of it is he's thousands of the men who are going to be the United States, so far as they can be the United States, that is, of course. Mr. Mack's no fool, no, he's a right smart chap, but he's not so smart as he thinks he is, because he's selfish, it's a short-sighted selfishness. Such men won't be a class, they won't feel any responsibility for a class, therefore, or for a society. They won't even be leaders. They'll be drivers, I suppose you could say; and they'll be examples."

"Examples of what, Uncle Hugh?"

"Of themselves and success. But, you see, what will be denied is that they exist at somebody's expense. It's a popular idea, I imagine, that ycu get something for nothing. But everything has its price. The English system of a leading class may mean starvation and wreckage for masses lower down. For the nation's sake it may be worth it. Or it may not. At any rate, everybody recognizes that it has its cost. But with us it will be different. People will pay for it, hope to get a slice of it, but never call it by a name, not till years have passed. Have you noticed the parallel between the cases for democracy and for slavery? Or, perhaps you judge, as Horatio says, ' 'twere to consider too curiously to consider so.' "

"What, Uncle?" Duncan said.

"Well, this: democracy, a good theory, a great human right, which works out none too well; slavery, a bad theory, a great human wrong, which works out none too badly. I endorsed democracy, I condemned slavery; and here I am with my house burned down and my colored people free, deceived with false promises, mixed up and robbed. Mr. Mack and his crew won't consume me, but that's only because he hasn't brains enough and hasn't enough life behind him. If I were mean,

I reckon, I'd have to laugh about that: these men just haven't enough life behind them to match me. I mean by 'life' tradition, forefathers and a system of living. Don't laugh at me for a professor or some common editor; but these people make you want to explain things you'd always taken for granted. When you begin to explain things that you've always taken for granted, you've already begun to lose them. Still I have to laugh. It's as if I stood on the ground and they didn't."

"What's Mr. Mack doing here, Uncle Hugh?" Duncan asked, in a matter of fact tone.

"What he's doing here says the whole thing; he buys land, exploits it, ruins it—what's the difference? is the way he sees the case—and sells it. In sum, Duncan, to Mr. Mack the land's no more than stocks and bonds. When he sees the land like that, he sees himself and his character like that; a quick turnover for what can be made. Sometimes I think of what— 'twould have been very different from such as Mr. Mack—my boy, if he'd been spared, would have wanted these next twenty years."

He did not say that all this seemed to him, sometimes, in his despair, only retchings of an old ideality.

"Damn the whole lot of them!" said Duncan.

"No, I reckon it's not damn anybody, damn 'em! But I've noticed that our people here'n this country—by way of defending themselves, I reckon—have already begun boasting of what they had, their former splendor, and so on. But what they would do better to speak of would be not what they have had but what they have loved."

"I see that, Uncle Hugh."

"It was not the elaboration of life, it's the simplification of life that expressed the aristocratic security."

Hugh scarcely recognized it, but he was saying to Duncan the things he would have said to his own son if life had willed it so. His intelligence saw the war not as any single issue, nor did he see it bitterly, either. He saw the war only as in the line that had begun in England with the Industrial Revolution and was moving onward toward its peak. This planter civilization had been in the way of it, and had to be destroyed. Just that.

"So they got us out of the way," he went on to Duncan, "for a time, till they break their own necks. I'm not saying we had the most desirable society, or that men should go back to it; I'm only saying give them three generations now and they'll have ashes in their mouths. At least we had some degree of peace and stability for a while; but that must not be endured, no. Now ours is demolished, we'll see where the other will end, and the society it develops, if it develops anything that can be called a society."

In the course of the war, Hugh went on, more than 36,000 citizens in the North had been imprisoned for their opinions. That was an emergency measure to maintain unity. We should see, he said, what sort of unity this led to—for unity in itself is not necessarily a virtue. Nothing can be more dangerous in itself than this idea of unity. It means finally either the purpose of the strongest or the will of the dullest.

As they talked William Veal approached from the house, meaning to ask instructions for some work going on in the stable-lot, but seeing the two so serious and occupied, he stopped in his path and stood still, watching them out of his old, wise eyes; then turned and walked slowly, his head bowed, toward the quarters and on into the thick shade of the mulberry trees.

"There's William Veal," Hugh said, catching sight of the retreating figure. "When all was safe he brought the silver back from where he'd hidden it in the woods, none of us knew where. We just told him to hide it and not tell us. I must say when he brought the crate of it in again, it didn't seem very important."

"No," said Duncan.

"I talked to William Veal about what he'll do. He won't talk, just says he never could get nigger religion."

"And Mamma," Duncan said, "still has jewelry buried out by one of the garden pavilions, says she's got things to bury yet before she begins digging things up."

"I haven't said these things to people, but to you, yes," Hugh said.

"Yes, sir," said Duncan, "I understand." He understood that Hugh meant he was to be like a father to him and Duncan to him a son.

"But I'll tell you. I've had considerable opportunity to watch this war at every angle: and I came to a conclusion. Doubtless it's the same in all wars; I've watched this one and studied it, I mean the statesmen, politicians, orators, generals, and military strategy, good and bad. And I'm talking of South and North, both sides. I find there's always some one thing in everything, and so 'twas in this war. And I saw——"

"And what, Uncle Hugh?" Duncan said, speaking he did not know why in a low voice.

"I saw that the marvel of the war is the people."

LXII

To Duncan, as he went about the place those first days of his return, Portobello seemed the same as ever. The Benjamin West painting in the parlor of the glowering Bedford ancestor with his small son and daughter had two sabre slashes crosswise and loosely pasted up from behind. On the shirtfront of Grandfather Tate where the soldiers had written obscene words the paint had been scrubbed off down to the canvas. The table top of black, inlaid with flowers and birds, had the mother-of-pearl dug out of it with a bayonet point; and there were heelmarks in some of the door panels. But Duncan had seen so much wreckage along the war front that these things meant little to him; the mattresses were good on the beds—he had no notion of how they had been replenished that summer, with feathers and shredded newspapers—the roses were in bloom, the food on the table good. Whenever she sat down his mother now had sewing to do, or she brought two pans with her, one for late peaches to be sliced for drying, one for the stones and peelings. The storeroom had begun to fill again with preserves, dried fruit and canned vegetables. She had taken his father's chair at the head of the table.

Duncan accepted it all. Only at the stables did he feel the great difference; there were the mule his father had brought home, the roan and the colt; otherwise the stalls were vacant. He would have raised money somehow for new horses but for his mother, who meant to start no debts. Gradually he would have horses again, Duncan said to himself; and from studying the colt in the stable lot he used to go sit in Mammy Tildy's cabin. She was feeble now and would sit close to the brushwood coals on her hearth, for there was nobody to bring her in hickory logs or post-oak; and Duncan would sit on the bed. Once he stretched himself out and went to sleep. It was a second's cat-nap; and he opened his eyes to look at Mammy, as if to say he remembered when he used to come home from the tavern and she would be waiting at the gate for him. She would bring him here to lie on her bed and sleep the whiskey off before his mother saw him. He said now, sitting up, "Mammy how are you?"

"I'm tol'able, lil Marse."

"Take care of yourself."

"Oh yassir, I does."

It was from Mammy Tildy that he heard things about his mother that neither she herself nor Valette were going to tell him. Last year, while Middleton was sick upstairs with a fever, his mother had found a soldier taking a young turkey from the coop. You can't have that, she said, said Tildy, it's the onliest fowl on the place and a little boy is sick. The soldier refused to give the turkey up. You shan't have it, sir, said his mother, snatching hold of one of the turkey's legs. The soldier would not let go and she would not let go, and they tore the turkey in two and she walked off with half.

Soon after the surrender one day a Yankee soldier had driven up to the gate with a nigger woman in a buggy beside him. Hey, he says, this lady wants a drink of water. If that black wench wants a drink of water she can go to the well and get it, says Ole Miss. The officer got out of the buggy and came up on the porch, how dare you? he says; and Ole Miss picked up a wicker high-chair and broke it over his head. She had had a court summons for it; but nothing had been heard lately about that; the courts in this country had enough trouble on their hands already. "I dunno you know it, Marse Duncan," Mammy said, "but right after your Pa died upstairs, and there warn't no niggers here, and no harness seem like, Ole Miss tied herself up a harness wid grapevines and strings and ploughed the gyarden herself. But she ain' tellin' it."

Duncan felt not pity, which his mother would have despised, but only a sort of fierce pride and understanding; the world was not for babies and weaklings. When he found that his mother carried a pistol now in the pocket of her skirt where-ever she went outside the house, he asked to look at it. "It's in good shape," he said, handing it back to her.

It was from Mammy Tildy also that he heard of his mother's going off to see people who were dying and sending messages by them to his father and Aunt Rosa and to the little girl Virginia she had lost twenty years ago.

When he heard these things Duncan went back to the house, where the daguerreotype was, with the colors tinted in,

and looked at the young girl with the castanets, in a bolero
jacket with an Andalusian hat, and little red boots with brass
tips. Alabama, that girl, how long ago——

His mother on her part looked at Duncan and saw how
much more of a man he had become: the war was a good
thing. A man died fighting, well—you had to die some day—
or he lived through it. What business was it of women's?

And she could just see Duncan Bedford some day, with a
white beard. He would be sitting in church, having done all
that a Christian could do, listening properly till the time for
the sermon to end, and then when he saw the preacher was
going on too long, snapping his watch. He had his father's
watch, and she had heard it snap, and don't you ever think
Duncan won't find out how it snaps!

"What are you smiling at, My Dumplin'?" said Valette,
who had brought her a cup of tea and was making her drink
it.

"Just at this Duncan. I'm thinking he'll be more likely at
railroad companies or enterprises that'll be starting up again
now."

"Than as a planter? I don't agree with you, My Dumplin'."

"I know. Duncan hasn't any faults. We'll just have to
choose among his virtues which ones we prefer."

"My Dumplin', you're always mocking me," said Valette,
throwing her arms around her neck and kissing her. "And so,
let you talk, people would think—I mean—" She stopped;
the words she said meant nothing; she was struck with the
dread that she would never be worth his mother's little finger.
"And some day Duncan would find that out," she said to herself.

"Child, if 'twere all like you this world would be full of
angels," Valette heard the husky little voice murmur in her
ear, with that odd, abrupt way My Dumplin' had of seeming
to read your mind and ease what was troubling you.

One morning when Duncan was out where they were burning brush on a field just cleared, a little darkey came to the house to tell Mrs. Bedford that a white man was at the side gate. "He say he Mr. Shaw," the boy said, showing the whites of his eyes.

"Shaw? What's he want?"

"I don' know'm, he 'es say he Mr. Shaw."

"You go tell him to wait."

When she went to the gate the man did not raise his hat, but she recognized Old Sam Shaw at once, the same small eyes and scraggly red beard. He had reined his horse up squarely in front of the gate. With one hand he wiped the tobacco juice from the corner of his mouth.

"Is that you, Mr. Shaw? What do you want?" she said, only half glancing at him.

"I got a paper to serve on you, Mis' Bedford."

"A what? You know better than coming here like this."

"Jes the same——"

"You think now there're no men here, you scoundrel, so you come here like this."

"Jes the same, here 'tis," Shaw said. As he peered into the pocket of his dirty coat, the scraggly red hairs on his chin were mashed into the neckband of a faded blue cotton shirt.

Sallie Bedford reached through the gate and caught hold of his horse's bridle, and with the other hand pointed the pistol from her pocket straight at his head.

"Now you just sit there," she said, "till my son comes. And keep your mouth shut."

After a while the little negro brought Duncan around by the grove, on the same side of the fence with Shaw. Noon had come. The bright light fell on the garden and the shining pistol barrel and made the hip bones of the skinny, misused gray mare stick up sharper.

"That's all right, Mamma," Duncan said, taking his hat off

as he spoke and putting it back again as he turned to the man who sat on the horse, still holding the paper in his hand.

"Sam Shaw, I know you," said Duncan, looking him up and down. "Even if the niggers hadn't told me."

"Wouldn't you remember him," said his mother putting the pistol into her pocket again, "when he used to come up whining for something? But that was at the bottom of the back steps. That's where he belonged and where he stayed."

The man looked at her with his eyes full of sullen hate, then at Duncan.

"What are you doing coming here?" said Duncan.

"No offense intended," Shaw answered, doggedly.

"What are you doing coming here like this?"

"He's serving a paper on us," said his mother.

"This is not a summons," Duncan said, smacking the sheet of paper that he had taken from Shaw's hand. "This is a bill, you fool! For a saddle blanket bought at Dicks'. How did you come to bring it?" He tore up the paper and tossed it on the ground.

"Mr. George Dicks hyerd me asayin' I was passin' this a way. I offered to leave it with Miss Bedford."

"Get out of here, and just let me hear of you or any of your trash coming to this place again, I'll make it hot for you."

He stood with his arm resting on the gate, as he watched Shaw give the bridle bit a savage jerk and without glancing at them, ride off toward the road.

As Duncan and his mother walked toward the house he asked her why she was silent. She told him she had been thinking of that look of hate in old Sam Shaw's eyes and how she realized she didn't hate him, she never thought of him at all.

"You know your father's idea of poor whites," she said.

Duncan repeated some of the opinions Malcolm Bedford had expressed, rating these people below the blacks.

"Yes, and this is it; no matter how high-handed you were with old Sam Shaw just now," she said, "and I myself was actin' too as if I wouldn't touch him with a ten-foot pole—every dog has his day, yes, darlin', every dog has his day. With so many of our young men dead now, you watch these people, the bottom rail will be on top. With free black labor, and land changing hands already, you'll see. Sam Shaw's crowd will run the State."

"They won't run me," said Duncan.

"Hugh McGehee and Agnes would talk about it more softly than I would, as any fool could see by this cut-throat eye of mine. But there's no difference between Hugh and Agnes and me; no honey, they'd feed old Shaw, just as your father used to do, or give him money if he begged it. But what has feedin' people or giving 'em money got to do with knowin' they even exist? Hugh can be mighty kind, but never think what people feel don't come through just the same, and even these poor whites know it and they intend to show us. And now the world's changed, you give 'em time, they'll swamp us."

"Well, not yet," he said, "and you don't think so either, Mamma, not by a long shot."

Valette left her bench on the gallery and came down the path to join them, splashing at one spot in the path through a cluttering drift of brown magnolia leaves. She and Duncan turned down one of the pavilion walks, and Mrs. Bedford went back to the rosebeds. The thought of Sam Shaw and his idea of getting even with them, or rather with the world, still embittered her. It touched the springs of that arrogance natural to her, along with her natural sense of justice. Meantime she looked about her, wondering if there would ever be anything but makeshift gardening at Portobello again. And, as she thought this, she could hear, in and out of the garden sounds and the wavering of her own attention to any one thing, the sound of Valette's voice and Duncan's laughter. And here was Duncan home again at last, and so much that was different! And since Duncan's return, it seemed to Mrs. Bedford that she could see Valette change, inch by inch, back into something more of a child again. She had seen on that pretty face the signs of suffering and anxiety, only half covered with resolution and bravery, at one time and another during these four years. And some of it was Duncan's fault—though who is perfect? At times she had seen in Valette's wastebasket, when Celie was bringing it down, those smudged and crumpled little letters, torn up thus to be rewritten. But now it was like the old Valette, somewhat out of practice but singing for them lightly and sweetly, as if a bird had flown in through the window and paused at the keyboard. Of all the women in the world, Valette was the right one for Duncan, his mother said to herself. If he married somebody like Lucy McGehee, shutting yourself up and going on, he'd kick the doorpanel out, some fine day he'd kill her. But Valette was one of those blest people whose natures are open. Whatever came up between her and Duncan would be in the open, Valette with her good sense and heart, Duncan so quick on the trigger. He would be the first to be sorry for anything he had done, so long as it was Valette; aye, he would always know where they stood with each other, which was the first thing Duncan asked of you. You measure people like Valette not just by what they say or do, but also by what they don't say or don't do. At every stage of her life, if life gave her a chance, Valette would be still finer. And just now she was touching, like a flower that is put where you can crush it.

"Are they like dolls to her?" the older woman thought, as she saw how Valette had the children always around her. "Are they like her dolls, or does she feel herself somehow their mother? And Duncan can look stormy once or twice, but he never takes his eyes off her, I notice that, the rascal!"

"I'll wager," Mrs. Bedford would reflect, squinting her eyes, for she liked to think of herself as observant and analytical, "there's not another person in the county, barring me, would know how happy the child is. It seems enough just having him back, just having Duncan again at home." She was in her own room upstairs and leaned her brow against the windowpane, thinking. "Yes, sir, she thinks the cup of happiness is full to the brim for her. But Duncan, no, he knows there's still more happiness for them. In time. Yes. But Duncan used to be so impatient with time. You can't tell me Duncan's changed entirely, oh, no, not Duncan!"

As she saw Valette nowadays flitting about so simply, so forgetful and free of all the small arts and graces by which women often choose to play their parts, Sallie Bedford heard another voice in her ear—was there not that Maxim? She took up the volume. It was number CCXLVIII:

Le plus grand miracle de l'amour, c'est de guérir de la coquetterie.

So 'twas, so 'twas. For the Lord had made it possible for women to control their passion, but the devil made it impossible to control their coquetry. Look at Valette now, how sweet she was and unself-conscious!

Yes, the greatest miracle of love is to cure coquetry.

Nevertheless, Mrs. Bedford sighed to think of the prospect just ahead; that mood of lyric dullness that envelops everybody when there is an engaged couple in the house.

LXIII

A WEEK before Duncan came home, Zack McGehee came down to stay at Montrose. He was Miles' youngest son, so plump that his Uncle Hugh said he would have been a preacher if he hadn't been a cotton expert. He was slowly making his way to New Orleans, where a good position with a cotton factor awaited him whenever he might arrive. It was not only because his father and uncle were, along with General Wade Hampton, among the largest cotton planters in the world; Zack himself had a gift for judging the market. He thought of himself as like his godfather, President Taylor, his father's friend, whom they called "old rough and ready"; but what suited Zachary best was to be waited on and, above everything, town life; and this, most of all, was what sent him now to the city. At Natchez there were not only his Montrose kin; the main object was Amelie Balfour, who had come down to stay with her cousins at Longwood, while her father, dismayed at the rack and ruin of his West Feliciana plantation by Sherman's troops, had gone to investigate Texas as a place to change to. After the death, ten years before, of Amelie's mother, he had not married again.

To look at Amelie herself you would not have guessed that a young man, five months before, had shot himself about her. The whole incident had been forgotten. He was a young man named Wilburn—some said it was Wilmer—from up somewhere around Black Creek, and Amelie had met him at a charity ball, and had doubtless been foolish enough to smile at him oftener than he could understand. He had yellow hair and narrow hips and could dance. She had even met him, later, of course, several times for a short stroll in the Longwood grounds. One Sunday, riding horseback, Amelie had

met him along the Natchez Trace somewhere and raced him
a mile; and then the young man had gone back to his room
above the drugstore and shot himself in the head. Nobody
had ever heard of the Wilburns, up around Black Creek; and
if you did not know very well what a Wilburn was, you could
not know very well how a Wilburn would feel. Nobody
would have put the case as brutally as that, but that was about
the size of it. People said "poor young man!" The whole
thing could not be fitted into any social scheme as Amelie's
people knew it; and so it was all left out and forgotten. Consciously and unconsciously, they had sense enough to know
there is no social system, or anything else, without its price.

People said that Zachary had addressed Amelie Balfour so
often that when she did accept him finally, he rushed for his
hat and lantern and ran out of doors. He returned next day.
Zachary, so people said who seemed to know, had begun pro-
posing as soon as he was home from the Army of Tennessee,
which was in April; and by June he had Amelie's promise to
marry him in December. It was partly to change the subject, her aunt Mrs. Balfour, said; who knew really that her
niece was slowly falling very much in love.

Late Tuesday afternoon, Duncan's third day at home,
Amelie came walking upstairs and into the dressing-room
where Valette was slipping into a yellow gown that had just
been turned for her out of one of Mrs. Bedford's.

"I passed the stable gate," Amelie said, kissing her friend
at the same time, "and Duncan was there. So I told him the
whole business."

Valette turned her back to ask how the flounces set, for she
had made the dress herself, and what was it Amelie had told
Duncan?

"And Duncan said," Amelie went on practising a little with
her large blue eyes, "that is certainly what he would like
the best in the world, but he would not ask you, Valette,

he wouldn't like to treat you that way. Just because you might be sweet and generous is what he meant."

The business, after they had kissed each other several times and laughed and there were tears in Valette's eyes, finally was clear. There was to be some cotton commission in Liverpool and Zachary McGehee that morning had received word that he was to go along. His father would be on the *Princess* tomorrow night, Wednesday; and Zack would join him, for the commission was to sail on Saturday by way of Havana to Liverpool. And so Amelie, after saying no at first, when this unexpected news came, had agreed to be married now instead of in December, and that meant tomorrow at six o'clock, from her cousin's. She had telegraphed to New Orleans for two bridal veils which would arrive early tomorrow, and one of them was for Valette. Miles McGehee had invited the two couples to be his guests on the *Princess* and at the St. Charles in New Orleans. Everything for the wedding was already arranged at Homewood.

"And the way anybody can hem tartleton ruffles, without a stitch," said Amelie, making a light motion of her thumb across her index finger, "a train, even, is nothing, nothing but a bagatelle; and just a satin bodice, my goodness! So you needn't worry. And where are all those clothes Duncan brought down here from the University of Virginia with him when he was so stylish? He's so thin now he could wear them still, with those velvet collars and all, he most certainly could."

Valette threw her arms around her friend's neck. "I do thank you, dearest Amelie, I do, I really do. But I object to double weddings," she said, blushing and catching herself before she blurted out that they reminded her of twins and twins made you think of animals. What a thing that would be to say!

"You object to!" Amelie said, moving away and starting to walk up and down as Madame Du Vaux used to do at school in New Orleans, when she lectured on young ladies' behavior. Amelie had always thought Valette had the spirit of the wind; which Valette, sitting huddled on the stool of the dressing-table with her face in her hands, resembled very little just then. "Valette, darling," she went on, "if you'd just think what a place for a wedding Homewood is, that great hall with the arches and the four double-doors! You enter by one door, I enter by the door opposite."

Valette looked up and saw tears streaming down her friend's cheeks.

"Amelie, don't cry. I do thank you, I do indeed, Amelie."

"Then why do you treat me like this, why won't you marry?"

Mrs. Bedford, when they finally went downstairs to consult with her, first sat quietly down on a straight chair, her hands folded in her lap, her eyes twinkling.

"Whatever suits Valette is agreeable to me," she said. "There's no sweeter child than the little thing's always been."

In her mind she was thinking also that there was not much to celebrate a wedding on just then at Portobello, and she had no great wish to undertake it. She could, if she had to, carry through something of a wedding; for it took more than a Sherman invasion to make you forget how to make cakes and ambrosia and punch. But she was tired in her bones and would like to sit down. These last few years there had been enough.

"It is mighty good of Amelie," she said, looking gently at Valette.

"I know Amelie's been an angel, My Dumplin'."

"Well, that you know more about than I do. But you and Duncan can visit New Orleans with Cousin Miles Mc-Gehee, as Amelie says: and you've waited a long time for Duncan to come home, darlin'. What does Duncan say to this?" She turned to Amelie. "Come on out here, let me see what those young turkeys are doing, just hatched last week, and tell me what Duncan said. We'll leave the child here. It's rushed you headlong, Valette, I know it has, sweetheart; you just go backward like the crab in *Hamlet,* and sit there and decide for yourself."

Valette, sitting there in the armchair sidewise, felt a strange obstinacy within her breast. Amelie was a captain, rushing her to the altar like that, and everybody else in the house marrying her off. And yet, after all that had happened—she still carried in her bosom that last letter of Duncan's—before the letters ceased and they thought Duncan was—and yet—. "I know of course I'll do it," she said to herself. "Right tomorrow. At Homewood with Amelie. I know I will. But still I haven't decided, I ought to think it over."

Then some time later Valette seemed awaking to listen: Duncan and the children had come around from the garden and he was playing with them. She could hear his burly voice mingle with theirs. She sat listening with her eyes closed, and felt something so tender, immediate and happy that she had never before known anything like it.

When Mrs. Bedford came in a moment afterward, Valette rushed to her and buried her face on her shoulder, holding the little body tight in her arms.

"Yes, yes, My Dumplin' knows." Sallie Bedford stroked the dark hair. "And how many yards of tarleton did you need for your dress, Amelie, we'll have to send in town tomorrow early."

That evening soon after supper, Duncan and Valette, walking up and down past the statues under the trees, were recalled to the house by the arrival of guests. Word of the wedding had got around generally and friends came out to call, to see just what this was that was happening at Portobello, and to offer their felicitations. Valette had to be kissed by everybody, and the ladies kissed Duncan. He sat in their midst and, without thinking anything about the matter, was the centre of the company. On his face was still the little scowl, as if to say he would fight where a fight was wanted; but his eyes were kind as a child's. And he was one of those rare people who have the power of giving off joy, so that everybody in the room was happy and was delighted with him and with all happiness.

Later on in the evening Middleton came running in to his mother with excited eyes, followed by Hugh McGehee, who had brought the little boy home after spending the day at Montrose. They reported that Zack had been out behind the house showing Middleton how to skin the cat, and the ladder fell with him. He was knocked unconscious; but when he came to was so afraid Amelie would put off the marriage that he sent a boy right off to Homewood with a note to say he would be on hand.

For most of the reasons in the world Sallie Bedford was glad that there were guests that night and that they stayed so late, in that house, at that time. "Celie," she said to the only one of the four Celie maids left from the old days, "light the night lamp for my room. I'll keep it lit tonight."

All night in that big room the beading on the chimney rim threw a circle of faint lamplight on the ceiling. But morning came and a bright air, and early breakfast, so that she was busy again. After breakfast Duncan went off to town to make various arrangements, first as to the marriage licenses and then certain Portobello affairs. The University of Virginia clothes would have to do for him. But his mother had given him the diamond cuff buttons. During the French and Indian War some soldiers digging a well had struck a coal vein in which were the diamonds, and Duncan's ancestor had them made into the buttons. They were cut flat with hair under them. It was all very vague but Duncan liked wearing them.

One of the negro sewing-women who had remained on the place came in to cut the tarleton flounces and help with the wedding dress, for which there was already an ivory satin bodice on hand from better days. There was Valette's travelling trunk to be packed; but for the most part new dresses were to be bought in New Orleans, with money scraped together for it and at shops that Mrs. Cynthia Eppes would know. When the fitting was over and the last touches were going on the wedding dress, Valette left the work in the sewing-room and wandered out of the house into the garden. From the window Mrs. Bedford could see her sauntering slowly along, stopping now and then to look at something, turning, coming around again by another box walk.

"Look at Miss Valette," Tildy said. "What you reckon she's studyin', Ole Miss? Ain' nobody think she have a weddin' today at six o'clock."

"That's all right, Mammy. You sit down and mind your business, Miss Valette's got her own thoughts."

"Yes, m'am, she sho' is too."

Nevertheless Mrs. Bedford herself sat wondering at Valette. Of all people you would have thought this child would be on tiptoe about her wedding. Why should she turn now as the children joined her in the garden, hanging on her hands, jumping up and down, and making her lean over to be whispered to? It might as well have been any day, when nobody was even thinking of a wedding.

Child, child, deeper than people think! But you are not going away for good. You and Duncan will be here with me. Perhaps you know how it will never be the same again, yet you love Duncan more than all the rest of the world put together. But still you are telling good-bye to something, and what are trunks and dresses? Good-bye to something——

And I have said good-bye too in my life.

But some people would not have thought it of you——

"We are often as unlike ourselves as we are unlike others."
Was this Valette, or was it not Valette?

Late that morning, when Celie came up with two hot flat-
irons to press ribbons, Mrs. Bedford learned from her that
Valette and the children were on the back gallery and that
Valette had ordered pitchers of hot and cold water brought
out there and a bowl, with soap and towels, and had scrubbed
each child's face and washed their hair.

LXIV

During the wedding ceremony, when the two brides and
two bridegrooms stood before the bishop, with the matron-of-
honor to one side, Hugh McGehee and Mrs. Bedford, standing
next each other, were thinking along similar lines. She
thought of Hugh. Years had shown her, out of her own experience and from watching him, that there was something
in him deep and steadfast—it might prove to be the foundation of all life among people together. But, still, he lacked
the right initiative. He was after all a McGehee man, needing
a woman to push him. This thought in her mind was crossed
by another about Valette. "You watch her," she said to herself, "she'll settle into a great woman one of these days.
These stages she goes through are right: plenty of blossoms,
plenty of harvest." Sallie Bedford observed the solemnity of
the light figure standing there before the clergyman, absorbed
with love and grown so quiet as she stood thus, giving her
imagination and her heart to Duncan.

Hugh looking at Duncan thought, "Some day he will grow
into a man who will be serene, at home in life, tender, surrounded by people that love him. And yet curiously free, not

turning to anybody. Clean and free." It seemed to Hugh
that most of the women in the room kept their gaze on
Duncan.

This was true. And yet it was true, also, that Zachary
McGehee looked so kind and jolly and so rosy with his senti-
ments, that everybody wished him, of the two bridegrooms,
more happiness.

"My own opinion is," Miss Mary Cherry said, as the guests
crowded round to salute the two brides and pay their compliments, some of these very serious and high-minded, "I was
saying my opinion is—" She rapped her neighbor, a tall old
man with an imperial—some cousin of the Balfours, who had
been visiting them since the fall of Vicksburg—on the arm
with her palm-leaf fan. By the time he came out of his
thoughts and turned to her, she had advanced toward Hugh
and begun to address him instead.

"I say, in my opinion, Brother Hugh, Zachary is stiff in his
joints, and will be for some time. His wife tomorrow mornin'
will have to help him dress."

"Well, Zack's fond of being helped anyway."

"Aye," she said, as she turned her head with her good eye
peering hither and yon over the company gathered at Homewood.

This house, built by her father as a wedding gift for Mrs.
Balfour, had been finished only a year before the war began.
It was said to have a million bricks in it, fired on the spot
by slave labor; and its iron balconies had been wrought by
negro workmen who had learned their art in Spain. The
house from the first opening of its doors had been famous
for its hunt breakfasts, balls, and entertaining, and was likely
to go on with them now, so long as the new times allowed.
Most people, now that the war and the devastation were
ended, had started off living as if things were the same as

ever. More than one guest that day found himself watching the festivities with the thought back of his mind that the ruin would soon begin.

But what every one at the wedding spoke of was how perfect Homewood was for the purpose: the square central hall with its arches leading into four corridors, the six lofty rooms, and the sliding doors, with their heavy mahogany and silver knobs and hinges, that threw all the first floor of the house into one. When these remarks were not addressed to the host or hostess themselves, the guests spoke also of the fair lady of Homewood, or the gracious master.

The four years in which they had been cut off from fashions were ended, and just now many of the ladies took every chance to hear what new toilettes they might have, some few from Paris by way of New Orleans shops as of old but most of them made up at home, either out of new goods or out of old dresses, and fashioned from such hints on the Paris modes as Jennie June's, whose New York letter was appearing again in *The New Orleans Weekly Times*. Hoops were smaller, corsages lower, Hercules braid was to be freely used; blonde hair, though less fashionable because of its universal adoption by stage ladies of questionable reputation, so wrote Jennie June, was to be fringed in front, but dark hair waved and worn smooth; in fact the most desirable hair was the chestnut or "Queen's" color. And ladies with old China crêpe shawls should cut nem up into tunics in the new Paris rage. Mrs. Balfour, the hostess, had done so, and pinned the tunic at the throat with a diamond brooch, seven diamonds set together, fifty years before, in a sort of Tudor rose, but not at all the fashion.

When Hugh McGehee joined the circle around the two brides, he bowed first to Amelie as the new member of the family. Amelie whispered in his ear:

"When he's like this now—that's when I—look at him now, Uncle Hugh, isn't he pretty? I mean with Aunt Agnes, look at the little thing!"

Hugh followed her glance to Zachary, who had made his way straight through the crowd of guests to Agnes, where she stood with the three Bedford children, beside one of the great bookcases of the library. Zack was scarcely a little thing, but he had linked his arm through hers and stood leaning over talking. On his round, soft face there was a look of pity and goodness which his effort, clumsy like a child's, to be gay and smiling only half concealed.

The name of the matron-of-honor was Mrs. Henry Armat. She was married to Amelie's cousin, who lived at Eldershade Plantation, a few miles down the Woodville Road. It had been arranged that the two bridal couples steal quietly away unnoticed by the company, to whom, also, the destination of the wedding-journey was supposed to be a secret. So that when Amelie and Valette were upstairs for their going-away dresses, Mrs. Armat, who was in her own wedding dress, all but the veil, which convention forced her to leave off, more or less took the floor. Her removable train, its sides turned back and joined the whole length by butterfly bows, had come loose twice already during the evening, but seemed now secure.

She was a lady whose large, romantic eyes struck around the room like chimes. As a rule her habit was to utter a series of words and then, when she understood what they meant, follow them up quite brightly, as if it were a topic she was anxious to discuss. But today she stuck to one subject. A propos of her dress, she told one person after another her story. "How different 'tis!" she would say, or "How fortunate girls are now!" Her own wedding had been hurried, the company was off to the war. The bridesmaids wore lilac, the bride white, "as you see," she would add, spreading out her sleeves. And then sooner than anybody thought, the trumpets blew; they had to hurry. And so the cake and wine had been put away; they were served after the war, four years later. Every one except Mary Cherry said that this was the most romantic thing they had ever heard in their lives.

Valette and Amelie stole down by the servants' stair to the court back of the house, where the two bridegrooms were waiting with the carriages. The rattly Montrose carriage with Zack and Amelie was the first to drive off.

As Duncan took her hand at the carriage steps, Valette turned suddenly and pointed toward the house.

"Look," she whispered. "See there? I knew it. I saw her move just then, I knew I did."

Duncan saw, where the shadow was deepest on the gallery, a slight form standing, and then Valette dragging his mother toward him, her arms around her as if she were lifting a child.

"Dearest, My Dumplin'," he heard that sweet voice saying to his mother, and his heart leapt, "here you are out here by yourself! Oh, I do love you, and he loves you and will come back to you, you won't know how soon! And never, never leave you, My Dumplin'. Sweetness! Duncan, she had her hands over her face, but she says she wasn't cryin'——"

"My goodness," his mother said, as he sprang to the other side of her, "now it's both of you tearing me apart! You see what you've done now, miss, you've got Duncan all stirred up."

"She was cryin', Duncan, don't you believe her," said Valette.

"I'm not—and if I did—I was not."

"Yes, *amo, amas, amat,* you're just goin' in the carriage with us, is what you're goin' to do. Isn't she, Duncan?"

"And be frozen to death, without my old dolman."

"Don't listen."

"She can turn her skirt up over her shoulders, Duncan."

They drove off with Sallie Bedford sitting between them in the carriage like a little girl.

For a part of the way each of them sat holding one of her hands, which were trembling at first but grew quieter. At length she drew out her hands from theirs and folded them on her lap, as she began talking of their return and what there was to do at Portobello. Some of the garden sadly needed resetting and trimming out; but that would have to wait, the plantations must come first. And there must not be any mortgages started, the way people were doing with their land all over the county. It does not take long for land to change hands; and you just lose your land and see where you are! And what your children will be, drifting about in towns!

Duncan was the one who seemed to listen, though he said only a word or so. Valette kept leaning forward to look out of the carriage window into the dusk, and now and then she sighed. "No," she said to herself, and kissed the wrinkled little cheek, "no, My Dumplin', I don't think this is what you're really thinking about—at such a time, now are you?"

"No, what I was thinking is that this reminds me of the time sister Carrie was married, my eldest sister. I remember it exactly, in Alabama, I was twelve years old. Because they caught me and painted my face."

When Mrs. Bedford slipped quietly into the company at Homewood again, she found that Captain Ruffin had arrived by the Princess and driven up in the Montrose carriage to join the company at Homewood. Miss Mary Cherry told her this.

"He's telling his stories," Miss Mary said. "He can remember whether it rained on the 3d of June twenty-five years ago, and what happened to him two years after that and every other time. But he can't remember how many times he's told the same story to the same person."

Mr. Balfour had contrived to put together a quartette of

town musicians, one of them a young veteran who had only a stub for a hand, and held his fiddle by pressing down his chin against it. People were crowded around the long table, with its high silver candlesticks, where supper was set out. In the late dusk the candle-light glittered brighter, the rooms seemed larger, and some of the faded or made-over gowns shone fresher because of it. The ladies were wearing the same tight shoes, so it still took Macedonian courage to put your foot down. Dancing had begun; and as they whirled, the gentlemen held up the ribbons to the ladies' trains.

LXV

Hugh McGehee went out by the tall glass doors on to the gallery. "There are so many candles burning, and so many flowers," was all he thought; but he did not walk up and down as he had meant to do. He stood leaning against one of the columns, slowly snapping his thumb and middle finger together, and was glad when he heard a gust of wind strike the trees and the scattering leaves. He saw the crowd of carriages and buggies drawn up along the drive; the horses stamped now and then, and their drivers moved about talking among themselves. Some of the Homewood negroes stood on the ground below the balcony and were watching the entertainment indoors. The late autumn night was cool and clear, and where some of the leaves had fallen from the trees the blue light of the sky shone through. It was almost full moon and all across the sky a glow had arisen from the east. The lush greens of the garden were black under it; the fragrance of the sweet-olive seemed as forgotten and natural as the coming moonlight and the air. He could still see in the dusk the white camellias sown thick amid their leaves; they reminded him of Montrose. How can one be homesick for a place a mile away? But it was so.

On the gallery near the other negroes a few of the more favored servants had been allowed to stand. Mammy Tildy had driven over from Portobello with the children, Duncan had seen to it. They had brought her a low hickory chair and she sat upright, a stiff white apron over her dress, on her head a new tignon.

Captain Ruffin came out to join Hugh. Since his wife's death his hair was white and he was thinner.

"Two years have passed, sir, since I had the pleasure of being in Natchez," he said, speaking in his slow and elegant manner but more quietly than once. As if by an effort to take his old place, he added, "And how fortunate I am to arrive when there is this festivity that makes 'the foot of time to tread on flowers.' "

"Yes," Hugh said, turning to look at the figures moving about the parlor, "and it's a good thing for a change. We've seen too much black. At church every other woman in mourning. But 'tain't worthwhile now to speak of that."

Captain Ruffin, whom time had begun to reduce, said nothing; and Hugh stood with his arms folded, gazing into the room. "In these people—they are my people—how much goodness there is!" he thought. He was right. Among them there was still goodness that comes of harmony. It rested on a physical harmony and manner of life in which the nerves were not harassed; and it arose from the natural springs of feeling, where interest, pressure, and competition have not got in the way. "How sweet people's faces are!" thought Hugh.

"Do your meditations resemble mine, my dear friend?" said Captain Ruffin suddenly, taking Hugh's arm and beginning a stroll along the gallery. "Looking at these young people, these young ladies of our country, I was wondering if there would come a time when that radiance will not be in girls' faces."

Hugh made no answer, though such a thought had more than once come to him as he considered the changes that lay in the future.

"My friend, what a fragrance in the air!" the old man added, as if he and Hugh were listening to music. "I suppose I oughtn't to complain if my world is gone. I've had my years." He sighed.

Old Tildy's voice interrupted them with a good evening.

"So your young master's taken himself a bride, Aunt Tildy," Hugh said, putting his arm affectionately through Captain Ruffin's whose spine immediately straightened into parade lines. "What do you think of that, Aunt Tildy?"

"I done say my say jes' now," the old woman answered, with the bold assurance of her place in the family. "When Bishop Thompson ax ef she gwine cherish Marse Duncan, I say 'An' well she mought.' And I said it loud, so I been hyerd."

"Yes, well she might. And so with him too."

"I done say already long ago how come he want to marry Miss Valette? Her folks talks long. I recollects her ma and I recollects her pa, befo' 'at yellow fever. Marse Duncan when he ain't found de word he wants, he gits on a horse. I ain't never misunderstood him, neither."

"God A'mighty, Mammy, he knows that," said Hugh.

"Miss Valette when she can' find 'e word she wants she jes' makes 'em up."

"Don't sit up too late, Mammy Tildy," Hugh said, kindly, and passed on with Captain Ruffin. The old woman gave a chuckle and folding her arms again, began to bob her head to the tune of the music that floated out to them.

Captain Ruffin had come to Natchez for the purpose of conferring with some of the landowners whose taxes were

being multiplied in a system intended to break them. His own
property had already been turned in to the Government by
default and he hoped for a professorship in law at some university.

"Look at your daughter," Mrs. Wilson, at the supper table,
said to Hugh, when he and Captain Ruffin approached. She
turned to Agnes, through whose arm she had twined her
own. "Pray, look! Dear, dear, dear!"

Lucinda passed near them waltzing with George McGehee,
The white muslin of her dress, its puffed sleeves and wide
sash ruffled with lace, and pink roses in the hair, seemed to
float and sparkle in the candlelight. Her mother had decided
to encourage an interest in clothes. It was a French dress and
the long white gloves were French, with six buttons.

Mrs. Wilson went on: "It's what I call wasting your sweetness on the desert air. First I see her dancing with some man
as old as the hills, and now it's with her cousin, who's a married man besides—and, from what you tell me, only too soon
to be a father." She turned to Mrs. George McGehee, who
had been a Miss Stewart from St. Francisville and smiled.
"Yes, a married man."

"And what are our young gals to do, may I venture to
inquire, Mistress Wilson, short of some special Providence?"
said Mary Cherry. She stood holding a plate with a slice of
cake which she alternately glared at, bit, glared at again, and
then took another bite of. So close to the many candles on the
table, the old grenadine showed even more the fading at the
cuffs and tops of the sleeves. "With so many killed in the
war—unless our girls marry trash— Here, take this—" she
handed her plate to a servant going by with his tray, "and
don't keep passing me things—marryin' trash is not in Lucy
McGehee's line."

Agnes drew Mrs. Wilson and her Irish temper away,
changing the subject to a letter from Francis Eppes in Paris

about General Lee's fame over Europe, where military academies were already studying his campaigns as classic strategy. Miss Mary addressed herself to Hugh and Captain Ruffin:

"It's the politicians got us into this war and nobody else," she said, her voice loud enough to be heard at the other end of the room. "Yes, I warrant you, the politicians dragged us in. And by the time I got good and mad, it was the politicians kept General Lee from carryin' out his plans."

The captain reddened to the roots of his hair.

"But, Miss Mary——"

"Then the wind-bags up and stopped the war."

"But, Miss Mary," Captain Ruffin repeated, "I have been a senator myself, as you may know. Doubtless there is a modicum of truth in what you say, but surely, surely——"

"I am not talkin' about you, Senator Ruffin," Miss Mary said, "I'm not talkin' about you. I'm talkin' about people exactly like you."

At this moment the music ended and Lucinda came up with her cousin George. Her manner now had become more open and carelessly affable, like a woman who knows at last that she will never have what she most wants in life or that it will never return to her. She got on now more easily with people; and this was because she asked less of any one person. More people would like her company now, and fewer could think of her with the notion of falling in love. If she seemed to have less of something rare and elusive about her, she was handsomer than ever.

"Well, daughter," her father said, smiling and gazing at Lucy until she blushed and looked down to see if the violets in her bodice were right, "your Aunt Lucinda was the prettiest girl in Georgia. Governor Gilman thought the fact so important that he recorded it in that history of his."

"Yes, and, Papa, you're the one always says his history is mostly lies, now, don't you?"

"Otherwise 'tis, otherwise 'tis," he said, "lies," and put her hand through his arm.

"If you want to see who Miss Callie Armat thinks is the prettiest lady," said Lucy, giving her lips a droll twist, "and the finest dress, look. Yon she is now." At the far end of the ballroom they could see Mrs. Armat stepping out and signalling the musicians with her fan, as if she meant to lead the cotillion.

George McGehee laughed. "Then it's just as well she didn't see the expression I caught on Duncan's face once during the ceremony. In fact I saw it more than once. Don't know if you saw it. I thought I'd die the way Duncan was scowling at her."

"I saw him," said Lucy. "If Duncan had got his say, Valette would have all three wedding dresses."

"That's more than probable," said George, laughing, as he took his wife's hand and began to swing it to and fro. "'Twould be like him." He let go his wife's hand and put his in his pockets, and stood there looking down at his boot-tips for a moment. "'Twould be like Duncan exactly." The sweet smile which everybody in the family had spoken of at one time or another came over his face.

"I remember the time I was at Montrose," he said, "and Ed was telling that story about Duncan. He was telling of a ride with Duncan. They had been into Natchez and were returning to Portobello when Duncan began to tell him of the sundry attractions of Miss Valette Somerville. Ed, by way of being agreeable, chimed in and enlarged upon the lady's many virtues, too. When there was a pause in the conversation, Duncan turned in his saddle and said in the most generous tone, 'Ed, do you want her? If you do, I'll go away and give you an opportunity to win her.'"

LXVI

THEY had promised at the wedding to send, and early next morning the carriage went off to Portobello for Mrs. Bedford and the children. Miss Mary Cherry was preparing to leave for the McGehees' in Panola and so did not come. Spending the day at Montrose, Sallie Bedford would be less lonely than she would have been right at first like this, without Duncan and Valette, and would not work all day merely to fill the time.

The large, plain room of the house where the McGehees now lived was furnished with the piano, sofa and four chairs saved from the fire. Scattered among them for necessary uses, were straight hickory chairs made on the plantation and a willow rocking-chair that still, when the weather was damp, sprouted at the knots. There were flowers everywhere, most of them in glass fruit jars except for the four great silver urns that William Veal had buried; these were filled with red and white camellias.

"Are the roses too heavy for you, Sis Sallie?" Agnes said. "Though the windows are open."

"I know how people go on, child, but nothing is ever too sweet for me, nothing that grows. The fire I'm glad of. I'm not cold, but lately somehow I like to see a fire."

"And so do I," Hugh said, giving the logs a kick and then glancing at the toe of his shoe. "Aye. And this chimney draws; they knew how to make chimneys."

The two little girls, Mary Hartwell and Frances, wore dresses of blue plaid gingham exactly alike; by now everybody was used to the idea of their mother's buying the whole bolt at a time, to save money. They sat at one end of the sofa, Middleton standing at the arm, while Hugh McGehee showed them an album made out of a penny copybook into which he had put examples of Confederate money for his grandsons, the two little Abners. There was, for special interest, a three dollar scrip issued by the West Feliciana Railroad, which their Woodville uncle owned, and a five dollar scrip of the Mississippi Central that their Panola uncle owned, the engine on it with the black stream of smoke was named for him. When the album was done with, Middleton stole out of the room; and the two little girls sat on, listening gravely to the conversation.

Hugh McGehee and Mrs. Bedford were talking of the governor of Mississippi. Except for the exercise of the war power, the President of the United States had no authority to appoint a governor of the state; and had finally done so by public proclamation, as commander-in-chief of the army; the salary was to be paid from Government funds. Governor Sharkey declined to be paid so, saying that he did not regard himself as an official of the United States nor even as a constitutional governor. He stated that he could arrange for his salary of $3000 out of the proper state taxes for such purposes.

"Yet we are not back in the Union," said Mrs. Bedford, contemptuously, "we were never legally out of it, but we are not legally in it."

Sharkey had it understood with President Johnson that the military still kept all over Mississippi would not interfere with the civil administration, Hugh said. "The North has its eye on what we will do. *The New York Times* says Mississippi's decisions are of peculiar interest because it was the state of Jeff Davis, was the second to secede, produced more cotton than any other state, and had nearly as many slaves as any."

"Yes, and you watch," Mrs. Bedford said. "Bro' Hugh, you know as well as I do the kind of people coming into this country and what's going on all round us. You watch. It will be ten years before they'll wreck themselves through their own greed and savagery, and Mississippi is sound again, you'll see. If it's ever sound again."

While this discussion went on, William Veal came to the door to ask directions for some work. He looked tired and old these days, his hair was white; and even Agnes no longer called him William, she said Uncle. For a moment she stood now conferring with him about the trellises that Aleck was to build along the west gallery, against the afternoon sun on so small a house. She did not return to the others but went down the steps and across the lawn.

Agnes took the walk that led past the half-ruined garden of the old house, toward the graveyard. For a long way she could still hear sounds from the parlor where the others were, and then for a moment Lucy, as she began singing. Then came only the country stillness. She went quietly along the path with her beautiful movements, still light and even.

Along a side path she saw Middleton coming a few yards away in her direction. He was walking slowly, trailing his fingers against the wall of a hedge that had belonged to the old house. Now he had seen her and hurried to take her hand. The boy looked up at her with something excited and far-away in his eyes.

"I know where you are goin'," he said, as he pointed with his right hand to where the tops of the marble shafts came into view, under the live-oaks and the hanging moss. "Will you let me go, too, Aunt Agnes?"

For a moment she seemed to see in those eyes looking up into hers the direct mystery of childhood and felt that she understood it, and that it saw into her soul this day. So she did not bend down to kiss him as she would usually have done, but only held his hand close, as she said,

"Why, yes, my darling, if you want to."

She said to herself how much a child's, how fresh and delicate, was that little face with the wide gray eyes.

In the family graveyard, for it was almost noon, there were few shadows, only the glancing light on the leaves; on the marble, the stains that time and the rain through the moss had made showed their pale rose-color touched with gray. Agnes and Middleton stood for a moment looking at Edward's grave, over which the lively green was already well grown. It was only another of Agnes' visits there, except that today especially he should not be forgotten. She had heard Hugh McGehee say, and she had known by instinct, that some sacred memory preserved through the years is the best education to live by.

Middleton leaned closer to her as he asked:

"Is Cud'n Edward there, Aunt Agnes?"

"No, darling. His body is here, but he isn't."

"Yes, but, then, he is here."

"Yes, my darling."

When they sat down on the iron bench with the fruits and leaves over the legs and seat and back, painted white, the little boy leaning against the arm at one end, she at the other, Agnes forgot that he was there.

"Shiloh, Shiloh, Shiloh," she was saying to herself, lovely old name from the Bible, a little meeting-house, peach trees blossoming in April. The battle of Shiloh, she thought. Shiloh, with all those half-trained boys and men on each side lost, seemed to her the epitome of war's folly, the symbol of men's childish urges. All that wild glory, folly, and pain in men must remain as women's dream and delight and fear when a child is going to be born to them. All that blood to be soaked up by the earth must rise again into women's breasts, from which life flows. And thus she could say, "In me, a woman, oh, glory and oblivion, is the life principle!" And by some long use of wisdom she could understand, as she sat meditating there at her son's grave, the relation—so different from what it is with women—of war to men, men to war.

Nearby Agnes heard a sound in the throat and turned to

look at Middleton. He sat with his eyes straight ahead, fixed on the trees beyond the cemetery wall and the sun pouring down into them. She was filled with doubt and compunction, as to having let him come. The little boy did not move his eyes save for one rapturous glance into hers; but he slid over and sat closer beside her, slipping his hand into her hand, as he sat gazing again across the flecked marbles into the trees and light beyond. And yet why, she asked herself, should he not be here, who should decide for another what life is? She saw, now, here at Montrose, the little plants at her feet, vervain, plantain, rabbit peas; everywhere about her at this morning hour almost no shadows fell, nor in the grove beyond among the trees, where the body of summer waited, still, definite, like the presence of some one walking there.

There was the other woman yonder in the house, happy that her son was found, Duncan with that new look on his face, back from the war, back to the life that waited for him. And now Agnes herself could feel suddenly the hard gravel under her feet at Shiloh. More than three years ago.

She had left her friend's wagon on the road and, walking for a long way, half stumbling through the wood in the darkness, had come to a hillock overlooking the field where the battle had been. You could smell the peach blossoms on trees not far away, the ground everywhere was wet from sleet and rain. Farther away she saw—perhaps it was only because the sentries, after they came up, had told her so—the grove and its small Shiloh meeting-house. Nearer, she could make out dimly over here, over there, the fallen timbers, the wagons left behind, their mules stirring about, and the guns, caissons, limber boxes, tents that General Sherman had not destroyed because he knew the Confederates could not remove them. This the pickets had also told her. But she could not go farther, not on the battlefield; she would have to wait till morning; the order about that was final. And how could she know, they asked, that her son had been killed? When her eyes grew more used to the darkness, she saw over that part of the field nearer them the shadows lying; for after the battle that day, night had fallen before the wounded could be cared for or the dead buried. Another sentry came up, who said he was from the Fifty-sixth Ohio, and Agnes stood there listening as the soldiers talked to each other. Neither army, the sentries said, was yet ready for fighting but somehow the fighting had to be. On one side General Grant had said that he did not expect any attack but would be prepared for it, and, according to the Confederate prisoners, General Johnston had said he would fight them if they were a million. So ran the talk. The prize was for the Mississippi River and the control of it down to the Gulf. With the Tennessee River and the creeks draining the lines of a great triangle, a vast plain for drilling and fighting was there; and the thick trees in places made surprise attacks easier to carry through. Around dawn the Confederates came pouring out of the woods. Everything went to pieces in the Union lines, and the Southern troops were rushing on toward the river landing. The division farther away from the attack scrambled into ranks, letting hundreds running from the front pass through their lines. But when Johnston's army caught up, even these rear divisions broke and the left Union flank was driven back to the river. After some hours Grant got there, and later Buell.

Then, after sunset, word came that General Johnston was killed, and General Beauregard was in command, and the attack ceased. The night got black as pitch and the rain poured down.

The Ohio soldier described how Grant's advance began next morning, with 25,000 fresh troops that had arrived to reinforce him; his gunboats from the river poured their fire into the valley. By six o'clock that night the Confederates began their retreat; the sentries spoke of the columns retreating in good order and taking along with them a great quantity of spoils. But it was a Union victory, just the same, and on April 7th, "Imagine now," the Ohio soldier kept repeating. "Imagine its falling on my own birthday!" Yet there was one thing he could never forget: you saw swamps and standing water and creeks, but there was one small stream where he had led his horse and found the water thick red with blood.

Agnes could hear again now all of a sudden the groans and cries of the wounded and dying that were left in that section. She could see faintly again their shapes lying together scattered on the field. With the groans and cries coming back to her again like that, her nerves tightened and her arms stiffened, and then she felt the boy at her side startle and look at her, catching her hand now in both his. From that on, instead of at the trees, the marbles, the sunlight, he kept his gaze on her face, his own face pale, his eyes absorbed and full of ecstasy.

Agnes only glanced at the child, seeing what was in his face, and stirred by it more than she knew. At the same moment memory was stronger—she returned to her thoughts. She was at Shiloh; but now she heard nothing, only the silence; then, inside her body, she heard her heart beating. Edward was among them somewhere but the others too were hers. She stood there looking out across the darkness and the field where the dead lay, as if they were all sleeping.